A Coldwater Warm Hearts Wedding

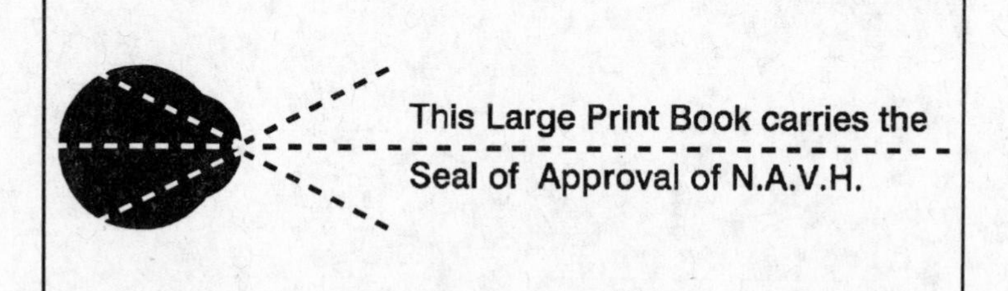
This Large Print Book carries the
Seal of Approval of N.A.V.H.

THE COLDWATER SERIES

A Coldwater Warm Hearts Wedding

Lexi Eddings

THORNDIKE PRESS
A part of Gale, Cengage Learning

GALE
CENGAGE Learning®

Farmington Hills, Mich • San Francisco • New York • Waterville, Maine
Meriden, Conn • Mason, Ohio • Chicago

The Coldwater Series #2.
Thorndike Press, a part of Gale, Cengage Learning.

Thorndike Press® Large Print Clean Reads.
The text of this Large Print edition is unabridged.
Other aspects of the book may vary from the original edition.
Set in 16 pt. Plantin.

LIBRARY OF CONGRESS CATALOGING-IN-PUBLICATION DATA

Names: Eddings, Lexi, author.
Title: A Coldwater Warm Hearts wedding / by Lexi Eddings.
Description: Large print edition. | Waterville, Maine : Thorndike Press, 2017. | Series: The Coldwater series ; #2 | Series: Thorndike Press large print clean reads
Identifiers: LCCN 2017015040| ISBN 9781432839086 (hardcover) | ISBN 143283908X (hardcover)
Subjects: LCSH: Large type books. | GSAFD: Love stories.
Classification: LCC PS3613.A7664 C654 2016 | DDC 813/.6—dc23
LC record available at https://lccn.loc.gov/2017015040

Published in 2017 by arrangement with Kensington Books, an imprint of Kensington Publishing Corp.

Printed in the United States of America
1 2 3 4 5 6 7 21 20 19 18 17

For my dear sisters, Cindy, Linda and Jennifer, keepers of my secrets and my forever friends. (I'm not too worried about the secrets bit. I've got enough on them to make this a mutually assured destruction pact!)

Chapter 1

Trouble makes us stronger, they say. It brings out the best in us and shows what we're really made of. But don't you just hate it when blessings come in disguise?
— Shirley Evans, after she got the news from her doctor about the Big C

"This was so not the time to take a surgical rotation," Heather Walker muttered as she scanned the lineup of procedures for the day. Not that she didn't love assisting. She did. It was truly rewarding to be part of the surgical team at Coldwater Cove's small hospital. She went home "good tired" every day. But it would be so much easier if she didn't know her patients personally.

And Heather knew everybody in town.

Today was worse than usual because the mother of her best friend, Lacy Evans, was on the schedule. Lacy pushed her way past one of the curtains that divided up the surgical waiting area and made a beeline toward Heather.

"Mom was supposed to be in surgery an hour ago." Lacy's nose was red, a sure sign she'd been fighting back tears.

"I know and I'm sorry, but it can't be helped. We had an emergency appendectomy this morning." Heather always tried to be calmly professional, however frazzled she might feel on the inside. No one would be helped if she joined in barely suppressed panic. She strove to be detached enough to get the job done. That was the goal anyway. It was a hard line to walk when her friend was obviously holding herself together with spit and baling twine. "Your mom is next on the list."

Lacy nodded. "OK. Maybe it's just as well there was a delay. Michael's not here yet."

Lacy's fiancé, Jake, had called in a favor with one of his Marine buddies who was in intelligence, and between them, they'd managed to track down the elusive Michael Evans. Lacy figured her brother deserved to know what was happening, even though he'd shown precious little interest in his family in the past few years. Lacy had confided in Heather that she was relieved — and a little surprised — to discover her brother wasn't in jail somewhere.

“Are you expecting him to come?” Heather asked.

“No, but Mom is.”

Her friend’s black sheep brother hadn’t been home in ages. Hadn’t called. Hadn’t even sent a postcard. Mike Evans had been in Heather’s class in school, but he ran with a totally different crowd, so their paths had rarely crossed. Her only sharp memory of him was when he christened her “Stilts” in middle school. Through no fault of her own, Heather had shot up to five feet ten inches by her thirteenth birthday, and she hadn’t been finished growing yet.

The name stuck. She was “Stilts” Walker all through high school.

But even that indignity wasn’t enough to account for the resentment simmering in her chest. According to Lacy, Michael had shamed his family many times over the years. If there was a way to go wrong, Mike Evans found it. Still, the frustration rising in Heather’s chest was unproductive, so she tamped it down. Her relationship with her own parents wasn’t anything to brag about. It was aloof rather than estranged, but in a pinch, she was sure the Walkers would come together.

Any guy who couldn’t be bothered to show up when his mother was facing cancer surgery deserved a swift kick in the backside.

Lacy's eyes went hazy for a moment. "She doesn't know how to swim."

"What?"

"My mom. Every summer she took us kids to the pool for lessons five times a week, and I mean *religiously.* At six-holy-cow-thirty a.m., we'd be hopping around by the side of the pool trying to warm up before they let us into the water." Lacy's voice trailed away. "Mom swims like a rock, but she made sure we all learned how."

"Maybe she can take lessons at the civic center as part of her physical therapy after surgery," Heather suggested. It was important for her friend to think positively about her mom's future.

"That's not the point," Lacy said with a sniff. "The fact is she's a terrific mom and I never appreciated her like I should have."

"She's still a terrific mom. Appreciate her now."

Lacy gave her a shaky nod. "But what if —"

"Hush now." *Forget being professional.* Heather gave her friend a hug. "You're borrowing trouble. Until after surgery, we won't know if the cancer has spread. And until we know that, it's hard to say what treatment

Dr. Warner will recommend."

Or if we caught the disease in time to make treatment worth the misery, Heather thought but didn't say. No point in rehearsing the worst-case scenario.

But Lacy had evidently been imagining it.

"Come on. I need to get your mom prepped." Pasting on what she hoped was an encouraging smile, Heather led Lacy to the surgical waiting room and drew back the first curtain. The scent of antiseptic cleansers and bleached linen was second nature to Heather, but hospital smells put most people on edge. Mrs. Evans wasn't troubled by it, though. She was always awash in a personal cloud of Estée Lauder. She wouldn't have smelled a skunk if it had built a nest under her bed.

Heather's patient was sitting up on the gurney, trying to wrestle a pillow away from Lacy's older sister, Crystal. Heather wasn't sure what offense the pillow had committed, but Crystal was doing her best to pound it into submission.

Everyone deals with stress in their own way.

"Good morning, Mrs. Evans," Heather said as she edged past Crystal to reach her patient. "How are we doing today?"

"Fine, Heather. Ready to get this over with." Mrs. Evans gave up and surrendered the pillow to her daughter. She was already festooned with electrodes monitoring her heart rate, and the pillow fight had sent her pulse racing. An IV pumped saline into her system. In a few minutes, Heather would add a drug cocktail to prepare her for the general anesthesia to come. Doc Warner called it the "don't-give-a-darn" drug.

Only he didn't say "darn."

"I'll see what I can do to move things along," Heather promised.

"Thank you, dear," Mrs. Evans said. "Crystal, for heaven's sake, stop worrying that pillow."

"I'm not worrying it. I'm trying to give it a little shape. It won't do you any good if it's flat."

"Flat or fluffy, it's not doing me a speck of good if it's not under my head."

"You heard your mother," Mr. Evans chimed in from the only chair on the other side of the bed.

With a sigh, Crystal stuffed the pillow behind her mother's shoulders. Heather suspected Lacy's sister didn't fluff and plump for her mom's comfort. She might not even be doing it out of nervous energy. Crystal had always been the sort who arranged things to suit herself.

Of course, everyone was entitled to their

own opinion, but if they wanted to be right, they had better agree with Crystal.

Looking gray and stretched thin, Mr. Evans retreated behind the *Coldwater Gazette,* rattling the paper noisily.

A prime example of the "ostrich with his head in the sand" way to deal with stress.

Then he began to quote snippets from the *Gazette* whether anyone was listening to him or not.

"Labor Day is fast approaching," he read, "the traditional time for all graduates of Coldwater High to gather for their class reunions. Like lemmings rushing to the sea, we expect a number of Fighting Marmots will make their way home for the festivities."

"I did *not* write that," Lacy was quick to point out, though she did work for the local paper. "That's my boss all the way. It's not enough that our high school mascot is an oversized rodent, Wanda has to lump us with suicidal ones, too."

Heather had been a Lady Marmot once, a star power forward on the girls' basketball team back in the day. But she'd often wondered who had first decided it would be a good thing for the Coldwater Cove teams to be named after a glorified ground squirrel.

"Looks like our class is hosting a supper at the country club on Saturday as one of the reunion events, Shirley." Mr. Evans glanced up from the paper long enough to make eye contact with his wife before focusing back on the *Gazette.* "Think we'll be able to make it?"

Classic denial, Heather thought. If George Evans acknowledged that his wife was about to undergo surgery, it would make the breast cancer real.

"Well," Shirley Evans said as Heather wrapped the blood pressure cuff around her upper arm and pumped it up. "I —"

"How can you ask that, Dad?" Crystal interrupted. "Mom will still be recovering this weekend. She might not even be out of the hospital by —"

"She might also like to answer for herself, if you don't mind," Mrs. Evans said, with an arched brow at her oldest daughter. "I'd like to go, George, but we'll just have to see. Buy a pair of tickets anyway. The class always gives any excess to a local charity, so whatever happens, you know the money will go to a good cause."

Whatever happens . . .

Heather had to either lighten the mood or get things moving, preferably both. When she opened Mrs. Evans's chart, her heart fluttered a bit. No one had gone through the pre-op documents with the patient. Of all the aspects of her job, Heather rebelled against this part most. She was a healer. She hadn't studied nursing to push papers. Especially not these papers that dealt with some of life's toughest decisions. "There are a few things for you to sign."

"What sort of things?" Mr. Evans rose. Since he was a retired lawyer, papers were his life.

"First, there's consent for treatment." Heather explained the procedure Mrs. Evans was about to undergo, the possible risks, and the expected outcome. They'd heard it all before, but Heather was required to repeat it now. When Mr. Evans nodded, his wife signed. Heather drew a deep breath. She hated this next part, but it was absolutely necessary. "Then there are advance directives to consider. Have you made out a living will or durable power of attorney?"

Mr. Evans snorted. "I wouldn't be worth my salt as a lawyer if she hadn't, would I?"

"Dear George made sure we took care of all that a few years ago when we were both healthy." Mrs. Evans patted her husband's forearm. "It's always easier to deal with the hard things when they seem a long way off, don't you think?"

Mrs. Evans gave Heather a tremulous smile. She was bearing up well for her family's sake, but it was hard to head into surgery not knowing if your worst fears were about to be confirmed.

"Lacy," Mrs. Evans said, "why don't you show Heather your wedding palette? I bet she hasn't seen it yet."

Heather *had* seen Lacy's colors. She'd even helped her pick them out one evening over a nice merlot. Heather was Lacy's maid of honor, after all. But to change the subject, she asked to see the swatches again. Lacy pulled out her cell phone and brought up the navy blue, pale pink, and ivory palette.

"You'll be in ivory, of course, Lacy, and Jake and the male attendants in navy," Mrs. Evans said with a wistful smile, her gaze fixed on a distant point as if imagining the wedding party in their finery. "And the bridesmaids' gowns will be bright pink."

"No, Mom," Lacy said gently. "We discussed this, remember? Jake will be in his dress blues. He deserves to wear the uniform."

Since Jake had lost a leg from the knee down in Afghanistan, Heather agreed. He'd more than earned the right to wear the blues. Besides, nothing looked better in wedding pictures than a groom in uniform.

Of course, in my case, any groom would look good. Not to mention surprise the heck out of my mother.

Heather quashed that thought. No guy in her life was better than the wrong guy. She was single by choice, she told herself. But her mother argued she was "single by choosy."

While Heather prided herself on being particular, it didn't put an extra place setting at her table. Or an extra head on her pillow.

"The bridesmaids' dresses will be navy, too," Lacy went on. "Pink is just the accent color."

Heather silently blessed her friend. A navy dress would help her blend into the background. As gangly as she was, a pink one — especially the violent pink Mrs. Evans favored — would make her feel like an overgrown flamingo.

The curtain enclosing the waiting area ruffled, and Mrs. Evans looked up expectantly.

"Michael," she whispered, but when she saw who it was, her smile turned brittle. Instead of her son, her future son-in-law stepped into the small space. Heather knew Mrs. Evans both liked and approved of Jake Tyler, but he wasn't Michael.

The one who isn't *here is always the one they want to see most.*

Jake gave Lacy a quick kiss. "I overheard you talking about the wedding colors again. Isn't it settled yet?"

"The devil's in the details," Mr. Evans said morosely.

"I tried to talk Lacy into jarhead camouflage, but she insists on navy. *Navy,* of all colors!" Jake shook his head.

"Hey." Lacy gave him a playful swat on the shoulder. "I could always go Army green."

Jake shook his head. "It's enough to make a Marine consider an elopement."

"I've got a ladder you can use, son," Mr. Evans groused. "This wedding is gonna cost the earth."

"Now, George," Mrs. Evans chided, "you'll love giving Lacy away in style and you know it. After all, she's the last daughter you have to walk down the aisle."

Heather had finished her nursing degree and moved back to Coldwater Cove to take a position at the hospital in time to be around for the wedding of the decade, the joining of Crystal Evans and Noah Addleberry. Years later, folks still talked about the event. The Addleberrys were one of the town's first families, so everything had to be just so. Mr. Evans had complained loudly and often to anyone who'd listen, and a few who wouldn't, that if the Addleberrys wanted to bankrupt someone over a wedding, they should start with themselves.

But the real driver of overspending was his own wife. Mrs. Evans got her way in the end, and the wedding was elegantly excessive. Everyone in Coldwater Cove had a guesstimate about how much the wedding had cost. On the low side of the gossip scale, Crystal's wedding could have provided a substantial down payment on a house. If you took Mr. Evans's complaints into consideration, the amount would have run a small country for a week.

He disappeared behind his paper again. Lacy and Crystal and Mrs. Evans nattered on about the color scheme. Heather injected the sedative into her patient's IV and waited for it to take effect.

"It says here in the paper that Levi Harper needs a liver transplant," Mr. Evans told Jake. The young Sooner quarterback was one of Coldwater Cove's favorite sons, a rising University of Oklahoma star. Then he'd gone on a mission trip with his church group to some backwater country over the summer and come home with an exotic parasite that demolished his liver. Now he was forced to sit out his junior year.

"That's a shame." Jake had been an all-conference halfback himself when he was in high school, so following college football was second only to following Lacy. "If Levi gets a new liver, will he be ready to play next year?"

"Hope so," Mr. Evans said. "He comes from good stock, I hear. Aren't the Harpers related to the Walkers, Heather?"

"Yes," she said. "Levi is my cousin several times removed. His mother's uncle was my grandmother's first cousin or some such thing."

Levi was eight or so years younger than Heather, but she remembered him from the big Walker reunions. Levi had been the self-proclaimed leader of a whole gaggle of little boys that styled themselves the "Monkey Troop." They terrorized the great-aunts piecing quilts and then made off with the pies before the rest of the picnic things had even been laid out. No watermelon was safe from their predations. No jug of Kool-Aid stood a chance against their not-so-stealthy marauding.

No one held those youthful indiscretions against Levi now. Since he was family, Heather had been tested for a possible partial liver donation. Unfortunately, she was not a match. If he didn't get a liver soon, he'd have more to worry about than missing a football season.

Heather focused back on her patient at hand. Mrs. Evans was trying to referee while Lacy and her sister wrangled about whether the bridesmaid dresses should be tea length or drape to the floor. Heather was grateful that their argument was distracting their mother. Once the box was checked to indicate whether or not the patient was willing to be a donor, no one going into surgery should be subjected to a prolonged discussion about transplants.

Mrs. Evans was blinking more slowly now. It was time.

Heather told the family. The good-byes took a while because there was a lot of kissing and hugging involved. Through it all, Mrs. Evans assured them that everything would be all right. She stared at the closed curtain once more, as if thinking hard about her son, Michael, would magically summon him. When he didn't appear, she sighed.

"I'm ready."

Heather pulled back the curtain and started pushing the wheeled bed down the hall.

Then Mrs. Evans waved her hand in the air and sang out gaily, "If anything happens, give my liver to that football player!"

Behind her, Heather could hear the Evans family chuckling despite their tears. Shirley Evans was a wonderful human being. She so deserved the support of her entire family.

If Heather ever ran into Michael Evans again, she'd happily lock him in an examination room with a first-year proctology resident and let the new doc practice till he got it right.

However long it took.

CHAPTER 2

Going back to Coldwater Cove feels like
returning to the scene of the crime.
Guess in some ways, it is.
— Michael Evans as he roared
into town on a big-ass Harley

Mike pulled off his helmet and swung it at his side as he strode toward the hospital entrance. A new wing had been added since he'd left town, but as far as he could see, Coldwater General was still a piddle-squat excuse for a hospital.

Why hadn't his dad taken his mother to Tulsa at least?

Cancer.

The word set his gut roiling. His parents had always ragged him about being a risk taker. Now they were the ones taking chances. If he'd had anything to say about it, his mom would have been transferred to the Mayo Clinic as quickly as he could arrange it.

He'd have gotten a second opinion. He'd have found the best oncology team on the planet. He'd . . .

No, he wouldn't. They never would have allowed it. Michael had burned his bridges to the watermark when he'd left town. It was a wonder anyone even bothered to track him down to let him know about his mom's illness. As it was, the news had come to him through a maze of contacts, like a twisted six degrees to Kevin Bacon thing. By the time he'd learned what was happening, there was no way to get back to Coldwater Cove in time to do anything.

Mike pushed through the heavy glass doors — no newfangled automatic ones for Coldwater Cove! — and headed toward the information desk. The strong scent of Pine-Sol wafted up from the old linoleum. Fluorescent lighting hummed overhead. But before Michael reached the blue-haired lady who volunteered behind the desk, his father rounded the corner. The old man was flanked by Mike's sisters. Crystal had draped herself over their dad's arm, while Lacy was hand in hand with a big guy who seemed vaguely familiar.

George Evans stopped dead and stared at Michael as if he didn't recognize him. That was no surprise. It had been nearly a decade since they'd parted.

Badly.

Mike wasn't sure he'd have known his dad either without Crystal and Lacy at his side. The old man seemed shorter than he remembered. Frailer. As if he'd shrunk into himself a bit. Dark circles ringed his eyes, and his cheeks looked damp.

His father had been crying. So had Mike's sisters.

Oh, God.

"Where's Mom?" he asked, panic rising in his throat.

Crystal kept her hand tucked into their father's elbow, more to prop him up than to steady herself, Mike suspected. But his sister Lacy left the guy she was leaning against, ran to Mike, and clung to his neck, sobbing afresh.

Oh, no. He was too late.

Lacy chanted his name between blubbering. Then she pulled back and smiled up at him through her tears. "She's going to be so happy."

She. "Mom's OK?"

"Yes, she's out of surgery and resting now."

"But you're crying."

"Well, that's partly your fault. I'm happy

to see you, you big dope." Lacy punched his shoulder. "As far as the rest of the tears go, we held tough for as long as we could, but once we got the good news about Mom, we sort of let go."

"So it wasn't cancer after all?" Relief washed over him.

"Oh, no. It was," Lacy said, giving him yet another tight hug. "She had a lumpectomy but the mass was pretty well contained. Doc Warner thinks he got it all. There were no cancer cells in the lymph tissue samples. That means he doesn't think the disease has packed its evil little bags and done any traveling."

Mike released a pent-up breath. "So that's it. She's going to be OK."

"What do you care?" His father finally found his tongue and barreled toward him. He stopped only inches away, glaring up at Mike. "You couldn't even be bothered to show up in time to see your mother before she went into surgery. It would've meant the world to her. God knows why."

"Dad, give him a break," Lacy chided. "He's here now."

His father snorted. "A day late and a dollar short. That's you, Michael. Always has been. Obviously, nothing's changed."

George Evans straightened his spine,

turned, and strode toward the exit with Crystal still attached to his arm. Mike's older sister didn't look back, and he didn't expect her to. When they were growing up, he and Crystal had been polar opposites. While she made the honor roll, his grades meant he was always in danger of being held back a year. Not that he was stupid. Far from it. Most of the time, school had simply bored Mike out of his mind.

"Don't take anything Dad says to heart. He's been through a lot these past few days." Lacy gave Mike another hug. It was easy to remember why she was his favorite sister. "He doesn't mean it."

"Yes, he does." Mike watched as the hospital doors whooshed closed behind his dad and Crystal. "And the old man is right. Nothing's changed."

"Well, a few things have." Lacy waggled her left hand in front of his face. A tasteful diamond in an antique setting flashed on her ring finger. She indicated the big guy behind her. "You remember Jacob Tyler, don't you?"

"Oh, yeah. The football jock." Mike extended a hand and Jake gave it a shake.

"We're getting married the Saturday after Thanksgiving," Lacy went on. "Say you'll be there."

"Heck, say you'll be the best man." Jake grinned and slapped him on the back. "May as well keep this thing on the Evans side of the family. That way I don't have to pick one of my brothers over the other. They can both be groomsmen. In fact, if they don't shape up, I may bust them back to being ushers."

"I don't know about being in any wedding." Mike took a step back. He wanted to stay long enough to make sure his mom was OK, but he didn't expect to be sucked back into life in Coldwater Cove. "I doubt I'll be around that long."

Lacy's brows drew together in distress. "Oh, Mike, you've got to be. Mom's going to need you."

"But you said she was going to be OK."

"Doc Warner is optimistic, but he can't say she's cured. He's ordered a full course of chemo and radiation," Lacy said. "And you know how mom is. She wants to do them both at the same time so she can get her treatments over with quicker."

Mike tried to suppress a smile and failed. "That sounds like her. Mom always tackles everything like she's killing snakes."

Lacy nodded in agreement. "And since this time she's killing cancer, I'm glad of it. But it's not going to be easy on her. That's why you need to stick around."

Obviously, his little sister believed he had nothing to go back to. That no one needed him elsewhere. Well, he couldn't blame her. His dad saw him as a shiftless drifter. It was no surprise that Lacy did, too.

She was just nicer about it.

"You can stay with me," she offered. "I've got a couch that makes out into a bed."

"Not necessary." She probably thought he couldn't even afford to take a room at the shabby no-tell motel out on the highway. In fact, Mike had already reserved the ranch house at the Ouachita Inn, a restored nineteenth-century treasure on the other side of Lake Jewel. "I got it covered."

Lacy looked pointedly at his helmet. "My couch may not be the Hilton, but it'll beat the pup tent you've got strapped to your bike."

Mike didn't wonder why Lacy hadn't suggested he stay at their parents' big house. Even though there was plenty of room, they both knew that wouldn't fly. "Let me worry about where I sleep, little sister. Now, where's Mom?"

"Second floor. Ask at the nurses' station. Before they could assign her a room, Mom shooed us all out while she was still fresh from recovery. Dad skipped breakfast this morning and lunchtime has come and gone. She was worried about him so we were taking him to the Green Apple for something to eat."

"Did he skip his coffee too?" Mike asked.

Lacy nodded. George Evans's brew was legendary, both for its strength and its awfulness. It was an acquired taste, but their dad had been drinking the stuff so long, anyone else's coffee was like a shriveled bean dipped in tepid water to him.

Lacy nodded. "So that accounts for his surliness toward you."

Mike cast her a wry smile. They both knew that wasn't true. Even if Dad had jolted down six cups of his coffee that morning, his reaction to Michael would have been the same. But Lacy's lie was kindly meant. "Guess I better find Mom."

"After you're done here, come by the Green Apple Grill," Jake said. "You can have supper on the house."

Great. His sister thought he couldn't keep the rain off his head, and his future brother-in-law felt the need to feed him. He didn't know which was worse, his father's bare antagonism or Lacy and Jake's suffocating overprotectiveness.

"I may drop by later, then," he said because they both looked so hopeful about it. Mike guessed he couldn't afford to alienate the one part of the family that was still speaking to him. Then before they could start making any other decisions for him, he headed toward the elevator.

He made it two steps before Lacy practically tackled him with another hug. "Oh, Michael, I can't tell you how good it is to see you. Thank you so much for coming home."

He hugged her back. The scent of his sister's hair flooded his mind with memories. She smelled of new-mown grass and crisp fall leaves and the long Indian summer evenings when they were kids, chasing fireflies on the lawn.

Had he ever really been that innocent?

Home, she says. Mike wasn't sure where that elusive place was, but he was pretty certain it wasn't Coldwater Cove.

Not for him. Not anymore.

Heather updated Mrs. Evans's records. She'd be released tomorrow, but she had a long row to hoe. Heather was still trying to convince her to give herself a little time to recover from surgery and do some physical therapy before starting her other treatments. A lumpectomy wasn't as invasive as a full mastectomy, but Mrs. Evans would have muscle weakness in her left arm where the lymph nodes had been removed. It could linger for some time. But even a week of regular exercises to regain her strength would help before starting on chemo and radiation. At the moment, her friend's mother was set on leaping into treatment right away.

Heather checked her schedule. No more surgeries were planned for the day, so she only had the two postoperative patients to manage for the rest of her shift. Aaron Bugtussle, the twelve-year-old who'd had the emergency appendectomy that morning, was still feeling pretty tough. He wouldn't touch so much as the lime Jell-O on his lunch tray. Tina-Louise "Grandma" Bugtussle had smuggled in a possum pie, which she claimed was his favorite, but even that hill-folk delicacy failed to tempt the boy's appetite.

Heather counted Aaron's refusal to scarf down possum as a sign of intelligence, but the kid still needed to eat.

"I hope the next shift can get some chicken soup into him," Heather told Glenda Scott, the CNA on duty.

Glenda nodded and looked up from her cell phone, a guilty expression on her face. "Sorry, Heather. This app is so addictive."

Glenda had been thumbing the small screen, popping the digital Bubble Wrap that served as her wallpaper. She shoved her phone into her pocket and tucked the strand of iron-gray hair that had escaped her cap behind her ear. If Glenda ever started coloring her hair, no one would believe the slender, energetic woman was in her fifties. "But the silly thing sure is a good stress reliever."

"You need to take a break?" Heather asked. Glenda was pulling a double shift since the hospital was woefully short staffed.

"Naw. Half a minute of popping bubbles and I'm good to go," Glenda said. "You know, while I was popping, it came to me that we ought to find out if the Bugtussle boy plays football. He has to be firing on all cylinders before we'll let him out of here. If he has a game coming up and doesn't want to read about it in the papers, he might start eating."

"Good idea." Heather cast a sidelong glance at her coworker. She wondered if it was Glenda's life outside the hospital that caused her to need a stress reliever. "How's it going with Lester?"

"There is no 'with Lester,' so there's nothing going," she said with a shrug. "He comes over on Sundays and mows my lawn.

I let him drink a glass of tea on the porch. That's it. Besides, I'm off men."

If she wasn't, she should have been. Glenda was still technically married to Lester, but her husband had been an alcoholic early in their marriage, and a homeless bum who'd deserted his family for a decade or so after that. Now Lester Scott was off alcohol, seeing a therapist for his PTSD and anger issues, and trying to turn his life around with meaningful work and better choices. Mowing Glenda's lawn every week was one of his small ways of trying to make amends.

Heather was all for second chances. In fact, she and the Coldwater Warm Hearts Club, a service group she'd founded, had been instrumental in helping Lester take his first steps back into society. But it wouldn't pay for Glenda to be too forgiving.

Not yet anyway.

"Trust, but verify, that's my motto," Glenda said. "After Lester replaces the shingles on my garage, I may give him an Oreo to go with his tea. But only if he cuts off that stupid man bun he's trying to grow and shaves his beard." Then she surprised Heather with a low whistle.

"Oh, my!" The older woman fanned herself with her hand. "Hottie alert on your six."

Heather frowned. "I thought you were off men."

"I *am* off men," Glenda admitted. "But that doesn't make me dead. Looking never hurt anybody. And this fellow's well worth a look."

Most of the men Heather met were too married, too old, too young, or too gay. If she met a new man that didn't fit into any of those categories at Coldwater General, it would be time to alert the media. Heather shifted slightly so she could get a glimpse of the guy in question from the corner of her eye without seeming to ogle him.

Glenda was right. He was worth two looks.

His dark hair was a couple weeks past needing a cut. Dressed in biker leathers, he was the poster boy for trouble on two legs. Some impressive ink crept from under his white T-shirt and up one side of his neck.

Heather normally didn't go for men with tats, but this guy's neck would have seemed naked without it. She didn't recognize the pattern. It flowed and twisted back on itself like a bowlful of long-tailed commas that had been dumped in a blender with a handful of mathematical symbols. The effect was both brainy and "whoa, baby!" at the same time. The unusual tattoo drew her gaze up to his angular face. His jaw was dusted with a couple of days' worth of beard. The eyes beneath his dark brows were gunmetal gray.

Her belly did a couple of backflips, but in that giddy endorphin-infused moment, Heather figured out who he was.

Michael Evans.

He seemed to know her, too, because one corner of his mouth turned up in a crooked smile. "Well, if it isn't Stilts Walker."

After all those years, the nickname still stung.

"That's *Nurse* Walker to you," she said icily.

"Is that an invitation to play doctor?"

Heather barely stifled the impulse to reach across the counter and smack his handsome face. She wasn't sure where he'd been for the last ten years or so, but he hadn't lost his easy drawl. Low and rumbly, it was disgustingly easy on the ears.

She drew herself up to her full five eleven and a half. Usually that was enough to cow most men, but she'd need to wear heels to go eye-to-eye with Lacy's bad-boy brother.

If Michael felt at all intimidated, he didn't show it. "What have you been doing with yourself? Besides getting prettier."

"Finishing my education and starting a

career," Heather said, trying to be all business despite the flutter in her belly. A compliment from a guy like Mike Evans didn't count for spit. She drew on her old basketball coach's advice. *The best defense is a good offense. Time to put him on the run.* "I've been taking care of people like your mother. She was hoping to see you before her surgery this morning, you know."

She wished she could whale into him about how crappy it was for him to have turned up late. He ought to know how his thoughtlessness had hurt his mom. If only he could have seen Mrs. Evans's hopeful face when she'd thought he was coming just before she was about to go under the knife. And then the way her face had changed when she'd realized he wasn't there after all.

It made Heather's heart ache for her.

But only last Sunday, Pastor Mark had reminded Heather and the rest of her fellow Methodists that they didn't need to get even with those who upset them.

God was the ultimate scorekeeper.

"Remember how the apostle Paul said: 'If thine enemy hunger, feed him; if he thirst, give him drink: for in so doing thou shalt heap coals of fire on his head,' " the pastor had explained. "Think of it as a sort of heavenly hotfoot!"

Michael Evans could use a singe around the edges. So instead of tearing into the man, Heather smiled at him. Sweetly.

"You must be tired after your trip from . . . wherever it is you've been. Glenda, please fetch a bottled water for Michael from the break room."

He leaned on the counter that separated them. "And here I thought you didn't remember me."

"A girl would be hard-pressed to forget a guy who called her Stilts."

He nodded. "Point taken. Sorry about that. I was kind of a jerk back then."

Only back then? Heather clamped her lips together to keep her thoughts from tumbling through them. *He disappoints his mother, and then he insults me with the first words out of his mouth. How is that not still jerk-worthy?*

"I shouldn't have teased you about being tall, Heather," he said. "But you sure make the height look worth the climb."

She looked away, wishing his voice wasn't so deep. It drizzled over her, rich as hot fudge on Häagen-Dazs.

"Well, if I can't get you to smile, I better go see my mom. Maybe I'll have better luck with her," he said. "Since you're taking care of her, you must know which room she's in."

"Mrs. Evans is in 201. End of the hall." Heather glued her gaze to the chart in her hands. It was safer. It kept the little flutters in her belly at bay. "Don't tire her out."

"I wasn't planning on making her run a five K."

She made the mistake of looking up at him, and Michael smiled.

It was the kind of smile a smart woman hopes never to see because it turns female insides to Jell-O. It was the sort of smile that stood the world on its head. It made her want to trust him, to swallow anything he said whole without pausing to wonder how or if it would go down. His smile was full of promise.

It's far more likely to be full of horse-hockey.

Michael had skipped town without a backward glance, deserting his family for years.

Heather didn't understand how he could have given up so much. Granted, her relationship with her own parents was strained at best, and had been since her twin died some years ago. But at least she was still talking to her mom and dad, still trying to maintain a connection, even if it felt like they were all tiptoeing around each other most of the time. Of course, it might help if they'd decide to stay in town for longer than a few weeks at a stretch. Her parents were consumed with travel, the more exotic, the better.

Running from their grief over Jessica.

Once Heather had finished her schooling, she hadn't felt the need to get away from Coldwater Cove for very long. Her roots were here. Her sister's grave was here. She had a life here, even if her parents often didn't.

Michael Evans had been in and out of trouble for years, but the final breach with his family happened after his grandmother died. Mike was suddenly gone, sliced from Coldwater Cove in one swift cut.

Heather never heard exactly why.

Now he was back. Heather told herself she didn't care, so long as Michael's reappearance didn't upset her patient.

"See you 'round, Stilts," he called over his shoulder as he moved down the hall in long-legged strides.

Yes, indeed. As long as he kept calling her "Stilts," it would be super easy not to care that Michael Evans was back in town.

Chapter 3

Finding a good man is as hard as sinking a game-winning three-pointer just as the buzzer sounds. No, on second thought, finding a good man is harder.

— Heather "Stilts" Walker, Long Shot Queen of the Lady Marmot basketball team, all-conference four years in a row

On Friday when her shift was over, Heather wished she could just kick back with a glass of sweet tea and a romance novel and put her feet up. Instead she wiggled into her one and only little black dress and shoved her tired size nines into fire-engine red pumps.

Every Labor Day weekend, a dance was held on Friday night for Coldwater alumni, regardless of when they'd graduated. The high school gym floor would be filled with octogenarians, twentysomethings, and folks from every decade of life in between. Her parents had insisted that she make an appearance.

Heather's mom and dad served on the organizing committee this year and had spent the better part of last week decorating the gym. A red torii gate fashioned of chicken wire and papier-mâché hung over the door. Paper lotus blossoms and origami storks dangled from the beams. Ever since the Walkers had visited Japan last year, her parents had been on a Zen kick.

"Besides, darling," her mother had said while she was twisting Heather's arm about coming to the dance, "how will you ever meet someone if all you do is go back and forth from your dreary little job to your dreary little apartment?"

Her mother had a point, but Heather wasn't about to acknowledge it. If it had been up to her folks, Heather would have become a trust fund brat. When she was in kindergarten, the wildcat drilling operation her dad had patched together had struck a huge oil deposit on the Walker ranch. Since then, the family had been swimming in cash and decided to diversify, snapping up most of the buildings that ringed the Square and becoming a powerful force in town. Heather could have ditched a career completely and spent her time blowing the generous stipend her dad tried to get her to take, but she wanted to make it on her own.

Besides, after her twin, Jessica, died in that senseless accident, Heather ached for her own life to *mean* something. There had to be more than shopping and flitting around the globe.

So she'd earned her RN through her own hard work. And she could afford the "dreary little apartment" on her hospital salary without touching the fund her parents had set up for her, thank you very much. As far as meeting someone went, as long as endless piles of Walker money followed her around, how could she ever be sure a guy was interested in her for herself, not just her burgeoning trust fund?

"There are bound to be some successful graduates returning for the reunion," her mother had said. "I hear Skyler Sweazy is back for the weekend. He went to Harvard, remember?"

Skyler belonged to one of the other founding families in the area and had the distinction of being the first Ivy Leaguer in the county. So the fact that Heather came from money probably wouldn't figure into the equation with him. But he'd also been her sister Jessica's boyfriend back in high school.

So that would be kinda weird.

Heather had spent most of her adult life trying to escape the shadow of her dead sibling. Just the thought of seeing Skyler as something other than an old classmate gave her the willies, but she promised her mom she'd show up for the dance.

Sometimes, you have to go along to get along.

Besides, one of the biggest complaints from returning alumni was that the classmates who lived in other parts of the country made more effort to attend the reunions than the ones who'd stayed in town.

There's a reason for that.

Reunions were mostly about bragging rights — who'd landed the best job, who'd married well, whose kids were the cutest, yada, yada, yada. Heather wasn't in a mood to make appreciative noises over pictures of someone else's little bundles of joy.

Her goldfish clearly did not count.

But tonight was a "command performance." After her parents had ponied up for the new mental health clinic at Bates College with a generous endowment when she'd asked them to, she couldn't very well brush them off.

Attending the reunion dance was such a simple request.

She didn't see them now in the milling

crowd gathered in scattered clumps around the gym. However, Junior Bugtussle spied her and waved her over to join him and his wife, Darlene, by the buffet table.

"Hey there, Heather." Junior pumped her hand with vigor. "Gotta thank you again for takin' such good care of our boy."

"It was a team effort. Aaron had a close call. Good thing you got him to the hospital so quickly," Heather said. A ruptured appendix was no joke, and Junior must have recognized it. The Bugtussles' truck had come flying up to the emergency room door with one of the sheriff's cruisers on its tail, sirens blaring. Junior had torn through the town's one stoplight and across the mayor's manicured lawn, destroying his prized pachysandra. Once the deputy realized the violations were committed, not out of malice or too much white lightning, but out of desperation, he ripped up the ticket he'd started to write and helped Junior get his boy into the ER.

Heather's gaze swept the crowd, still looking for her parents. She couldn't slip away from the dance until they'd seen her there. She found them across the gym floor under one of the basketball hoops. Her mother was deep in conversation with the retiring Judge Preston and the new judge who'd been appointed to replace him. Everyone was curious about Barbara Mueller, a former Oklahoma City prosecutor, and wondered how she'd adapt to life in Coldwater Cove.

Heather's mother looked up and spied her next to the Bugtussles. She sent her a furious frown. Heather could almost hear her scathing thoughts from across the wide space.

"Why are you spending time with those ignorant hillbillies when you could take your place with the quality folk of the county?"

Heather had tried to explain to her mom that she had a totally different idea about what "quality" meant, but her mom never quite understood. If honesty and "salt-of-the-earthiness" counted — emphasis on "earthiness," it must be admitted — then the Bugtussles had "quality" in spades. She turned back to face them.

"Aaron's doing pretty well considering how serious that surgery could have been, but he's not eating much," Heather told the Bugtussles as she helped herself to some of the goodies on the buffet table. Shrimp tempura, sashimi, egg rolls, and vegetables with wasabi.

Say what you will about my folks, but they do know how to lay out an impressive spread.

"If your son eats a good breakfast tomorrow and continues to improve," Heather said, "he could be going home by suppertime."

"Well, don't tell him that or he won't never eat a bite," Junior drawled. "He let slip to his ma that he kinda likes only having to share a room with one other kid."

"Aaron has four younger brothers," Darlene said, beaming.

"And the trailer ain't got but two bedrooms, so the boys have to bunk together. Anyways, Grandma's with the little 'uns tonight and what with Aaron well looked after at the hospital, Darlene and me thought, being as how I *almost* graduated, we'd come to the reunion dance."

Junior ran a hand over his gel-slicked hair, as if to highlight the fact that the Bugtussles knew how to gussy up for an occasion. His overalls were worn, but clean, and his boots had been freshly hosed off. He must have doused himself with Old Spice. The cloud of scent swirling around him made Heather's eyes burn.

Darlene was pretty in a windswept-prairie sort of way and would have looked fine if she'd just come as she was. Unfortunately, she'd done her best to try to look "nice." Heather doubted even a Wizard-of-Oz-style twister could budge a single strand of Darlene's heavily sprayed do.

"I'm glad you came," Heather said with sincerity. Just because her parents had become world-class snobs didn't mean she had to be. "Have you tried the food yet? My folks were on the reunion committee. They had sushi shipped in especially for the occasion."

"Sushi, huh? Is that what that is?" Junior eyed the buffet table with suspicion. "I thought somebody done laid out a couple a trays of bait."

"Be nice, Junior," Darlene said, elbowing him with a quick poke to the ribs.

"Ow!" Junior rubbed his side and edged away from his wife a bit. "I'm always nice. I'm just saying, what's wrong with havin' them little Vienna sausages wrapped in a biscuit?" He pronounced it "Vy-Anna," making sure the tiny wieners sounded Ozarkian instead of Austrian. "Maybe some fried okra on them fancy colored toothpicks. That's all."

"This here is an uptown shindig, for sure," Darlene told him. "Stands to reason, the food needs to be way more fancier than pigs-in-a-blanket and okra on a stick."

"Well, fancy or not, when a feller don't know what somethin' is, he oughter think twice about putting it in his mouth."

"Junior, I've watched you stuff your face for the last twelve years or so. Don't nothing make you think once, let alone twice. I swear you'd eat the putty out of the winders when you're sharp-set." Darlene rolled her eyes at her husband and turned back to Heather. "When do you think they'll get the fiddle player and caller going?"

The Bugtussles were obviously expecting a different sort of dance.

"I think the big band is playing tonight," Heather said. A local crew of instrumentalists got together to play standards at the Opera House on the Town Square once a month. They weren't exactly Benny Goodman's orchestra, but they had fun making music and made sure their audience had fun, too. Even recent grads, who might be expected to be more at home at a rap concert, didn't seem to mind trying a foxtrot for the reunion dance. As part of the phys ed program at the end of their senior year, everyone who graduated from Coldwater High learned a little ballroom.

Unfortunately, Junior and Darlene hadn't made it to that particular finish line.

"Well, shucks. Bet they don't play nothing we can square-dance to," Junior said morosely. "Come on, Darlene. Let's get us some grub then."

"Be sure to try that sushi stuff, Junior," his wife said, tugging at his elbow. "Just because you ain't never tried it don't mean you won't like it."

"I ain't never shot myself in the foot but I'm pretty sure I don't want to try that neither."

With a smile, Heather watched the Bugtussles move down the buffet line. Then a different male cologne overpowered Junior's Old Spice. This new scent was like a civet cat stalking her from a musky jungle. With a low note of stale Febreze.

"Hope the music starts soon," came a voice from behind her to go along with the cologne. "I bet you remember how to do a good West Coast swing, Heather."

She turned to find Skyler Sweazy, her sister's old flame. Too much Axe spray aside, he looked like a *GQ* cover model in skinny-cut khaki Dockers and a navy Izod polo shirt. She wondered if he had his brows waxed back East. Not so much as a nose hair was out of place.

He must spend hours in front of a mirror.

Skyler had always struck her as being self-absorbed. In that respect, he hadn't changed much since she'd seen him last. Heather thought a good-looking guy who didn't know it was always more attractive than one who knew he turned female heads.

Still, Jessica had been wild about the guy, so there must be something to him.

Skyler grinned at her, displaying a set of blindingly white teeth.

If those aren't veneers, I'll eat my goldfish.

"How could I forget?" Heather said. "Mrs. Kady spent the better part of that last semester in gym class making sure we could all dance."

Skyler stretched his spine, standing as tall as he could, but Heather still topped him by a couple of inches. She and Jessica had been fraternal twins. Her sister had been much shorter, the crown of her head reaching only to Skyler's shoulder height. Everyone said they made the perfect couple.

Maybe if I were in flats . . .

She wiped that thought away. It was something straight from her mother's playbook. Marcia Walker was all about women making unreasonable accommodations for the men in their lives. It sometimes seemed as if she were more an extension of Heather's father than a person in her own right. Over Skyler's shoulder, Heather caught sight of her mom, smiling and giving her a surreptitious "thumbs-up." She'd obviously steered Jessica's old boyfriend over to her.

Nuts to that. Heather adjusted her posture to ramrod perfection. If Skyler's neck hurt from looking up to her, so be it.

"What have you been up to since you left town?" she asked pleasantly. It wasn't his fault he'd fallen into her mother's nefarious plans.

"Making partner at Dunham and Howe in Cambridge, Mass.," Skyler said with no hint of his former Okie drawl. He hadn't quite mastered a Bostonian accent yet, but he dropped plenty of *r*'s in the attempt. "And in record time, too."

"Well, good for you, Skyler."

"Got that right." Now he sounded more like the boy she'd known. "Nothing worse than being beholden to family money."

That set her back a step. His family was easily as wealthy as hers. The Sweazys had made their money in cattle back when Oklahoma was still a territory. Later, they'd branched out into trucking and shipping, both domestic and international, to bring their beef to market. The fact that Skyler didn't want to be folded into the family business raised him a notch or two in her eyes.

But not her nose.

If only he'd ditch that heavy aftershave . . .

"You're right about family money," she said. "I steer clear of it as much as I can."

She didn't expect anyone else to understand how she felt about the Walker fortune. Most people would kill to have what her family could hand to her. But what they didn't realize was that nothing in this life is free.

Her parents' money came with shackles. The shackles of someone else's expectations for her life. Heather wouldn't allow herself to be manacled by them.

She found herself telling Skyler about going to the state university instead of a private college to get her nursing degree because she could pay for it herself between part-time jobs and scholarships. He made approving noises.

"So aren't you going to ask why I didn't go to med school and become a doctor instead?" she asked. Most people did.

"No, I get it," Skyler said. "You want to be the first line of care for people who need you, not someone who just breezes through on rounds."

Heather felt an unexpected rush of warmth toward Skyler. He understood her. A little, anyway.

Maybe Lacy's right. Maybe I have been too choosy. Is there a time when a girl should stop thinking about settling down and just settle instead?

Her mother was in her head again. She gave herself an inward shake.

Skyler shifted his weight, clearly impatient. "So when's the party starting anyway?"

"Don't get your knickers in a knot. Folks will think you've gotten all citified. I know things move faster back East, but here in Coldwater Cove, everything happens when it happens," Heather said.

"Can I help it if I'm looking forward to dancing with you?"

That gave her a rosy glow. A compliment was a compliment, and she'd not had many of late.

That stuff Michael Evans said so *does not count.*

"The band is just now getting set up," she said. "Besides, the reunion dance can't start until we sing the fight song."

As if on cue, Mr. Whittle, a round little man who'd been the high school principal since the Flood, stepped up to the microphone. "Welcome home, Fighting Marmots!"

The gymnasium erupted in cheers.

"We're so glad you've all come back to the place that gave you your start. We're proud of you and it does our hearts good to see that you're still proud to be one of us," he said. "I know you'll all do your best to join me now as we sing the school fight song!"

"Oh, no," Skyler said under his breath. "If I remember right, Mr. Whittle sings like a buzz saw."

"You remember right. But it's OK." She pointed surreptitiously to where her father had stationed himself next to the sound equipment. "My dad has it covered. As soon as the singing starts, Mr. Whittle will be losing his microphone."

Skyler laughed. It was a pleasantly male sound. Heather found herself laughing with him. Then Mrs. Paderewski, the town's piano teacher, struck a chord on the upright near the stage at the end of the gymnasium, and the singing began.

The Coldwater Cove fight song borrowed its tune from "Go U Northwestern," but the lyrics were uniquely altered to reference the team name.

Go, Fighting Marmots, squeeze right
through that line,
With your tails a-flying, we will cheer you
ev'ry time,
Hey! Rah, Rah!
Go, Fighting Marmots, made for victory

Spread far the fame of our proud name,
Go, Fighting Marmots, never tame.
(whistling and foot stamping for four beats)
Go, You Marmots, go!
(Shouted) Hit 'em hard! Hit 'em low!
Make 'em wish they weren't so slow!
Fighting Marmots, go!

When the song ended, the clapping and whistles rattled the rafters. Mr. Whittle's microphone mysteriously began working again as he thanked the crowd for that rousing rendition and ordered them all to have a good time.

Heather caught her dad's eye from across the room. He winked at her. His electrical sleight of hand had spared the principal's feelings by not exposing the fact that he couldn't carry a tune in a bushel basket and, at the same time, spared the gathered crowd from having to listen to him try. Her father's action was thoughtful, well-timed, and best of all, sneaky in a good way.

Dad and I disagree on a lot, but when he gets it right, he's my hero.

Skyler chuckled again. "That fight song is so stupid, I can't believe people sing it with a straight face. I'd almost forgotten how ridiculous this place is," he said. "If the other partners could see me now, they'd demote me back to the mail room."

Heather was ready to demote him back to "unwelcome outsider" status. She loved Coldwater Cove, despite its oddities.

Or maybe because of them.

The band struck up "In the Mood," and Skyler grabbed her hand and twirled her onto the dance floor. Before she could object, they were spinning and dipping around the room. All the steps Mrs. Kady had pounded into her came back to Heather. To her surprise, Skyler was a good dance partner.

"Remember, boys," Mrs. Kady had said in every class, "the gentleman's main job is to make the lady look good."

Skyler remembered. He went out of his way to lead her with assurance and show her off with each turn. Soon a circle formed around them as others stopped dancing to watch. Despite having been irritated with Skyler when they first started, by the time the trumpet blasted its last cadenza, Heather was having a ball.

Then when they came to a swinging stop, Heather felt a strange ripple down her spine. It was the same sensation that raised the hair on her neck when she had to walk a dark alley, the same instinct that warned the browsing doe to lift her head because a hunter had her in his sights.

Someone is watching me. Even as the thought flitted through her mind, she knew it was silly. *Everyone* was watching her and Skyler. And everyone applauded their dancing.

Everyone except Michael Evans.

She spotted him leaning on the doorjamb under the torii gate, next to the table where folks were supposed to pick up their name tags. His expression was carefully blank as if he were completely bored and couldn't decide whether or not it was worth his time to come all the way in. In addition to the biker leathers, he was wearing a pair of dark glasses. Heather couldn't see his eyes behind them, but she'd bet her trust fund those steely grays were trained on her.

No one else could make her feel so spied upon. Or give her such tingly prickles while they were doing it.

Chapter 4

We should not judge other people based on their clothing. We should look at them as if they had no clothes. Oh, wait . . .
— from Pastor Mark's sermon on "Judge Not Lest Ye Be Judged."
Note: Please make sure the congregational laughter is cut from the tape before it's delivered to shut-ins. Mrs. Chisholm and the rest will not be amused by their pastor talking about naked people from the pulpit. Even if he didn't mean to.

The circle around Heather and Skyler closed in so folks could heap compliments on their dancing skill.

"Yes, indeed," Darlene Bugtussle gushed as she pushed through the crowd to add her two cents. "It was like watching *Dancing with the Stars,* only gooder 'cuz we know who you are. Seems like Junior and me don't never know any of them TV folk what are s'posed to be so famous. Oh, law, would you look at that. Junior's too close to that punch bowl. Don't think he smuggled a flask in, but you can't never be too careful."

Darlene zipped across the gym toward her wayward husband while Heather's parents made a beeline toward her and her dance partner.

"Oh, Skyler, it's so good to see you again," her mother said, her eyes sparkling with excitement. She'd always hoped for a match between Jessica and the heir to the Sweazy fortune. Of course, Jess and he had been too young to get serious in high school, but even so, Heather's mom had encouraged Jess to apply to Brown, so she could follow Skyler to New England. But the accident ended Marcia Walker's dream of joining two of the most prominent Coldwater families.

"I gather you've done well for yourself back East." Her father shook Skyler's hand.

Oh, my gosh! It's like Dad's angling for a merger, too.

"Well, of course, he has. All it takes is one glance at him and anyone can see that," her mother said with a pointed look at Heather. Clearly, a new dream that involved Skyler Sweazy and a Walker girl was blossoming in her mother's mind. "Isn't it good to see him, Heather?"

"Yes, Mother," she said dutifully. The prickly sensation in her spine had only gotten worse. She was sure there were eyeballs on her and she was just as sure, without knowing how she knew, that they belonged to Mike Evans. "Thanks for the dance, Skyler. Excuse me, please."

She turned away and headed toward the town's original bad boy, with every intention of giving him what for. No one was going to make her uncomfortable in her own skin.

"Hey, wait —" She heard Skyler call from behind her, but she pretended she didn't. Not only was it a relief to get away from his cologne, but Heather was on a mission. She was out to prove to herself that Michael Evans was just another guy. He had no special draw for her. That tingly feeling was a fluke.

"Nice dance. You sure know how to use those long legs," he said when she stopped before him. He crossed his arms over his chest. Michael, unlike Skyler, didn't seem to be wearing strong cologne, but Heather caught a faint whiff of worn leather and an open-road sort of freshness.

The tingles grew more insistent. "What

are you doing here?"

"Hey, I graduated. I'm entitled to be here."

Only just, she almost said. Michael was supposed to be a year ahead of her and Lacy, but when she was in second grade, he was held back. Every fall, she wondered if he'd advance with the class or have to repeat another grade.

The fact that she remembered more about Michael than she'd originally thought made her feel even pricklier.

He took off his shades and stuffed them into the inside pocket of his jacket. His eyes were more unsettling than the sunglasses had been because now there was no mistaking that he was looking at her.

As if I were the last biscuit on the plate.

"Besides, even if I hadn't graduated," he went on, "I wouldn't be the only one here who didn't."

He nodded in the direction of Junior Bugtussle, who, amazingly enough, was headed back to the buffet table. Once there, he heaped his paper plate with so much sushi, Darlene had to pull him away before he emptied the platter.

"No," Heather said, refusing to be distracted. "I mean, why are you *here* instead of with your mother?"

"They kicked me out."

She blinked in surprised. "That's not hospital policy. Visiting hours don't apply to family. As long as the patient is able to rest, we generally allow family to stay."

"I wasn't kicked out by the hospital."

"Oh." It was fleeting, but Heather thought she detected pain in his eyes. Then a wall rose up behind them, and he looked as cool and bored as ever. Even though his relationship with his folks was clearly strained, a hospital bed was a great place to mend fences.

Or start to.

The band began a slow tune in three-quarter time. From the corner of her eye, she could see Skyler making his way toward her, obviously intent on claiming her for a waltz. Behind him, her mother and father looked on. Their expressions were an odd mix of concern and hope. The first was about the guy in front of her and the second for the one headed her way.

They so tried to micromanage her life.

Imagine how much worse they'd be if I ever accepted a nickel from them.

"Dance with me," she said impulsively. That would put a kink in her parents' plans, big-time.

"What?" Michael stopped leaning on the wall.

"You heard me. Dance. With. Me." She took one of his hands. "Now."

"I'm not sure I remember how."

"It's easy. Just do what I do, except facing forward, in flats, and on the other foot. How hard can it be?" She arranged him into a waltz hold. "I'll lead."

Michael resisted the urge to pinch himself as they began to move in time around the room.

I'm dancing with Stilts Walker.

He'd thought about her over the years, wondering where she was, who she'd ended up with. He never thought he'd be lucky enough to have her in his arms.

There has to be a catch.

"OK," he said. "Why did you want to dance with me?"

She looked pointedly at the bleacher side of the gym, where Mr. and Mrs. Walker were frowning worriedly in their direction. "Because I couldn't think of a better way to tick off my parents on such short notice."

"All right." He should have figured it didn't have anything to do with her wanting to be with him. "I'm up for being a way to punish your parents."

He pulled her closer. Her hair smelled so sweet, a light combination of honeysuckle and lavender. And she was soft in all the right places. He pressed gently on the small of her back, drawing her in tight, until there wasn't room to slip a paper clip between them.

"What are you doing?" The whites showed all around Heather's big brown eyes.

"If we dance closer, it'll really upset your parents."

She pulled back a bit. "I think they're suffering enough."

Michael was getting comfortable with the basic box step and decided he remembered enough of Mrs. Kady's dance lessons to try an overhead turn. Heather followed his lead beautifully. They weren't putting on a show like she'd done with Sweazy, but they were staying together better than Mike had expected.

"Why do you want to make your parents suffer at all?" he asked. "What did they ever do to you?"

"They're trying to make decisions for me."

"So you thought it would be good for them to have a ringside seat while you made a wrong one?"

"I'm sorry. You're not a wrong decision. I didn't mean to imply that you . . ." She bit her lower lip and her cheeks bloomed in a rosy blush.

"Yeah, you did. It's OK. I know who I am. A parent's worst nightmare. Always have been."

"No. It's not that. It's just that they want me to do something else besides . . . dance with you."

She hadn't meant to insult him. That was something, anyway. Besides, she wasn't wrong. Among the assembled Coldwater grads, he was the baddest of bad choices.

"What makes you think you're a wrong decision?" she asked.

"Lots and lots of practice."

Her lips turned up at the corners.

Yeah, those lips. Parts of Heather Walker had featured prominently in his dreams over the years. Her delectable mouth was a headliner.

The mouth started moving. "Well, I do seem to remember Mr. Whittle claiming that you raised bad behavior to an art form."

"Yeah, that sounds like me. What did I do that time?" Mike asked with a grin.

"I think that was when you put a cow on the roof of the new library."

"You have to admit they left themselves wide open for it. What with all those signs with longhorns on them, asking if we were in the ‘mo-o-o-d’ for reading.”

Heather’s lips twitched as if she wanted to smile again, but didn’t want to encourage him.

They danced without speaking for a few measures. The silence began to be oppressive.

“What have you —” “So are you —” They both started talking at once and then laughed together.

“Ladies first,” Michael said. “Another thing I learned from Mrs. Kady.”

“So since we’re at a reunion, are you going to tell me what you’ve been up to?” Heather asked.

He shrugged. If he told her the truth, she wouldn’t believe him. He barely believed it himself. Granted, he’d worked hard to get where he was, but he’d been blessed by some pretty spectacular luck, too.

“Well, tonight I had supper at the Green Apple Grill and got to size up my future brother-in-law,” Michael said. “A wounded warrior, a generous guy who adores my sister, and best of all, he makes a mean hamburger.”

“You should try Jake’s meatloaf.”

“Think I might.” If Michael stayed in town long enough. He had responsibilities, people who were depending on him. He couldn't let himself be sucked into such a little backwater. They were probably still limping along with dial-up here. "Jake doesn't let that prosthetic leg get him down much, does he?"

"I think your sister has helped him with that."

"Jake and Lacy are good together, aren't they?"

"Yes, they are, but you're dodging my question," Heather said with dogged persistence. "What have you been doing with yourself since you left Coldwater Cove?"

"I did some traveling." That much was true. When he'd first lit out, he wandered around the country on his motorcycle until his money dried up and he was forced to sell his wheels to keep eating. Then he thumbed his way from place to place, taking odd jobs to keep body and soul together, before ending up homeless on the streets of New York City.

Hitting bottom has a way of making a guy realize he's reached the end of himself.

For Michael, it meant he finally stopped long enough to take stock of things and make some changes.

"Did you ever . . . meet anyone?" she asked so softly he barely heard her over the music.

"I met lots of people."

"I mean anyone special."

Michael knew what she meant. He just never thought Heather Walker would care enough to ask. "Everyone I meet is special in some way."

He knew it was a tease, but he enjoyed making her brows draw together a bit. Her brown eyes were usually warm and sexy looking, but now they were about to spit sparks. He decided not to tease her anymore.

"I never got married or anything, if that's what you're wondering. Not even close," he admitted. "How about you? Anybody special in your life, Stilts?"

OK, maybe I'm not done teasing her yet.

Then she stiffened in his arms, and he wished she hadn't.

"I really haven't had time for a serious relationship," she said.

"You should make time," Michael said, realizing he was preaching to himself as well. "Time is all we really have, you know."

"Says the man who couldn't tell time well enough to get here before his mom went into surgery."

Now it was Mike's turn to stiffen. "I apologized to her for that already. I'm not sure I owe you one too."

She lowered her gaze. "You're right. You don't."

The message about his mother's cancer surgery hadn't even reached him until the wee hours of the morning. He'd woken his staff, canceled meetings, and had his assistant arrange for him to travel from the Big Apple to "Middle-of-Nowhere," Oklahoma, almost as fast as if he'd been able to say, "Beam me up, Scotty." He'd have explained his situation to his mother in more detail that afternoon, but his father had come back from his late lunch quicker than Michael had anticipated.

"I really wish I could have spent more time with her today," he said.

"You mean that?"

He nodded.

Heather searched his face for a moment and seemed satisfied with what she saw. "Do you think your dad has gone home for the night?"

He released her hand to check his watch but kept doing a basic box step. "It's after nine o'clock. If Dad isn't in his pajamas with his feet up waiting for the news to start, it'll be a first."

Heather stopped dancing and grabbed him by the hand again. It was getting to be a habit with her. He was beginning to like it.

"Come on, then," she said as she led him through the still-crowded dance floor and headed for the exit. "I'll get you back into the hospital."

As they left hand in hand, Michael saw that her parents were watching in bug-eyed horror. As far as they knew, the bad boy of Coldwater Cove was making off with their darling daughter. He couldn't resist giving them a wave and a quick thumbs-up sign.

Mrs. Walker's face paled to the sickly beige of a trout's belly. If she didn't faint dead away, Michael would be surprised. She'd always seemed the dramatic sort.

Someday, I've got to quit going out of my way to irritate people.

As if on cue, Mrs. Walker collapsed back into her husband's waiting arms. Michael snorted.

Just not today.

Chapter 5

Life can change you into the person you swore you'd never become. It depends on whether you think your problems are roadblocks or speed bumps.

— On a plaque in Michael Evans's office at MoreCommas.com

I'm only here because of my patient, Heather tried to tell herself. She and Mike were no longer holding hands. That had only lasted as long as it took to get to her car. He'd wanted to see her on the back of his Harley, but there was no way she was climbing into a "bitch seat" wearing these heels. So Heather had driven them to the hospital in her clean but aging Taurus.

"Thanks for getting me back in," he said as they boarded the elevator that would take them to the second floor of Coldwater General. The doors whirred closed.

"I'm doing this for your mother," she

reminded him. Those little flutters in her belly had nothing to do with it whatsoever. "She was anxious to see you this morning."

Michael and Heather stepped off the elevator into a corridor whose lighting had been dimmed for the night shift. In addition to the intermittent beeping of monitors and the low white noise of the hospital's HVAC, a soft popping sound was coming from the nurses' station.

When the LPN on duty looked up and saw Heather, she guiltily shoved her phone into her pocket.

"Sorry," she said, pulling it back out, realizing there was no point in trying to hide. The phone's wallpaper was covered with what looked like Bubble Wrap. When the nurse's thumb slipped onto it, the phone emitted a noise that sounded like a single kernel of corn popping. "I just finished rounds. Everyone's resting comfortably so thought I'd take a quick break."

"Glenda Scott was messing with that same thing earlier today," Heather said.

Michael grinned, nodding toward her phone. "Kind of addictive, isn't it?"

The LPN smiled back at him.

Well, what girl wouldn't? The man is terminally attractive. Heather smacked down that opinion and reminded herself that he still called her "Stilts" every chance he got.

"Yeah, real addictive," the nurse said, leaning an elbow on the counter and cupping her cheek in her palm, clearly smitten. "But you know, playing with it isn't completely wasted time. It's not like a regular video game. You don't have to think about it while you're popping away so you can think about other things. We've been having some issues with the supply closet and I actually thought up a new way to organize it while I was playing with this silly thing." Then she glanced at Heather, straightened abruptly, and wiped the smile from her face. "I was only doing it for a little while. Honest."

"It's OK this time," Heather said. "I hear it's a good stress reliever, but save it for the break room from now on. If a patient's family member catches you playing with your phone, they won't be impressed, no matter how many supply closets you mentally reorganize with it."

"Hey!" Michael objected. "It doesn't bother me and I'm somebody's family."

"Then it's time you acted like it." She rolled her eyes at him and started down the hallway, not caring whether he followed or not. She never should have left the dance with him. This was a mistake.

So are these darned heels. My kingdom for

a pair of white ScrubZones.

The offending heels clicked like she was pounding tacks into the linoleum with every step.

"Way to undermine my authority," she whispered when he fell into step beside her.

"Your authority? What are you, head nurse or something?"

"Or something." Her actual title was "supervisor of nursing" for the entire hospital, but since there had been cutbacks, she had fewer staff members to supervise these days. She hated to ask her parents to give the hospital another grant, especially so soon after they'd funded the new mental health clinic at Bates College, but she just might come round to it if more state money didn't roll into the hospital coffers soon.

"If your mother's asleep, you shouldn't wake her," Heather whispered.

"I won't. It'll be enough just to see her."

How many times had Mrs. Evans checked on Michael at night when he was a kid, just to make sure he was still breathing? Now he was doing it for her. Heather wasn't sure when that shift between parent and child happened in life, but she'd seen it demonstrated plenty of times. Eventually, the caretakers became the ones who needed care.

Michael seemed ready to step up for that. It raised him a notch or two in her eyes.

If only he'd stop calling me Stilts!

But Mrs. Evans wasn't quite out for the night. Her bed was propped in the upright position. Lit by the flicker of a TV screen, she was breathing slowly, her eyes half closed, clearly skimming the surface of sleep, but not there yet. A reality show about people at a tattoo parlor was scrolling across the screen. Mike picked up the remote and clicked it off, plunging the room into semi-darkness.

Evidently, the sudden silence roused Mrs. Evans. When she recognized Michael's silhouette backlit by the slab of light that spilled in from the hall, she was instantly alert, and as bursting with energy as a kid on Christmas morning.

She clicked on the room light with her call button.

"Oh, sweetheart," Mrs. Evans said, lifting her right arm to him so he could hug her on that side. Her left would still be sore from where Doc Warner had removed about twenty lymph nodes. Michael gave her an unhurried hug and a kiss on the cheek.

A happy tear slid down that cheek.

Heather was glad she'd brought him there. Michael's presence was the best medicine she could give his mother.

"I was so afraid you wouldn't be back after what —" Mrs. Evans pinched her lips into a tight line to stop herself. "Dad didn't mean what he said to you this afternoon."

"Yes, he did," Michael said.

Mrs. Evans's head bobbed from side to side in a post-drug-induced version of a shrug. "Well, maybe you're right. Your father can be awfully stubborn sometimes. He doesn't like change."

"Doesn't believe I'm capable of it, you mean."

Mrs. Evans waved her hand as if to wave away his comment. "But now that you're home, I'm sure my two men will find a way to bury the hatchet. Sit, son."

Mike didn't agree with her, but he did sit on the end of her bed. Heather started to slip out of the room, but he caught her by the wrist, silently asking her to stay.

She understood. Sometimes it was easier for family members to deal with the illness of their loved one if a third party was present. Another beating heart in the room sucked the intimate awfulness out of disease and forced people to behave as if this horribly abnormal situation was perfectly normal.

"Don't you look pretty, Heather. Kind of

fancy for the hospital, though," Mrs. Evans said with a confused expression. Then she brightened. "Oh, that's right. The reunion dance was tonight, wasn't it? Did you kids have fun?"

Heather nodded, though she wasn't sure someone who was knocking on thirty still qualified as a kid. "We had a good turnout. Lots of alums from out of town."

"Oh, how I wish George and I could have been there. We won the Lindy Hop competition last year, you know." She smiled wistfully. "That man of mine can still cut a rug."

When silence fell over them, Heather felt compelled to fill it. "How are you feeling, Mrs. Evans? Any pain?"

That might account for her still being awake.

"No, just a little indigestion," she said, "but I suppose that's my own fault."

"I don't see how. You didn't eat anything except what the hospital gave you, did you?" Heather asked. Family members often smuggled in favorite dishes that were spicier or richer than postoperative patients should have.

Like possum pie.

"No, it was the ice cream at dinner," Mrs. Evans said. "That sweet little nurse on duty brought me four cups since they're small, two chocolates and two vanillas. That way I could share some with George when he came back this evening."

Heather nodded. It sometimes stimulated a patient's appetite if their visitor had something too.

"Well, I meant to just eat one and save the other three for your father," she said to Michael. "But my taster has been a bit off today so I didn't know which one I wanted."

"Probably the aftereffects of anesthesia," Heather said. "It can mess with things until it works its way out of your system."

"I usually like chocolate best, you know," Shirley Evans went on, "but vanilla was sounding pretty good to me. So I tried a bite of this one, and then a bite of that one. Even when I opened the third cup, I still couldn't make up my mind which one I liked most." She laughed and tossed her hands in the air. "Wouldn't you know it? By the time I figured out that the vanilla tastes best, every bit of both of them was gone!"

Mike laughed softly with her and patted her blanketed shin. "I'll sneak you in some Green Apple Grill homemade vanilla tomorrow. Jake served me some after supper tonight with warm blackberry cobbler. It's the best stuff I ever tasted."

"No, don't," his mother said. "According

to Heather, I need to make healthy choices while I'm going through chemo and radiation."

"That doesn't mean you can't have a treat sometimes," Heather said. Chances were good that Mrs. Evans's appetite would be dicey once she started treatment in earnest. She might as well enjoy a forbidden goody now.

"Well, if you won't let me tempt you with the tastiest ice cream on the planet, what can I do for you?" Michael asked.

"Look, son," Mrs. Evans said, suddenly serious. "I don't know what finally caused the break between you and your father all those years ago. He never confided in me."

Michael's brows shot up for a second. Secrets were hard to keep in Coldwater Cove. If gossip were an Olympic sport, the town could field a world-class team every time. It wasn't so much that people were nosy. It was that they were so *interested* in the lives around them.

That, and what else did they have to talk about besides what was happening to their neighbors and friends?

But if even his mother didn't know, no wonder I never heard what happened.

"Whatever it was, I don't need to know," Shirley Evans went on. "What I do need is for you and your father to finally get over yourselves. If you want to do something for me, don't bring me ice cream. Bring me peace."

That had all the finality of a deathbed request to Heather's ear.

"It takes two to make peace," Michael said.

"But it only takes one to make the first step toward it. Say you'll do this little thing for me, Michael," his mother said, her eyes pleading. "Then whatever happens with the cancer, I'll be fine."

Heather got the feeling it was not so little a thing for Michael to do, but the way Mrs. Evans had framed the request, she didn't see how he could deny her.

Evidently, neither did he. "I'll try."

"That's all I ask, dear. Oh! Lacy told me Jake has made you his best man." Mrs. Evans was all smiles again. "Isn't that wonderful?"

Heather's gaze darted to Michael at that news. As the maid of honor, she'd be walking the aisle with him in November. And there were plenty of prewedding activities they'd need to coordinate before then. She wasn't sure she wanted to spend that much time with the guy.

Something about him . . . irritated her.

The way she'd been aware of him watching her at the dance made her feel uncomfortable in her own skin. And her stomach hadn't stopped doing weird little flips when he was around, usually when he caught her looking at him.

Oh, my gosh, could I be any more middle school? I may as well text him "If U ♡ me like I ♡ U, stop in the hall & nod."

She gave herself a mental shake. This was so not like her.

"That best man stuff isn't official yet," Mike said.

"Well, there's no time like the present. They want you in the wedding. *I* want you in the wedding," his mother said with force. "Make it official now."

Clearly, Mrs. Evans had missed her calling as a hostage negotiator. Cancer was a heavy club, and she wielded it with devastating conviction.

"All right, Mom. You win. I'll do it."

"Oh, good. I just knew you'd do the right thing," she said as if she'd actually given him a choice. "It'll be so wonderful to have you home now that fall is upon us. Remember how lovely Coldwater Cove is once the trees start to turn? And with any luck at all, I'll be done with my treatments in time for the wedding." She covered a yawn with one hand and slid down on the bed's incline. "Won't that be grand?"

Then she sighed contentedly. Her eyes closed, and she drifted away from them with a soft snore. Michael bent over his mother and brushed her cheek with his lips.

The simple gesture made Heather's chest constrict. The bad boy of Coldwater Cove had a tender heart he didn't let the world see.

If you want to know how a man feels about women, watch how he treats his mother. It was her own mother's voice in her head, but this time, Heather agreed with her.

She pushed the button that lowered her patient's bed into a level position and tucked the blanket around Mrs. Evans's chin. Then she slipped out of the room, with Michael on her heels.

"Good thing she fell asleep," Michael said as he waited for Heather to board the elevator first. For a bad boy, he still had good-boy manners. "She'd have had me agreeing to move back to Coldwater Cove for keeps in another minute or two."

"Would that be so terrible?" Heather punched the down button, grateful he hadn't opted for the stairs. Up or down, the heels she was wearing would be a royal pain on that many steps.

"Coldwater's not New York." The elevator shuddered its way to the ground floor, and the doors wheezed open.

"That's where you've been living?"

"For the most part."

Heather had visited the Big Apple once for a nursing seminar on critical care. After the initial rush of adrenaline over being in such a gigantic metropolis, she found the city exhausting. Granted, there were great museums and plays and incredible architecture, but there were so many people all jostling against each other at all hours of the day and night. Her hotel was nowhere near Central Park, so she didn't see anything green all week, not so much as a blade of grass. The rolling, forested hills around Coldwater Cove were restful to her heart, and even in the flat parts of the state, there was something majestic about a long horizon. She loved being able to see what she called "the edges of the earth" in all directions. When her plane landed back in Oklahoma, Heather had narrowly resisted the urge to kiss the ground.

"Doesn't it get lonely in New York?" she asked.

"What do you mean? There are people everywhere. In case you haven't heard, it's the city that never sleeps."

"It's possible to be alone in a crowd."

He nodded. "Yeah, I guess. But if you stay busy enough, you don't have time to notice. You have to slow down to realize you're lonely."

"So have you?"

"Once or twice." He gave her a long look. She got the sense that he could see past the assured face she tried to present to the world. That he was able to look inside her, to comb through her hurts and insecurities and see the real Heather, the one she hid from everybody.

No, if he could do that, surely he wouldn't still be calling me Stilts. Michael Evans may be trouble, but he's not intentionally cruel.

When they reached her car, he opened the door for her. "What about you, Miss 'Or Something' of Nursing? Do you ever take your scrubs off long enough to realize you're alone *without* a crowd?"

"What do you mean?" she said as she folded her legs into the space below the steering wheel. Even with the seat set as far back as it would go, it was still a tight fit. Especially in heels. "I have a full life, a *very* full life, thank you."

She pulled the car door closed, slamming it a little harder than she intended. He'd struck a nerve.

He rounded the car and climbed into the passenger seat. "So you're just not willing to share this *very* full life with anybody."

"That's not true. I have friends. Your sister, for one." The Taurus sputtered to life, and she peeled out of the hospital lot. The sooner she dropped him back at the high school, where his motorcycle was parked, the better.

"As long as you mean Lacy, I'll count that," Michael said. "Crystal doesn't have friends. She has minions."

"That's a terrible way to talk about your sister."

"She's sort of a terrible sister."

"You're not winning any 'Brother of the Year' awards yourself."

"Point taken." He raised his hands in surrender. "But you've still only named one friend."

"Then there's Jake and Glenda and all the members of the Coldwater Warm Hearts Club and the folks in the Methodist choir. Which reminds me." *Time to put him on defense again.* "You used to sing in glee club. Our director is always looking for more men and we're starting Christmas music next Wednesday. Since you're staying in town at least until the wedding, you may as well sing with us till then."

"Last time I looked at a calendar, Christmas comes after Thanksgiving. I only agreed to stay till the wedding."

"Your mother would be so pleased." Heather played her trump card. "And by then, she might actually be done with her cancer treatments and feeling well enough to enjoy seeing you in the choir."

"Don't start. Man, a guy can't get a break around here. It's one thing when my mom guilts me into things. I don't need you to do it, too."

Heather pulled back into the high school parking lot and stopped beside Michael's Harley. If he was the poor homeless guy Lacy had told her to expect, how was it he was riding such an expensive machine? "I wouldn't have to guilt you into anything if you'd just say yes."

"All right. I'll do it." He opened the car door, but didn't get out. "On one condition."

Score! She still had that competitive edge, and she didn't need to be "Stilts" to win. "What condition?"

"On your next day off, you and me, the Talimena Byway and" — he hitched a thumb in the direction of his Harley — "the hog."

CHAPTER 6

The hardest part of coming home is the last few steps.
— Lester Scott, formerly homeless Vietnam vet and recovering alcoholic who discovered he still loves his wife

Michael turned on the lights in the Ouachita Inn ranch house. The great room was a study in old leather and wood with a heavy patina. A Remington bronze of a bucking bronc and a cowboy hanging on for dear life dominated the space from its perch on the deep mantel. A cowhide served as a rug in front of the river-rock fireplace.

Mike strode in and plopped down on the couch before the flickering fire. It had been upgraded to gas, one of the few outward concessions to the current century.

Speaking of this century . . .

Michael pulled out his cell phone and

punched the number before he thought about the time difference on the East Coast.

"Hey, Jadis. Sorry to be calling so late."

"Not a problem," his assistant answered. "I was up anyway, working on the graphics you requested. Sending them to you now for approval."

His phone gave a happy little chirp that said it had received the data. "So if you're working, I should be working too?"

"Something like that," she said. "How is your mother?"

"She came out of surgery OK. The doctor doesn't think the cancer has spread, but he has no way to say for sure. Mom's taking no chances. She'll start chemo and radiation soon."

"The company jet is still in Tulsa. Do you wish me to have it reconfigured for patient transport so your mother can be transferred to the Mayo Clinic? Shall I have a mobile nursing team assembled for the flight to Rochester as well?"

That had been Michael's first inclination. He'd wanted to whisk his mother off to someplace where she'd have world-class care. But he realized she wouldn't be happy away from her family and friends while she underwent treatment. Home was a powerful medicine all its own.

"No, I think the hospital here has it covered." Besides, with Heather in charge of the nursing staff, he was sure his mother would get more personalized care at Coldwater General, where everyone knew her. "I'll talk to her doctor and see if there's anything more cutting edge than chemo and radiation for my mother's type of cancer."

"Researchers are making great strides with gene therapy," Jadis said.

"Look into it and whatever it costs, I'll foot the bill. We can hire a concierge oncologist and fly the meds in along with the people to administer them if we have to. Either way, my mom will be OK in Coldwater Cove."

"Very well," Jadis said. Michael heard the soft click of keys that told him she was taking notes on their conversation. "I will also send some white light in your mother's direction."

Mike's assistant was pretty eclectic in her faith. They'd had a few theological discussions, but Jadis refused to be pigeon-holed into any one belief system.

"It is a wise person who knows that they do not know, Michael," she'd always say. "No one can claim exhaustive knowledge of God."

Mike would settle for understanding the

little he did know of God. Regardless of their differences, Jadis had the most calming presence Michael had ever encountered. He wondered what his mom would think about the "white light" headed her way. Shirley Evans was a pretty dogmatic theologian. "I'll tell her you said a prayer for her. She'll understand that."

"As you wish. The intent is the same. My hope for your mother is great good health."

"Now to business. I'm happy to report the Bubble Wrap app has gone about as far as it can go," Michael said. "They're even using it here in Coldwater Cove."

Jadis laughed. "If it has reached maximum saturation, it is a good thing MoreCommas has another set of apps coming out."

"Yeah, but I had no idea the reach of this thing was so huge," Michael said with excitement. "Tell marketing and get them to up the price of ads on the next-gen apps first thing tomorrow."

"I assume low-key, soft-sell rules still apply?"

"Of course." There was no point in a relaxation app that constantly bombarded consumers with blatant "Buy Me!" pitches. "And preference will still be given to products meant to encourage the user to take a pause and make healthy choices."

Jadis made approving noises. "You have come a long way since you first discovered what your grandmother meant when she said you need more commas."

Michael's grandma had been suffering from Alzheimer's at the time, so when she'd told him he needed more commas, it hadn't made any sense. Then he finally realized she wasn't talking about punctuation. She meant *his life* needed more commas, more pauses for reflection, more chances to consider what needed changing.

Maybe his mother's illness was another one of those commas. If it was, he needed to embrace the speed bump it represented.

"When can we expect you back in New York?" Jadis asked. "You have a meeting with the investor group on Thursday."

He wanted to tell her to push it off, but he couldn't. The group had been clamoring to meet with him for months. "That's early, isn't it?"

"7:00 a.m. Breakfast meeting at Blue Fin. Private room. Sales says the investor group is getting concerned about our reluctance to accept advertising from the highest bidder. It may take some convincing on your part to get them to understand your vision."

"That's because they don't get the MoreCommas brand. It's a different business model than most. If they aren't ready to come on board without demanding a say in how I do things, I don't want their money." If Michael had to sell his conscience, he'd look for investors elsewhere. He'd already made enough to self-fund the company for a long time, but he didn't have the liquidity to expand toward an IPO. Besides, taking on investors was Michael's idea of paying it forward, spreading around the opportunity that had been so good for him.

"Put the flight crew on standby for a turn and burn," Michael said. "I'll leave here Wednesday night in time to be there for the meeting on Thursday morning, but afterward I'm coming straight back here."

The silence on the other end of the connection was eloquent.

"The company doesn't need me on-site," he said.

More silence.

"Things are . . . delicate with my mother right now. Once she starts her treatment, I should be able to pull away more, but in the early phases, I need to be here . . . for a couple of weeks, anyway."

It wasn't only for his mother's sake. He'd made that deal with Heather Walker, too.

"One ride on the Harley and you'll sing with

the choir for Christmas?" she said, eyeing him as though she could tell what was true and what was bullroar.

"One ride." Of course, he hadn't specified how long the ride was going to be.

"All right. I'll do it. On my next day off."

"You got a deal. The Methodists will figure you earned a star in your crown, Stilts. You bagged another baritone for your choir and at the low, low price of a motorcycle ride."

She rolled those big brown eyes. "Why do I get the feeling I just made a deal with the devil?"

Heather was so sure he was still the bad boy of Coldwater Cove. Michael smiled to himself. He wasn't that guy anymore.

Not most of the time, anyway.

"You are the heart's blood of MoreCommas, Michael," Jadis reminded him, pulling him out of his Heather daydream. "The team will not function as well without you."

"But it will function. Make it work without me for a while," he ordered his assistant in a tone that brooked no refusal. "I'll be in touch."

Then he punched out of the conversation and turned his phone off completely.

What was the point of being the boss if you couldn't act like it sometimes?

■ ■ ■ ■

Judith Hildebrand drummed the eraser of her pencil on the desk and stared at her phone as if that would make it ring. She'd paid enough for this investigator. It was time for him to come through with something more damning than pictures of the subject tipping his doorman at the trendy SoHo building where he occupied the penthouse loft.

Judith, on the other hand, shared a pint-sized studio with her African gray parrot, Emmy. The apartment was located in a part of Manhattan so sketchy, an invisible force she called "condo gravity" kept her inside once the sun went down.

That and the occasional drive-by shooting.

"This is all Michael Evans's fault," she complained to Emmy. The bird was molting, and not looking its best made it even more bad tempered than usual. Emmy was named for the award Judith had hoped to win once she was promoted from general gofer to producer. Unfortunately, her career was more tattered than Emmy's feathers at the moment.

"Stiletto Girl, Stiletto Girl," the bird

chanted.

"Shut up," she said sourly. "Stiletto Girl" was the nickname Michael Evans had given her on camera when he made a brief appearance on the reality show at a tattoo parlor she was working for some years ago. The homeless guy with his cowboy accent had taken issue with her spiky Manolo Blahniks and made her a laughingstock. And not just with viewers of the show.

Yeah, like all ten of them at the time.

Her producer and the rest of upper management made sure the nickname stuck. Even though the show did OK for a season, no one took her seriously after the "Stiletto Girl" episode.

She was a joke. A sound bite. Judith had used up her fifteen seconds of fame when she flipped off Michael Evans on camera. Since that time, she couldn't beg, borrow, or steal a chance to show what she could really do.

But it wasn't her fault. It was Michael Evans. He was the start of her downward spiral. The guy had a gift for getting under people's skin and making them crazy.

While her career took a nosedive, the life of Michael Evans suddenly skyrocketed after the show was taped. Judith had recently learned that somehow, he'd quietly put together one of the hottest new dot coms to hit Wall Street since Facebook. MoreCommas was a back-to-the-basics, discover-the-secret-to-life phenomenon, and the man behind it had successfully remained in the shadows most of the time.

Who knew the heart of a mathematical and marketing genius lurked beneath the T-shirt and leather jacket she'd made him wear for the show?

No one.

Michael Evans was not Steve Jobs. He was no grandstander. He shunned the spotlight. For years, it was hard for anyone to find out who had even started MoreCommas. His employees were fiercely loyal and, worst of all, tight-lipped. Even once he was outed as the CEO, the man himself had flown under the radar, refusing to give interviews or even acknowledge that, yes, he had once been part of a reality show that featured people telling their stories while getting a tattoo.

After a while, most media outlets wearied of the chase.

Not Judith. She was determined to get some face time with him in front of a camera. There must be a reason he was harder to gain an audience with than the Dalai Lama.

Michael Evans had a secret.

And it must be a doozy.

Toward the end of his reality episode, when Evans had removed his shirt for the tat, the cameraman had gotten a close-up of a wicked scar that sliced across the guy's ribs. He'd adamantly refused to answer the tattoo artist's question about the scar.

Judith's crap-detector began pinging.

Secrets were a reality producer's best friend. If she could only uncover how he'd come by that scar, she could go back to the network and pitch her idea for a new series — a show-all, tell-all, where-are-they-now exposé of past reality stars called *Reality Bites Back.*

And what better way to kick off the series than with an undercover sting on the elusive self-made multimillionaire Michael Evans?

Reality Bites Back would be bigger than *The Bachelor.* Judith would get that Emmy for sure.

The sudden blast of her ringtone shattered Judith's dreamy musings.

"Yeah," she barked into it.

"Your boy made an unexpected move."

"What? Did he tip the doorman a fifty instead of a hundred this time?"

"No, he flew out of state in the corporate jet."

"Let me guess. Off to Fiji for some R & R."

"No. I pulled some strings and got a look at the flight plan. He headed to a general aviation airstrip in Oklahoma."

"Back to his roots, huh?" Judith twirled her pencil through her fingers like a mini baton. "Interesting."

As far as Judith had been able to discover, Evans hadn't returned to fly-over country since she'd crossed paths with him. Something important must have happened to send him racing back there.

Maybe it had something to do with how he got that scar. . . .

"So, look, you haven't paid me for the last week of surveillance," the PI said.

"Oh, did you send an invoice?" It was lying on Judith's desk along with her delinquent rent, unpaid utility bill, and a cancelation notice on her Visa card.

"I sent you the bill twice," the man said gruffly. "I'm done being your eyes until I see some green."

"You're done anyway unless you plan to follow him to the Land of Oz."

"You're thinking of Kansas. Or maybe Australia. Anyway, I'm telling you, the guy went to Oklahoma."

"Whatever. I can't pay a bill I haven't

received. And write up a decent report if you expect to see a dime." She clicked off, and when her phone rang back immediately, she let it go to voice mail. Judith tucked the private investigator's bill under the stack of other unpaid ones.

"Get in line, buddy."

She stood and started pacing her studio apartment.

"Get in line, buddy," her parrot repeated. "Get in line."

"Shut up."

The bird turned its back to her and tucked its head under a wing, clearly in a sulk. Judith wondered how much she could get for Emmy if she decided to sell her. The parrot wasn't good for anything except eating, pooping, and mind-numbing chatter.

Kind of like most of the people I know.

Judith opened her browser and checked her bank account online. It was more depressing than a month of rainy weekends.

Michael Evans could fly anywhere he wanted in his fancy corporate jet. Judith made do with the subway to get around. But the MTA didn't stretch clear to Oklahoma, and that was where she had to go.

She couldn't afford to hire a cameraman and certainly couldn't pay for one to accompany her all the way to the back of beyond. She'd need to make do with a concealed camera she could wear on her lapel.

After searching multiple airlines for a cheap coach seat, she decided even that was too rich for her blood at the moment. After all, she didn't know how long she'd have to camp out in some horrid little motel while she tracked down the secret of Michael Evans's scar. She was going to have to get to Oklahoma by alternate means.

"Whoever said getting there was half the fun never had to travel thirty-seven hours on a bus."

"On a bus, on a bus," came from the cage in the corner. And then before Judith could beat Emmy to it, the bird screamed, "Shut up!"

CHAPTER 7

DARLING DAUGHTER,
YOU WERE OUR DREAM.
WE WOKE TOO SOON.
— from Jessica Walker's headstone

People say winter is the most depressing time of year to visit a graveyard.

"Like there's really any good time," Heather muttered to herself.

But in winter, the ground is like iron. The wind slices through your parka, no matter how highly rated it was in that outdoorsy big-box store. And your nose hairs freeze with each breath. You can't even leave any flowers to brighten up the starkness. They only wilt before you can hightail it back to the car.

Heather parked near the entrance to the Coldwater Territory Cemetery and sat there for a few minutes while the engine sputtered and knocked. She knew she should go and get it over with, but a nameless something held her in the safety of her not-so-charmingly-mature Taurus.

Winter was bad, but autumn was even worse.

The graveyard where her twin rested was unnecessarily beautiful in the fall. It taunted the coming winter with a last hurrah of vibrant days. All the trees blazed up in a final burst of color. Dry leaves skittered down the worn paths, whispering secrets to each other as they swirled into mini tornadoes and then settled again. It was the time of harvest, the pinnacle of growth. But even though the seasons were winding down, fall was still full of life.

And life was glorious.

Jessica had barely made it out of the spring of hers.

"So not fair," Heather said under her breath as she switched off the car and hauled herself out. She retrieved a box of gourds and corn sheaves from her trunk. Since she tried to visit her sister's grave at least once a month, she'd started leaving appropriate decorations for the time of year.

Jess would've liked that.

She was always the "fixy" one, the budding designer. Even in high school, she'd decorated and redecorated her room according to the whim of the moment. Jessica was constantly changing things around.

Since her death, their parents had preserved the space untouched. It was exactly as Jessica had left it on her last night in this world. Like a time capsule, it proclaimed the unrealized goals of its former occupant. Her prom dress still hung over the closet door, the corsage Skyler Sweazy had given her still pressed between *The Collected Works of Mark Twain* and *Moby Dick,* the two heaviest books Jessica could find. A Harvard pennant was pinned to the wall, even though Jess had never been officially accepted there and was planning to attend Brown later that year.

To the Walkers, Jessica's room was a shrine. It was there they communed with their lost one, not in the Coldwater cemetery. Grief was a private thing, her mother had said, not to be laid out like a buffet for lookee-loos and small minds to feast upon.

Heather thought it would be healthier for them to turn Jessica's room into a study or a craft room or even set up a Ping-Pong table in there. Anything would be better than that morbid space that looked like it was waiting for Jess to return any moment. And it wouldn't hurt them to visit the grave once in a while.

But she didn't blame her parents for trying to hold on. Of course, they couldn't let go of their golden child.

Jess did everything right. Unlike her gawky twin, she was blessed with petite loveliness. So feminine, so charmingly delicate, Heather always suspected Jessica was hiding a pair of wings under her too-cute clothes.

Academically gifted, Jessica sailed through school barely breaking a sweat. Heather had made the honor roll too, but only with much suppressed weeping and wailing and gnashing of teeth. "Suppressed" because it wouldn't do to be caught struggling. Walkers didn't struggle. They vaulted over life's challenges. They sought out new adventures. They excelled in everything they put their hand to. Struggling, in school or in life, was for lesser beings.

Heather slogged up the hill to the corner section of the graveyard, where the dear departed Walkers had ceased their struggles.

Heather didn't have that luxury.

She wrestled with the awful feeling that if her parents could have chosen, they would have kept Jessica instead of her.

It wasn't rational, and she was *almost* sure it wasn't true. But right or wrong, the feeling persisted.

Almost wouldn't let her rest.

As she neared her sister's grave, she saw

that someone had beaten her there. Michael Evans was standing before the headstone, hands folded before him, head bowed.

Was he praying?

Time to alert the media. Long before he skipped town, Michael had been skipping church.

A twig crunched under her tennis shoe and he raised his head. That smile she dreaded, the one that turned her insides into a quivering puddle, spread across his face.

"Careful, Nurse Walker," he said in a lazy drawl. "Folks will think you're following me."

"What? No." How dare he! The quivering stopped in a heartbeat. "This is my sister's grave. What are *you* doing here?"

"Just paying my respects. That's allowed, isn't it?"

He was right, dang it. Heather felt peevish for scolding him. To avoid looking at him, which any normal woman would want to do more than she wanted to take her next breath, she dropped to her knees and took a wicker basket out of the box. After she put a couple of bricks in the bottom to anchor it against the wind, she assembled the gourds and Indian corn into a semi-artsy fall arrangement.

"Your sister is the only classmate we've lost. Why wouldn't I be here?" Michael almost sounded defensive. "Besides, I knew Jess."

Everyone knew Jess. She was a cheerleader, smart as a whip, and holder of a permanent seat at the cool kids' table. Of course he knew Jess. She glanced up to see him staring at the engraving on the stone. His brows nearly met over his fine straight nose. Under his T-shirt, his chest lifted in a sigh.

He knew her better than I thought. "You and Skyler were pretty tight back then."

Jessica and Skyler had been the power couple of Coldwater High — prom king and queen, voted most likely to have an Ivy League happily ever after. . . . After she died in that freak accident, Skyler had probably unloaded his grief to Mike.

That's how he knew her. That's why he looks so sad.

Then Mike's gaze switched to her, and the pained expression disappeared. Instead, he smiled at her. Open. Honest. And so yummy looking, she could barely keep from licking her lips.

How does he do that?

Michael had gone from almost ready to shed a tear to poster boy for Hotties-R-Us in the blink of an eye. Did men have a toggle in their hearts that let them turn emotions on and off as easily as a light switch?

Where do I sign up for one of those?

"Yeah," he said. "Sweazy and I hung out a lot back then. Did a bunch of stupid things together."

"Like the time someone let those goats loose in the high school library?" Heather smiled at the memory. It was right to smile, even though she was arranging gourds on her sister's grave. Jess had thought the goats were hilarious at the time. "That was you and Skyler, right?"

Michael raised his hands in mock surrender. "Suspected, grilled until we were crispy, but never officially charged, Your Honor."

The goats in question had a number 1, 2 or 4 painted on their respective sides. It took Mr. Whittle and the other school officials several hours of frantic searching to figure out that despite the numbers, only three goats had been released to wander the stacks and munch away at the periodical section.

"So have you and Skyler kept in touch all these years?" she asked.

"No. I didn't really keep up with anybody.

Getting away from everybody was sort of the reason I left town," he admitted. "Besides, people change. Or maybe you never really knew them in the first place. Anyway, they'll surprise you every time . . . and, like as not, *not* in a good way."

Michael Evans had surprised her since he'd returned to town — falling in with her sudden need to dance with him, being sweet to his mother, and agreeing to be in Lacy's wedding. Even showing up at the cemetery to pay his respects at her sister's grave was a shocker. Except for the whole "Stilts" business, Mike had been astonishingly well behaved. Guess she hadn't really known him.

"Someone made you cynical," Heather said, casting a sidelong glance toward him. "Who surprised you in a bad way?"

He opened his mouth as if about to say something, but then shook his head. "Never mind. I just lost touch with everybody after I left. Even Sweazy and I took our own paths after high school."

"Skyler went to Harvard. What was your path?"

"The path of least resistance. Nothing like the Ivy League, that's for sure. I never earned a degree or anything, but I did learn a few things along the way."

"Like what?"

"Like when a girl agrees to go riding with you, you don't let her off the hook. I've got a helmet for you, so you're without excuse."

He extended a hand to help her up after she finished placing the last acorn squash. A little zing arced from her wrist to her elbow.

The casual contact created such a charge in her system, Heather bet if someone plugged her in, she could light up a Christmas tree. She tugged her hand away, but gently. Not so much because she wanted to, but because she knew she should.

Michael Evans might not be as bad as she'd thought, but he was still hazardous to a girl's heart. After all, he'd only promised to stick around for a few months.

"You free now?" he asked.

She shook her head and checked her watch. "I work three to eleven today." It was nearly two thirty and she liked to arrive at least fifteen minutes early so she could change into her scrubs and look over the charts before her shift started. She was cutting things close, but she couldn't bring herself to hurry off.

"When's your next day off so we can take that ride?"

"Thursday."

■ ■ ■ ■

Crap on a cracker. He was supposed to be at that breakfast meeting at the Blue Fin in New York on Thursday. If he told her he had a high-powered meeting with some movers and shakers in the Big Apple on the day he'd promised to take her riding, she'd never believe him. Besides, he wasn't ready to explain his success to her.

Women got weird when they realized a guy had money. He wanted to keep things simple with Heather. Either she liked him or she didn't.

But that hard lump in his chest hoped she did.

She bent to pick up the box of leftover oddments. A few spare gourds and ears of corn didn't make the cut to adorn her sister's grave.

Why do women do that? If Jessica could see them, wouldn't she be more touched by the visitation itself than the stuff left behind?

Michael chalked up the decorations as something Heather needed to do for herself. But that didn't stop him from taking the box from her and carrying it down the hill to her car.

They walked together in easy silence.

Michael breathed in the peace of the place. Living in the city, he'd forgotten what it was like to hear leaves rustle on trees. Or how good it felt to be quiet with someone without feeling the need to fill the space between them. It already seemed to be filled with a comfortable understanding. They were easy with each other.

A guy could get used to this.

"Don't forget. Choir meets on Wednesday at seven," she reminded him.

Double crap. He'd told the flight crew to be on standby for a turn and burn, but this was going to be cutting it close. He'd have to sleep in the Cessna Citation on the way out and back if he was going to make this work.

"We're starting the Christmas music this week," she said. "You are coming, right? That was the deal."

Could he sing "Silent Night" and prepare for the investors' group at the same time? He could try. "Wouldn't miss it."

"Good. No choir. No ride."

"You're pretty black and white about things, aren't you?"

"And you're all about the gray."

"Only when black and white isn't working."

That made a small frown furrow her brow.

She was the sort who always knew what was right. Michael was still working on that.

"So if you show for choir, when should I expect to put my life and limb at risk on the back of your bike?"

"Hey!" He moved in close, pinning her between his body and her car door. "I'd never risk a single one of your lovely limbs."

She blushed to the roots of her hair. She was even prettier when she did that. He liked the way she smelled, too, all fresh and clean without the need for any flowery fragrance to cover up the pure scent of Heather.

She wiggled away from him and opened the door. "OK. I still need a time for our ride. When?"

Michael did some quick calculations — two hours for the meeting (maybe he could squeeze thirty minutes off that), a quick helo ride to JFK, another three and a half hours to Tulsa in the Cessna Citation, a couple of hours on the hog getting back to Coldwater Cove, factor in gaining an hour since he'd be traveling west from New York, better add a little more time for a cushion in case there was a glitch . . .

"Let's make it a sunset ride," he suggested. "I'll pick you up at five."

"Sounds good." She climbed into the car.

He leaned on the open window. "Heather, I don't think I told you at the time, but . . . I was sorry about what happened to your sister."

"I miss her every day." Her eyes glistened and her lips twitched. She covered his hand with hers for a moment. "It helps to know others are sorry about it, too."

Then she started her car and drove away. Michael watched until the Taurus topped the hill and disappeared from sight.

He was sorry about what had happened to her sister, all right. She had no idea how sorry.

CHAPTER 8

Labor Day is past. It's nnot too soonn to prepare for the Christmas canntata. Our director, Don Marianno, invites everyonne who enjoys sinninn to joinn the choir.
— Seen in the Methodist church bulletin
Note: Pastor Mark is looking for the donation of a new keyboard, hopefully one with a *g* key that works and an *n* that doesn't stick.

The church smelled of mothballs and lemon-oil polish. Just like he remembered.

As he walked down the center aisle of the sanctuary, Michael noticed a small stain near the left side of the altar rail. He snorted.

Still there after all those years.

It was grape juice. He'd managed to lose his grip on his teeny first communion cup. His parents had threatened him with trials just short of the Tribulation if he ruined his new suit. He'd quickly jerked out of the way of the tumbling cup so as not to let a drop fall on the navy polyester.

The carpet had not been so lucky.

He made a mental note to send the church an anonymous donation to cover recarpeting the entire sanctuary. Even if there'd been no stains, it was past time to replace the worn red wool. With any luck, the trustees would get it done before his sister's wedding in November.

Maybe he'd have to stipulate a certain color of carpeting so it wouldn't interfere with Lacy's much-debated wedding palette. She and his mother were still trying to hash out who was wearing what shade of navy, pink, or ivory.

"Michael Evans, as I live and breathe, is that you?" Marjorie Chubb waved to him from where the alto section was gathering in the choir loft. She was the captain of the prayer chain and had probably missed him sorely. Michael used to provide the "prayer warriors" with plenty of spiritual battles to fight.

"Surely no normal child could get into so much trouble unless there was a dark power at work," Marjorie had often told his mother.

Emphasis on "normal child." Michael was

more inclined to blame ADD for his ability to create havoc. It was another thing, along with dyslexia, with which he'd never been officially diagnosed, but which he suspected was part of how he was wired. It would explain why numbers had made sense to him when the written word remained a frustrating mystery and why he never could seem to sit still.

Marjorie climbed over several other choir members to get to the side aisle. She blocked the way so she could give him a hug, stopping him from heading up to the back row, where the basses sat. "I hear you're going to be the best man for Lacy and Jake's wedding."

"Where did you hear that?"

Marjorie cocked her head and shrugged. "You know what they always say: 'Telephone, telegraph, or tell Shirley Evans.' " She clapped a couple fingers over her mouth before hurrying on. "Not that your mom's a gossip. Not at all."

"Of course not," he said with a grin. He really did love to tease members of the prayer chain, Marjorie in particular. "Because then you'd have to admit to gossiping, too, since you listen to her."

"Well, that's not it at all. Never think that's what we do when she and I get together. We *share* things. It's just that she's thrilled to have you back in town and can't help letting anyone who'll listen know about it."

Michael would bet Marjorie was thrilled too. Fresh fodder for the prayer chain.

"I call your mother every day, the poor dear. Just to cheer her up and keep her up to speed on what's going on," Marjorie went on, blithely unaware she'd just admitted to gossiping again. "Shirley puts on such a brave face, but you can tell me. How's she doing, really?"

Michael had been on hand when his dad brought his mom home, in case they needed help. He and his father barely grunted at each other, but at least there was no shouting as the two of them settled into an uneasy truce for his mother's sake.

"Mom seems to be doing fine."

"*Seems* to be?"

Even if there was good news, trust Marjorie to latch on to the slightest ambiguity about it.

"She's fine," Michael assured her. "Happy to be home. The physical therapist has given her some exercises she can do to strengthen her left side."

He'd stood beside his mother while she walked her fingers up the kitchen doorjamb to increase the range of motion of her left arm. There, dug into the layers of white paint, were marks showing how tall he and his sisters had been at various times during their growing up. The year he shot up past Crystal had been a banner year. Height was the only thing he'd ever excelled at.

Michael had added to the family-legend wall by marking the spot where his mom's reach ended each day. After she managed to stretch a little higher on Wednesday than she had on Tuesday, she'd shot him a tremulous smile. When he praised her efforts, the smile bloomed across her face. It was as if he'd handed her an Oscar or something. In that slice of a moment, their roles had reversed. After years of making his lunches and cleaning up after his messes and praising his meager accomplishments, his mother needed someone to encourage and lift her up now.

"She's getting stronger each day," Michael told Marjorie. *If the prayer captain feels the need to "share" Mom's progress with her minions, she can share that.*

"Well, bless her heart." Marjorie leaned toward him confidingly and whispered, "Has she lost her hair yet?"

Shirley Evans's hair was her crowning glory. It was pure white. Like cotton or paper or snow or swan's down — Mike ran out of worthy descriptions pretty fast. Even at her age, his mom could be mistaken for the *Frozen* Disney princess with that hair of hers. There wasn't a single strand of her original warm brown. Not even a hint of silver. The shocking whiteness of it was so beautiful even total strangers stopped her to ask who colored her hair.

"God," she'd say with a mischievous smile.

"Mom hasn't started chemo yet. Her hair is fine." Michael was glad he'd already put a plan into motion to deal with that indignity when the time came. "Well, I'd better find a seat."

He edged around Marjorie and moved on up to sit next to Jake in the bass section. He didn't see Heather anywhere yet. If he remembered right from high school, she was a soprano.

The soprano section was located in front of the lucky tenors. He wished he could give the tenor line a try just to find a seat closer to her, but there hadn't been a high note in him since his voice dropped when he was twelve. He slid into the seat next to his future brother-in-law.

"See you made it through the Marjorie gauntlet," Jake said, handing him a three-ring notebook full of anthems they'd be expected to learn.

"The woman's a ghoul," Michael said.

"She means well."

"Yeah, like a wrecking ball means well."

Jake shrugged. "Marjorie may say the wrong things, but she also does plenty of good. I happen to know she took supper to your dad every night while your mom was in the hospital. And she organized a group of volunteers to rotate coming in to clean for your folks once a week until your mom's done with her treatments."

Why hadn't he thought of that? Michael wished he could kick his own butt up between his shoulder blades. With his resources, there were plenty of things he could do to help his mom and dad. Yard work, paying bills, laundry . . . all the things that have to get done whether there's illness in the family or not. Of course, they might not accept the help if they knew it was from him.

He'd have to give that some thought.

A loud jangling filled the sanctuary, and Michael jerked at the sudden clashing racket. From up in the loft, a bell choir of about a dozen people was ringing for all they were worth.

"Bell practice is just finishing up. Last time through the introit for Sunday," Jake explained. "They'll be done in a minute."

"The noise is . . ."

"Excruciating. Yeah, I agree." Jake opened his choir folder and looked over one of the pieces. "That's why they need to practice."

Mr. Mariano waved his arms in front of the bell choir and shouted something at the top of his lungs, trying to be heard over the clamor. He repeated the phrase over and over. Michael strained to make sense of it, but he couldn't believe his ears.

I'm willing to believe church has changed a lot since I was here last, but not that much.

"Um, what's he saying?"

Jake looked up at the loft and cocked his head. "Given the way the sound's bouncing around, he's probably shouting 'Damp those bells!' They forget to do that a lot."

From his short time in bell choir as a kid, Michael remembered damping required the ringer to touch the rim of the bell to the cushioned table or their shoulder to stop the sound. Nobody seemed to be doing it. One chord bled into the next, with very unpleasant results.

"Hmph." Michael nudged Jake. "Somebody should probably tell Mr. M that nobody can hear the *p* when he shouts 'Damp those bells' over all that noise."

"You think he cares? The man's Sicilian,

for Pete's sake."

Whether it was true or not, the rumor that Don Mariano had mafia connections persisted in Coldwater Cove. Despite that, he was not only the Methodists' director of music, he'd also headed up the high school band and choir program for the last twenty-five years. Mr. Mariano whipped the marching band into crisp formations for halftime at every football game. And the varsity choir consistently rated high in state contests. So the good townsfolk were willing to overlook the gossip about Mr. M's dubious past.

But nearly all of them believed it.

Not Michael.

When he was in school, he'd suspected Mr. M had spread those rumors himself. Cross a mafia don in class? Not a healthy choice if you believed your director might make you an offer you couldn't refuse. Was there a better way to corral a rowdy bunch of teenagers on risers or get them to blow their clarinets while marching in straight lines?

"Basta!" Mr. Mariano shouted at the bell choir after the piece clanged to its noisy conclusion. He swiped his face with a white handkerchief. Evidently, captive audiences like high school kids were less work to control than church volunteers. *"Basta"*

didn't mean what Michael had originally thought it meant. Mr. M wasn't calling anyone's parentage into question. He was simply saying "Enough, already" in his own unique, un–Coldwater Cove–like way. The director shouted it a few more times when a bell or two continued to toll away after the rest of the group had stopped abusing their instruments.

His head must still be ringing, standing right in front of them like that.

"Be here at eight on Sunday morning so we can run through it again," Mr. M told the bell choir in a more normal tone. "Now, before you put away your instruments, are there any prayer requests?"

Several hands slipped up, and after a few minutes, Mr. Mariano led them in prayer.

If anyone was surprised at a suspected wiseguy praying, they'd remind themselves of how often the Godfather went to church in the movies. When Mr. Mariano left the loft and joined the assembling choir at the front of the sanctuary, Michael noticed that Mr. M had put on quite a few pounds.

Looks like he's more "fries guy" than "wise-guy."

Michael chuckled to himself.

"What's so funny, man?" Jake asked.

"Nothing." He sobered immediately. At

one time, Mike would have made sure everybody heard that little joke. If he couldn't be a good student, he'd settle for class clown. If that didn't work, he was happy to be thought bad instead of stupid.

But now he had nothing to prove. He knew who he was. And he didn't need to poke fun at anyone else to feel better about himself.

Jake's younger brothers, Steven and Mark, filed in and plopped down in front of Mike. Steve turned around and slapped Mike on the knee.

"So we hear you're going to be our brother's best man," he said.

"Guess so." Mike still wasn't sure how he'd been roped into the whole wedding business. Usually, he avoided such occasions as if the cake afterward were laced with the Ebola virus.

"Better him than one of us," Mark said.

"Got that right," Steven agreed. "Being a groomsman means we don't have to do anything but show up and look pretty for the pictures."

Jake snorted. "In that case, the wedding is totally fubar already. Your ugly mugs are guaranteed to break the camera."

"Whatever." Mark leered at Jake, making an L on his forehead. Then he turned to

Mike. "What are we doing for the bachelor party?"

"I don't know. Haven't thought about it yet." Michael didn't remember much about the few bachelor parties he'd attended in the past. Probably had something to do with the vast quantities of liquor he'd consumed, but he vaguely remembered there'd been strippers. And any number of risky decisions by the bridegroom-to-be that totally would have blown the wedding if any of them had remembered exactly what happened well enough to bring it to light.

Jake was marrying Michael's sister. His *favorite* sister. He didn't want to see the guy stuffing dollar bills down some bimbette's G-string or falling down drunk.

"What did you have in mind?" he asked Jake. *He'd better give the right answer or I'll knock him into next week.*

"Poker, beer, and pizza at my place would be fine. It doesn't have to be anything complicated," Jake said as the choir loft continued to fill with latecomers. "I just want to marry your sister, Mike. The rest is a bunch of hoops I have to jump through to be able to do that."

Right answer.

Michael scanned the soprano section. Lacy had wandered in and, after blowing a kiss to Jake, took a seat in the front row of the alto section.

Heather's still not here.

Mike heaved a sigh. The time-suck known as choir practice would last an hour and a half.

If it ever gets started.

He'd almost forgotten how laid-back folks in Coldwater Cove were about pesky little things like time. He had a tight schedule to keep if he was going to make that breakfast meeting in Manhattan tomorrow and shoot back here like a rocket for his first official date with Heather.

Jake shifted in the seat beside him. "Lacy's mom — well, your mom, too — was asking me about the bachelor party this afternoon. She seems to think everything connected with this wedding has to be over-the-top."

"That's my mom. *Excess* is better than *success* in her book. Actually, it's sort of the Evans family motto. I'm surprised Lacy hasn't told you. If a little is good —"

"A lot is a whole bunch better," Jake finished for him.

"I see you've been initiated."

"Any other Evans family quirks I should be aware of?"

"I think I'll let Lacy handle that. Some things are better if they're a surprise. You haven't signed a prenup, have you?"

Jake rolled his eyes.

Michael glanced down at his sister, who'd been cornered by Marjorie Chubb and had no chance of escape unless Mr. Mariano called the choir to order.

Still no Heather among the gaggle of sopranos.

Mr. Mariano climbed on the orange crate he called his "podium" and signaled the rehearsal to begin.

The gathered Methodists belted out "What Child Is This?" at a volume level guaranteed to wake sleeping babies for several blocks in any direction. Michael kept one eye on the door.

What was the point of living up to his side of the bargain if Heather wasn't there to see him do it?

CHAPTER 9

> I tried bein' open-minded once, but I decided to give it up. If a feller ain't careful, his brains could fall out.
>
> — Junior Bugtussle, after the sushi at the reunion dance went to war with his colon

Heather kicked off her ScrubZones as soon as she closed the door to her apartment behind herself. She flexed and curled her toes, wishing she could slough off the tension in the rest of her body as easily.

She was strung as tight as a piano wire, and she knew why. When she was a student nurse in Tulsa, working her first week on the pediatric floor, they'd lost a nine-year-old. The nursing team had done all they could, but it wasn't enough. Since then, she'd avoided peds like the plague.

But she hadn't been anywhere near pediatrics today.

She'd pulled a shift and a half because her young surgery patient, Aaron Bugtussle, was returned to the emergency room by his frantic parents. Darlene was almost incoherent as Heather tried to draw out a quick history of the onset of the problem.

"The trouble started yesterday, 'cuz my husband don't know when to say when." Mrs. Bugtussle shot Junior an accusing glare. She'd been tending to Junior, who was still suffering from the aftereffects of too much sushi. Left to their own devices, the Bugtussles' rowdy brood had run amok. Darlene had to break up a scuffle between Aaron's younger brothers that resulted in bloody noses and black eyes all around before she separated them.

The bored, recuperating twelve-year-old, who couldn't take part in the fight, took advantage of the distraction. Aaron had decided the weather was warm enough for one more dip in the pond near his house.

A pond that was regularly swelled by runoff from the hog pen and cow pasture.

His unhealed incision was an open invitation to every stray bacterium that wanted to hitch a ride. By the time his terrified parents could get Aaron back to the hospital, his temperature was 106 degrees and climbing. The boy was a shivering, sweating, hallucinating mess.

And his mother was almost worse. Junior was too green around the gills to be much trouble, but Darlene was so hysterical, she was a disruption to her son's care. She and the uncooperative patient both had to be physically restrained while the team inserted an IV.

Doc Warner prescribed the most virulent antibiotic the hospital had in its arsenal. Heather was burdened with the miserable task of getting the Bugtussles to sign a release. After convincing them the infection was more dangerous than the cure, they agreed to remove the hospital from all legal liability if the antibiotic should happen to destroy the boy's bone marrow while it killed the bad bugs.

Then as the meds dripped into Aaron's system at a maddeningly slow pace, Heather and her nursing staff fought the fever. If it rose to 107.6 and stayed there for any length of time, the boy could suffer permanent brain damage. But the fever was also doing its part to fight the infection, so Heather had a narrow path to walk. She and her staff had to keep the fever from continuing to climb, but not let it sink much below 105, so it could continue to cook the infection.

When Aaron's fever finally stabilized at around 104, Heather clocked out with the knowledge that her staff would keep a close eye on the boy through the night. Aaron wasn't out of the woods yet. Such a virulent infection could take an unexpected turn.

Heather felt for all those under her care. She had to. Empathy was what made a good nurse, but when the patient was very young, it hurt her heart more.

Her phone made a tinkly sound, so she checked for a text as she flopped onto her couch. It was from her mother:

Levi is worse.

"Trust Mom to be the bearer of bad tidings," Heather muttered. Like the old saw about Siberians enjoying bad weather, her mom seemed energized by negative news and couldn't wait to pass it along.

This has been the crappiest of crappy days.

First, her patient. Then, her cousin. And to top it off, she'd missed choir, so she had no idea whether Michael Evans had kept his word and added his voice to the bass section. True, the choir had plenty of willing men, but they were like sheep without a shepherd. Mike's sister Lacy was the best alto of the lot. If there was anything to genetics, Michael could help lead the bass section. If he'd bothered to show.

Probably didn't.

He wasn't the sort of guy a girl could depend on. Everything in her that screamed for self-preservation urged her to walk wary around him.

Too bad another part of me urges something else entirely.

A knock on her door dragged her out of her dark thoughts. Heather lived in an apartment on the upper floor of a building on the Town Square, above Gewgaws & Gizzwickies, a consignment shop for bargain hunters who thought of other people's trash as their treasure.

The G & G shoppers also had far more tolerance for clutter than Heather possessed.

But the location, while central to everywhere Heather wanted to be, also offered her a great deal of privacy. Hardly anyone who didn't live in one of the upper-story apartments bothered to climb the wrought-iron stairs at the back of the building to reach the long deck she shared with her neighbors.

The knock became more insistent.

Though she didn't take money from her parents, she did come from money. Her folks lectured her constantly that if she wouldn't live at home, where the security system was state of the art, she ought not to make herself a target. Granted, Coldwater Cove wasn't exactly teeming with potential kidnappers, but the repeated warnings had made her cautious.

She checked the peephole and was surprised to see Michael's handsome face distorted by the fish-eye lens. She opened the door.

"I never told you where I live."

"I know," he said, one hand on her doorjamb, the other in his jeans pocket. He looked long and lean and delicious. Heather tried hard to remind herself she didn't need his brand of trouble. And failed miserably. She found herself grinning at him like a starstruck freshman.

"Your address is more closely guarded than a state secret," he said. "But I'm not above a little blackmail."

Heather glanced along the deck she shared with her neighbor to see Lacy unlocking the door to her apartment. Her friend waved and grinned sheepishly before darting into her own place.

"Don't blame Lacy," Michael said. "She wouldn't spill at first. Not until I reminded her how often I'd taken the blame for things we'd done together when we were kids."

"Apparently, I can trust no one," Heather said wryly as she stepped aside and waved him in.

"You can trust me. Here's the music you missed in choir." He held up a black three-ring notebook filled with anthems. "I grabbed an extra copy of everything for you."

"You went to choir?"

He smiled like a frat boy after a panty raid. "And you didn't. Want to tell me why?" Then his brows drew together in concern. "You're OK, aren't you?"

Suddenly, she wasn't.

She'd worn a stoic mask while Aaron's parents faced the scariest of gut punches, the terror of a desperately ill child. She hadn't let her emotions get in the way. She'd done her job. Even when she had to bully them into signing that waiver so treatment could start.

Then that cryptic little message from her mom. Her cousin was worse. That meant he was nearing critical. She knew in her head that Levi would die without a transplant. Now she knew it in her heart.

She'd been tough. She'd taken care of others all day. She was done.

Heather burst into tears.

■ ■ ■ ■

OK, that's not the reaction I expected. He'd kept his promise to show up for choir. She was supposed to fall into his arms.

Then she sort of did.

He wrapped his arms around her, while her shoulders shook with silent sobs. The only thing he was sure of was that this wasn't his fault. He'd done exactly as promised. He'd shown up to sing with that vocally challenged choir.

Someone else had made her cry.

He wished he knew who it was so he could hang the bum up by his thumbs.

The front of his T-shirt was becoming increasingly damp, but he wasn't about to complain. He was holding her, Heather Walker, the girl he'd never dared to ask out back in high school. This was even better than dancing with her. She felt exactly as he'd imagined she would. Most of the women he knew in New York could pass for starving refugees. Heather's body was strong and fit, but soft and yielding in all the right places.

He drew his fingertips down her back and pulled her in closer. Except for the fact that she was crying her eyes out, he was finally holding the woman he'd dreamed of having in his arms.

"Hush," he found himself whispering. "It'll be all right."

"You can't know that."

"Why don't you tell me what's wrong, then?"

He wished he hadn't said that, because she pulled away from him. Then she scrounged in her pocket for a tissue and blew her nose like a trumpet. Even red faced and crying, she made his chest tighten.

"I'm sorry. I'm usually not such a puddle."

"I like puddles. My mom always says she couldn't keep me out of them when I was a kid."

She swiped away the tears. "I must be your dream girl, then."

She was, but this wasn't the right time to tell her so. Not when she was so obviously upset. A guy only got one chance at that sort of declaration, and he didn't want to blow it by rushing things. "So what happened to make you turn into a puddle?"

"Where do I start?" Then the words came spilling out of her, tumbling over each other so that he had to really concentrate to follow the disjointed phrases and leaps from one topic to the next. She was worried about a patient. She was distraught over her cousin's condition and how hard it was to find a liver donor.

"It was touch and go with Aaron today. And Levi is nearing the . . . the end stage of his condition."

"Doesn't that bump him up the transplant list?" Michael didn't know much about such things, having been ridiculously healthy all his life. Even when Lacy and Crystal came down with chicken pox, he didn't catch it. His dad claimed Mike was ornery enough to scare the germs away.

Michael wasn't sure he was kidding.

"Yes, Levi's condition will move him up, but he's hard to match," Heather explained. "His blood type is O negative. He could donate part of his liver to anyone no matter their blood type, but he can only receive a transplant from another O neg. And the donor would also need to be someone of compatible size and tissue match."

"Sounds like he has a few strikes against him."

"He does. And what about Aaron? I practically forced his parents to sign that waiver. If that antibiotic destroys his bone marrow —"

"Hush." Michael put two fingers to her lips. They were soft and warm. "You're borrowing trouble."

"I know, but they're both so young. It's just not fair." She collapsed onto her couch, slouching down into the cushions. Michael sat beside her.

She didn't object.

"I know you're all about taking care of people, but there's one person you're neglecting."

"Who?"

"You. You're working more hours than you should."

"You're right about that. I'd be much more pulled together if I got enough sleep." She straightened to sit upright. "But it can't be helped. The hospital's short staffed. Funding doesn't come in from the state like it used to."

She went on to tell him that many rural hospitals were closing. Lots of small towns no longer had adequate health facilities. If things didn't turn around soon, Coldwater Cove might be joining them.

"Seems to me," he said, artlessly propping an arm along the back of the couch, "a problem that can be solved with money isn't much of a problem."

"Unless you don't have the money." She shot him a wary glance. "I know what you're thinking. My parents have more money than God."

"Never crossed my mind." He was actually thinking he was glad he'd founded MoreCommas and made a boatload. He could make a generous donation to Coldwater General, more than enough to make up for the missing public funds. He made a mental note to get his assistant on it first thing tomorrow. He wished he could make the grant in his mother's honor, but it was more important to keep the donation anonymous.

Still, there were some problems money couldn't solve. His relationship with his father was a case in point. Introducing the money Mike had made into the equation would only make things worse.

"Actually, my parents have been very generous already," Heather said, and started telling him about the Walker endowment for the new mental health clinic at Bates College. "So you see, even if I wanted to, I really can't go back to them for more."

"I suspect they'd want to help if they knew about the trouble the hospital was in."

"Maybe, but they can't hear it from me."

She stifled a yawn. She was still in her scrubs, a cute little blue number with panda bears on the pockets.

"Have you had supper?" he asked.

"Supper? Who has time?"

"You do, and right now." Michael stood, took her hands, and raised her to her feet. "Why don't you take a shower and get comfortable while I see if I can rustle up something in your kitchen?"

She lifted a skeptical brow. "You cook?"

He cocked his head. "Not exactly. I'm not in Jake's league, that's for sure. But my omelets have been known to keep the wolf away from the door."

"OK." She headed for her bedroom and bath. "Back in a few."

"Take your time." *Man, she looks great walking away. Even in scrubs.*

While he searched the refrigerator for eggs, milk, and cheese, guilt tapped him on the shoulder. He had planned to head out of town right after choir. The Cessna Citation crew was standing by in Tulsa ready to go wheels up. All they were waiting for was him. If he delayed much more, it was going to crunch his already tight schedule.

But he couldn't leave a damsel in distress.

She'd knock you sideways if you called her that.

He smiled to himself as he pulled a bowl from her cupboard and began cracking eggs. He'd see her fed and then make a speedy exit. If he pushed the hog a bit, he could make up for the lost time. He hadn't built

MoreCommas by not taking chances and snapping up opportunities when they came his way.

And Heather Walker was the best thing that had come his way in a long, long time.

Chapter 10

Marjorie Chubb, captain of the Methodist prayer chain, has offered to teach a class for those who are feeling low. She guarantees you'll feel better or the prayer chain will lift you up until you do.

— from the Methodist bulletin

Michael loved watching Heather eat. The little groan of pleasure when she first tasted the food he'd cooked, the way she ran her tongue over her bottom lip between bites, the way her eyes closed and she sighed contentedly as she sopped up the last bite with a piece of crisp toast. He'd never seen anyone get so much enjoyment out of such a simple meal.

"Feeling better?" He took her empty plate from the bistro table and carried it to the sink.

"Mmm . . ." She wiped her lips with a napkin and took another sip of the hot cocoa he'd fixed for her. "Who wouldn't feel better after eating the omelet from heaven? Honestly, I can't believe you made that with what I had on hand."

"You don't cook much, do you?"

"No. I rarely have the time. And when I do, I usually just open a can of soup or something. It's a lot of trouble to cook for one." She leaned an elbow on the table, cheek resting in her palm. "My mother bemoans the fact that if I ever do marry, which she seriously doubts will happen, my poor husband will face nothing but 'burnt offerings' for the first year at least."

"I have a feeling he won't mind."

The corners of her lips turned up. "That's sweet. But how did you learn to cook? I mean, you don't exactly have a gas range strapped to your motorcycle."

She thought he was nothing but a biker bum, just as his sister Lacy did.

"It's part of the biker code. We're supposed to carry eleven secret spices with us at all times," Mike quipped. "Seriously, I can't take much credit for that omelet. Hunger makes the best sauce. You must have been sharp-set."

Heather downed the last of her cocoa, rose, and wandered into her small living room. Then she settled onto the overstuffed couch, folding those long legs under her. After her shower, she'd changed into yoga pants and a T-shirt that was too big for her. The effect was sloppy and comfortable and totally adorable. "Michael Evans has a modest streak. Who knew?"

"Why are you surprised?" He joined her on the soft, worn leather.

"Are you kidding? When we were in school, you got off on attention — good or bad. You always seemed like . . ."

"Like a tool," he finished for her. "Maybe even a power tool."

She scoffed and then shrugged. "If the power cord fits."

Would it kill her to disagree?

"Hey, is that any way to talk to the guy who just made you the omelet from heaven?"

"You're right." She hung her head, looking contrite, except for the mischievous quirk of her lips. "Sorry."

"No, you're not. But it's OK. I own what I was. I just hope you'll let me show you what I've become."

"And what's that?"

Dang! Why had he led the conversation that way? He wasn't ready to tell her what he'd been up to for the past few years. He wanted her to fall all over him because of . . . well, him, not because of the success of MoreCommas. He wanted her to *know* him, warts and all. And if by some miracle she didn't run away screaming, well, he'd see what came next.

But for now, he had to turn this conversation around pronto.

So he started telling the most harmless tales he could about his traveling days — when he'd bounced from town to town, taking odd jobs.

"All that wandering . . ." Heather shook her head. "What were you looking for?"

"A place to fit in, at first. But after a while, I started to appreciate being an outsider," he admitted. "It gives you a unique perspective on things."

He told her about how surprised he was to discover that people in other parts of the country thought about their world in a totally different way from the folks in Coldwater Cove. He'd met people of all colors, religions, ethnic backgrounds, and education levels and soaked up as many new ideas as he could.

"And I learned something from all of them." Even if sometimes it was what not to do. He wouldn't burden her with stories of strung-out junkies or the pickpocket who was in trouble with the law so often, he could recommend which jails up and down the Ohio River offered the best grub to their prisoners. "I picked up a few interesting skills along the way."

"Such as?"

When he was really down-and-out, he'd learned to pinch a penny until it squealed, but that wasn't likely to impress her. "Well, one Christmas I took a temp job giving foot massages to shoppers in a mall near Newark."

"Ooh! Show me." She propped her feet up on his lap, and he demonstrated his expertise until she was all but purring. Conversation flowed easily between them. They discovered they both loved The Ring trilogy, but hated what filmmakers did with *The Hobbit.* They agreed to disagree about whether soccer was a real sport or not, but were in complete accord on the subject of pumpkin pie.

It was the dessert voted most likely to make them both feel "yammy."

After the massage, at some time during the talking, somehow Heather had ended up snuggled next to him, her head resting on his shoulder.

This was, bar none, the best night of his life.

She smelled so good, like fresh-cut grass

and cool linen. "I hated seeing you unhappy earlier," he murmured into her hair.

"I had reason to be."

"Yeah, sure, you did. I know you're worried about your patient and your cousin and all, but I bet you have tough cases all the time. Why do these two get to you?"

She told him about her student nursing experience and how they'd lost a child that first week.

"That's rough." He wished he hadn't turned the conversation to something so serious, but maybe she needed to talk about it. Women were always wanting to talk about things. Whether talking did a speck of good or not made no difference at all to the need to verbally chew a problem to death. Michael supposed, in the long run, it would do her good to talk it out.

She launched into a monologue about kids and illness and how much easier it was to deal with death when the patient was older.

"Not that my older patients are any less valuable," Heather was quick to add.

"Do you think it's because adults have had a chance to live and the kids you work with haven't?"

"Maybe, but life is precious at every stage. No matter how many days someone has had, most of my patients want at least one more." Heather's fingers clenched the hem of her T-shirt into a tight bunch. "And I desperately want to give it to them."

"That's biting off a little more than you can chew, isn't it? I may have ducked out of Sunday school more often than not, but isn't God supposed to decide that sort of thing?"

She sighed. "You're right. But at least I can make sure however many days they have, they're as comfortable as I can help them be."

"Now that's something I'm sure you can handle," Michael said, hugging her a little tighter. "You've sure made me comfortable."

"Me too."

He wished she didn't sound so surprised about it, but the fact that she stayed snuggled up next to him still made it a win.

Heather went quiet for a moment. The rhythm of their breathing fell into sync as Michael stroked her arm. He was almost sure she'd drifted off to sleep, when she started speaking softly again.

"I've never told anyone this," she said. "It borders on mania and I hate it in myself."

"I can't believe there's anything to hate in you."

She sighed. "Obsessive-compulsive tendencies don't work every time they're tried."

"What do you obsess about?"

"Every time I work with a young patient, I start thinking about Jessica again. And not the good memories from when we were kids together," she said. Tension growing, she stiffened in his arms a little. "I replay that horrible time in my head."

Not good. Michael kept his face carefully blank. Maybe he *should* tell her about MoreCommas. Anything to keep her from revisiting the night her sister died.

"There was nothing you could've done to change what happened to Jess," he reminded her.

"I know. The trouble is, I couldn't ever do anything to change things for my parents either."

"How do you mean?"

Her shoulders shook again, and he held her closer. "Gosh, I really thought I was over this."

"Over what?"

"Over wondering if they wish it had been me in that car instead." She didn't make any noise, but he knew from the tremor in her shoulders that she wept.

"I know they don't wish that. They couldn't."

She turned in his arms and, eyes glistening, frowned at him. "Have you even met my parents?"

"Not really, but I know they can't think that. Not for a minute."

"Well, I guess I don't make it easy for them," she said. "Whether it's about money or where I live or who I date, I fight them at every turn. I'm not the 'good daughter' and never have been. How could they not wish to have Jessica back?"

When Michael was wandering, he'd met lots of people, but none with more going on upstairs than Jadis Chu, who was now his right hand at MoreCommas. She'd given him some words of wisdom in that maddeningly no-nonsense way of hers, and they'd stuck.

"Someone once told me that it's possible to care deeply for someone, to love them even," he said, "and still not like them very much."

The thought had given him hope that his family wasn't completely dead to him. His dad might not like him a bit, but somewhere, deep down, Michael had to believe he still loved him.

But his words didn't seem to comfort Heather. "You think my mom and dad don't like me?" she asked.

"No, I didn't mean that. Of course they like you. They love you or they wouldn't be trying to fix you up with Sweazy." Though if the Walkers knew Skyler as well as Michael did, they'd stop pushing their darling daughter toward him in a skinny minute. "It's just that parents are people and people have favorites. God knows my folks do, but even so, I can't believe they'd ever want to choose between their kids. Neither would yours."

"I guess," she said with a sigh. "Everyone loved Jessica, you know. She was so easy to love because she did everything right and made it look effortless. You'd think I would have been jealous of her, but it wasn't like that. We were more than sisters. We were best friends from birth. Jess was the keeper of all my secrets."

Michael would bet any amount of money that Heather didn't know all of Jessica's. Beginning to end, that horrible night happened because of a secret that would rock the town.

"Maybe it was because we were twins, but even though we weren't identical, it was like we were two sides of the same coin," Heather said softly. "When she died, part of me went with her."

Mike wondered how he'd feel if he lost one of his sisters. He had no doubt he'd grieve for Lacy. She'd been his partner in crime and, since he was older than her, she sort of hero-worshiped him when they were very little. No guy can resist that. But if something happened to Crystal . . . well, he and she were so different, it was almost as if they shared no DNA at all. His older sister had merely tolerated him. He was an annoyance to be borne, and swatted aside when their parents weren't looking.

Still, would he grieve for the relationship they never had?

"At the funeral, I felt like an outsider," Heather went on. "I had to be strong, for Mom and Dad, you see, so I couldn't let myself feel anything. It was all so surreal. So . . . so . . ."

"Obscene," he suggested. "Death is the last obscenity."

"Yes." She shot him an amazed look. "That's deep."

"Surprised?"

"Well, yeah. Sorry."

"It's OK. I get that a lot. One good thing about being underestimated is that you get to surprise people often."

"I don't underestimate you. I just expected you to be different, that's all." Heather laid her head back down on his shoulder. "Of all the people in the world for me to trust with this stuff, I never thought it would be you."

She trusts me. Dang, that feels good! Now, how do I not blow it?

Her breathing slowed. She'd fallen asleep for real this time. He closed his eyes and imagined what it would be like to lie beside her every night. To listen to the soft sounds of her breathing, to know he could reach out and touch her whenever he wanted . . .

Before he realized it, he was skimming the surface of sleep, too. Then between one breath and the next, he dived headlong into blackness with her.

One of the red Fiesta's headlights was still burning, sending a shaft of light through the dark water of Lake Jewel. A largemouth bass swam by to inspect the sudden illumination and then darted back into the shadows.

The passenger-side window was down, so water gushed into the interior. It was cold. Soul-sucking, body-numbing, ball-freezing cold.

Just before it closed over her head, Jessica screamed.

Michael jerked awake, sucking in a quick lungful of air. He'd been holding his breath in his sleep. Heart pounding, he forced himself to stay still, willing it to slow to a normal rhythm.

It took him a minute to realize where he was. Jessica Walker's car was no longer at the bottom of Lake Jewel. They'd pulled it out the next morning. Jess had been pulled out the night before, but it was too late. She was dead.

And now, years later, here he was, all tangled up with her sister on an old leather couch.

Michael used to have that dream, or some sick variation of it, at least once a week. It hadn't troubled him in months. Guess he should have expected it to return, what with being back in Coldwater and all.

He checked his watch and stifled a curse. It was past midnight. According to plan, he should already be airborne and on his way back to New York for that breakfast meeting.

He'd hoped to be able to check in with Jadis and run through the numbers once more before sitting down with the investors. Now he'd have to wing it. Even if he was roaring out of town this instant, he might still be late for the meeting.

Despite the way he'd jerked awake, Heather slept on.

She must be exhausted.

As gently as he could, he moved Heather

and rose from the couch. She shifted onto her other side but didn't wake. Michael was pretty good at reading other people, but he had trouble identifying emotions when they were his own. Something he guessed was tenderness made his chest heat. He covered her with an afghan and slipped out of the apartment. Then he took the stairs two at a time, climbed onto his motorcycle, and kicked it into high gear for Tulsa with no thought of speed limits at all.

Over the whine of the bike, the road surface seemed to be saying in a repetitive stream "She trusts you, trusts you."

Mike hoped Heather never learned anything that made her rethink that trust.

Chapter 11

I always thought money would solve everything. Of course, that was before I had money.
— Michael Evans, who still has trouble with the concept of "can't"

"I'm a little behind schedule," Mike said to his private pilot as he supervised the crew, who loaded the Harley into the Cessna Citation that had been specially reconfigured to accommodate it. The crew was being paid to treat the hog like gold and they did. "Can you still get me back to the Big Apple in time for my seven a.m. meeting, Captain?"

"Yes, sir. We got lucky in that respect. The weather service reports winds aloft that are favorable at the altitude we'll be flying. It'll be a heck of a tailwind," the pilot said. "But I can't say the same for making the return trip to Oklahoma on the original schedule."

"Why not?"

"I won't be eligible to fly then. I'll have timed out before we finish the flight plan. Per your request, I've been on the clock since 21:30. According to regs, I can only be on duty for fourteen hours without rest," the pilot explained. "If we had Garcia with us, it would be different."

Michael's company copilot was out on maternity leave, and he hadn't thought to hire a temporary replacement. Until his mother's illness, he hadn't taken any trips that didn't involve an overnight layover. This requested turn and burn was out of the ordinary, but he was paying handsomely to have a flight crew at his beck and call. He assumed the timing of his travel would always be his decision.

"That's unacceptable," Michael said.

"Those are the rules, sir."

"Why didn't you tell me when I first requested this trip?"

"Sir, if we'd been wheels up by 22:00, we'd have been in NYC long enough to rest the crew. I could've filed a new flight plan for the return trip. But starting this late . . ." He let the sentence dangle unfinished. "Once we get back to New York, I can see about finding a replacement pilot for you."

"That won't do." Mike wouldn't admit it

to anyone, but he was a white-knuckle flyer. He'd hired Captain Russo because he was retired Air Force. If the military trusted him with a fighter jet, Michael figured he could trust him, too. The idea of a rent-a-pilot made his gut churn.

"If you're willing to wait for the required rest period, I can have you back in Tulsa by early Friday," the captain said. "Will that be acceptable or do you wish to scrub the flight tonight?"

Mike rubbed his forehead. If Heather had been at choir, he might have been able to talk to her during the break Mr. Mariano insisted upon for coffee and cookies. Then he could have sneaked out a little early. He certainly could have left soon after the last chord sounded. If he hadn't decided to take her music to her before he left town . . . If he hadn't taken the time to make the omelet from heaven . . . If he hadn't fallen asleep with the girl of his dreams . . .

So he could make the investor meeting or his date with Heather, but not both.

Well, this is a no-brainer.

Of course he couldn't stand up Heather. A guy only got so many shots with a girl like her. She'd confided in him. She'd let him hold her someplace besides a dance floor. She *trusted* him.

Besides, if you want to get technical about it, we freaking slept together!

He couldn't let her down.

But then he remembered the other people he couldn't let down. When Michael first started making serious money with MoreCommas, he'd thought that meant more freedom. Actually, the greenbacks came with more responsibilities. He had employees — hundreds of them. And they all expected him to make decisions that would grow the company. His people counted on him to ensure that their paychecks and health insurance and 401(k) plans and vacation days and maternity leave, and yada, yada, yada would continue without interruption.

The investor group's money would enable MoreCommas to expand. His hundreds of employees would balloon to thousands, maybe tens of thousands. The company would thrive until it was ripe for an IPO. Then everybody associated with the start-up — all those brainiacs who'd worked beside him for beer and the promise of stock options in the beginning, and later for princely salaries and benefit packages so Google wouldn't poach them away — would win the Wall Street lottery.

Big time.

Michael had worked hard, but he'd be first to admit he'd also been blessed. When his company went public, he'd be paying it forward. Lots of families' lives would change because of him.

Then maybe he'd tell his dad what he'd done and see if it made any difference.

But the main issue now was the old Star Trek dilemma — the needs of the many outweighing the needs of the few.

Or the one.

It's hard to argue with Spock. He made a low growl in the back of his throat and climbed into the Cessna. "Get this bird in the air."

A shaft of sunlight poured into Heather's little living room and teased her eyelids open. She stretched, mildly disappointed to discover she was alone. In her dreams, she'd been cuddled up with Michael Evans all night.

It had felt so right.

As Glenda at work might say, "Who'd a thunk it?"

Being with Michael was like standing at the edge of a limestone cliff — wildly exciting, and the view was terrific, but it could be dangerous all the same. Then last night she'd seen a different side of the town's bad boy, a side that made omelets and listened to her troubles without needing to fix them for her.

It showed a measure of respect she never expected from someone who released goats into a library. What had changed him?

But this was not a day for such questions. It was her first day off in a couple of weeks, and Heather intended to enjoy it thoroughly. She fixed herself a leisurely cup of coffee and a steaming bowl of oatmeal with raisins and cinnamon while she listened to the local morning show on the radio.

"The Rotary Club is building a corn maze on the edge of Lake Jewel just in time for Halloween in a few weeks," the announcer said in his pleasant drawl. "It'll be open October twenty-fifth to the thirty-first from sundown to ten each night. Admission is two canned goods apiece, which will be donated to the good folk at the Coldwater Cove food bank. You can get in for just one can if it's some kind of potted meat."

Heather snorted. "Bet half of what's donated will be pork brains in gravy," she said to the radio as if he could hear her.

For some inexplicable reason, the unusual dish was considered a local delicacy. Even the convenience store out on the highway stocked cans of Mama Hopper's Pork Brains in Milk Gravy on the shelves at all times.

Heather had never been able to bring herself to try it.

"Guess I've never been that hungry, thank God." She switched off the radio and fed her goldfish, whom she pointedly refused to name. After losing Errol Finn, she didn't have the heart to name his replacement. No point in naming something you might have to flush down the toilet someday, but she did enjoy watching him make tight circles in the bowl and gobble up the fish food floating on the surface.

"Life is good, eh, Fish?"

He answered her with a bubble.

She took her lazy time about getting dressed. Her day was almost a blank slate. First, she was lunching with Lacy and her mom and Jake's sister, Laura, so they could work on plans for the wedding together. Then she'd have most of the afternoon to laze around and get ready for her ride with Michael at five.

Standing before her long mirror, she imagined what she'd look like tricked out in full biker leather gear. She pictured herself with a bandana corralling her hair, a ring in her nose, and a wicked-looking tat on her upper arm.

Heather giggled at her reflection. "I *so*

don't have the attitude for a biker chick."

Instead, she pulled on worn jeans, enjoying the feel of old denim on her thighs, and topped it with what she called her *Matrix* sweater. It wasn't like the slick, cool stuff the character Trinity wore in the movies. It was more like Trinity's everyday kick-arounds on the *Nebuchadnezzar.* The sweater was a little frayed at the edges, but far too comfortable to toss out. She toed on her oldest pair of loafers, gave her hair a quick brushing, and called it good.

Then she practically skipped down the iron stairs before climbing into the Taurus and heading over to Mrs. Evans's house to meet up with Lacy. Mr. Evans was out in his front yard, puttering around with something, when Heather pulled up. A handful of fallen leaves scuttled across the driveway in front of her.

"Hey, Mr. Evans, how are you doing this fine fall day?"

"I'd be better if I could get rid of these dang squirrels," he said grumpily, and bent over to monkey with something on the side of his house near the foundation. His faithful little Yorkie, Fergus, was nosing about in the mums nearby.

Lacy had told Heather about her father's fixation with what she called "The War of

Squirrel Insurgency." The Evanses' yard didn't have more fluffy-tailed rats than anyone else in town, but Mr. Evans was convinced the ones in his oak trees held a special grudge against him. He claimed they chewed off small branches and littered his lawn with them out of pure spite. To protect himself against a possible barrage of acorns that might rain down at any minute, he always wore a football helmet while he mowed.

Paranoia much?

"Shirley doesn't want me to use poison to get rid of them," Mr. Evans explained. "Deputy Scott has warned me against using the shotgun in town anymore. And my homemade squirrel repellent . . . well, let's just say it repelled more than squirrels."

The whole town had heard about Mr. Evans's experiment gone awry. His pest-repellent concoction had smelled like moldy tacos in an outhouse. The odor lingered in the Evanses' kitchen, where it was created, and front yard, where it was applied without the desired effect, for weeks. Lacy's mother had moved to her daughter Crystal's house until the stink cleared. Heather covered her mouth so Mr. Evans wouldn't catch her smirking over the memory. Or worse, laughing aloud.

Instead, she peered down at the device he'd plugged into an exterior electric socket. "Pests Be Gone" was plastered across the metal side of something that looked a little like an old popcorn popper, minus the oil and kernels.

"What is that?"

"That," he said proudly, "is the latest development in vermin eradication. I got it off the Internet."

"What does it do?"

"It fights squirrels with sound waves." He flipped a switch and stood up straight, beaming down at the device like a father surveying his newborn for the first time.

From the corner of her eye, Heather saw Fergus give a startled shake and begin chasing his tail in frantic circles.

"It's all very scientific." Mr. Evans grinned. "And it should drive all those furry devils over to Mayhew's yard."

Alfred Mayhew was a notorious fussbudget, but he'd lived next to the Evans family since Lacy and Michael were kids. Crystal too, though Heather always had a hard time remembering her as a child.

She was sort of born old.

Heather cocked her head, listening. "I don't hear anything."

"That's the beauty of it," Mr. Evans said.

"The sound waves are emitted at a frequency beyond human range. Only the critters can hear it."

At that moment, Fergus stopped circling and plopped his little Yorkie bottom on the ground. Then he pointed his nose at the sky and howled like a miniature wolf. Up and down the street, all the dogs in the neighborhood joined the mournful chorus. Even Mr. Mayhew's cat, who'd been stalking crickets in the grass, leaped two feet into the air and yowled wildly. Then he made a beeline for Mayhew's slightly propped open garage door, trying to get away from the Pests Be Gone sound waves. Songbirds roosting in Mr. Evans's oak trees took wing, like bats shooting out of a cave at dusk.

The only animals that didn't seem adversely affected by Pests Be Gone were the squirrels. A trio of them chattered down at Heather and Mr. Evans from the safety of a high branch. Their furry little heads bobbed in time with a pulsing rhythm Heather couldn't hear.

"Like headbangers at a rock concert," Heather said in disbelief.

"The darn things like it!" Mr. Evans quickly bent over and turned off the device. Fergus stopped howling, and Mr. Mayhew's cat peered out from under the garage door, trying to make sure the coast was truly clear. A brisk wind ruffled by, and a hail of acorns rained down from the oak tree. When Heather looked up, the squirrels were nowhere to be seen.

"Did you see that? Those dirty sons of bi— biscuits," Mr. Evans amended with a guilty glance in Heather's direction. "They just threw acorns at me."

"Surely not." Even as she said it, Heather was doubtful. The timing was too precise. At the risk of jumping onto the crazy train, she was beginning to be on Mr. Evans's side. "It could have been the wind."

"Coulda been, but we both know it wasn't."

CHAPTER 12

If a problem can be solved with a little power shopping, it's not really much of a problem, is it?

— Shirley Evans, while poring over a wig catalog

Mr. Evans stomped over to his front door and held it open for Heather. "Let's go in. It'll be safer there. Guess you'll be wanting some coffee," he added with a note of hope in his voice.

Heather had been warned about Mr. Evans's "Take No Prisoners" brew. Lacy claimed her father's coffee was stout enough to carry its own mug across the table and had been known to make grown men cry.

If Mr. Evans could only find a way to introduce his coffee into the squirrels' water supply, they'd probably run themselves into the next county on the jolt of caffeine alone.

She decided not to suggest it. Mr. Evans

had already shown himself willing to go to extremes to win this undeclared war.

"No thanks, Mr. Evans. I've had a cup already and one's my limit."

"Well, a single cup won't do for me. That's why I always make a big pot. Shirley and Lacy and Laura are in the family room."

Laura was Jake's sister. She had the same dark Tyler eyes and hair and was going to be a bridesmaid alongside Lacy's sister, Crystal. Laura was pretty and petite and would look great in whatever dress Lacy chose for them to wear.

Even the hurt-your-eyes pink one.

"Expect they're looking for you," Mr. Evans said. "But I warn you, they've been all a-twitter since the UPS man came this morning."

Once inside, they passed by the formal living room to the right and headed toward the informal dining space at the back of the house. Mr. Evans peeled off toward the kitchen on the left. Heather followed the sound of feminine laughter to the right, into the family room that adjoined the eating space.

Her friend Lacy, Laura Tyler, and Mrs. Evans were seated in various versions of the lotus position in the middle of the space, surrounded by lavender boxes, some open, some yet to be. Lacy was holding a mirror for her mother, whose hair had somehow turned pumpkin orange and grown into a shoulder-length pageboy overnight.

"What in the world?"

"Oh, Heather, there you are." Shirley Evans turned to greet her, but didn't rise from her cross-legged posture on a pillow on the floor. "Come and see. It's the most wonderful thing."

Jake's sister, Laura, grinned at her. "I'll bet you had a hand in this, didn't you?"

"In what?" Heather asked.

Shirley waved a piece of paper in the air. Heather couldn't make out the company logo on the letterhead, but it seemed to be decorated with a long string of free-flowing commas and mathematical symbols.

It reminded her of Michael's tattoo.

Now you're being a goose, she scolded herself. *Stop looking for him everywhere. You'll see him soon enough tonight, silly.*

"Now don't be modest, dear. Somehow" — Shirley winked hugely at Heather — "this company received my name as a new cancer patient and I was chosen to try out a whole line of wigs."

She pulled off the orange pageboy to reveal a completely bald head. Not a head full of wispy clumps. Not the thinning hair with the scalp showing through of most cancer patients. Mrs. Evans's head was bare as an ostrich egg.

Heather gasped. "But . . . you haven't been on chemo long enough to lose it all. What happened to your hair?"

"Well, when I received notice that these wigs were coming, I decided not to wait for it to fall out. I mean, would there be anything more depressing than having your hair come out in handfuls?" Shirley shuddered. "Anyway, I decided to — oh, what is it the kids say nowadays? Oh, yes! — go big or go home. So I had Lolita from Hair Today Gone Tamale come over and just lop it all off."

"Hair today gone to what?"

"Oh, surely you know Lolita Alvarez."

"Yes, we've met," Heather said. Lolita was a licensed barber who volunteered at the hospital. She came in once a week to give haircuts and shaves to patients who'd been there long enough to need one.

"Well, she and her husband, Hector, recently opened a new business that combines both their talents. Hair Today Gone Tamale. It's out on the highway. They renovated the old Sinclair station, you see. She cuts hair in the side where they used to sell Skittles and Jujubes and motor oil. And

Hector turned the garage bay into a commercial kitchen and take-out place. He makes the best tortillas in town." Shirley rolled her eyes expressively. "And his churros are to die for."

Heather knelt down between Laura and Lacy, surveying the dozens of boxes. There were wigs in all colors and hair lengths. "But what's the deal with all these wigs?"

"Well, according to the letter that came with them," Lacy said, "Mom is supposed to try them all on and keep the ones she wants. Any that don't suit her can be donated to the hospital. I expect there are other cancer patients who need one or two."

Heather nodded. The lady who ran Simply Chic on the Square gave classes on the many ways to wear a silk scarf, but a wig would help patients who were going through chemo feel far more normal than the most artfully tied piece of cloth.

"The hospital will be glad to accept whatever you can spare," Heather said, taking Mrs. Evans's hand and giving it a squeeze. "I'm glad to see you in such good spirits."

"Why wouldn't I be with all these goodies?"

"When was your last treatment?" Heather asked.

"It's been a few days," Shirley said. "I won't lie. I felt like I'd been rode hard and put up wet that first day. But as you know, the farther I get from chemo, the better I feel. I refuse to let it get me down. It's meant to do me good in the long run."

Heather smiled and nodded, but she knew Mrs. Evans was putting up a brave front. She'd seen it often enough with her patients. Most of them made little deals with God whether they were even aware of it. If they were nice enough to everyone, if they maintained a positive outlook, if they hid how horrible they were actually feeling, nothing bad would happen.

"Your mom has a great attitude," Jake's sister told Lacy.

"And why shouldn't I? I have my family and friends. I know people are praying for me. I've always been a big believer in living each day as it comes, and cancer is *not* going to get me today," Shirley said with a tremulous smile that brightened into a real one. "Besides, what woman wouldn't be thrilled with all these wigs?"

"*I* would have bought you a wig, Shirley," Mr. Evans said as he came from the kitchen to settle at the round oak table in the eating space. He bore a copy of the *Coldwater Gazette* and a steaming mug big enough to be mistaken for a beer stein. The fragrant aroma of arabica beans that had given their all emanated from it. Heather would have been tempted to try a cup if she hadn't been strongly warned against it.

Good thing his coffee doesn't taste as good as it smells. Otherwise, it would have to be a controlled substance.

"I know you would have bought me one, George," his wife said. "But this way, I can have one for each day of the week."

Ah! The Evans family motto in action. Just like Lacy says: If a little's good, a lot's a whole bunch better. Wonder if Michael thinks that, too? She gave herself an inward shake. *And there I am thinking about Michael again.*

Mr. Evans rattled his paper before disappearing behind it. "Just don't keep that red one," he grumbled. "If folks see me squiring a pretty redhead around town, they'll think I'm cheating on you."

"Oh, do you really think so?" Mrs. Evans blushed and shot him an impish grin. "What fun!"

"Shirley!" He lowered the paper so he could lift a reproving eyebrow in her direction.

"Well, if they're gossiping about us, they'll be giving someone else a rest," she said. "Let them talk. I know you love me and you know I love you. Our marriage is rock solid and that's all that counts."

He made a *hmph*-ing noise, but Heather suspected he was secretly pleased, because the corners of his mouth kept turning up before he dived behind his paper again.

"Speaking of rock solid," he said, "I was reading the other day about the negative relationship between the cost of a wedding and the length of the marriage."

Mr. Evans kept his paper up this time.

Sort of like a shield.

"According to this study, it seems the more you spend on the wedding," he went on, "the less likely the couple is to stick together. They had all the figures and charts and graphs to prove it, too."

"Oh, that's nothing but twaddle," Shirley said.

"No, it's not. It's science."

"And how did science work for you with the squirrels today, dear?" she asked with syrupy sweetness.

Without a word, Mr. Evans drained his gigantic coffee mug, rose from the table, and stomped back into the kitchen.

Probably for a refill.

"You know," Shirley said as she put on a long wig that would have looked more at home on the bootylicious Beyoncé, "I hear tell some couples enjoy pretending they don't know each other. Take a look at this wig, George. This could make pretending you don't know me easier, don't you think?" When he popped his head in from the kitchen, she stood and gave her hips a seductive shake.

"Shirley! Not in front of the children . . ." Red-faced, Mr. Evans waved his hand toward Lacy, Laura, and Heather.

"They're hardly children, George. In fact, now that Lacy's getting married, we owe it to her to share what we've learned about staying together in our many years of marriage. And one of the biggies is that every relationship needs a little spice from time to time."

He blinked at his wife as if she'd suddenly sprouted a second head. Then he headed for the front door.

"Where are you going, George?" Mrs. Evans stood, the long locks flowing in bouncy curls down her back.

"To Cooper's Hardware to see if he'll take that blasted Pests Be Gone off my hands."

"All right, dear."

He slammed the door behind him.

Then Shirley pulled off the long wig and substituted a short-haired one in her own glorious white color. She looked like herself again.

"And that, girls," she said as she smoothed down the bangs, "is how you make a husband be gone. Now, then. Let's clear out these wigs and make plans to spend some serious money on Lacy's wedding!"

Chapter 13

The beauty of reality TV is that it gives the illusion of letting viewers spy on a stranger's life without being arrested as Peeping Toms. It's gold for the networks because we can fill airtime cheaply without bothering to pay those pesky union wages to writers and actors and the rest. But don't kid yourself. There's nothing real in a reality show. If there was, who would watch it?

— Louise Katzman, producer
for Forget-Me-Not Features
and mentor of Judith Hildebrand,
aka "Stiletto Girl"

"A PhD in Cinematic Arts, Theory, and Practice, years slaving away as a gofer for people with less talent in their whole bodies than I have in my pinkie finger, and where did it get me? Stuck in this pitiful fleabag!"

The Heart of the Ozarks Motel and Car

Wash was the bus line's drop-off point for Coldwater Cove. It wasn't quite as bad as Judith made it out to be. The linens were worn, but they smelled faintly of bleach and the windswept freshness of having been line dried. The hardwood floors could have benefited from a resanding and staining, but they were much cleaner than any sort of carpet would have been. A small refrigerator chugged away in the corner, and near the sink, which was located separately from the rest of the bathroom, sat a coffeemaker with the basic fixings for a caffeine delivery system, if you weren't too picky.

Starbucks, it is not!

The motel's biggest fault was that it was old and tired. Pretty much everything Manhattan was not. In Judith's mind, that was synonymous with worthless.

She hefted her oversized roller bag onto the chest of drawers. The vintage piece of furniture listed an inch to the left but stayed upright under its load. She decided then and there not to unpack her bag. Not only was she hoping to get what she needed on Michael Evans and get the frack back to civilization ASAP, she really didn't want to open any of those drawers. She'd surely be overcome by the scent of mothballs and lace doilies.

At least, there was no evidence of bugs.

In her week and a half of riding the bus, she'd seen more cockroaches in terminals than she'd known existed in the world. Of course, it wasn't supposed to take that many days to travel from New York to Oklahoma. But she boarded the wrong bus in Chicago and ended up in Memphis for a day and a night.

The flat Midwest accent and its hard *r*'s gave her trouble. To her ears, everyone west of Ohio was growling all the time. As she traveled south, a bit of a drawl crept in, and that made it worse. She caught herself listening to *how* people said things, not what they said, so she was a step and a half behind in most conversations.

She was usually the smartest person in the room. It irritated her to be so out of her element.

Of course, Michael Evans had warned her that everybody in Oklahoma sounded like him. Why had she ever thought his rough cowboy baritone was hot?

Even worse than the people was the land. It was so empty. Barring Chicago, of course, she could travel for hundreds of miles in any direction and not see anything she would remotely class as a city. Even the places that claimed to be were more suburbia than central core. There was too much sky. Too many trees and endless cornfields and hills and hollows. They all looked alike.

The empty vastness of the plains made her feel so exposed and, though she'd never admit it, so alone. She was a city girl. She needed the friction of all those lives rubbing up against each other. Without that constant static prickling around her, she felt drained and adrift.

"How do people live out here?" she wondered aloud as she checked her watch. *Only three in the afternoon.* Since she wasn't going to bother unpacking, there was still enough time to get some work done.

She fastened on the little lapel camera that was disguised as a pin and scooped up her laptop bag, making sure the computer was on. The camera would feed into a file on her Toshiba. Then she headed out the door, being careful to lock it behind her with a real key.

Not a code, not a key card, a fricking metal key with the name of the motel and the number of my room on it! May as well leave the door ajar and invite the locals to help themselves.

She dropped by the motel office and rang the bell on the counter. A middle-aged woman with impossibly blond hair and far too much lipstick for the amount of eye shadow she wore ambled out through the long strings of beads that formed a curtain between the lobby and backroom.

"I need a cab," Judith said.

"Sugar, you are plumb out of luck. We don't have no taxi service hereabouts," the woman said. "But if you're wantin' to go to the Walmart for some things, you can borrow my Buick. It's parked out front."

Like many lifelong New Yorkers, Judith had never learned to drive. And she'd sooner vote Republican than be caught in a Walmart.

"What? Uh, I mean, no, I don't think so." Judith almost stammered in her surprise. Why would a total stranger offer her the use of her car? How did the blonde know she wasn't some serial killer on the run and lying low in this backwater? Judith could very well take her car and disappear with it into the wasteland of fly-over country. The Buick might never be seen again. The bleach in the motel clerk's hair must have fried her brain.

What's wrong with some people?

But the clerk continued to try to be helpful. As it turned out, the motel was only located a few blocks from what the woman called "the Square."

"And you'll find half a dozen cute little shops along the way if you take Maple Street." The clerk drew the route onto a touristy little map with oversized versions of shops that had sponsored it marking their locations. "O' course, if you're worried about gettin' lost, I can put up the BE BACK SOON sign and drive you across town to the Walmart."

Lost in this teeny excuse for a town? Don't make me laugh.

"I'll walk." Judith snatched up the map and headed for the door.

"Well, if you get turned around, sugar, just ask anybody for directions. Everyone knows where Heart of the Ozark is. They'll set you to rights."

Judith was from New York. She'd never be foolish enough to let anyone know she was lost. *If you don't look like you belong, you're an easy mark.*

"Have a nice walk, now," the woman said cheerily.

"Thank you." Judith blinked in surprise at the words that had popped out of her mouth. She wasn't in the habit of saying "thank you." It was rare when anyone did something for her that deserved thanks. But foolish or not, the woman had suggested Judith use her car. And then followed it up with the offer to give her a ride. So she guessed that called for a "thank you."

And besides, everything I say is being recorded. If I want to banish my Stiletto Girl image, I'd better be professional at all times.

She was aiming for Diane Sawyer meets Julie Chen.

And likeable. I have to be frickin' likeable. Louise always said that was my biggest problem. That reality show made me the person people love to hate.

The woman gave her a friendly wave and hurried back to catch the rest of *The Price Is Right.*

Judith set out, feeling like she was about to invade the enemy's stronghold — because Michael Evans was the enemy, no doubt about it. Her career, which may not have been stellar up to the time she first laid eyes on him, was at least on an upward trajectory. After he christened her "Stiletto Girl," Louise made her embrace the bitchy persona for that reality show about getting tattoos. She became a walking punch line in the film community. She'd been grateful to get a job fetching some director's coffee.

Even an *indie* director.

Judith walked on, wishing she'd left her heels in New York. They didn't work well on cobblestones. There were sidewalks a-plenty, but many of the crosswalks were paved in brick laid in a herringbone pattern. The effect was charming, she had to admit, but oh so treacherous for her red-soled designer pumps.

Maple Street turned out to be aptly named. Trees on either side of the lane had blazed into glorious color.

"Not bad," she murmured. "It's not New England, but it's not bad."

There. The camera's mic should pick that up.

That kind of commentary would make her more likeable, wouldn't it?

At first, the street was lined with older homes, but then after a block or two, businesses began to pop up, interspersed between residences. She passed by Unique Boutique, a women's clothing store with surprisingly cute outfits displayed in the window.

A fellow with a small "man bun" and scraggly beard was sweeping the sidewalk in front of Cooper's Hardware on the next block.

Whoa! Shades of Deliverance.

Despite looking like a cross between a *Duck Dynasty* reject and an old hippie, he stopped sweeping to let her pass. The man nodded to her and smiled.

"Have a nice day, ma'am."

Ma'am! What is it with these Okies?

Michael Evans had called her ma'am, too, and way before she deserved it. She hadn't been quite thirty when he first ma'am'd her on camera. Now that she was knocking on forty, and arguably might have earned a "ma'am," she still hated the word. It reminded her how old she was without very much to show for the passage of years.

But because she knew she was being recorded, she found herself saying "You, too" back to the broom man.

Finally, she reached her destination — the local newspaper office, such as it was. She pushed open the ornately carved Victorian door of the *Coldwater Gazette,* expecting a sedate atmosphere and the smell of old newsprint.

Instead, she stepped into minor pandemonium. A phone was ringing, with no one bothering to answer it because almost everyone already seemed to be talking on their headset phones. The clicking of keys on multiple keyboards beneath the multiple one-sided conversations sounded like an infestation of insects.

However, one conversation wasn't one-sided.

"I'm telling you, Wanda, we can't run this

ad." A blue-haired matron scuttled after a woman who was skinny enough to fit in on Fifth Avenue. Unfortunately, the woman — obviously named Wanda and just as obviously in charge — ignored Judith as she strode past on the way to a cubicle occupied by a bespectacled kid. He flinched as Wanda drew closer.

He's gotta be the resident techie. They always have that "startled mouse" look whenever anyone notices them.

"Are you listening to me?" Blue Hair waved a piece of paper and then began reading from it. "For rent: one bedroom in my house. Possible bathroom and kitchen privileges for the right tenant."

"What's wrong with that?" the fashionably thin Wanda asked.

"We could be sued. That's what's wrong. You can advertise a property and give all the specifics you want to about the place, but you can't advertise for a particular type of renter."

"Mrs. Chisholm didn't specify any particular type," Wanda pointed out.

"She said the 'right tenant.' " Blue Hair repeated, poking her finger at the offending page. "That means she'll be discriminating against anyone who fits her idea of 'wrong.' I'm telling you, Wanda, we can't run it. Unless you want to lose the *Gazette* in a lawsuit."

"I don't see the ACLU lining up outside our door. Besides, Mavis Chisholm has a fabulous old house. She's right to be picky about who she chooses to accept as a boarder."

"She can be choosy by running a background check or credit report. She can refuse to accept a pet, but knowing Mrs. Chisholm, she'll reject a renter if she thinks their eyes are too close together. Then she'll be in hot water and we'll be there with her." Blue Hair arched a brow at the woman who was obviously her boss and shook her head in disapproval. "You know I'm right."

Judith would never have gotten away with that with Louise.

"All right," Wanda said. "Tell Mavis we can't run her ad, but we'll do a little scouting for her on the QT and come up with someone she'll find acceptable."

Blue Hair gave a pursed-lipped smile of triumph and flounced back to her cubicle.

Judith filed the information about the available room away for future use. If this Mrs. Chisholm's house was anything like some of the charming older homes she'd walked past on Maple Street, she'd happily give up her situation at the Heart of the

Ozarks motel for a more bed-and-breakfast-type arrangement.

For the moment, though, Judith was being totally ignored by the entire office staff. However, it wouldn't do to go all "I'm walkin' here!" on them. Professional. Likeable. Those were the watchwords.

"Ahem," she said.

No one even glanced in her direction.

"My computer is being stupid again, Deek," Wanda said accusingly to the shivering techie.

"What did you do to it?"

"What do you mean, what did *I* do? It's the computer that's not working." Wanda's voice strayed upward half an octave and doubled in decibels.

"What was the last button you pushed?"

"I don't care what button I pushed. The computer should do what I meant!"

"I quite agree," Judith said, matching Wanda's pitch and loudness. "Whether it's a computer or an employee" — she shot a scathing glance at Blue Hair — "anything that doesn't work should be replaced."

Deek gulped loudly enough to be heard across the room.

"Oh, for pity's sake, I'm not going to replace you, Deek. Just go reboot my computer and fix it," Wanda said to the kid, who skittered across the chopped-up space and disappeared into the only office with a door. Wanda walked over to Judith.

"Sorry for the general confusion. You caught us on one of our low-staff days." She held out her hand. "I don't believe we've met. I'm Wanda Cruikshank, publisher of the *Coldwater Gazette.* And you are Ms. . . ."

"Actually, it's Doctor." Judith shook her hand and then fished out a business card. She'd only had a hundred made up, but they looked pretty impressive, if she did say so herself. "Dr. Judith Hildebrand."

She'd worked hard for that PhD, even if it was in a slightly esoteric field. She might as well use it. Like a club, if she had to.

"And how can we help you?"

"I'm doing research on the sociological impact of small-town life, particularly as it relates to young males aged fifteen to twenty." That should cover the age range that would include Michael Evans when he lived here last.

"We do a whole section on high school activities once a week."

"Commendable," Judith said because she needed the woman's help. Privately, she couldn't imagine anything more stupefying than reading about the antics of a bunch of pimply faced hicks on such a regular basis.

"However, I need to track certain markers and behaviors over time, going back several years."

She pulled out a tablet and pretended to scan the page that popped up for data. Actually, it was the horror novel she'd been reading on her Kindle app.

"I think a decade or so will give me a sufficient baseline," she said importantly. "Of course, your paper will be recognized in the acknowledgments section when I publish my findings. Might I have access to your digital archives for the purposes of my research?"

She'd type in "Michael Evans," do a search, and in a few minutes, she'd know a good deal more about the man who ruined her career. And how he came by that scar he didn't want to talk about.

"We should be able to work something out, but I warn you, our archives probably won't be what you're used to."

I wouldn't be surprised if they still use dial-up modems out here. But Judith didn't have to worry about getting on the Internet. The data was no doubt on a couple of flash drives someplace.

Wanda looked at her wristwatch. "Most of what you're looking for is probably in the dungeon."

"I beg your pardon."

"That's our affectionate term for the storage area in the basement. The paper has only been digital for the last three years. Before that we recorded editions of the *Gazette* on microfiche, and the really old stuff is still hanging in paper files."

Judith was no stranger to having to dig through things to get dirt on a subject. Once when she worked a temp job as part of the negative research team for a political campaign, she routinely went through the opposition's garbage. She was grateful she didn't have to climb into a Dumpster after the old issues of what was surely a ghastly local paper.

"Working through your basement stacks will be fine. Now if you'd be so good as to direct me to —"

"Hold your horses, Missy."

"That's Doctor. Dr. Judith Hildebrand."

"Great, you're a doctor," Wanda said. "I'm betting you can't do a thing for my sciatica."

Judith shook her head. "I'm not that kind of doctor. The work I do is" — *covert, sneaky, downright mean, and just shy of slander if I do it right* — "scholarly research."

"Well, scholarly or not, I can't turn you loose in our files unsupervised. We have our own organization system here and, if you don't mind my saying so, you're bound to mess it up."

Judith flinched in surprise. She'd never considered that her request might be denied. She expected these hayseeds to be overawed by her credentials and fall all over themselves trying to help.

"But don't get your knickers in a knot, Dr. Hildebrand. Lacy is off today, but she'll be back tomorrow," Wanda said. "She can help you then."

"Lacy?" Years ago, when Michael Evans's reality episode was being shot, he mentioned having a sister named Lacy. *If this is the same Lacy — and face it, how many Lacys can there be in a town of this size? — I can get close to Evans through his sister without him suspecting a thing.*

Could Judith be that lucky?

"You say her name like you know her," Wanda said shrewdly.

"No, it's just that Lacy is a rather unusual name." Judith made a mental note to walk warily around Wanda. It was tempting to downgrade her estimate of a person's intelligence if they spoke with a Southern accent. Wanda might sound like a simple country girl, but there was obviously nothing simple about her mind.

"Lacy might be a tad unusual, but Hildebrand isn't exactly Smith either."

"No, you're right. I meant no disrespect."

"None taken. Lacy will do a good job of steering you in the right direction. She's in charge of our 'ago' columns, so nobody knows more about the old editions than she does."

" 'Ago' columns?"

"Yes, we reprint old stories from past issues," Wanda explained. "You know, five years ago, ten years ago, fifteen and so on. It's like literary recycling, but our readers love it."

Judith thought calling anything about this local paper "literary" was pushing it. She doubted she'd be able to stand reading through the *Coldwater Gazette* once, let alone slog through repeats from years past. But if she could find some clue in old news stories about how Michael Evans got that scar across his ribs, it would be worth the trouble.

"Fine," she said. "I'll be here at nine o'clock tomorrow."

"You'll be here at seven if you want Lacy's help," Wanda said in a take-no-prisoners tone. "Fridays are her busy days, what with taking Thursday off. It's her catch-up day and the day she plans all the features she's responsible for in next week's editions. As it is, I'll have to call her tonight and get her to come in early for you."

Why would this Lacy person come in to help a total stranger? If they asked Judith to reimburse her for her time, she'd have to give some plausible excuse of why she couldn't. Maybe she could convince them that her grant to do this research was still awaiting approval, but she'd been assured it was being fast-tracked and she'd pay as soon as it got the green light.

"Do you think she'll come in early?" Judith asked.

"Sure. I'll call you if she can't." Wanda glanced at Judith's card again to make sure there was a cell number on it. "Her mother's got cancer and just started treatments, so if she needs Lacy for some reason, all bets are off. But other than that, I'm sure Lacy'll be here. She used to live in Boston and really slurps up any chance to talk to anybody from back East. That is where you're from, isn't it?"

"I'm from New York," Judith said with a sniff. Only someone from fly-over country could lump Boston with the greatest city in the world.

"Well, that explains it," Wanda said dryly.

"Explains what?"

"Those shoes. We only wear heels that

high for weddings and other special occasions round here, but mincing along on those things every day is misery for the sake of it. Wear something sensible tomorrow. You're like to break your neck on the stairs to the basement in those things."

Judith would have gone off on her, railing at Wanda for being a fashion reject who couldn't rock a pair of designer heels if they were made specifically for her feet, but then she remembered that she was being recorded and thanked Wanda Cruikshank for her concern.

She headed back toward the Heart of the Ozark, striding like a New Yorker, in her red-soled stilettos. She did just fine, thank you very much, until she reached one of those crosswalks paved with bricks laid in a herringbone pattern. One of her heels caught in the grout and snapped right off. She stumbled a bit but didn't fall.

She almost wished she had. Anything not to have destroyed her best pumps. It was all she could do not to collapse onto the road and weep. Those shoes had cost eight hundred dollars. Ten years ago.

She'd never be able to afford replacements.

She picked up the sad, broken remains of her footwear, toed off her good one, and walked barefoot the rest of the way. As she neared the motel, a thought struck her that made her smile.

At least I learned one good thing today. Michael Evans's mother has cancer.

Chapter 14

They say a relationship without trust is like a rusted-out vehicle. You can stay in it till the bottom drops out, but it won't take you anywhere. I had a truck like that once. And a husband.

— Glenda Scott, whose estranged husband makes a pretty good part-time gardener and handyman. She's not sure she dares count on him for anything else.

"Are you really going to let your mom have her way about the bridesmaid dresses?" Heather asked as she and Lacy climbed the iron staircase that led to their side-by-side apartments. They were in and out of each other's places so much, they often joked about asking Mrs. Paderewski, their landlady, to put in an adjoining door.

"Don't worry about the dresses," Lacy said.

They'd had lunch with Lacy's mother and then spent several hours poring over bridal magazines for ideas about how to decorate everything from the church vestry to the groom's pickup. Mrs. Evans and Lacy had seemed to agree on pretty much everything except the color of the bridesmaids' dresses. Then before that discussion could escalate into a full-blown fight, Lacy had folded.

"That pink dress your mom wants will be the kiss of death on me."

"And that particular shade doesn't work with my palette at all, but I only said OK to humor her. Actually, I caved on almost everything. Take her idea for paper napkins at the reception instead of cloth. I mean, folding the napkins into origami cranes is craziness for the sake of it."

"Then why did you let her think you're all right with it?"

"She *is* going through a lot right now, you know. I don't want to argue with her about the small stuff," Lacy said. "I may not get my way with anything else, but when the time comes, I'll make sure the bridesmaids' dresses are navy."

"Good." Heather hadn't been keen on standing beside Lacy at the altar rail in shocking pink. She'd look like a gigantic breast cancer awareness ribbon. *Hmm . . .*

maybe that's why Mrs. E is so set on that shade. "Don't feel guilty for getting your way sometimes. It's your wedding, after all."

"How naïve you are," Lacy said, shaking her head. "It may be my wedding, but it's Mom's production. She's determined to make a statement with it. Shirley Evans and Wonder Woman are cut from the same cloth. She's out to show folks that she can put on the wedding of the decade and still whup cancer's butt in her spare time."

"Guess she feels a little out of control, so she's controlling what she can," Heather said.

"That's the charitable view. Except for allowing me to pick the color palette — which she's playing pretty fast and loose with — she's charging ahead with everything else. Full-blown formal everything, with a reception at the Opera House. This wedding is going to scream Shirley Evans."

"What kind of wedding did you want?"

Lacy sighed. "Something simpler. Smaller. It would have been nice to use the chapel instead of the big sanctuary. Or something even tinier. When I was a little girl, I imagined walking down the staircase in my family's house and getting married in the living room surrounded only by my closest family members and friends. Mom's set on inviting most of the county."

"Why don't you tell her what you want?"

"Are you kidding? People are still talking about Crystal's wedding. Mom feels honor bound to up the ante. Besides, the invitations have already been sent."

Heather's shoulders slumped. "Then I better get used to the idea of looking like a giant bottle of Pepto-Bismol."

"I promise I'll take care of it," Lacy said with conviction. "If nothing else is my choice, I will win this one at least."

"Seems to me you're only postponing the argument." Heather sighed. And later, Lacy's mother might not feel as well as she did now. Chemo — like guilt over not letting a cancer patient have her way — was a cumulative thing. "You can deal with it now or deal with it later, but the problem is still the same."

"I'm way ahead of you." Lacy tapped her temple. "When I place the order for the bridesmaids' dresses, I'll specify delivery for the day before Thanksgiving. When the navy dresses arrive, I'll just tell Mom the company made a mistake. What with the holiday, there won't be time to return them, so at that point" — Lacy made an imaginary waving motion with her arm — "we'll just have to go with the flow."

"What a perfectly devious plan," Heather said, grinning as she opened the door to her place. "I like it."

"I'm afraid it's genetic. Everyone in my family has been known to occasionally stoop to skullduggery to get our way," Lacy admitted. "And we're doggedly determined when we set our minds to something."

"I've seen that quality in your dad."

"Exactly! He's been a committed squirrel fighter since I was a little girl."

Heather tactfully refrained from saying he might benefit from commitment of a different type, but in fairness, mental health was not her field.

"You'll have to start thinking like an Evans if you intend to keep going out my brother."

"What do you mean? I'm not dating Michael." She waved Lacy into her apartment and then followed her in.

"You left the reunion dance with him and the pair of you didn't come back."

Lacy settled on one of the stools by the kitchen peninsula while Heather hung up her sweater in the closet near the door.

"Well, yes, Michael and I ducked out of the dance together, but that was only so I could make sure he was allowed back into the hospital to see your mom."

"A technicality. It still counts." Lacy

helped herself to a banana from the bowl of fruit on the counter. "And were you or were you not seen strolling through the territory cemetery with him a few days ago?"

For someone who took a reporter job at the *Coldwater Gazette* only under duress, Lacy had developed into a world-class snoop.

"That was a totally chance meeting," Heather protested.

Or was it? Had Michael learned about her weekly visit to Jessica's grave and timed his accordingly? If so, Heather didn't know whether to be flattered by his determination to spend time with her or annoyed that he'd manipulated her with her own schedule.

"Chance meeting, she says! A likely story," Lacy said, sounding like her lawyerly father. She finished off the banana and three-pointed the peel into the garbage bin beside Heather's pantry. "He followed me home after choir so he could track you down. And by the way, you also convinced him to join the choir *and* made him agree to stay in town long enough to sing the Christmas stuff in December."

"What? Do you have a drone following me around or something?"

Lacy laughed and shook her head. "Don't deny the choir bit. I have your arm-twisting on good authority."

"Whose?"

"Michael's. He's my brother, after all. We talk. At least we do since he came back to town," Lacy said. "So give. What did he make you agree to in exchange for shoring up the Methodist bass section?"

"What makes you think there was a deal?"

"Because you've been checking your watch every fifteen minutes since three o'clock. You've got something going on, and I'll bet you half your last banana it's with Michael."

Almost involuntarily, Heather checked the time again. Four thirty. She was cutting things close.

"Since you neither confirm nor deny the allegation, I'll take your silence for a yes," Lacy said. "OK, so when's he coming?"

"In thirty minutes."

"Well, let's get moving, then." Lacy slid off the bar stool and made a beeline for the closet in Heather's bedroom. The prosecuting attorney was instantly gone. Heather feared that Lacy had donned her designer hat. "We don't have much time."

Heather followed her and plopped down on the end of her bed. "After trying to wrestle control of your own wedding from your mom all day, do you really think you ought to take over my date with your brother? And, may I add, without even asking if I want help?"

"Mirror, mirror, on the wall. I am my mother, after all," Lacy singsonged. Then she shot Heather a wicked grin. "And I got you to admit it's a date!"

Heather clamped her lips closed. Lacy could probably get her to admit she'd thought about little else since she woke this morning. If she half closed her eyes, she could still feel Michael's solid warmth beside her. And how much she missed it when she woke to find him gone.

Please God. Don't let her find out how late he stayed last night.

"As far as asking for my expert advice goes, you need my help, whether you want it or not." Lacy started pawing through Heather's clothes. "So what are you two lovebirds planning on doing?"

"We're not lovebirds. I haven't even given him my phone number yet." Heather stood and took the sequined tank Lacy was admiring away from her. Then she rehung it before her friend could insist she wear it. Heather's mom had given her the shimmery thing for Christmas last year. Apart from wearing it for an obligatory meal with her parents, the thing might as well still have the tag on it. She wasn't about to go riding with Michael looking like a mirror-ball trophy strapped to the back of his bike.

"If you must know —" she began.

"And I must," Lacy said.

"Your brother is taking me for a ride on his motorcycle."

"OK. So we don't have to spend much time on your hair, but let's do it now so we don't forget about it completely. If you're not dressed when he comes, he can wait. If you still need to do your hair and makeup, I know you. You'd just go without."

"No, I" — she sighed — "probably would."

Having a friend who knows you inside out is both a blessing and a curse.

"I rest my case." The daughter of a retired lawyer was back in full force. Lacy picked up a brush from Heather's vanity. "And now with intent to commit flawless grooming, might I suggest a ponytail?"

"I guess."

Lacy pointed to the only chair in the room, the seat before Heather's grandmother's old vanity, and Heather obediently sat. The piece was a terrible space waster, but Heather kept the vanity for sentimental reasons. When she was a child, Heather watched her grandmother give her waist-length iron-gray hair its nightly hundred strokes at that vanity. Sometimes, she'd let Heather play with those soft tresses.

Now it was Lacy's turn. Her friend began running the boar-bristle brush through Heather's hair as she gathered it in her other hand.

Heather relaxed into the attention. After seeing to the needs of others all week, it was ridiculously nice to have someone take care of her for a little while.

"You have such thick hair," Lacy said admiringly.

"Yeah, it makes up for the mousy color."

"There's nothing the least mousy about it," Lacy said with conviction. She was a world-class designer, after all. She should know a thing or two about color. "Your hair is ash brown with plenty of high- and low lights. It's a perfectly good color that plays well with a medium-cool to warm palette."

Lacy's expert assessment aside, ash brown sounded pretty middle of the road to Heather. Ordinary.

Jessica's hair had been golden blond, the color of eternal summer.

"It works great with your skin tone, too," Lacy went on.

"If you say so."

"I do. Never color it." Lacy held Heather's

hair off her neck. "High or low?"

"Low," Heather decided. "It'll be easier with a helmet."

She was already imagining flying down a winding road with her thighs around Michael, her arms wrapped around his waist. If she didn't wear a helmet, she could rest her head on his back and listen to his heartbeat thunder under her ear.

A little thrill shivered through her. Then she tamped it down. Of course she'd wear a helmet. Head trauma was no joke. What was she thinking?

I gotta lay off those romance novels.

Lacy divided a section of Heather's hair up front and clipped it to give her a bit of a pouf.

Heather turned this way and that to consider the effect in her grandmother's mirror. "Isn't that a little too Jersey Shore?"

"You're right." Lacy unhooked the clip and smoothed Heather's hair into a low ponytail, which she fastened with a brown elastic band. "And now back to the closet. What are you planning to wear?"

"Jeans and a denim jacket."

"All right. I'd have suggested you go shopping and get some leather pants if I'd known about this sooner, but jeans will do," Lacy said. "What about under the jacket?"

"I was thinking this." She whipped out a beige cambric shirt. Lightweight and cool, it was her go-to top when she didn't know what to wear.

"Bleh! Let's get some color on you." Lacy took the offending beige top and tossed it on the bed. Since her artistic designer urges had been thwarted enough in the matter of her wedding, she was ready to give them free rein now. She pulled out a pale blue tank, a warm orange peasant top with lace along the hem, and a black-and-white geometric print blouse with multicolored polka dots interspersed between the bold black slashes. It wasn't what Heather usually wore, but the sales clerk at Unique Boutique had talked her into it a few weeks ago.

"Let's get you out of your comfort zone, shall we?" the clerk had said. "This print just shouts, 'I'm strong and assertive,' doesn't it?"

Unlike the sequined tank, the tags were still on this one. She'd worn the mirror-ball top once, but Heather hadn't felt strong and assertive enough to leave the apartment in this geometric and polka-dot explosion yet.

"Which one do you like best?" she asked her friend as they considered the three tops spread out on the bed.

"Either the blue or the orange." Lacy narrowed her eyes at them as if visualizing Heather in each. "Both will work well with jeans and a jacket, though I'm leaning toward the orange."

"Then why did you even pull out the print?"

"Because you should burn it, and whoever sold it to you should be horsewhipped."

"Gee, I wish you had an opinion." Heather picked up the print blouse and stowed it back in the closet. Maybe Unique Boutique would let her exchange it for something she felt comfortable in.

Probably something beige.

"What about shoes?" Lacy asked.

"I was thinking I'd wear my sneakers." Heather pulled her pair of lavender tennis shoes from the bottom of the closet.

"No. Those won't work."

Heather wanted to ask why, but was afraid Lacy would tell her to burn them, too. They were her favorites.

"Got any bright green heels?" Lacy asked. "The higher, the better."

"Heels?"

"Nothing's hotter than jeans and heels. And don't worry. Michael's tall enough that your height won't intimidate him a bit."

"No, it won't, but heels will just give him

a chance to call me 'Stilts' again."

"I told him he shouldn't do that, but I think he means it in the nicest possible way."

"Whatever. Anyway, I'm not wearing heels to ride a motorcycle." She felt awkward enough without having to worry about whether or not she'd sprain her ankle on the dismount.

"You're probably right. How about boots?"

Like any good Coldwater Cove girl, Heather had a couple pairs of cowboy boots. She dug them both from the bottom of the closet. One was glossy black leather with silver tips and the other was an impossible shade of lime green with turquoise insets — another of her mother's Christmas presents she'd worn exactly once.

"You know, you could really rock those green ones with the orange top," Lacy said.

"No."

"Come on. You'll hardly see them from way up there."

"Is that a tall joke?"

"Little bit." Lacy grimaced and shrugged her shoulders. "Sorry. Come on. Wear the green boots and I'll never ask you for anything else as long as we live."

Heather eyed her doubtfully. "You're sure."

"Trust me." She rifled through Heather's jewelry and came up with the leather bag that held her grandmother's pearls. "These will be great — a little class to go with the casual. Put it all on and come model when you're done." Lacy headed back into the living room, closing the bedroom door behind her. "And don't keep me in suspense."

Heather peeled off the clothes she'd worn all day and hopped into the shower for a quick scrub. Then she set a land speed record for toweling off and putting on the outfit and accessories Lacy had picked out for her.

She made plenty of decisions at work, but she felt confident about those. It was all science, and she'd always excelled in classes where the answers were clear-cut and provable.

Fashion strayed into the artsy world of personal preference. That had never been her strong suit, so it was a relief to leave this choice to someone else. Especially someone like Lacy, who had both a flair for design and Heather's best interests at heart. After she tugged on the last green boot, she joined her friend in the other room.

"Well?" Heather turned in a slow circle,

hands extended palms up. "What do you think?"

Lacy had helped herself to a glass of sweet tea while Heather dressed. She set it down on an end table now and gave her an open-mouthed once-over. "You look fantastic, Heather. No lie. Totally hot. It's like you stepped from the pages of *Cosmo* or something. You are so far out of my chuckle-headed brother's league, it's not even funny."

Heather found that hilarious. Lacy was exaggerating, but it gave her spirits such a lift. She had never expected to feel so . . . fluttery over a guy, least of all someone like Michael Evans, someone who lived to flout the rules and made her mother faint dead away.

But after spending last evening with him, she was beginning to think he didn't deserve his bad-boy reputation. At least, not anymore. Michael had a surprisingly sweet side that he didn't show to many people. He'd shown it to her. And, whether it was wise or not, she'd felt safe to trust him with some of her deepest secrets.

So it wouldn't hurt for her to dress to impress him. If Lacy's reaction was any guide, she certainly would.

Heather glanced at her wrist and discovered she hadn't put her watch back on. "What time is it?"

Lacy pulled out her phone. A frown drew her brows together. "Five thirty."

Michael was late. Well, she ought not to make a big deal about it. After all, she hadn't made it to choir at all last night, and he hadn't seemed upset.

Heather went to the kitchen and got a glass of iced tea for herself.

"He should call if he's going to be late," Lacy said sourly. "When we were growing up, punctuality was next to godliness at our house. Honest, I used to tell people I'd rather be caught pregnant out-of-wedlock than show up after curfew to face my dad. Seriously, Michael knows better. He ought to at least call."

Heather's insides spiraled downward and then zipped back up when she remembered why he couldn't. "Maybe he wants to, but can't. I didn't give him my number."

"Oh." Lacy nodded. "That was smart of you, actually. Play hard to get. Guys like the chase."

Lacy launched into a one-sided diatribe about her mother's idea of wedding décor again. Heather suspected it was just to keep her from wondering what was keeping Mike, but she was grateful for the distraction. Another thirty minutes went by.

Still no sign of Michael.

"Well, this is getting annoying. I was hoping to get in some sisterly ribbing when he showed up." Lacy thumbed her phone. "He may not have your number, but I've got *his.* Let's see where he is."

Lacy punched a few buttons and held the receiver to her ear. She frowned. "It went straight to voice mail."

"Well, if he's on a motorcycle, he wouldn't hear a phone ring, would he?" Heather said, hoping that was the reason, and he was on his way.

Lacy punched a few more buttons. "Oh! Looks like I've got a voice mail."

"From Michael?"

"No, from work." Lacy put the phone back to her ear and listened for a minute. Then she clicked off and pocketed the phone. "I have to go in early tomorrow. There's some lady with a doctorate who wants to crawl around in the dungeon and I have to babysit her."

"The dungeon?"

"It's the basement where the archives are kept. Wanda can't stand for a stranger to mess up her files. As if there was any semblance of order to them in the first place."

Lacy rose, collected both of their tea

glasses, and put them in the sink. "I need to get home to feed the attack cat before Jake shows up for his supper."

When Lacy had moved into her apartment last spring, she'd inherited a semi-deranged Siamese, abandoned there by the previous tenant. She often described her new pet Effie as "a one-person cat that's still looking for her person."

Lacy and Jake were keeping separate apartments until after the wedding, mostly for the convenience of their pets. If the animals were left alone, Lacy was afraid that Effie the Terrible would decide to eat Speedbump, the homeless little mutt Jake had rescued from traffic. Until an all-species truce was declared, the feline/canine visits were heavily regulated.

"After Jake's been cooking at the Green Apple all day, I try to give him a break, but I'm not nearly as good as he is," Lacy said as she headed toward the door. "Guess I never saw the point. I mean, why spend so much time and energy on cooking when somebody's just going to eat it and it'll be nothing but a memory?"

"What is life but a collection of memories?" Heather said, trying to keep the mood light. As a nurse, she'd seen her share of worst-case scenarios. The last thing she wanted to do was infect Mike's sister with her what-ifs. "Put a sprig of parsley on the plate and it'll look like you tried to get fancy."

"Ever the wise woman." Lacy stopped with her hand on the doorknob. "I'm sorry Mike's so late. If he doesn't arrive with a dozen roses in apology, I will personally kick him in the nuts for you. Or better yet, I'll have Jake do it. Titanium packs quite a punch."

"Not necessary, but I may threaten him with it so he won't be late again," Heather said, forcing a smile. She was past irritation over Mike's tardiness and beginning to worry in earnest that he was lying in a ditch someplace. "If you're sure Jake doesn't mind playing the enforcer . . ."

"My Marine was born to kick butt and take names. He'd be happy to teach my idiot brother some manners."

Jacob had returned from Afghanistan with part of his left leg missing, but he still had protective masculine instincts in spades. Heather was happy to be included in the circle of those he defended. She appreciated Lacy and Jake's support.

She just wished she didn't need it.

Lacy waggled her fingers in farewell and closed the door behind her.

Heather slumped down on the couch, not caring if she rumpled her "right out of *Cosmo*" outfit.

Minutes ticked by.

Hours.

She didn't want to call the hospital to see if any emergency cases had come in. Depending on who answered the phone, she'd be grist for the gossip mill in short order if they found out she was looking for a missing date. She narrowly resisted the urge to call Dan Scott, an old classmate of hers who was now a sheriff's deputy, to see if there'd been any accidents reported in the county.

Michael was beyond late. He wasn't coming.

Finally, she stripped out of her clothes, letting them lie where they fell, and climbed into bed buck naked. She'd told him things she wished she hadn't. She felt so hollowed out, she didn't care enough to put on a pair of pj's.

She'd let herself hope. She'd let herself trust.

"Michael Evans, of all people."

She covered her head with a pillow. The walls were thin between her place and Lacy's. She didn't want anyone to hear her sobs.

CHAPTER 15

An uncluttered desk is the sign of a diseased mind.
— Words to live by from Wanda Cruikshank's coffee mug

Standing in front of the *Coldwater Gazette* office, Judith shifted her weight from one foot to the other. Her second-best heels were a little shorter than her beloved and now ruined stilettos, but she'd still had to tread carefully over the brick pavers as she made her way from the motel to the newspaper at a ridiculously early hour. The only activity around the Town Square seemed to be people heading into the diner with a sign over the door that read GREEN APPLE GRILL.

Wonder if they realize the initials spell "GAG?" If that doesn't scream "greasy spoon," I don't know what does.

The manager at the Heart of the Ozarks

had told Judith she ought to try the Green Apple's Green Plate special.

"The Hungry Man Grits and Gravy they serve on Friday is my favorite. But don't let the name fool you. You also get two eggs anyway you want 'em with fresh side, which is frankly the best thing this side of heaven." The manager laughed. "Side this side of heaven, that's rich." She chuckled again at her own very small witticism. "You ever had any, honey?"

Judith had shaken her head.

"Well, let me tell you. It's thick-sliced pork belly. Sort of like bacon that ain't been cured yet. Make sure Jake Tyler's doing the cookin' if you decide to try it. He's that hunky guy who owns the Green Apple and whoa, baby, if I was thirty years younger, I'd be getting myself some of that, yessiree bob. Where was I? Oh, yeah, the way Jake cooks the side is he rolls it in flour and fries it up in Crisco with a little salt and pepper and the cookin' magic that drips from his fingers and I'm here to say, it's good eatin'."

Judith hadn't been able to find a retort that wouldn't be considered "unlikeable." Wearing a hidden camera meant she self-edited. A lot.

"Anyways, you also get homemade biscuits so light they practically float away. And the grits and gravy, of course," the manager had finished up. "Think about me while you're havin' it!"

Just thinking about such a heavy breakfast was enough to give Judith a full-blown reflux attack. She had no idea what "grits" were and was afraid to ask. Breakfast in Manhattan was a light meal on the run, croissants or Greek yogurt, for choice, washed down with a Styrofoam to-go cup of the most bitter coffee she could stand in line for.

"No self-respecting croissant would be caught dead in this town," she muttered.

She checked the time on her phone. Five minutes to seven.

What an ungodly hour!

Judith was a night person. Her creative juices didn't really start flowing until well after midnight. It was torture to force herself out of bed and into her "visiting academic" persona so early, but she did it to accomplish her goal. The only strawberry in the situation was that she wasn't the only one who had to brave the chill of a foggy fall morning.

It was a comfort to know she was inconveniencing someone else as well.

She'd heard that the farther south one traveled, the more likely the people one encountered were to take a la-di-da approach to things like appointments and schedules and wasting other people's time. She was ready to deliver a scathing setdown to this Lacy Evans person when she turned up late, but just as her phone alarm beeped a reminder that it was 7:00 a.m., a disgustingly cheerful-looking young woman in sensible but cute, ballet flats came jogging up to her.

"Hello. You must be Dr. Hildebrand." She stuck out her hand, forcing Judith to shake it. "I'm Lacy Evans, a reporter for the *Gazette.* Call me Lacy. Wanda asked me to take care of you this morning."

"I do not need to be 'taken care of,' you patronizing little twit" complete with air quotes almost tumbled out of her. Just in time, Judith remembered the small camera pin on her lapel and adjusted her expression, if not her attitude.

"If by taking care of me you mean you'll be providing coffee," Judith said, "my caffeine-starved brain thanks you."

There. Tell me that's not likeable. Years after the fact, Louise's criticism of her as being unlikeable still stung. And after the maid at the Heart of the Ozarks had left only decaf in her room, Judith thought her behavior this morning had been not only likeable, but pretty fricking gracious, too.

"Oh, sure! We always have coffee," Lacy Evans said as she fiddled with the lock on the office door. After a few gyrations and a considerable bit of yanking and twisting, the door shuddered open. "Wanda says a newsroom runs on caffeine. Give me a minute and I'll fill up the pot."

Lacy opened an antique wardrobe that stood in mahogany majesty along one wall. It had been repurposed to hold a coffee-maker and small refrigerator. The shelves stored not only assorted sweet and salty snacks and bags of coffee beans, but real cups — not the Styrofoam kind — and a mismatched set of spoons thrusting up from an oversized mug.

"How do you usually take it?"

"From Starbucks," Judith said without thinking. Her eyes widened. Even to her ears, that sounded pretty snarky, but instead of being offended, Lacy laughed.

"Oh, gosh, me too! It's one of the things I miss most about Boston. Of course, there it's more Dunkin' Donuts than Starbucks, but I learned to love both their brews. Still, we make do here in Coldwater." As if to prove her point, she dumped some whole beans into a grinder and hit the switch.

"You mean you left a real city for —" Judith stopped herself. There was no way to finish that sentence without slamming Lacy's home. *And sounding unlikeable.*

"For a sleepy little backwater like Coldwater Cove?" Lacy Evans finished for her.

"Well, yes."

"I understand. I felt that way about it, too, at first. In the beginning, Coldwater Cove was just a soft landing after my business in Boston hit a rough patch, but I've grown to love being here again."

"Why? Forgive me, but there's no theater or culture or nightlife." *Or anyone important who can grease the wheels for your career.* "What on earth do you find to do here?"

"I live," Lacy said simply. "The people I love are here. I've made or rekindled more friendships in a few months than I made in years back in Boston, though that's probably my fault. Not that there's anything wrong with a city. I used to really feed off the energy of so many lives intersecting."

"I know what you mean." Against all expectation, Judith began to feel she'd finally met someone with whom she could have an intelligent conversation.

"But there's a certain anonymity in a city." Lacy's tone made it seem as if that were a bad thing.

"What's wrong with that?" Judith was

never happier than when she was blending in with a crowd. Preferably an upscale, mover-and-shaker-type crowd.

"The facelessness of a city is sort of like the Internet. People say hateful things to strangers online that they'd never say to someone's face. They may be nice people in person, but being able to hide behind their computer lowers their inhibitions, and they start spouting the first thing that pops into their heads, without caring how it affects the one they're directing the meanness toward," Lacy said.

In Judith's experience, people were the same, whether in person or online. Given a chance, they'd all be mean to her. It paid for her to be mean first. Lacy was eyeing her with speculation. It was time to say something that sounded like sociology was her thing.

"Interesting. The sense of anonymity would explain why cyberbullying has become such a problem."

"Exactly. In a city, you likely won't see the people you meet ever again," Lacy went on. "It has the same lowering effect as hiding behind a computer screen. If someone cuts you off in traffic, why not lay on the horn, and yell, and flip them off?"

Reacting to idiots who shouldn't be driving made sense to Judith. It was a point of honor not to suffer fools gladly. "People don't do that here?"

"Sometimes," Lacy admitted with a self-deprecating grimace. "But if I do, someone will likely tell my mom, and trust me, I don't want that. Or I'll run into the person I yelled at in the grocery store or at church, and because I'm no longer upset over being cut off, I'm embarrassed by my bad temper. So I end up apologizing."

"Why? You were the wronged one in that scenario."

"I'm still responsible for me. If I let someone else's actions change mine for the worse, I'm in the wrong. Living here has reminded me not to get upset about the small stuff and to give others the benefit of the doubt."

When Judith tried that, it only made it easier for others to steamroll over her. But she was supposed to be a visiting sociologist, so she said, "An insightful take on causality of inappropriate behavior in rural and urban environments."

"Don't get me wrong. There are great things about living in a city. For one thing, people aren't all up in each other's business. Sometimes, it's nice to keep your private life . . . private," Lacy said. "Here, you can't set foot out of your house without someone wanting to know where you're going and what you're up to."

"I couldn't stand that."

"You get used to it. Here in Coldwater Cove, we've elevated nosiness to an art form, but we mean extremely well." Lacy set out a matching sugar bowl and creamer set. She filled the creamer with half-and-half from the refrigerator. "If the trade-off is that small-town living tends to help me behave a little better, I'll take it. I need all the help I can get."

"Don't you miss the opportunity for advancement?"

"A little. There are exciting things happening in cities. In fact, a design firm in Cambridge has been trying to woo me into moving back East and to tell the truth, sometimes I'm tempted," Lacy said wistfully.

"Design? But you're a journalist."

"By accident. Not by trade," Lacy said. "And wait until you've read a few editions of the *Gazette* before you decide there's anything remotely like journalism going on around here."

The coffeepot stopped belching, and Lacy poured a cup for herself and Judith.

"I think you'll like this," she said, handing

a steaming cup to Judith. "Mr. Bunn went to Jamaica with the Royal Order of Chicken Pluckers last month to help rebuild a church after it was demolished by a tropical storm. He came back with dozens of bags of Blue Mountain coffee for all his friends."

"Excuse me. The Royal what?"

"Order of Chicken Pluckers. How they got their name is a long story, but they're basically a Lutheran men's service club. They help the ladies bake chicken pies to raise money for missions, but they lend a hand with a hammer when it's needed, too."

Judith needed a hand with her coffee. "I don't suppose you have artificial sweetener."

"I'm sorry. No one in the office uses it. We sort of go natural around here. We have brown sugar, if you'd prefer that. Unless you're diabetic, why don't you try a little of the real stuff?"

Judith hadn't consumed any real sugar in the last twenty years. At least, not knowingly. She forced herself to smile at Lacy. "I'll just drink it black. You know what they say. You can never be too thin."

"They don't say that around here," Lacy told her with a grin and a quick once-over. "In fact, my dad would say you need to weatherboard up a little. But you're not here for dietary advice. What can I help you find in the dungeon?"

Now we're getting somewhere.

"Our conversation about city versus country has been quite helpful because I'm researching the sociological impact of small-town life. On young people specifically and particularly males, aged fifteen to twenty."

"Hmm. Comparing the rural experience to that of urban youth would make a fascinating study," Lacy agreed. "Come on. I'll show you where everything is."

Judith remembered to say thank you, both for the camera's benefit and because she felt small-town etiquette seemed to demand it.

When in Rome . . . or its rustic outskirts.

Judith's guide opened the door next to a Victorian-style bathroom. She flipped a switch that was probably from the same era and led her down a rickety staircase.

Judith was expecting a dank, foul-smelling space, but the basement was pleasantly cool and dry. Rows of unusually deep filing cabinets lined the walls. A table long enough to seat a small army of country bumpkins was situated in the center of the room under a bank of fluorescent lights. An old microfiche machine dominated one end of the table. Its electrical cord, which was not connected to any power source, had been wrapped with duct tape in several places. A tired-looking Hewlett-Packard PC was plugged into an electrical socket mounted to an exposed floor joist above their heads.

Judith was willing to bet there were all kinds of building code violations in that basement.

If there are such things as building codes in Coldwater Cove.

"Wanda said you were interested in going back a decade or so. The microfiche sparked out on me last week. I haven't had the heart to tell Wanda yet. She's on a cost-saving rampage of late." Lacy turned on the computer, which emitted a low whine. "It takes a while for this dinosaur to wake up, and the files on disc only go back a few years. But in paper, we have every edition of the *Gazette* since its first one in 1898. I recommend starting with the paper documents."

"Agreed. Let's go from oldest within my parameters to newest."

Lacy crossed the room to the appropriate file cabinet. "You'll probably find the 'Fighting Marmots Notes' most useful."

"The what?"

"Fighting Marmots Notes. It's the special section, usually an entire page, for news about our high school. And yeah, I get how weird it is for school teams to be named for a rodent. But people laughed at the Mighty Ducks, too, until they made a movie." Lacy lifted a ten-year-old copy of the *Gazette* from its place in the file. It was still draped over the wooden dowel that allowed it to hang instead of being folded. After laying it out on the table, she checked the time on her cell. "I can only give you until nine this morning."

"You don't need to stay."

"Yeah, I do. Wanda's rules. She wants to make certain everything is filed away exactly as it was."

"Then maybe you can direct me to the most pertinent information," Judith said. "Societal change often follows upheavals. Have there been any . . . catastrophic events involving the young people in this town?"

"When I was a little girl we had a tornado come through. I guess that's usually catastrophic, but this one only touched down on the edge of Lake Jewel and took out the marina." Lacy directed Judith's attention to the wall-sized map of the town that had been découpaged onto a moveable blackboard on casters. "Mr. Simmons — he owns the place — said it was a blessing in disguise because the old restaurant and docks were about to fall into the water anyway. He rebuilt with the insurance money and now it's a real showplace. The construction provided a lot of jobs, but . . ." She ground to a stop like a wind-up monkey on its last twist. "I'm guessing that's not the sort of thing you're looking for."

"How perceptive." A little flattery might get Judith what she wanted sooner. Plus, it made her seem more likeable. "The events I mean are of a sociological nature — gang turf wars, for instance. Maybe involving, oh, I don't know . . . knife fights?"

If Michael Evans got that scar fighting for some motorcycle gang, well, that would make for a spectacular exposé.

"There aren't any gangs in Coldwater Cove. Not yet, thank God. There was a bit of a dustup a few years ago when some drugs started making their way up from gangs in Texas, but the sheriff and his deputies ran them off before they could get a toehold."

"Really? I hope they didn't employ unnecessary force." Judith hoped the exact opposite. Police seeming to overstep their bounds stirred the pot and made for good, controversial television.

"The folks around here didn't ask how the sheriff did it, but they were glad he did. One day the bikers were roaring around the Square and the next they weren't. I suspect folks would say whatever force was used was necessary. Protecting the kids in this town is high on the list for everyone." Lacy smiled. "Even those of us who don't have any yet."

"What about school shootings?" Judith persisted. On the surface at least, Coldwater Cove was coming over as a cross between Mayberry and Lake Wobegone. Surely there was some hidden black stain on this little town's soul.

"We haven't had any. Again, thank God. Well, not unless you count the time Junior Bugtussle was dropping off his kids for school, and spotted an eight-point buck grazing on the football field," Lacy said. "He pulled the rifle out of the gun rack in his pickup and brought it down with one shot."

"Oh!" *Gun violence! Now we're getting someplace.* "I hope the man was arrested for endangering children like that."

Lacy shook her head. "Junior's a dead shot. The only thing in danger was the buck. But you'll be happy to know he did get a citation. It wasn't quite deer season yet."

Where's the outrage? Judith's face heated. "Still. Even having a gun so close to a school. Surely there's a law against that. Was the rifle confiscated at least?"

"No." Lacy referred to the map again, pointing out the school grounds and their proximity to the rising hills. "What if it hadn't been a deer on the football field? There are a few mountain lions and bears up in the Ouachitas, and once in a while, they wander down our way. The school kids would be in more danger from one of them than Junior Bugtussle with a Browning."

Judith shuddered. *Give me London any day. Not even the bobbies carry guns there.*

"Anyway, Junior donated half of the meat from the buck to the food bank, so everyone seemed satisfied." Lacy moved across the room, checking the dates penciled on the drawer labels. "The write-up about the incident would be in the September 2013 or '14 file. I'm not certain of the year since I only moved back to Coldwater Cove last spring."

"No, no. That's not what I'm looking for." She had to get Lacy Evans back on topic. Then once the woman found a usable file or two for her, Judith would casually ask her if she had any siblings in the area. "Have any bad accidents happened to teenagers?"

"Well, aren't you a ray of sunshine?"

"I don't ask out of morbid curiosity," Judith said. "It's a sociological construct that when one young person is seriously injured, it impacts that person's entire peer group."

There. That sounds properly scientific even if I am just making it up as I go along.

Lacy was silent for a moment. "You're right about that. We were all devastated by Jessica Walker's death."

"Oh?" Judith's vulnerability detector pinged. This could be the secret Michael Evans didn't want to talk about.

"She was in my class at school. It happened a few weeks before graduation." Lacy rifled through a file cabinet and came up with several yellowing editions of the *Gazette.* "This should get you started on it."

"Why don't you tell me about it instead?" Judith urged.

"No. I'd rather you read the official report. I can't be objective. Jessica Walker was my best friend's sister."

Better and better. And if her brother had something to do with it, when I get to the bottom of things, the destructive ripples will just keep rolling.

Judith checked the date of the paper. The incident fell into the right time period. This Walker girl had died in the spring of the same year Judith had met Michael Evans. Cold winds had been whistling down the man-made canyons of Manhattan when she first laid eyes on him.

His scar had still been angry then.

Maybe he got it in the same accident that killed Jessica Walker.

Judith crossed her fingers and started reading.

Chapter 16

People always wonder what they'd do in
a real emergency. Would they be the hero
or the goat? I wish to God I didn't know
the answer to that question.

— Not quite a month before
Michael Evans surprised everyone
and actually graduated from
high school

About a decade ago . . .

The sun hadn't risen yet, but it was on its way. The eastern sky was painted a telltale shade of yellowish gray. Michael quickened his pace through alleyways, across yards, and over fences. He'd carefully left the back door to his house ajar when he'd sneaked out last night. He slipped into it now.

Wincing at the overly loud sound of the click, Mike latched the door behind him. Then he toed off his sodden shoes to keep from squelching across the mudroom. He pulled off his torn, wet T-shirt and jeans and stuffed them into the washer.

He couldn't start a load yet. The pipes in the old house banged something terrible when anyone used hot water. But in an hour or so, he could pretend to rise from bed and dump some detergent into the washer before his mother rose. She'd be pleasantly surprised that he'd started a load of clothes before he left for school. He usually avoided doing his laundry until it was either face the suds or face going around town buck naked.

But soapy water was the best way to get rid of the evidence.

He was still bleeding badly. The jagged cut across his ribs probably needed stitches. Lots of them. Michael pulled a beach towel from the line strung across the laundry room and wrapped it tightly around himself. He didn't think there was a gauze pad in the family medicine chest upstairs big enough to cover the wound. If he raided his sisters' stash of "lady pads," he might be able to tape a couple to the gash and stanch the bleeding.

The trick was getting up the old house's creaky stairs.

It was lighter now. Michael wouldn't have to flip any switches to see where he was going. He tiptoed into the kitchen, but froze almost immediately.

In shades of gray, Michael could make out his dad. He was standing at the sink, filling the coffeepot. His father must have felt eyes on him, for he turned and gave Mike a long, narrow-eyed glare. He frowned, probably at the fact that his only son was wandering around the house wearing nothing but tighty-whities and a beach towel at oh-dark-thirty in the morning.

Then light filtering through the plantation shutters on the front of the house began to strobe in flashes of blue. A sheriff's cruiser had pulled into the drive.

How did they connect me with Jessica so quick?

At least the cops didn't have the siren on. That would have brought the entire neighborhood out to see what was going on.

It was a small mercy, but he knew it wasn't on his account. The sheriff played poker with his dad on Wednesday nights, and the pair of them took turns being the president of the Rotary Club. He wouldn't embarrass Michael's dad if he could help it.

His father sighed. The weight of disappointment in that sound nearly crushed Michael to the ground. And the worst of it was, there was tons more to come as soon as the county mounty came through the door.

Mike didn't think he could bear it.

"Anything I should know, son?"

The last thing he could tell his father was the truth.

Present day . . .

Time to see if the truth really does set you free. It's likely to be the only thing that'll square me with Heather, Michael decided as he parked his Harley in the hospital lot. For good measure, he stopped by the gift shop on his way in and bought the biggest bear on the shelves. He didn't see the charm in it himself, but if the advertisements around Valentine's Day were right, women were supposed to go crazy for the fuzzy things.

Deciding not to wait for the elevator, he headed up to the second floor, taking the stairs two at a time.

Look out, Heather Walker. I may not want you to know who I was, but I'm about to tell you who I've become.

He hoped it would be enough. She wasn't the sort to be impressed by the money he made. He was sure of that, but she'd understand that he had responsibilities. He wouldn't have blown her off if it hadn't been absolutely necessary. His meeting with the investors' group had gone better than he'd hoped. MoreCommas had the backing it needed to move to the next level. The people who depended on him for their livelihood were as secure as he could make them.

He stopped when he reached the second-floor landing and looked through the window in the door. The nurses' station was about fifteen feet away. Heather was there, head bent as she studied a chart. She tucked a lock of hair that had escaped her cap behind her ear. Mike wished he could nuzzle that sweet lobe. Her lips moved, and the other nurse standing next to her nodded and then hurried away.

Probably to do her bidding. Give me a chance, Heather. I can do your bidding too, girl. Say the word, and I'll Aladdin you off wherever you want to go.

He started to push the door, but then the elevator opened and Glenda Scott stepped out. She hurried over to Heather, clearly distraught and jabbering a mile a minute.

Michael took a step back from the window, lest Heather catch him watching her. She might think he was being stalkerish, which, if he were honest with himself, he sort of was. But he had a good reason. Since he had a serious apology to deliver, he wanted to make sure he had a clear field to talk with her uninterrupted for a few minutes. Long enough to get her to agree to let him take her out after her shift ended.

He'd wait until Glenda was gone.

In the meantime, there were worse ways for a guy to spend his time than watching Heather Walker.

"I'm so, so sorry. Honest. I'm hardly never not on time," Glenda said, leaving Heather to sort through the bewildering maze of double negatives and qualifiers. "I hate being tardy. Always have."

The CNA tugged off her cardigan and draped it over the back of her chair. Then she typed in her password and started updating charts. "Since I started working here, I haven't been late before, no not once."

"Take it easy." Heather placed a hand on her shoulder. The woman was trembling. "It's OK."

"It's just I want you to know I'm not the type to be late without a good reason."

"I know you're not. That's why I've been covering for you." Heather handed her the rest of the charts Glenda was supposed to update. Actually, she'd been grateful for the mind-numbing task. It helped her take her mind off the fact that Michael Evans was a shiftless, lying . . . At this point, she was tempted to veer off into bed-pan contents metaphors and decided she needed to change her thoughts.

"O' course, I can't claim to have good reason today," Glenda admitted.

"Have you at least got a bad one?"

"It's a doozy." Middle-aged Glenda blushed like a tween in the throes of a first crush. "It's all Lester's fault."

"You were with him."

The blush again as she nodded.

Oh, my gosh! I wonder if that means she was really *with him.*

"What's he doing at your place on a Friday morning?" Heather asked. "I thought he only came over to mow on Sundays."

"He did. He does," Glenda answered, still clearly flustered. "But this morning, he turned up at my house just after sunup, and started pounding away on the garage roof. I was hoppin' mad at him making such a racket so early."

"Well, they say that's the best time of day to do roof work. It gets too hot later on, even at this time of year."

"Yeah, that's what he said." Glenda's eyes went soft and dreamy. "But it wasn't his argument that shut me up. Once I got a good look at him, all the wind went out of my sails. He cut his hair, you see, so he doesn't have that silly man bun thing anymore and he was clean-shaven for a change."

Heather hid her smile. She'd happened to run into Lester at the Green Apple and mentioned how much Glenda disliked his new look. Evidently, he'd taken her words to heart.

"Anyway, he looked so much like the man I fell for all those years ago and . . . oh, I don't know what it is about a guy swinging a hammer, but I do love to see a man work up a sweat, don't you?"

Heather wondered how Michael would look chopping wood or building something with his very capable hands. Judging from the way his body had felt next to hers on her sofa, he was pretty ripped. But then she remembered how crappy he'd made her feel and decided, whether he sported a six-pack or not, he just wasn't worth the misery.

"Isn't Lester supposed to be working at the hardware store on Fridays?"

"Mr. Cooper gave him the morning off so he could repair my shingles." Glenda sighed, a totally smitten sound. "Lester promised he'd do it before winter comes and by golly, he did it."

"I'm glad he's keeping his promises. Trust but verify, you said." *That puts a formerly homeless recovering alcoholic miles ahead of Michael Evans.* "But how did he make you late for work?"

"W-e-e-l-l," Glenda said, knotting her fingers together. "Seeing as how he was there so early, I went to the trouble of fixing him eggs and bacon just the way he likes it. I had the best of intentions, Heather. Honest. I was going to make him eat it on my front porch, just like I make him drink his iced tea outside when he mows the lawn. But I set out a TV tray for him this time, because I was feeling kind of mean about making him stay outside. I mean, he's showed up faithfully every Sunday to mow all summer. I told him so and you know what he says to me?"

"What?"

" 'Glenda Scott,' he says, 'I'd rather sit here on your porch and eat whatever you make for me than dine in splendor with the Queen of Sheba.' Guess they've been studying about Solomon in his Sunday school class so that's why he was talkin' so fancy about queens and all."

Heather chuckled. "I'm still not hearing anything that would have made you late."

"I'm getting to it," Glenda said, touchily. "Well, after he ate his breakfast, he asked if he could come in and wash his plate and stuff. I'd done the cooking so it was only fair for him to do the cleaning."

"That sounds reasonable."

"Exactly." Glenda nodded vigorously. "So I let him. Only I said I'd wash because I'd fed him on one of my grandma's china plates and didn't want it to get nicked. So Lester dried."

That was a major tell. Glenda wouldn't have laid out her good china if she didn't care for him. No wonder Lester had asked to come into her house. She'd practically rolled out the red carpet.

"You're such a neatnik," Heather said. "I'm sure you always wash your breakfast dishes before you come to work and it doesn't make you late. What was different about this time?"

"Well, I was all done washing up and somehow or other, I couldn't get the bung out of the drain. It's an old house and I never did have one of those fancy metal stoppers. So Lester reached into the soapy water to help me and our fingertips sort of accidentally-on-purpose touched." Glenda's eyes closed and she sighed deeply. "And . . . oh, Heather, it was like I was seventeen again. You know what that feels like."

I wish I didn't. Then maybe I'd be smart enough not to care when a guy who makes my insides flutter more than an aviary stands me up.

" 'Glenda, love,' Lester says to me. And let me tell you, when that man said my name, it sent shivers into places I forgot I had. 'I know I don't deserve a second chance,' he says, 'but I want to warn you that I'm gonna do everything I can to win you back.' And then" — she paused for effect — "he kissed me."

"No," Heather said in mock surprise.

"Yes, he did, too, and before I knew it, I was kissing him back."

"What's wrong with that? After all, you *are* still married to the man," Heather said. "Technically."

"Yeah, but we haven't 'technically' shared a bed — I mean, a roof — since our son was in high school."

"So you're saying you shared a bed with Lester?"

The tips of her ears turned red as a beet. "Without even drawing the blinds to make the bedroom darker."

Heather stifled a giggle. "Well, I can see how that would make you late for work."

"Are you going to write me up?"

Glenda was a hard worker. She deserved some happiness — provided Lester could be trusted not to destroy that happiness again. When the Warm Hearts Club had appealed to Judge Preston with a detailed plan for rehabilitation that would keep the old veteran out of jail, Lester had grabbed the lifeline with both hands. He was working steadily for the first time in years, probably because he was going to AA meetings and staying clean. He even volunteered at the senior center so he could pay it forward by giving to others.

But could he keep it up?

Glenda's a big girl. Guess she can decide for herself if she's ready to let her ex back into her life.

Heather shook her head. "I won't report you for being late. Just tell Lester to come for supper instead of breakfast next time."

"Oh, there's not going to be a next time. I told him as much. He just caught me in a moment of weakness, that's all. We have miles to go before I take that man back."

"Good. Play hard to get. Men like the chase," Heather said, repeating the advice Lacy had given her. Too bad it hadn't worked on Michael. "But you *are* planning to forgive him eventually, aren't you?"

"Oh, I've already forgiven Lester for what he did to me and our boy."

Heather's breath hissed over her teeth in surprise. From the little she knew about the situation, Lester had not only been a drunk, but an abusive drunk. It was a mercy to his family when he abandoned them. The fact that he'd never been treated for acute PTSD after his tour in Vietnam was a mitigating factor, but still . . . Surely a few months of mowing lawns and fixing a garage roof couldn't make up for years of pain.

"You're a better woman than me," Heather said. "If I were in your shoes, I'm not sure I could forgive him."

"I had to. For my sake. Carrying around that load of bitterness would have broken me." Glenda sighed. "Besides, love isn't like a light switch, you know. You can't just cut it off. Even when you want to sometimes."

"And that's why I'm avoiding it like a flesh-eating virus," Heather said.

"Yeah, you let me know how that works out for you, honey," Glenda said, morphing from nervous coworker to confiding friend in a few blinks. She waggled her eyebrows and grinned at someone to the left of Heather's shoulder.

Heather turned to see Michael Evans striding toward her with a ridiculous stuffed bear in tow.

Chapter 17

"If it be possible, as much as lieth in you, live peaceably with all men." That's the lesson Pastor Mark tried to teach us last week. Obviously, he's never met Michael Evans.

— Heather Walker's take on the Book of Romans

"Think I'll go check on the Bugtussle boy in 208. According to his chart, he's responding well to treatment. Last night, Doc Warner said he might remove his IV today and start him on antibiotics by mouth if the fever is under control," Glenda said, and skittered down the hallway, leaving Heather to the wolves.

Wolf, she corrected herself. There was a feral glint in Michael's eyes as he approached. Almost a proprietary gleam.

"Hi." He propped the stuffed animal on the counter between them like some furry peace offering. The words "I care beary much" were embroidered on a stupid little heart sewn to the middle of its chest. "I want to —"

"Are you here to see someone?" she interrupted.

"Sure am. I'm here to see you, beautiful."

If she could trust a word coming out of his mouth, she'd have blushed more deeply than Glenda had. She dropped her gaze. *He's too darn hot for my own good.* "I'm busy."

"I can see that. This won't take long."

"It'll take no time at all. If you aren't here to visit a patient, you have to leave. Hospital policy."

"Heather, I'm trying to apologize."

" 'Trying' is the operative word. I haven't heard anything that convinces me you're even a little sorry for leaving me hanging."

"You haven't let me get a word in edgewise."

"So this is my fault?"

"I didn't say that."

"You haven't said anything."

His mouth lifted in that guaranteed-to-make-a-girl-forget-her-own-name smile and he leaned an elbow on the counter. Then he jerked a thumb toward the stuffed bear. "I thought I'd let Yogi here do the talking for me."

Heather glared at the bear and then back at him. "Yogi says you're an idiot."

Something passed behind Michael's eyes. It flashed and was gone, like sunlight glinting on Lake Jewel and then disappearing when clouds roll in. Heather was attuned to reading her patients' micro-expressions. She recognized pain when she saw it.

Stricken, she realized her words had hurt him. That wasn't like her. "I'm sorry. I didn't mean that."

"Yeah, you did and you'd be right. I was always the class idiot."

"Don't try to change the subject," she said. No way he was going to trick her into defending him. "You might have called, you know."

"You never gave me your number. I had to follow my sister home to find out where you lived."

"You could have called Lacy."

"I didn't have cell service."

"Where were you? Outer Mongolia?"

"I'll tell you in a minute, but first, let me say I'm sorry. Truly, deeply sorry," Mike said, his gray eyes sincere. "I didn't mean to stand you up, but it couldn't be helped."

Heather drew a deep breath. If Glenda could forgive Lester, whose sins were legion, she ought to at least hear Michael out over his one and only screwup. "OK. Where were you last night when you were supposed to be with me?"

Michael had hoped he wouldn't have to tell Heather about MoreCommas. At least, not yet. In his experience with women, money was always a game changer — and not for the better. He could never be sure if they wanted to be with him or his credit score. He counted on Heather being different.

Moment of truth time. "I was probably at about 35,000 feet."

"Come again?"

"Flying in the company jet, somewhere over Ohio, on my way back from New York."

Heather scoffed and shook her head. "If you don't want to tell me, that's fine. I have work to do." She sat and focused on the terminal in front of her, ignoring him completely.

"Honest. I rode hell for leather to Tulsa after I left your place Wednesday night. Then I flew to New York so I could make a breakfast meeting with an investor group," he said, figuring he'd better not explain that he'd put his employees' interests ahead of her. "After that, we had an issue with the flight crew not having had enough rest, so we had to delay the return trip."

"*We?* Is that the royal 'we' you're using or do you have a mouse in your pocket?" Heather said without looking up.

"Look, I'm trying to explain —"

"Mmm-hmm, so you're saying you actually have a job that lets you flit around in a jet."

"No, I actually have a *company,*" he said, louder than he'd intended out of frustration. "I'm the CEO and owner of an app development group called MoreCommas."

She met his gaze for a long moment. "Obviously, you think I'm gullible, but I didn't figure you took me for a fool."

"I'm telling you the truth."

"And I'm telling you to leave, Michael. Don't make me call security." She stood and pointed to the elevator. "Old Mr. Leland is getting up there in years and he doesn't need the aggravation."

Fighting the urge to swear the air blue, Mike kick-started his Harley and roared down the street. He turned onto the highway, barely slowing enough to make the curve. Beyond Lake Jewel, the road rose steeply into the hills. Michael leaned into each twist and turn, hoping the rush of air and the whine of the engine would settle him down.

It didn't help.

He was still angry with himself. He should have found a way to tell Heather he wasn't going to make it when he'd first learned about the glitch in his plans. But once he hit the ground running in Manhattan, there'd been dozens of people clamoring for his time. MoreCommas didn't run itself. He couldn't spare a moment to think about anything or anyone else until he was wheels up and flying west again.

By then, it was too late.

Even if he had been able to call her, she probably wouldn't have believed him. He'd kept such a low profile, outside his company very few people realized he was "Mr. MoreCommas." He valued his privacy. The corporate website didn't have a directory listing him as its owner and CEO. He didn't even carry business cards. They weren't his style.

Unless he could spirit Heather away to New York and show her the office, he had no way to prove himself to her.

Michael pulled off the highway and rode up the dirt track that wound through deep forest to the Ouachita Inn ranch house. Designed like an outback station house, it was a long, low structure. Though it had been built in the late nineteenth century, the ranch house and the outbuildings had been updated about ten years ago. The structures retained their rustic character, but the plumbing and electrical panels definitely belonged to this century. It even offered access to satellite Internet.

Mike got a twitch between his shoulder blades. It reminded him of how he'd felt when he first came up with the Bubble Wrap app. An idea started to gel.

He put through a call to his assistant.

Jadis answered before the second ring. "So, you arrived alive."

"Pretty much." This thing he was trying to get going with Heather was DOA, but that only meant it was time to try something different.

"Everyone here is still excited about the investment group's decision to back us. The legal team projects that we'll be ready for our IPO in eighteen months."

Michael paid his people well, but an IPO meant a windfall for all of them. They'd be able to pay off student loans, buy first homes in the insane Manhattan market, or squander their newfound wealth in riotous living, if that's what they chose.

Michael massaged his temple. If he'd learned anything about money since he started making boatloads of it, it was that it couldn't fix everything. Just the thought that he now had a legal department gave him a headache. But it reinforced that he was doing the right thing by delegating his company's expansion to people who understood how the financial and regulatory wheels turned.

Michael was an idea guy. A code guy. A "stay up all night to get it done if you have to" guy.

He could no more slog through the reams of legalese needed for the IPO than he could perform brain surgery.

But he did know how to put together a winning team.

"We can keep things humming here for a while," Jadis said. "But when do you plan to return?"

"That's just it. I don't think I can break away from Coldwater again until December at the earliest."

"I thought your mother was doing well."

"She is. As well as anyone on chemo and radiation treatments can be."

"Did she receive the wigs?"

"She should have. I'll make certain. She's going to love them, but . . . I need to stay close for a while." Jadis didn't need to know he was also staying so he could get closer to Heather Walker. And she sure didn't need to know he was willing to sing in any number of sorry choirs to make it happen. "Here's what I'm thinking. Why don't you and the design team come out here for a month or so?"

"A month?"

"Yeah. We can get a lot accomplished in that length of time, and then you can all go back with plans laid out for the next few quarters to come. After that, you can send out the marketing group for a couple of weeks. Then graphics, then HR, you get the idea. We'll rotate whatever team needs my attention." Even as he said it, he realized that plan would put him in Coldwater Cove well past the time he'd agreed on with Heather. It didn't bother him a bit, but he knew his dad would have a different take on the situation.

"Michael, have you thought this through?"

He looked around the ranch house great room. If he half closed his eyes, he could see the place transformed into multiple work stations, with space for brainstorming sessions around the big fireplace, a break and snack room in the massive kitchen. "It'll work. Look, I've got a big place rented where we can set up shop. Plenty of rooms for everyone to stay."

"I hate to break this to you, but your employees do have lives outside of work, even if you do not."

"Really, Jadis? What do you do but doodle in your sketchpad and wait beside your phone in case I need you?"

Silence. Their relationship was more than boss/employee. Jadis was his best friend. His sounding board and confessor. The sister he wished Crystal had been. But Jadis didn't give her confidence easily and held herself apart. It was partly how she was wired. And partly what had happened to her. Michael never wanted to add to that old hurt.

"I'm sorry. That was uncalled for."

"The truth requires no apology," she said in her maddeningly calm tone. "But as for the others, you cannot ask them to leave their families for that long."

"Bring them all — wives, husbands, kids. Call it a corporate retreat/family vacation," Mike said, getting more excited by the second. The Ouachita Inn had several bunkhouses that had been turned into guest rooms. He could take over the whole thing if he had to. Heck, now that the investors were on board, he could buy the place using funds from MoreCommas' petty cash and not blink twice.

"Very well. We will see what we can do. But some people will not be able to uproot for that long."

"Make it optional, then. We can accomplish a lot with video chats and e-mail. It'll be good for the teams to learn to work together remotely." The thought of bringing part of his life in Manhattan to Coldwater Cove gave him hope. It was his best chance to show Heather he was telling the truth. And maybe convince his dad that he wasn't a waste of skin after all. "Get as many of the design team as you can to head this way as soon as possible, say a couple of weeks to give them time to make arrangements."

It would take him that long to transform the ranch house into his command center. His sister Lacy had been itching to stretch her design muscles.

Maybe I can hire her away from the Gazette *so she can help me with it.*

"MoreCommas will likely double the population of Coldwater Cove," Jadis warned in mock seriousness. "We will most certainly eat up all the bandwidth available in several neighboring states."

"Come on." Mike laughed at her exaggeration. "I'm the only one who can dis my town."

"I thought the Big Apple was your town."

"It was. It is," he corrected himself. *It will be again.* "Let me know when you've got everything arranged for the MoreCommas migration. It won't be forever." He knew better than to try to lure his people permanently out to the back of beyond. For most of them, there was nothing between the East and West Coasts of note except for Vegas. "For now, I need to be close to home."

Even though they came out of his mouth, the words surprised him. Years ago, he'd stopped thinking about Coldwater Cove as home. Not since that day at his grandmother's graveside.

If a guy is very lucky, God will give him someone who believes in him no matter what. Gran was my gift. Wish I could have called "no take backs."

"All right, boss." Jadis's voice in his ear pulled him back into the moment. "I hope you know what you are doing."

"So do I."

Then she hung up. She always seemed to know when he'd drifted away from the present to rehash something in his head. She was clairvoyant like that.

Mike almost called her back. Anything to keep the memories of that last day from washing over him afresh. It had happened about four months after he'd graduated from high school. And like all life-changing events, he remembered every detail with knife-sharp clarity.

The air was crisp, the sky cloudless and blue.

It was like a bad dream.

But Michael wasn't going to wake from this one. On this heartbreakingly beautiful fall day, he was burying his grandmother.

Gran had been his rock. The one person in the world he could count on for unconditional love. Even when she developed dementia toward the end and stopped recognizing him as himself, he visited her every day. Everything about her was special, from her spicy gingersnaps to the kind, encouraging words that always dropped from her lips.

Gran was love in an apron.

Now she was gone. And the sun was so bright, it hurt his eyes. Of course, that might be because he was hung over, but there was no excuse for the irrationally cheerful sunshine beating down on him.

How could the world be so uncaring? Where was the leaden sky he expected? It would be so much more fitting if the slight breeze sending fallen leaves skittering across the cemetery was strong enough to rip through his rumpled suit and tear his heart out.

The crowd around him began to thin as mourners placed their floral tributes on the polished casket and returned to their cars at the bottom of the hill. Mike could hear them, speaking in soft tones to each other as if regular speech would disturb those sleeping in the graveyard. He strained his ears, but none of the words made sense.

His mother kissed his cheek, and, with his sisters at her elbows, she began walking away. Only he and his father remained at the graveside. After a few silent minutes, the last of the other mourners was well out of earshot.

"How could you come to your grandmother's funeral drunk?"

"How could you come sober?" Mike shot back.

That was probably unfair all around. They were both hurting. His father grieved in his way, surrounded by his church and family. Michael grieved with his best friend, Jack Daniel's. Neat.

"This whole thing about her being . . ." Even standing over her grave, Mike couldn't bring himself to say the word "dead." "It's just . . . obscene."

"Yes," his dad agreed. "It certainly is. And it's the last straw. I've had it with you. I want you out."

"Fine." His bag was packed. He'd already made arrangements with one of his buddies at the construction company where he worked to couch surf at his apartment for a few days.

"I'll find my own place."

"No. Not just out of the house. Out of town."

"What?"

"I always said you'd get into more trouble than I could get you out of someday."

When the sheriff's cruiser had showed up the morning after Jessica's death, Mike's dad had used all his lawyerly skills to keep him out of jail. Even when the sheriff said they'd found Michael's pocket knife in the submerged car, his father defended him and found a way to get his wounds stitched without drawing public attention to his injury. Through his father's legal and law enforcement connections, the fact that Michael had been somehow involved in the tragic death of a teenaged girl was swept under the rug.

It had been months since the car went into the lake. In that time, no blame had been laid at Michael's feet. Jessica's death had officially been ruled an accident, but there were still a few rumblings. His father pulled every string and called in every favor to distance Mike from Jessica's death. In private, he never bothered to conceal his loathing for his son on account of it.

"She was pregnant, Mike," his father said, tight-lipped. "The lab in Tulsa has been backed up for months, but the results came in this morning. The sheriff told me before your grandmother's service. Did you know?"

Oh, God. Now he'll hate me forever.

While Michael couldn't tell his dad the whole truth of that terrible night, he wouldn't lie when asked a direct question. He nodded, unable to find his voice.

His father growled an obscenity Mike didn't think was in the old man's vocabulary. The next thing he knew, he was lying flat on his back. His dad had blindsided him with a punch to the jaw.

"Just when I thought I couldn't be more ashamed of you." Then his father pulled out his wallet and threw down five one-hundred-dollar bills at him.

"Don't come back."

CHAPTER 18

The trick to beating cancer is never to let it think it has you. Don't talk about it as if you own it. I'd rather be horsewhipped than say "my cancer." I never even say, "I have cancer." Instead, I tell myself, "The doctor found cancer, but most of the awful stuff is gone. And thanks to the chemo and radiation, whatever escaped Doc Warner's knife is feeling even sicker than me."

— Shirley Evans to her bathroom mirror as she adjusts the red pageboy wig George didn't want her to keep

Michael knocked on the front door of his parents' house. It was probably unlocked. Nobody in his neighborhood locked their doors during the daytime. It wouldn't be considered friendly. Still, he couldn't bring himself to turn the knob without an invitation. He'd sneaked a glance in the garage window and noticed his dad's car was gone.

Mom might be with him, but if she wasn't, this was the perfect opportunity for Mike to spend a little time with her. Not that he was afraid of the old man. He just wanted to avoid a confrontation that would upset his mom. So he knocked again softly.

Fergus didn't bark.

That was unusual. And troubling. Since Mike had come home, the yappy little guy had announced his arrival in a frenzy of yips each time he rapped on the door. Instead of posting a sign saying the house was protected by an antitheft system, Mike thought his parents should hang a sign that said ALL BURGLARS, PLEASE KNOCK. Fergus would certainly raise the alarm.

But since the dog didn't let out a peep, a wave of worry swept over him. He turned the knob and pushed the door open. "Hello?" he called in a stage whisper.

Fergus's soft growl came from the family room at the back of the house. Michael hurried there, a sense of disquiet making his gut churn.

His mother was stretched out on the couch with the little Yorkie resting, chin on paws, across her abdomen. One puppy eye was closed and the other fixed Michael with a protective glare. His mother's chest rose and fell, and she made little puffing noises between each breath. She was asleep.

Thank God. For a second, he'd let himself imagine the worst.

She didn't have a wig on, but her bald head was covered with a soft-knit beret. Shirley Evans was usually the vivacious sort, the life of any party. She was never happier than when she was the center of attention. Even as she grew older, she didn't look her age because her ornery little face was always so full of fun.

Now every one of her years was etched on her features. The deep lines between her brows, even in sleep, were the remnants of pain and exhaustion. She wasn't wearing a stitch of makeup. Michael had never seen her so pale.

He sank into the rocker across from the couch, wincing when it creaked. His mother's eyes fluttered open, and she smiled at him.

"You caught me being a lazy bug. Riley's coming later and I need a nap before she gets here." His mother chuckled. "Sometimes after she goes, too."

Lacy had told Mike that Crystal and Noah's son Ethan was a third grader who'd been born old. The boy liked computers, built things with his mechanized erector set that looked like they belonged on the space station, and could hold his own in any adult conversation. Clearly, a gifted kid.

However, the Addleberrys' younger child, Riley, was a whirlwind with feet. Mike hadn't met his niece and nephew yet, but anyone could see his mom needed rest, not a visiting cyclone. "When is Crystal bringing Riley over?"

Mom glanced at the cuckoo clock on the wall. "Crystal isn't. Noah will be dropping her by in about fifteen minutes. I've been taking care of her a couple of afternoons a week since Crystal became the dean of admissions at Bates College."

As wealthy as Noah's family was, Mike was sure Crystal could afford adequate day care. "You might want to punt on that until you're back on your feet, Mom. You deserve to take it easy."

She deserved so much more. He crossed over to give her a kiss on the cheek.

His mother sat up to receive it. "What I deserve is a pint of Jake's homemade ice cream. I sent your father off to get some."

"The chemo isn't making your stomach upset?"

"Just the first day after treatment mostly. Then it gets better. As I understand it, the way chemo works is that it targets the cells in my body that are growing rapidly. Unfortunately, that means more than just the cancer cells. Did you know the cells in your mouth grow quickly too?"

Mike shook his head.

"I'm learning more than I ever wanted to know about my body," Shirley went on. "Anyway, that means I have a few mouth sores. Ice chips would probably be soothing, but why have ice chips when I can have ice cream?"

Michael smiled. "If you're gonna go hog, you might as well go whole hog." It was something she'd said often when he was a kid.

"Ordinarily, your father doesn't hold to that. Not that I'm accusing him of being tight, mind you," Mom said. The most Mike's dad would ever admit to was being the frugal sort. "But right now, he can't seem to tell me 'no.' " She grinned impishly. "Needless to say, I'm taking full advantage of the situation."

"Who are you trying to kid?" Mike said with a laugh. "Dad never says no to you."

"He did once." Her eyes were unnaturally bright. She blinked hard. "When I asked him not to send you away."

"Don't blame Dad," Michael said. "He

had his reasons."

"I'm sure he did. I was there when you were little, remember? But oh, Mikey, honey, whatever it was that caused the break between you, it was a long time ago. Surely there's some way for my two men to make peace."

Michael shook his head. "I'm not sure there is." His dad grudgingly tolerated his presence, and only when his mother was with them. There was never a chance for private words with him. Mike's father made sure of that.

"But there must be. Don't you remember how Jacob made peace with Esau?"

"It's been a while since I was in Sunday school, Mom."

"Well, that's something you can fix." Then she launched into a retelling of how Jacob had stolen his brother's birthright and blessing and then ran away from the family for years. "When Jacob decided to come home, Esau gathered his fighting men and went out to meet him on the way. Now, your dad has no fighters to gather —"

"Unless you count the squirrels," Michael suggested with a grin. "If you can't beat 'em, join 'em. Maybe Dad could become their general."

"You're not taking this seriously."

He reached over and took his mother's hand. "Yes, I am, Mom. Go on."

Slightly mollified, she gave his fingers a squeeze. "Well, anyway, the Bible tells us that Jacob sent gifts to his brother ahead of his arrival."

"So you think Dad wants me to give him something?" Michael could afford practically anything, but no *thing* would make this better.

"No, that's not the point," his mother said. "The gifts were Jacob's way of acknowledging that he'd wronged his brother. It was his first step toward finding forgiveness."

Mike studied the hardwood between his shoes. He'd let his father down plenty of times over the years. Michael couldn't blame him for washing his hands of him.

But his dad didn't have all the facts.

"An apology won't fix this, Mom. Otherwise, I'd do it in a heartbeat."

She sighed. "All right, honey. But it couldn't hurt." Her eyes brightened, but her coloring was still off. The chemo was washing her out. "Lacy tells me you're singing in the choir again."

"Yeah, as long as I'm in town, I may as well be useful."

"That's an understatement. That poor

bass section is like sheep without a shepherd. Jake does the best he can, but he's dragging a lot of dead weight behind him. Mr. Mariano must be thrilled to have another strong voice in the choir," she chattered, sounding more like her usual self. "And I'm tickled to pieces to have two of my children — well, three after the wedding and I can count Jake, too — making a joyful noise."

"Noise just about sums the choir up."

"Nonsense," his mother said, beaming like a mother hen whose chicks were all gathered under her wings. "My children have given me so much to look forward to. First Thanksgiving all together, then a wedding, and finally the best Christmas cantata this town has ever heard. I couldn't ask for more."

Michael could. He sent a silent prayer skyward that the chemo and radiation would work.

Every Tuesday morning, the Coldwater Warm Hearts Club met for breakfast at the Green Apple. Even Mr. Bunn, who was habitually the last to arrive because he tended to fall into pleasant but long-winded conversations along the way, was already sipping his first cup of coffee when Heather hurried in.

"You're late," Lacy said as Heather slid into the big corner booth Jake always reserved for the club.

Everyone else was present and accounted for.

Valentina Gomez, a dispatcher for the sheriff's department, and Mr. Cooper were huddled together, working on the crossword puzzle in the latest edition of the *Gazette* until the meeting came to order. Marjorie Chubb, captain of the Methodist prayer chain and Lacy's coworker at the *Gazette,* was diving into a serving of Belgian waffles and therefore was not gossiping about anyone at the moment.

As a senior in high school, Ian Van Hook was the youngest member of the group. He and Mr. Bunn were deep in a spirited discussion about laugh tracks and percussion stingers for comics on TV.

"What's with the 'ba-dum-chhh' anyway?" Ian wanted to know.

"That's to let the audience know when it's time to laugh," Mr. Bunn explained.

Ian shook his head. "If you have to be told when to laugh, the joke's not very funny."

"Some comics made their reputations on jokes that weren't funny," Mr. Bunn said. "Johnny Carson used to get bigger laughs for the expression on his face after a joke bombed than when it went well."

"Johnny who?"

"Kids," Mr. Bunn said, shaking his head.

"It's not like you to be late," Lacy whispered to Heather. "Everything OK?"

Heather nodded. Now was not the time to admit she was losing sleep over Lacy's brother. Except for Sunday morning, when they were singing in the same choir, she hadn't seen him in days. And she'd made it a point to avoid talking to him even then. Michael Evans had no right to sneak into her dreams and make her wake with a blush, but he'd managed it last night.

More than once.

The first part of the Warm Hearts meeting was always dedicated to updates on the members' projects. The goal was to do someone good, while realizing they were blessed to be able to help. It was always a win-win. The principle of sowing and reaping was built into the fabric of the universe. You always get more than you give.

"What did I miss?" Heather asked.

"Well, so far just the news that you're going to have to find another project," Lacy said. "Mrs. Chisholm won't need you to come over on Thursdays to spell her niece anymore."

"Really? Why?" The fact that Heather donated her time to mind the old curmudgeon once a week was the only way Peggy Chisholm got a break from perpetual caregiving for her demanding aunt.

"Mrs. C has a boarder now," Lacy said. "It's that Dr. Hildebrand. You know who I mean. I told you about how she's doing that study using the *Gazette* archives. Anyway, she was looking for a more permanent place to stay while she completes her research. For a good deal on the rent of one of Mrs. Chisholm's spare bedrooms, Dr. Hildebrand has agreed to keep the old lady company on Thursdays."

Mrs. Chisholm was the retired town librarian. She'd always been a stickler for how things were done, demanding perfection from everyone around her. Now that she was confined to a wheelchair, she was even more persnickety. Her poor niece had the harried look of a rabbit at a greyhound track most of the time.

"I hope Mrs. Chisholm's boarder knows what she's in for," Heather said doubtfully.

"I'm sure she has no idea," Lacy said with a semimaniacal grin. She was always happiest when she was stirring the pot, just like Michael. Evidently, the tendency to promote mayhem was genetic in the Evans siblings.

"Otherwise, Dr. Hildebrand would never have agreed to live with Mrs. C."

"Wait a minute." Valentina looked up from her crossword. "Did you say Dr. Hildebrand?"

Lacy nodded.

"She came into the sheriff's department the other day, asking for copies of an old incident report. I told her those weren't available to the public. I'm not supposed to pull them up unless an officer asks for them or there's a court order to produce them." Valentina cocked her head at Heather. "She was asking about your sister's accident."

"Jessica? Why would she want that?" Heather asked.

"Oh, I think I know," Lacy said. "She's a sociologist. She's looking for trauma that affects young people."

"Jessica Walker's death affected more than young people," Valentina said.

And the trauma had lasted. Even ten years after the accident, Heather was still living in its shadow.

"Anyway, I thought you should know this doctor person is all up in your family's business," Valentina concluded.

As if everybody in Coldwater Cove isn't all up in everyone else's business.

Heather thanked her for the heads-up

anyway. She hoped Dr. Hildebrand didn't bother her parents about Jess's death. Some wounds never healed, and it certainly wouldn't help to pick at this one.

Lester Scott came over to the booth, coffee carafe in one hand, menus in the other. "Can I warm up anybody's cup?"

"I thought Jake had you learning to cook," Heather said.

"Well, he did, but Ethel's feeling a mite puny, so she put me to work waiting tables."

Ethel, Jake's geriatric waitress, watched Lester from her high-backed stool at the counter. The expression on her winter-apple face reminded Heather of a tabby near a mouse hole. Ethel was clearly enjoying having someone to supervise.

In addition to working a couple of days a week at the Green Apple, Lester put in a few days with Mr. Cooper at his hardware store, too. The employment was part of Lester's court-ordered rehabilitation. It went along with support from his AA sponsor and regular sessions at the local mental health clinic for dealing with his PTSD. He did odd jobs and gardening in exchange for the use of the studio apartment over Mr. Bunn's garage. On Saturdays, Lester volunteered at the senior center with Marjorie Chubb, teaching the octogenarians to play new card games.

Heather hoped one of them wasn't poker.

Other than making his estranged wife, Glenda, late for her shift at the hospital, Lester's transformation from homeless alcoholic to a clean-and-sober member of society was one of the Coldwater Warm Hearts Club's finest achievements.

Homelessness was all it was cracked down to be and difficult to break out of without help. Heather didn't believe Michael's outlandish story about being some hotshot CEO for a second. But she worried about him. She knew Mike wasn't staying with his folks or camping out on Lacy's couch. She wondered where he was laying his head.

Just because I don't want anything to do with him doesn't mean I can't care about him as a person, she told herself piously.

Yeah, right, the part of her that enjoyed those dreams he'd invaded fired back.

"Say, Lester," she said, keeping her tone carefully neutral. "The weather's turned colder. Do you know if there's anybody sleeping on the streets in town?"

The old vet smiled as he filled the coffee cup in front of her. Now that he was clean-shaven, his strong jaw made him agreeable to look upon in a weather-beaten, older-man sort of way.

Heather understood why Glenda had been late for work.

"I ain't seen anyone out and about. Not so's I've noticed," Lester said. "But now that I keep what you might call more regular hours, I don't know half of what goes on in this town. Tell you what. I'll ask my son when I see him next. If there's anybody who isn't finding their way to Samaritan House to bed down for the night, Danny will know."

Lester's boy, Daniel, was a sheriff's deputy. Since the old vet had gotten clean, he'd begun rebuilding a relationship with the son he'd abandoned years ago. He'd even been allowed to spend supervised time with his baby grandson. But though Lester's life was on an upward trek at the moment, he was first to admit that he was always one drink away from losing all the ground he'd gained.

"Have you got someone in mind you want to help, Heather?" Marjorie asked between bites of waffle delight. A light dusting of powdered sugar lined her upper lip, but it didn't last long. She licked it clean. Marjorie often claimed that Jake's waffles were good enough to be served at the heavenly "Marriage Supper of the Lamb."

"Well" — Heather shot a glance at Lacy — "I was wondering if your brother had a place to stay."

"Mike?" Lester chuckled. "Does he ever! Didn't you hear? Lacy's brother done rented out the Ouachita Inn — all of it."

"What?"

"It's true," Lacy said with a shake of her head and wonderment in her voice. "Evidently, Michael is Coldwater's version of a captain of industry. He's built a very successful company based in New York. But right now, he wants to stay close to home while Mom is going through her treatment, so he's bringing out a team of his employees to work from here." Her eyes danced with excitement. "And I get a chance to use my design skills. He's asked me for help in reconfiguring the ranch house great room as a corporate workspace."

Heather felt gut punched. Michael had told her the truth. "But why didn't he say anything about it? At first, I mean. All this time he let me think — I mean, let *us* think . . . well, did anyone here believe he did more with his life than wander around on his motorcycle?"

Everyone shook their heads and gave a collective shrug.

"Why did he hide his success?" Heather asked.

"Maybe you should ask him," Valentina

suggested, her expression shrewd.

"Look, Heather. My brother may not be homeless, but he's still Mike the Mess. If you're looking for a new project, well, let's just say, he'll give you plenty to work with," Lacy said. "At the risk of making a very old joke — 'Take my brother . . . Please.' "

"Ba-dum-chhh!" Ian added a paradiddle with his fingers on the table and pantomimed striking an air cymbal.

The club erupted in laughter.

"How 'bout that?" he said. "It worked, even for that lame joke."

The group laughed again. Heather didn't join them. Taking Michael Evans was what she really wanted to do.

Chapter 19

There are obvious holes in the reporting about the death of Jessica Walker. This little town may look like something out of the *Andy Griffith Show,* but a whiff of corruption oozes from the cobbled streets.

— from Judith Hildebrand's notes for her exposé on Michael Evans, dot-com king or heartland horror

"Yeah, that's good," Judith said to herself as she scanned her notes. It pleased her that the wording subtly trashed the bricked walkways of Coldwater Cove for ruining her Manolo Blahniks. Of course, in the end, the sacrifice of her beloved stilettos might be worth the trade. Michael Evans was guilty of something. She wasn't sure what, but it had to be something terrible.

The only fly in her ointment was that she didn't have a scrap of proof.

Judith had rifled through every bit of newsprint surrounding the unfortunate accident involving that teenaged girl, certain she was on to Michael Evans's secret. The timeline fit. The scar fit. If he'd been in that submerged car with her, hopefully in the driver's seat, he could easily have been injured.

Somehow, he was responsible for the Walker girl's death, and the whole thing had been covered up.

Just because she'd found no proof didn't make it not true.

She gave herself an inward shake over all those double negatives. Still, the premise of her project was sound.

But she'd exhausted the *Coldwater Gazette* information on the subject. When she'd tried to pump Michael's sister for her recollections of that time, Lacy had stonewalled her with general memories of high school angst and grief.

"You know how it is. We took Jessica's death as a personal slap. When you're eighteen, you think you're immortal," she'd said. "It made all of us realize we're not. Everything became suddenly more important. More urgent. In fact, if Jess hadn't died, I might not have found the courage to leave town to study back East."

After that, Lacy Evans could only talk about the design business she'd built in Boston, and Judith had failed to turn her back to the topic at hand.

But Judith had gained a couple of things from her time spent grubbing in the basement of that two-bit excuse for a paper. She'd arranged to stay with Mrs. Chisholm, a delightfully eccentric old lady with a sprawling Victorian overlooking the town park that bordered Lake Jewel. The woman was a shut-in with a broad picture window.

It was a recipe for a committed snoop.

On the first day Mrs. C's drudge of a niece left them alone, Judith left her notes in her newly rented room and took the opportunity to pump the old lady for information.

"I expect you see a good deal of what goes on in town from here, don't you?" Judith adjusted herself to make sure the lapel camera was focused on Mrs. Chisholm in her wheelchair.

"Of course, I do. What else do I have to do but watch?" Mrs. Chisholm's words spewed out like bullets from a repeater rifle. "Heat up my tea, would you? There, just a little more in the cup. No, no, not too much. Do you want me to scald myself? What was I saying? Oh, yes, I can tell you which mothers watch their children on the monkey bars and who should be investigated for neglect. Honestly, it's a shame they let some people have children these days."

"I don't think anyone controls who can have children." *At least, not in this country.*

"Really? Well, more's the pity, I say. There ought to be a law."

"Right." Even to Judith's ears, eccentricity was edging toward the crazy train, looking for a spot to jump on. But Mrs. Chisholm's picture window faced out on the exact place where Jessica Walker's car had entered the lake all those years ago. She had to find out if the old lady had seen anything. "I guess you see . . . well, how can I put this delicately? . . . things that might be considered scandalous."

"Oh, all the time." The old lady waved a crabbed hand in the air. "Even more now than when I was a librarian. People thought they were being cagey, with their secret trysts in the stacks, but they didn't fool me. No one's that interested in old periodicals." She tapped the side of her nose.

"It's clear you're a keen observer of human behavior, but I was wondering more about your vantage point now."

"From here, I see plenty of who's meeting who for a picnic, even if they're spoken for elsewhere. And if they'll eat a hot dog on a park bench together out in front of God and everybody, it makes a body wonder what they'll do when they're alone. Well, am I right?"

"Surely," Judith said, making a note to herself never to be caught in Mrs. Chisholm's crosshairs. "Of course, you probably only watch the park during the daytime."

"Land sakes, no. When you're as old as I am, you don't need more than three or four hours of sleep a night." She took a noisy slurp of her tea, her false teeth clicking loudly on the china. "I often get up and come into the parlor so I can watch the lake in the moonlight." The old lady sighed like a young girl. "It soothes me."

"How nice of your niece to get up with you."

"That lazy thing? No, Peggy can't be bothered. At night, I have to get myself up and into the chair. And I don't mind telling you, that's no small feat."

But if she can manage it at night, why does she make her niece lift her during the day? Judith wondered.

"Why, I could fall and be lying on the floor in a pool of my own blood and Peggy wouldn't hear a thing."

“That must be so trying for you.” Judith gave a small shake of her head in what she hoped passed as sympathy. Actually, she found herself pitying someone besides herself for the first time in years. As her aunt’s full-time fetch-it girl, Mrs. Chisholm’s niece was stuck in the sorriest situation Judith had ever seen.

“I’ve tried ringing a bell. I even had one of those newfangled baby monitor thingies installed so I can call out when I need her, but nothing rouses her.”

If Judith were in Peggy’s shoes, she’d have the batteries out of that monitor so quick, their little electric poles would spin.

“After midnight, Peggy sleeps like the dead,” Mrs. Chisholm complained. “Or says she does. My cup’s empty. More tea, girl.”

Judith jumped at her sharp tone and obeyed on reflex. “Well, it’s a good thing your bedroom is on the main floor so everything is conveniently located for you.”

“Pish. It’s conveniently located for Peggy, you mean. I’m sleeping in what used to be the dining room. But as we never entertain, she insisted we change it to my bedroom. When she first came to live with me, Peggy would carry me up to the lovely bedroom I had when Mr. Chisholm was alive.” A smile lifted the corners of her mouth and then dropped them back into her usual scowl. "Of course, she was much younger then."

And perhaps you were much lighter, Judith thought, eyeing the old lady's ample girth. "I wonder if I'm renting the room you shared with your husband."

"Oh, we never shared a bedroom. When I was young, it simply wasn't done. The husband might visit his wife's boudoir on occasion," she said with the same expression she reserved for sour pickles, "but proper married people always had their own rooms."

That explains why Mrs. Chisholm is cared for by a niece instead of a daughter.

"My room upstairs is the one that overlooks the front lawn. It has pretty much the same view as the parlor, but up a level. You're in Mr. C's old bedroom." She arched a wiry brow. "Or at least, you'd better be."

"Oh, I'm sure I must be. My room overlooks the side yard."

"Yes, that's Herman's room. The one with the gramophone. Peggy sleeps in one of the old servant's rooms on the third floor."

Judith turned her lips inward to hide her smile. Mrs. Chisholm's overworked niece had commandeered her aunt's coveted upstairs bedroom without her knowledge. That explained why Peggy crept around the space in stockinged feet and closed the door with such care the latch didn't make a sound. She was trying to avoid being heard by the sharp-eared old lady below.

It was a small bit of insolence, but Judith liked Peggy better for it. The powerless needed to take what they could from their oppressors. And if the oppressors were unaware they'd been plundered, so much the better.

What Mrs. Chisholm doesn't know won't hurt Peggy.

But Judith needed to find out what the old lady *did* know. "In my research of the *Coldwater Gazette* archives, I discovered an account about the tragic drowning of a teenage girl. It happened about ten years ago."

"Going on eleven, in point of fact."

"Oh, then you remember it."

"I should hope to shout. I'm not feeble, you know." Mrs. Chisholm leaned forward confidingly. "I watched the whole thing happen right from this chair, but did anyone think to ask me? Not once."

"Then here's your chance." Judith nearly leaped up in excitement, but she forced herself to keep up the calm, detached persona of a visiting scholar. "Tell me about it. Every detail you recall."

Mrs. Chisholm set down her tea cup. "Well, it was around May Day. I remember because several of the neighborhood children had cluttered up my porch with their tacky little homemade baskets filled with flowers and candy and —"

"Mrs. Chisholm," Judith said more sharply than she ought. She modified her tone as she went on. "If you could please just stick to an account of the accident . . ."

The old lady gave an injured sniff. "You might have said so in the first place. I thought you wanted every detail."

"Every detail about the accident, yes."

"Very well. I had the most excruciating migraine that night, you see. Peggy had left some of the downstairs windows open and the pollen — from those infernal May Day baskets most likely — had unleashed havoc on my sinuses. And —"

"And this is connected with the accident, how?"

"It's why I was awake that night," Mrs. Chisholm explained in the same tone she'd take with a not-quite-bright child. "If Peggy had done her job, or if people didn't allow their children to spread pollen around the neighborhood willy-nilly, why, I'd have enjoyed the sleep of the just that night." Then Mrs. Chisholm's indignant expression softened. "Instead, I'm left with the memory of that poor girl's last moments. Oh, it's a terrible burden to carry, let me tell you."

Tell me. For the love of all that's holy, just tell me! Judith wanted to scream, but instead she said, "Take your time and share it with me. Perhaps the burden will seem lighter."

Where had that idea come from? Oh, yes. It was something from the silly little paper in the "Words to Live By" column that was authored by all the pastors in town in a round-robin sort of arrangement. Yesterday's words were: "A burden shared is a burden lightened."

But however hokey Judith found the saying, it seemed to do the trick. Mrs. Chisholm stared out the window and began speaking.

CHAPTER 20

Put three sticks of wood into the cookstove and bake them little cakes until they're done. Or maybe longer.
— from Grandma Higginbottom's recipe for "Good Enough for Company Cakes"

Shirley Evans was determined to make petits fours from an old family recipe for Lacy's bridal shower. As maid of honor, Heather was equally determined to make sure her friend's mother didn't wear herself ragged. According to Lacy, her mom tended to go after everything "like she was killing snakes." So Heather had volunteered to help bake and decorate the little cakes.

"Just wait till you taste one," Shirley said. "So light and airy, they practically float off the plate."

The only problem was that Grandma Higginbottom had never been very forthcoming about how she made those slivers of heaven. She'd worked hard to perfect her recipes, and it was a point of honor not to share. If she ever wrote anything down at all, it was riddled with vague directions and always left out one or more key ingredients so no one could ever duplicate her results.

And since Grandma Higginbottom had "gone on to glory" years ago, she'd taken her kitchen secrets with her.

"But that doesn't mean we can't figure them out with a little trial and error," Shirley had assured Heather.

The error part was what worried Heather, which was why she was waiting on the Evanses' front steps that morning.

Shirley had left a note on the door saying she'd run down to the Piggly Wiggly for a few last-minute items they might need — spices and Crisco and whatnot. This morning's batch of cakes was the trial run to make sure they had the recipe right.

If there was an error, Mr. Evans, like any retired lawyer worth his salt, had volunteered to eat the incriminating evidence. Or in the worst case, take it down to share at his Rotary Club meeting that evening.

"Those fellows will eat anything," he'd assured them.

Mr. Evans wasn't at the house now either.

If there was experimental cooking going on, he wanted no part of it and had promised he could be found drinking coffee at the Green Apple until his services as "Head Taster and Quality Control" were needed. Heather was glad he'd made himself scarce, when Michael roared into the driveway on his Harley.

Heather waved sheepishly once he turned off the motorcycle. She hadn't spoken to Michael since being so horrible to him at the hospital. It wasn't like her. She usually gave everyone the benefit of the doubt. It bothered her that she hadn't done so with him. "Hey."

"Hey, yourself." A slow smile spread over his handsome face as he removed his helmet.

He didn't seem to be holding a grudge, but he didn't seem to be walking toward her either.

"Guess you're waiting for an apology."

"Nope." He headed her way.

"Well, I should have believed you. For what it's worth, I'm sorry."

"It's worth a lot." He ran a hand over his dark hair, but he needn't have bothered. He didn't have a smidge of helmet head going on. His hair was still longer than it should be, but Heather was beginning to like it that way. "To be fair, I didn't give you much to work with."

That was true. He certainly didn't dress to match his income. Didn't flash his status around town. Didn't even tell his family about his success.

And certainly doesn't waste money on pricey haircuts.

A strange lump glowed in her chest. There was nothing sexier than a man who didn't know how sexy he was. And a rich guy who acted like he didn't measure himself or others by their bank accounts was also curl-your-toes hot. Add in the tender care he lavished on his mother, and Michael was a triple threat to Heather's heart.

"Your folks aren't here," she told him, "but your mom will be back from the store soon."

He nodded. "Gone to buy more stuff for baking, no doubt. Why have two bags of flour on hand when you can have three, or four, or six? Too much is never enough in my family." He sat down beside her on the steps. He didn't crowd her at all, but Heather felt warmth emanating from his thigh next to hers.

"Mom asked me to come over to help," he said.

"You know how to bake?"

"Me? Naw. But I can beat eggs and whip batter into submission all day long. Mom used to coerce me into helping her when I was a kid," he said. "Back then, my reward was licking the beaters."

Heather imagined him as a little boy, standing on a chair next to the counter so he could stir the batter. She smiled at the thought. "What did she promise you this time?"

"That I get to see you."

He looked at her so intently, it was as if he was trying to memorize her. A warm flush spread over her skin. He leaned toward her.

In the romance novels Heather read, they always talked about how the hero and heroine's attraction to each other was almost magnetic, as if they were drawn together by an invisible force. She'd never believed it could really happen.

Until now.

She closed her eyes.

Oh, my gosh. He's going to kiss me.

She wanted him to with a fierceness that surprised her. It had been so long since she'd been kissed, she wondered if she'd forgotten how. Her lips tingled in anticipation. His warm breath feathered over her mouth. Excitement shivered over her.

Then a car honked sharply three times, and the spell was broken. Heather's eyes flew open to see Michael turn away from her as his mother's van pulled into the driveway.

"I can't catch a break," he muttered as Mrs. Evans turned off the vehicle and climbed out.

"Oh, good! You're both here. You can help me unload."

Shirley's color was high. Heather figured she must be almost a week away from her last treatment. As long as her white blood cell count held, she could keep up the rigorous chemo schedule. Heather hoped she wasn't taking on too much with Lacy's shower and wedding plans.

"I thought this trip to the store was just going to be a quick run, but Piggly Wiggly was having such a good sale, I decided to stock up the pantry a bit."

Shirley went around, opened the rear hatch, and handed the first two bags to Michael. Then Heather and she gathered up a bag apiece and carried them inside. It took several trips before the back of the van was empty and the pantry was full to bursting.

"Oh, wait a minute!" Mrs. Evans looked down around her ankles, her face a mask of worry. "Where's Fergus? Has anyone seen him?"

"He's not in the house?" Mike asked.

"No. He whined so much when I started to leave, I took him with me to the store," Shirley Evans said as she hurried out the front door to check for him in the van. "I do that sometimes. Fergus is a good traveler. He usually just curls up in the backseat and goes to sleep, but he's not there now." She made a megaphone with her palms and called his name, but no furry ball of fluff came running. "Did either of you see him when I arrived?"

Heather shook her head.

"There's nothing in the van, Mom," Michael said after checking under the seats.

"Oh, no." She sank down onto the back bumper. "He must have hopped out at the store when I wasn't looking. Your father will never forgive me if I lose him. I've got to go look for him."

Visibly shaking, she started to climb into the van.

"No, Mom. Let us go. You're too upset," Mike said. "Besides, someone needs to stay here in case Fergus comes home on his own."

"How can he do that?" she asked as Michael led her toward the front door. "He wouldn't know the way. Besides, it's a good three miles to the store."

"Dogs have been known to cross continents to get home," Heather offered with hope. *Of course, those dogs don't generally have legs that are only three inches long.*

"We'll find him," Michael promised. He grabbed Heather's hand and started toward the motorcycle. "Come on."

"No, let's take my car. It's less noisy."

"You're right. The hog might scare him off." He went around to the driver's side and held the door open for her.

"I didn't think guys did that anymore."

"You're not going to go all commando feminist on me, are you?"

"No." Of course, she was perfectly capable of opening her car door herself. She was as independent as they came, but it was a nice gesture all the same. "Being polite isn't sexist."

Wonder if he only did it because his mom is right there.

No, it had seemed natural.

Next thing you know, he'll be putting a hand to the small of my back to guide me across a room.

That spot at the base of her spine, just above her bottom, tingled a bit, and she wished they were back in the high school gym for the reunion dance. If they were a regular couple, he'd probably touch her like that. It was a subtly intimate gesture. It sort of said, *"See, this is my girl. I can touch her like this in public and you can't."*

No one had ever touched Heather like that. She wasn't the fragile sort that encouraged guys to offer that kind of gentlemanly shepherding. Girls who were nearly six feet tall didn't get to feel soft and feminine that often. But Michael made her feel that way.

And she didn't know why in the world she was thinking about it now when they were supposed to be looking for a lost dog. It was probably because Michael had been so close to kissing her. She was sure of it. All her nerve endings were still firing with pent-up frustration.

She floored the Taurus as she pulled away from the Evanses' drive.

"Hey," Michael said, pumping imaginary brakes on his side of the vehicle. "I've got nothing against fast chicks, but at this speed, we could zoom right by Fergus and not see him."

"You're right." She let up on the accelerator. "We could use some extra eyes, too. Got a phone?"

He pulled a slim one from his pocket.

"Bet that thing is loaded with all the bells

and whistles," she said.

"It does everything but take out the trash."

"Funny. I just use mine to call people," she told him. "For example, call 911."

"For a lost dog?"

"Remember where you are, Michael. A lost dog may well be the most exciting thing that happens in Coldwater Cove all day long."

He punched in the numbers and hit speaker.

"911. What's your emergency?"

"Valentina? It's Heather."

"That's an out-of-state number you're calling from," the dispatcher said. "Who you with, *chica?*"

"Michael Evans."

"Ah! As in 'take my brother, please' Michael Evans?"

What? Michael mouthed silently.

"Never mind," she told him with a shake of her head. "Look, Valentina, Mrs. Evans's dog is missing. Yorkshire terrier, probably got a collar, answers to Fergus, last seen at the Piggly Wiggly. Have you gotten any calls about a stray?"

"Matter of fact, there was a report of a little dog nosing around the Dumpster behind the store, but the stock boy couldn't catch him. Said he ran down the alley, making for the Square."

"We'll head there now," Heather told her. "Let me know if you get an update on his twenty."

"His twenty?" Michael said incredulously. "What? Have you got a CB handle or something?"

Valentina's laughter crackled over the phone. Heather grimaced at him.

And to think I was mooning around about wanting him to put his hand on my back!

"I'll let you know if someone sights him again," Valentina sang out. "Gotta go. The switchboard is starting to light up."

As they neared the Square, they rolled down their windows and called out for Fergus every few yards. Michael put two fingers between his teeth and gave an ear-splitting whistle. Several big dogs started yapping from backyards as they passed, but there was no sign of Fergus.

Once they entered the Square around the courthouse, Heather spotted Jake standing outside the Green Apple Grill. He waved his arms to flag them down. Heather slowed to a stop.

"Heard you were looking for Fergus."

"Where did you hear that?"

"It's on the radio," Jake said. "They interrupted Swap Shop to put out a public announcement about it."

"Only in Coldwater Cove," Mike said, shaking his head.

"Valentina said Fergus was seen on the Square." Heather leaned out the window.

Jake nodded. "Lester spotted him when he was taking out the trash and tried to catch him, but that little devil is fast. He lit out heading north on Maple."

"Thanks." Michael thumped the side of the car twice to signal they should go.

"Good luck," Jake called after them.

"We're gonna need it," Heather said. "If the dog doesn't want to be caught, this could go all day."

"Well, I can think of worse ways to spend a day. After all, I was ready to be up to my elbows in cake batter for a chance to spend time with you."

And the tingle at the base of her spine was back.

But she couldn't indulge the feeling just then. She was still calling for Fergus and driving like a turtle to avoid missing him.

He was nowhere to be seen.

Michael's phone rang. It was Valentina.

"OK, here's the rundown," the dispatcher said. "Fergus was seen playing with some kids at the gazebo down by the lake. Then he allegedly wandered into Mr. Cooper's hardware."

"Allegedly?" Michael said.

"Hey! Innocent until proven guilty, *chico.* It's the American way."

"Well, good," Heather said. "We can pick him up at the hardware store."

"No, you can't. He beelined out the back door when they tried to slip a feed bag over him." The phone crackled as Valentina seemed to be flipping through some papers. "Then a small dog was seen doing tricks for bites of churro from folks in the take-out line at Hair Today Gone Tamale. Oh, wait a minute. Daniel just handed me a report of another sighting. Are you sure there's only one dog missing?"

"As far as we know," Mike said. "Where was Fergus seen last?"

"The Heart of the Ozarks Motel."

"Thanks, Valentina," Heather said, and Michael clicked off. "Shall we head out there?"

"No, he'll probably be gone by the time we get there." Michael drew a circle in the air in front of him and made little checks for each sighting. "Piggly Wiggly, Town Square, the park, Mr. Cooper's, the Mexican take-out place —"

"And beauty salon," Heather interrupted. "Don't forget the hair part of Hair Today

Gone Tamale."

"Noted. Anyway, Fergus seems to be making a loop," Michael said. "He's working his way back to Piggly Wiggly."

"So we'll head him off at the pass." Heather took the first left turn and wound through the tree-lined streets to the grocery store. They still called out in every block, but if Fergus was crouching under a juniper bush or behind a picket fence, he didn't respond.

When they reached the store parking lot, Heather slowed the car to a crawl. She drove up and down each lane as Michael called and whistled.

"Fergus!" She added her voice to his. "Here, Fergus!"

Just as she started down the last aisle of cars, Mr. Mundy, who'd been watching them from the door to the store, waved her to a stop. He was an avid fisherman who didn't like spending money on equipment. Fortunately, as the husband of the town librarian, he had easy and pretty much unlimited access to all the rods, reels, and lures that had been donated to the Coldwater Cove Library and Repository of Useful Items. When he wasn't checking out the fishing tackle to use in the latest bass tournament, he was making a surprise visit to the emergency room for a fish hook caught on some unpleasant part of himself.

Heather sent a quick thank-you heavenward that the town fathers hadn't allowed Junior Bugtussle to donate his old set of filleting knives. Mr. Mundy surely would have chopped off something important by now.

"Who's Fergus?" Mr. Mundy wanted to know.

"My mom's little dog," Mike said.

"Is it *that* little dog?" The man pointed behind them. " 'Cuz if it is, you can stop casting and reel him in. Poor little guy's been following your car since you pulled into the lot."

Mike hopped out, and Fergus limped up to him, tongue lolling. His chest was heaving, and he smelled of churro, all cinnamon and sugar and flour and grease, but he was unhurt. When Michael bent to scoop him up, he didn't try to run away. Once they climbed back into the car, the Yorkie collapsed in a puppy heap on his lap.

"Looks like he's had enough adventures for one day," Michael said.

"He'll perk up. Just wait until he smells those little cakes your mom and I are going to bake," Heather said with a laugh. "Fergus will find his second wind."

"Speaking of a second wind, we need one,

you and me. Sort of a reboot." He reached over and took her hand. "Now that all my cards are on the table, can we start over?"

Now that he wasn't trying to hide his wealth, maybe he wanted to do something outlandish like spirit her off to Paris for a weekend. Michael Evans had his own jet. She hadn't believed him when he told her, but now that it had been confirmed on the Methodist prayer chain as "additional information" to aid the prayer warriors in lifting up Mike's mother in particular and the Evans family in general, Michael's high net worth was an established fact.

No, she didn't want to go to Paris even if he offered, she decided. He had nothing to prove. Whether he had money or not made no difference. But she wished he hadn't felt the need to hide so much from her.

"What did you have in mind?" she asked.

"Now that I'm going to be in town for a while, it seems I'm expected to take part in family things," he said. "Mom's orders."

"I know how those 'command performances' are. My mom can turn on the guilt tap at the drop of a hat and before I know it, I'm agreeing to do lots of things I'd rather not. What does your mom want from you?"

"My niece, Riley — that's Crystal's daughter — has a dance recital on Thursday. If you come with me," he said, "I think I can sit through it without disgracing the family much."

"Well, that's not exactly a weekend in Paris." She pulled her hand away from him and clapped it over her mouth. What had gotten into her?

"You want to go to Paris?"

"Yes. I mean, no. Well, maybe someday, but no, forget it. I'm being silly. I can't get away from the hospital anyway. We're too short staffed."

Ah, the safe haven of a job where I'm needed!

"So, 'no' on the recital?" he asked.

"No. I mean yes, I'll go with you." A weekend in Paris might be world shaking. A kids' recital in the refurbished Coldwater Cove theater should be safe enough. "It'll be fun."

"Oh, I can pretty much guarantee it won't be. It's a bunch of little kids hopping around in tights. We're talking strictly parental consumption here. But I can promise you one thing."

"What's that?"

"Riley's recital will be better than a poke in the eye with a sharp stick."

"Ouch."

"Yeah, well, if I set the bar low, I have a better chance of exceeding your expectations."

"That's the way to tempt me." She laughed as she pulled into the Evanses' driveway. "Bet you use that one on all the girls."

"There are no other girls, Heather. Never have been." He climbed out of the car and set Fergus down so he could mark the front yard. Michael came around and opened Heather's door for her. "There's just you."

She didn't know what to say. She wished she could believe him, but he'd been so good at keeping secrets.

It made her wonder what else he hadn't told her.

Chapter 21

Whoever suggested someone should "Dance like nobody's watching" ought to be strapped to a chair with their eyes taped open and forced to sit through a ballet recital.

— Noah Addleberry, after he learned how much Crystal had spent on Riley's dance lessons

"Uncah Mike!" A blurry froth of pink came skittering across the lobby of the old theater and nearly knocked Heather over in its haste to clasp Michael's knees.

"Hey, you!" Even though he was wearing a suit so well tailored it must be bespoke, Mike reached down and hefted up his niece, sending her momentarily airborne. Riley squealed with delight before he caught her again. Heather moved back a step so she could watch him with her.

Dang, the guy is good with kids, too. Could

he be any more perfect?

"How's my Riley-girl?" he said as he set her back down on her tiny slippered feet.

"I'm not Riley today." She pronounced her name "Riwee" because she couldn't say her *l*'s.

Crystal is such a perfectionist. I bet that small speech impediment must rub her raw.

"Today, I'm a princess, Uncah Mike. See my crown." She pointed to the sparkly tiara held in place with half a dozen bobby pins.

"Of course, you are. My mistake." He gave her a mock-serious bow. "You're a princess every day in my book. A thousand pardons, Your Highness."

Riley giggled again as Crystal and her husband Noah caught up to them. Perfect little Ethan followed behind them, his hair slicked down and his bow tie rigidly horizontal. Once he stopped walking, he pulled an iPad mini from his cargo pants pocket and resumed a game, ignoring his parents, his sister, and virtually every other human on the planet.

Heather could read stress in a person's body language. She had to since her patients seldom admitted how they really felt. From Crystal's tense posture to her darting gaze, she had all the signs of someone being held together with duct tape.

"Don't encourage her, Mike." Crystal crossed her arms over her chest. "She's not a princess and she knows it."

"Lighten up, sis. Let the kid have some fun. It's only pretend."

"I'm just saying she needs to be a team player today, not a princess. Moving in perfect synchronicity is everything in a dance ensemble. She has to fit in."

"And yet there are those who find fitting in boring."

Shut up, Mike. You're making it worse. Heather gave his bicep a squeeze.

"Besides, Riley doesn't need you making her feel like she's something special." Crystal bent down, licked the pad of her thumb, and wiped a smudge off her daughter's cheek. "It'll spoil her."

"She could use a little spoiling," Mike said. "Besides, she is something special."

Heather agreed with him. Crystal was being more unpleasant than usual. It wasn't wise to poke this particular bear.

Certainly not in public.

"Heather, it's good to see you." Noah stuck out his hand, and she shook it, realizing he was trying to change the subject. "What did this ugly mug have to promise you to get you to come to this thing?"

"I'm taking her to Paris afterward," Mike

said, straight-faced.

"Oh!" Crystal blinked in surprise.

"He's kidding," Heather said quickly. "I'm looking forward to seeing Riley dance."

"You'd be the only one," Noah muttered under his breath. "Don't expect the Bolshoi."

Crystal shot her husband a glare that ought to have immolated him.

Riley tugged on her mother's hem. "You haf to tell Miss Bartwett. Tell her, Mommy."

Because of the lisp, "tell" came out "tewah," and the way Riley pronounced Miss Bartlett sounded like someone's dog had had an accident on the floor. Crystal winced.

"Tell her what?" Noah asked.

Crystal sighed in obvious exasperation. "Riley has been having a running battle with her teacher over where she's supposed to stand on the stage. There are little numbers in masking tape on the floor so the kids will be properly spaced. Riley is supposed to stand on three."

"But I'm not three. I'm four." Riley held up the correct number of fingers.

"It's not about how old you are," Crystal told her. "It's just where Miss Bartlett wants you to stand when you start to dance."

"But I'm not three." Riley stamped her foot.

She looks just like her mother, but she's as stubborn as her uncle.

"Better tell that teacher to move the kid," Noah said under his breath.

"If I've told you once I've told you a thousand times, we can't give in," Crystal told her husband. "Riley is a willful child and we'll never break her if we let her have her way all the time."

"Sis, you can break a horse. You can break a teacup. You can even break wind." Michael waded into the argument between his sister and her hubby with both feet. Heather gripped his arm and gave it another hard squeeze. She wanted to yank him aside and warn him not to barge in where even angels fear to tread, but there was no stopping him. "I don't think you're supposed to break a child."

Crystal's narrow-eyed gaze shifted to her brother. "Says the man who's never taken responsibility for anything in his life."

"Crystal, this isn't the time or place for you and Mike to get into it." Noah put a restraining hand on Crystal's arm, but she brushed it off.

"It's exactly the time." She cocked her head at her daughter, who was playing ring-around-the-rosy with Michael's knees. "How does Riley even know you anyway?"

"She and I got acquainted over at the folks' house," Michael said. "I've been helping Mom look after her when Noah drops her by for the afternoon."

Heather's eyebrows shot skyward. Crystal was making her mom babysit while she was going through chemo?

Looks like she's trying to break her parents, too.

"I don't think it's good for you to spend time with Riley without me there," Crystal said. "You know nothing about children."

"Only that I was one once."

"Don't kid yourself, Michael. You may shop in the men's section now, but you're still a child." Crystal's lip curled. "And if Mom and Dad had only been a little tougher on you, maybe you wouldn't have had to go away for all those years."

"Crystal, don't," Noah said, glancing around the lobby. He was clearly embarrassed at the looks his wife was getting from the other recital goers.

"Why shouldn't I say what I'm thinking? No one else has the courage to do it." Crystal turned back to Mike. "You've always been nothing but trouble. Why are you even here?"

"Don't worry, sis." Michael tousled his niece's curly hair, taking care not to disturb the tiara. "I'm here for Riley, not you."

Crystal's eyes bugged out a little, making her look like a deranged praying mantis. But before she could launch into what promised to be a blistering setdown, Mr. and Mrs. Evans, along with Lacy and Jake, hurried up to join them.

"Oh, look, George. The whole family's here. Isn't it wonderful?" Shirley Evans said as she gave each of them a hug in turn. Even Heather.

This wasn't a meet-the-parents type date. Heather already knew the Evanses well. But Shirley had managed to make her feel like part of the family. Despite the current blowup between siblings, Heather was glad to be included.

"Let's go find our seats before the good ones are all taken." Shirley led the way, counting on her family to fall into step behind her like a gaggle of geese.

"Invisible towing tendrils," Mike leaned down to tell Heather. "Mom's always had them."

The Regal Theater had started out as an Oklahoma territory watering hole, a glorified saloon with a stage. In its heyday, acts from as far away as St. Louis or Memphis had played the Regal to a foot-stomping crowd. There were still a few bullet holes in the ceiling where a rowdy cowboy or two had shown his appreciation by getting a shot off.

The theater had been updated in the 1950s with a sloping floor, padded seating, and a screen that scrolled down in front of the velvet curtain. It was home to second-run movies and the best popcorn with real butter in town. Kids could get into the Saturday matinée by bringing in canned goods that were earmarked for the local food pantry. And occasionally, the Regal was lent out to Miss Bartlett's dance studio or Mrs. Paderewski's piano students.

"In support of the arts," Mr. Van Hook, the owner, was quoted in the *Coldwater Gazette.*

Heather noticed that he didn't support them by actually *attending* the recitals.

The building was showing its age, but in the right light, the Victorian curlicues and gilt cupids above the curtain were charming in a blast-from-the-past sort of way.

Following Shirley and George, the Evans family filled up most of the third row. Lacy and Jake were next to her parents, with Noah and Crystal after them. Heather found herself seated on Crystal's right, with

Michael taking the aisle seat beside her.

"Location is everything," he whispered as he settled in. "I can make a quick getaway from here."

Crystal leaned forward and tossed him a pursed-lipped glare. Heather narrowly avoided the urge to cringe since she was definitely situated to catch cross fire.

The lights dimmed, the heavy velvet curtain parted, and Miss Bartlett's oldest students kicked off the recital with a rendition of "Getting to Know You" from *The King and I.* The Thai costumes were delightful and full of color, but the dancer who played Anna tripped over her hooped skirt when its swaying momentum built up too much.

Then Riley's class of youngest dancers trouped onto the stage.

"Oh, no," Crystal whispered.

"I told you Miss Bartlett should have switched her to four," Noah said testily.

It might not have mattered. Riley had abandoned the number system altogether. She chose her own place. It was dead center stage, about five feet in front of the rest of the class.

As the music started, Heather leaned toward Michael. "It's like she's the prima ballerina and the others are her backup dancers."

"Just as well." Michael shook his head and shrugged. "She's not in sync with the rest of them anyway."

Sure enough, when the class did a series of neat toe points, Riley did a sloppy arabesque. When the rest of the little girls pirouetted, Riley balanced on one foot like a tutu-clad stork.

From the corner of her eye, Heather saw Crystal shift uncomfortably in her seat. She knew it wasn't nice of her, but it was hard not to feel a little gleeful about Crystal suffering such a public embarrassment.

Then Riley seemed to have a wardrobe malfunction. She began scratching at her hips where the tutu rested as she danced, rocking back and forth and hitching it up and down on one side. Evidently, she wasn't satisfied with that adjustment, and, on her next whirling turn, she grabbed the pink netting with both hands. Then Riley hiked the tutu up under her armpits and continued to dance, keeping time to the music in her own unique way. It was a safe bet Miss Bartlett had never dreamed up this armpit tutu choreography.

The audience erupted in laughter, and Crystal slipped down in her chair a little more. Heather suspected she wished she could melt away, trickle beneath the seat, and disappear altogether.

It couldn't happen to a nicer stage mom.

Riley, however, didn't appreciate the audience's reaction to her dance. She fisted her hands at her waist and glared at them with a ferocious scowl, as if to say, *Hey, you! This is serious. I'm trying to dance here!*

"Keep dancing, Riley," Mike called out. "You're doing great."

A smile bloomed across her face, and she resumed her freeform movements. She leaped. She turned. She balanced on one foot and winked at her "Uncah Mike." Never once did she fall into step with the rest of the dancers.

It was actually a little brilliant. No one could fault her musicality and creativity, but she definitely wasn't a team player. At her preschool, Riley would be voted "Most Likely *Not* to Color Inside the Lines."

Heather sneaked a glance at Michael, who was grinning ear to ear as he watched his niece dance.

He really likes her, and I can see why. She's just like him. Fitting in is not something either of them does well. Doubt they'd want to if they could.

Then the music ended, and the audience applauded politely. In unison, the rest of the class dipped in a graceful, perfectly timed curtsy, but Riley's tiara chose that moment to slide off her head and bounce onto the hardwood behind her. She whirled around and bent to retrieve it. With her pink-clad bottom smiling at the ceiling, Riley mooned the entire auditorium.

Then when the audience howled with laughter, along with the resounding applause, she turned and dipped in her own solo curtsy. The rest of the class exited stage left, but Riley remained at center stage, waving to the audience and blowing kisses with both hands. They laughed and clapped all the harder.

"Noah," Crystal hissed to her husband. "Do something."

"OK." Noah stood and continued to clap for his daughter. Michael joined him in a show of solidarity. Heather did, too, not sure if she was clapping for Riley's dancing or for Noah's refusal to bend to Crystal's demands.

"That's not what I meant." Crystal stood and poked at his waist.

"I know."

"But Riley's making a fool of herself. And of us."

"Crystal, she's just a kid. She's having fun. But you're right about one thing," Noah said under his breath. "We're the fools for forking out good money for those dance lessons."

A stiff smile on her face, Miss Bartlett finally appeared on-stage. Dancer-slim and pretty, she took Riley by the hand and gently led her off.

"Thanks for bringing me," Heather whispered to Michael as they settled back into their seats. "This has been surprisingly entertaining."

"As advertised. Better than a poke in the eye with a sharp stick." He leaned toward her as he whispered back, his warm breath feathering over her neck. He took her hand. "Crystal's not having much fun though."

Heather glanced at the smoldering stage mom at her side. Crystal's knuckles were white where she grasped the hem of her skirt, and her face looked so brittle she might break. A wave of pity for her washed over Heather.

"Don't be so hard on her, Mike. She's hard enough on herself," Heather said, enjoying having to snuggle in close so their whispers couldn't be overheard. "The pursuit of perfection is tough."

"Yeah, and if she's not careful, she'll find my brother-in-law thinks perfection is overrated."

The way Noah's gaze had tracked Miss Bartlett's progress across the stage, Heather wondered if Michael might not be right.

Chapter 22

He's a sharp-edged puzzle that would take a lifetime to solve. He's a lousy son to his father and a potential heartbreak to his mom. He's a terrific uncle to Riley and a so-so brother to her mother. Wish I knew what he is to me, but if Michael's taught me anything, it's that people are never only one thing.

— from Heather Walker's diary

Time spent chasing a missing terrier or watching Riley's unique style of dancing didn't really count as a way to show a girl a good time. Mike was determined to fix that.

Heather had been a good sport about it, but she deserved to be wined and dined. She deserved to be swept off her feet. Short of whisking her off to Paris, which was sounding less like a joke every time it crossed his mind, dinner at the upscale restaurant — upscale by Coldwater Cove standards — that operated on the main floor of the old Opera House was the best option open to him.

After a supper of Kobe beef and nice California merlot, he could see her begin to visibly relax. Her posture was no longer hospital rigid. She laughed more easily at his jokes and even cracked a few of her own. And before he knew what was happening, she was getting him to tell her things he never thought he would.

"You said there were no other women in your life, but I have a hard time believing that." She ran her fingertip around the top of her wineglass. The crystal hummed softly. "Unless, of course, you have a habit of giving them all horrible nicknames that stick."

"You haven't forgiven me for calling you 'Stilts' yet?"

She grinned at him. "The jury's still out, but I'm leaning toward an acquittal."

"Good." He reached across the table and took her hand, enjoying her warmth and smooth skin.

She shook her head and smiled. If that wasn't a mixed message, he didn't know what was.

"What?" Had he screwed up without realizing it?

"Every time I turn around, you surprise

me, Michael. When we were in high school, I had this, oh, I don't know, this image of how you'd turn out in my head."

"I'm guessing it didn't include winning a Nobel Prize."

"Not unless they opened up a category for contributions to the field of jerk-ology."

"Ouch."

She squeezed his hand. "What I'm trying to say is that I was wrong. You're not the show-off smart ass you were in school."

"Gee, I don't know how much more of this sweet talk I can take."

"I'm doing this badly. What I mean is, you're a really great guy. You're kind and thoughtful, and, well, I certainly didn't imagine you as a dot-com king."

"I didn't think money mattered to you one way or the other."

"Because my family has buckets of it? Yeah, there's that, but I admire the way you made yours. You had an idea and you built something with it. My dad made his money by getting lucky. He just happened to hit a big old pool of oil on the land he inherited from my granddad. It was like winning the lottery," Heather said. "Guess I always thought that was sort of a cheat."

"No, it wasn't. Your dad took a risk and that's not nothing. It costs plenty to drill.

He could have spent all that money wildcatting and come up empty," Mike said. "Did you ever ask him how many dry holes he dug before he hit a gusher?"

"No."

"Well, ask him sometime." Mike bit off the end of a chocolate mint stick. "Parents deserve the benefit of the doubt as much as 'Nobel Jerk Laureates' do."

"Does that go for *your* dad too?" she asked. "I noticed he didn't say a word to you at Riley's recital. Obviously, the two of you haven't buried the hatchet, but it was like you weren't even there."

"Don't blame my father. You don't know the whole story." The conversation was taking an uncomfortable turn. "Frankly, neither does Dad."

"You should tell him."

"Maybe I will."

"If you want to practice on somebody, I'm a good listener."

That was so not happening. Michael shifted in his seat and tried a trick he'd learned from Lacy — letting silence reign until the other person felt compelled to fill it.

"You know, I'm still wondering why in all your wandering you never found somebody to love," she said.

"Who says I didn't before I started wandering?" Mike leaned forward. "Heather, I really have always had a thing for you."

"But you must have met tons of women in New York."

"Yeah, but they never measured up to my memory of you."

She looked away as if he'd embarrassed her.

Mike glanced out the big window at the night sky. "The moon's come up. Want to walk down by the lake?"

"Actually . . ." She paused, picked up her wineglass, and downed the last of the merlot in one gulp. "The deck at my apartment has the best view of Lake Jewel you could ask for."

She was asking him up to her place. He didn't need to be invited twice.

Mike signaled for the check, and they were out of there before she could change her mind.

A crisp October breeze ruffled over them. Heather shivered as they walked across the Square to her building. As she'd hoped, Michael took the hint, peeled off his jacket, and draped it over her shoulders. He was attentive enough to pick up on the little things.

There's another check mark in his favor.

Whenever Heather had a big decision to make, she always did a plus-versus-minus-style balance sheet, listing the pros and cons. She hadn't gotten around to committing Michael's ledger to paper yet, but it was starting to take shape in her head.

The lining of the jacket still held his warmth, and it smelled of him — all leather and evergreen with a hint of citrus. When he put his arm around her, she found herself leaning into him.

It wasn't just because of the bottle of wine they'd split. She was leaning on him because he was dependable enough for her to lean on. Michael Evans wasn't the screwup everyone thought him to be. He didn't have to trumpet how important he was, but he provided jobs for a lot of people. He didn't have any reason to be good with kids, but he was. He obviously loved Riley and understood her instinctively. Heather had never realized that could be such an attractive quality in a guy. He could have been a major player in New York, in greater demand than a rock star. His brand of wealth attracted its own set of groupies.

But he'd always remembered *her.*

A bunch more check marks on the good side of the ledger.

Something inside her shivered in a way that had nothing to do with the brisk weather.

Heather and Mike climbed the iron staircase to her second-story apartment in perfect step with each other. When they reached the deck above, she leaned on the filigreed railing, and he joined her. Since the Square was on an elevated patch of land, they looked out over the rooftops of Coldwater Cove as the ground dropped toward Lake Jewel.

"See," she said, pointing eastward. "The lake is just over there."

Michael frowned in that direction. "What's all that stuff down by the shoreline?"

"Don't you remember? The Rotary Club always does a corn maze for Halloween," Heather said. "Only it's more like hay bales with dried corn stalks strapped to them. It's how they raise money for their Christmas projects — you know, the toy drive and extra goodies for the community food pantry."

Michael's mouth lifted in a smile tinged with mischief.

"Oh, yeah. I remember helping Dad and the rest of the Rotarians build it one year. Skyler was in on it, too. He and I hollowed out a secret passage from one section of the maze to another, so we could hide from Wally Mushrush and his gang."

"Really? I don't remember him being a bully."

"He wasn't to the girls. But he got his growth spurt early, and he made sure all the guys knew it. He was a big kid with a tough mouth. Anyway, he and his toadies had been taking our lunch money pretty regular that year. Wally had double-dog dared us to meet him in the maze. Guess he figured it would be a good place to show us once and for all who was boss."

"And you naturally had to go."

"Like a moth to flame, but a moth with a plan." Michael leaned his elbows on the rail. "I knew I couldn't take him in a fist fight, especially not with his gang jumping in, too. So Skyler and me made ghillie suits out of corn shucks. We hid in our secret passage and jumped out at Mushrush from behind the stalks. We scared him so bad." Michael chuckled at the memory. "The poor kid screamed like a girl. He even peed his pants."

"Good times," Heather said sarcastically.

"I was a boy and boys find that kind of thing hilarious. Sue me. But the plan worked and I didn't have to give him a black eye to prove my point. Wally never took another nickel from me or anybody else."

"And now he goes by Wallace instead of Wally. He works with Danny Scott as a deputy sheriff."

"No kidding? Guess I scared him straight."

"Guess you did."

Silence stretched between them, but Heather didn't mind. There was no tension in the quiet. No sucking need to fill it with anything. It was satisfying just to stand beside Michael, to rest her head on his shoulder and feel her breathing fall into rhythm with his. They could simply *be* together. It was enough.

Almost.

If only he'd kiss me, he'd have so many checks on the good side of the ledger, I'd never even notice anything on the bad.

"Look," she whispered, not wanting to disturb the silence. Still, the lake was so beautiful she had to say something. "See the way the moonlight makes a jagged silver line across the water."

"Why, Nurse Walker, I didn't know you were a poet."

"Burns is a poet. Whitman is a poet. I am *so* not a poet."

"What do I know? It sounded pretty.

Besides, I always did better in subjects that involved something besides words."

The intensity of his gaze plucked at something deep inside her. She felt herself falling into his eyes. She'd wanted him to kiss her, but she was afraid he might and she'd lose herself in him. And if she did, would she ever be able to find her way out?

"Well, I guess I'd better go in," she said, edging toward her door.

"In a minute." He stopped her with a hand on her forearm.

Then he made her wish a reality. Very slowly, he cupped her cheeks. Michael bent his head, and his lips found hers.

In her dreams, a perfect good-night kiss was a mint-flavored treat in the pool of yellow light at her door. But that's only where this one started.

Michael's mouth was warm on hers, and the kiss began so gently, it was as if he feared she'd break. Then the kiss took a deeper turn, and he carried her to a dark, hot place she hadn't suspected was inside her.

His jacket slipped off her shoulders, but neither of them seemed willing to break off the kiss to pick it up. But at the same time, Heather realized they were pretty exposed out on the long deck she shared with all her neighbors.

I can't kiss him like this in front of God and everybody.

Of course, there was no everybody. And God could surely still see them if they were inside her apartment, but she'd feel better if He were the only one who could.

Her hand found the key in her pocket, and she fumbled with the door. Even when she shakily pulled away from Michael long enough to unlock it, he pressed baby kisses along her nape. She was back in his arms as they pushed through the open doorway, weaving in a drunken waltz though neither of them was the least buzzed from that wine at dinner.

He kicked the door closed behind them without stopping their kiss. Then he walked her backward to the nearest wall until her spine was flush against it. His body felt wonderful against hers, all strong and hard, but protective at the same time.

She'd always thought a kiss would tell her everything she needed to know about a guy. Michael's kiss said he was tender. And tough. That he knew how to give and how to take. He seemed to know what she needed before she did, and he was there to shower her with it. There was balance in his kiss. A solid comfort that made her want to trust him with everything, and that hint of danger that made a bad boy so irresistible.

She was so wrapped up in him, she didn't hear the insistent rapping on her door. It opened with a long creaking sound.

"Heather, what are you doing there in the dark?" a snuffly voice said. The lights flickered on. "Oh! I thought you were alone. I can come back later."

Heather came up for air, peered over Mike's shoulder, and saw Lacy framed in the doorway. Mike turned.

"Hey, sis. You don't believe in knocking?"

"I did knock. A lot." Her nose was red, a sure sign she'd been crying. Lacy was a pretty girl, but she wasn't a pretty crier. Unshed tears made her eyes overbright as her face crumpled. "I'm sorry I bothered you."

"What? No. You're no bother."

"If we're taking a vote here . . ." Michael began.

Heather silenced him with a look. "Come on in, Lacy. What's wrong?"

"I think Jake and I may have . . ." She sighed so deeply, she must have drawn it clear from her toes. "Well, I don't think there's going to be a wedding."

Heather blinked in surprise. Lacy and Jake were the most solid couple she knew. "Of course there'll be a wedding. Whatever's wrong, you'll work it out. I'm sure it's just a misunderstanding."

Lacy didn't look convinced. "Oh, no. I understand him perfectly."

She came in and plopped down on one of the bar stools at Heather's counter. Then Lacy's chin quivered as she folded her arms on the soapstone. She buried her face in them, sobbing as if the world were ending.

"Go find Jake and convince him to apologize," Heather whispered to Mike, pulling him toward the door.

"But what if it's not his fault?"

"Trust me. Even if he didn't do anything wrong, he probably still needs to apologize."

"Words for a guy to live by," Michael murmured. "Do you want me to bring him back here?"

"No. She's too upset. Let's let things simmer down," Heather said, "but by tomorrow we need to get those two back together."

"What do you know? Our first maid of honor/best man mission. And here I thought it was only going to be about the shower and the bachelor party." He pulled her close. "I liked the direction things were heading before Lacy turned up."

"Me too. Rain check?"

"Oh, yeah." He pressed a kiss to her temple. "But I gotta tell you I'm getting pretty tired of not catching a break."

"Giving up?"

"Fighting Marmots never say die."

She giggled. "Well, then, who knows? You may catch that break next time."

"OK. You. Me. The corn maze?"

There were plenty of quiet romantic spots hidden among the twists and turns. "As long as no corn shuck ghillie suits are involved."

"Done." He gave her a quick kiss. It was delicious with promise. Then he disappeared through the door. Most women would say he looked awfully good walking away. Heather thought he'd look even better if he was walking toward her, but Lacy needed her just then.

She sighed and turned back to her friend. "OK, Lace. What's up? Spill."

Lacy lifted her head and sniffed. "Jake is being a pigheaded jerk."

"No doubt. I hear there's a lot of that going around in the male population." Heather pulled a tissue from the dispenser on the counter and handed it to Lacy.

She blew her nose hard. "He won't even consider my side."

"Your side about what?"

"About me taking that job in Cambridge."

Heather couldn't have been more surprised if Lacy had said she wanted to flap her arms and fly to the moon. "But I thought you didn't want to move back East."

"Well, no, I don't. I love it here, but the job's in Cambridge." She balled the tissue in her fist. "And, oh, Heather, it's my dream job. I'd have complete artistic autonomy, no reporting to the partners before I implement a design. That's how much they trust me. And they must really want me, too, because every time I turn them down, they up the ante. You won't believe what they offered me."

Heather's jaw dropped when Lacy named an astronomical figure. It had been a big deal when Lacy found an unknown Erté a few months ago. The discovery had sent shock waves through the design and art world and sealed Lacy's reputation as a first-class tastemaker. But Heather had no idea a design firm would have such deep pockets.

"I'm a rainmaker, they say. Just my name on the company letterhead will bring in high-end clients," Lacy explained. "But I can't ride the Erté find forever. If I don't follow it up with some first-rate work that gets noticed by the right people, it might as well not have happened."

Lacy's work won awards and had been featured in tons of glossy design spreads. She had a unique way of fusing Old World architectural elements with industrial kitsch. But as she often told Heather, a designer was only as good as her last project.

"And you'd have to work in the Boston area?"

Lacy shrugged. "At some level, every artistic field is about networking. It's hard to meet the type of client that needs my services in Coldwater Cove."

"OK, I get that." Heather's chest constricted. In the few months Lacy had been home, they'd become so tight, Lacy had started to fill up the empty spot Jessica had left in Heather's heart. It hurt to think she might lose her best friend, too, but she couldn't dwell on that. Lacy obviously needed her support. However much it cost her. "What would Jake do back East?"

"Whatever he wanted to do. I'd be making enough that he wouldn't even have to take a job if he didn't want to."

Jake was the most industrious guy Heather knew. Even with a prosthetic leg, he could work most men under the table. "Bet that idea went over like a lead balloon."

"Why? Because the man's supposed to be the breadwinner?"

"No, of course not. But Jake's justifiably proud of the Green Apple and it's not like he can pack it up and take it with him." She didn't add that any man, not just a wounded warrior, wouldn't like the passenger seat much. Jake was a driver. He'd never be satisfied with being a kept man. "You may have given him the idea that you think what he does isn't important."

"I don't think that."

"But you want him to abandon everything he's worked for since he came home from Afghanistan."

"What about everything I worked for? I studied with a passion to get where I was before. . . . oh, I don't want to go into all that junk again." Lacy waved away the sorry mess of how she'd lost her once-successful design studio in Boston when her partner embezzled from their clients. "But I so miss being able to be creative, Heather. It's like part of my soul is shut off without it."

"I wouldn't know anything about being creative. I can't operate a glue gun without burning all ten fingers." Heather put the kettle on. This was shaping up to be a full pot discussion. "But I thought you were OK with not being a designer anymore. Didn't you tell Jake you wanted to stay in Coldwater Cove?"

"Yes, but that was before I got a taste of working with light and space and color again."

Heather cocked her head at Lacy in puzzlement.

"Michael has leased all of the Ouachita Inn — and I mean all of it, bunkhouses, barns, everything — and I've been helping him redesign and make over the space into a creative working campus — sort of a mini-Google."

"Why is he doing that?"

"He wants to be around while Mom is going through chemo and he's well off enough to be able to bring a large portion of his office here. His development team is coming in next week."

"Mike's planning on staying in Coldwater?" If she'd had a heart monitor on, it would have been beeping like crazy. "For good?"

"I don't know about for good, but his company will definitely have a local presence for the foreseeable future. He took out a multiyear lease on the ranch. Maybe he's thinking about using it as a corporate retreat after Mom is doing better." Lacy shrugged.

"It'll take five years of clean mammograms

before we can use the word 'cure' with your mom," Heather said cautiously as she put tea bags into the kettle to steep. Was Michael planning to stay that long?

"Anyway, the fact that Michael is stepping up for Mom has let me do some rethinking about things. And getting to do design work has made me feel . . . like I'm myself again." Lacy knotted her fingers before her. "After months of pecking away at the *Gazette* in the same job I did when I was in high school, it feels so good to be playing with textures and fabrics and letting my imagination soar. It's like I was handcuffed before and now I'm free."

"But do you want to be free of Jake?"

Lacy's eyes welled. "No. I love him with all my heart. But why should I have to choose? Why can't I have Jake *and* a job that feeds my soul?"

"In a perfect world you could, but the world is far from perfect. What will you do?"

"I don't know. This thing in Cambridge is a limited-time deal. The contract with the design firm is for two years, renewable if both parties agree. But if I pass on it now, it's gone for good."

"Men are sort of like that, too, I hear. Do you think Jake will wait while you're back East?"

"I don't know. What would you do if you had to give up nursing to be with the man you love?"

That struck a nerve. Healing people was what Heather was born to do. She drew her friend into a tight hug.

Definitely a full teapot of a problem.

She hoped Mike would have better luck with Jake.

Chapter 23

Be careful before you say "I do," son,
because I'm here to tell you,
you surely will.
— Grandma "Tina-Louise" Bugtussle
to Junior before he and Darlene
tied the knot

Mike pounded on the back door of the Green Apple until Jake came down the stairs to glower at him through the screen.

"Heard you had a rough night." Michael hoisted a cold six-pack as a peace offering and Jake waved him in. Michael followed him up the stairs to Jake's place above the grill. For the first time, he was aware of Jake's titanium leg because he climbed up with such labored steps.

Jake's shaggy little dog, Speedbump, met them at the top of the stairs and circled nervously. The mop with feet was clearly picking up on his master's mood.

"I don't want to talk about it," Jake said.

"Good. I don't want to listen." He popped the top off one of the longnecks and handed it to Jake. "Let's just drink."

"Roger that."

Jake tipped back the bottle and downed half of it before he came up for air. "Why is it women think they have to change a man?"

OK. Turns out we are talking. "Don't know. Do you?"

"Yeah. It's most likely because we need changing." Jake sank onto the leather sectional. A football game played across the big screen on the wall, but the sound was muted. "If you repeat that to your sister, I'll knock you into next week."

"Hey. I'm the best man. That means I'm on your side. Bros before . . ." He stopped himself as he settled on the opposite end of the sectional. He couldn't say "hos." This was his sister he was talking about. His favorite sister to boot. He finished the thought with "Twinkle Toes."

"Huh?"

"Twinkle Toes. I used to call Lacy that back when we were kids and she was taking dance lessons. She sucked at it, by the way."

"If she did, it's one of the few things. She's really pretty incredible at everything she does."

"Glad to hear you say so." They knocked longnecks in a silent toast to a woman they both loved.

"I'm the luckiest man on the planet to have her. I'd do anything for her, you know."

"I do." Mike nodded.

"I'd take a bullet for her in a flat minute."

"Of course you would." Michael found himself thinking about Heather. He couldn't come up with anything he wouldn't do for her either. Did that mean he loved her?

"But Lacy's asking too much this time."

"Got that right," Mike said to be agreeable, then wondered what it was he was agreeing to. "Maybe you want to catch me up on what she's asking?"

Jake explained about Lacy's job offer. "She wants me to give up everything — my family, my friends, the grill, everything I have. It's too much, right?"

"If you think it is, it must be." Michael wondered if he could give up MoreCommas for Heather. If she'd ever expect him to. No, it wouldn't come to that. Just like he dealt with Wally Mushrush without full-blown fisticuffs, he'd find a work-around. He was already trying to figure out how to spend the lion's share of his time in Coldwater Cove. With teams rotating out from the Big Apple, he'd be able to stick around in town until his mother was done with her cancer treatments at least. After that, he hoped to find the sweet spot between telecommuting to the New York office and flying back there only when his physical presence was absolutely essential.

But Jake couldn't exactly man the Green Apple Grill from Cambridge. There had to be another way for him and Lacy.

Now Mike had to help Jake find it.

The time spent digging through the dungeon at the *Coldwater Gazette* yielded an unexpected ally for Judith. She had accidentally befriended Deek Atwater, the bespectacled computer nerd of the newspaper staff.

She'd done this without intending to when she didn't offer to shake his hand at their first meeting. As it turned out, the kid was a germophobe on steroids. He took her refusal to give him the conventional greeting as an invitation to a strangely one-sided friendship.

Deek had found a kindred spirit.

While she was combing through the records in the basement, the young man made excuses to come down often, and he tended to hover. He didn't so much as brush her with an arm hair, but he certainly invaded her personal space more often that she'd have liked. He watched her when he thought she wasn't looking, his gaze darting away guiltily whenever she glanced his way. Once, she was sure he'd even followed her back to Mrs. Chisholm's grand old house, always staying a block and a half behind her.

It might have seemed a little stalkerish except that there was nothing the least threatening about Deek. It was as if she were an exotic new species who'd invaded his lonely little world and he couldn't help but be drawn to study her.

Deek had no sense of ordinary interactions with others. Judith never heard him in casual conversation with any of his coworkers, but they all had plenty to say about him. He could make a computer dance across the table, they all agreed. Lacy Evans suspected him of being a hacker in his spare time. But if Deek did cyberinvade places he wasn't supposed to be in, Judith suspected he was the sort to treat the Internet as if it were a national park.

Take nothing but pictures, leave nothing but footprints.

Deek would likely do one better. He'd take nothing but screenshots and leave an electronic footprint so faint no one would ever know he'd been there.

His coworkers used many words to describe him. Second only to "weird," "brilliant" was the one used most often.

Judith decided to add "useful" to the list.

She discovered with no surprise that he lived with his mother.

Probably in the basement. There's a grain of truth in every cliché.

Mrs. Atwater, a round little woman with her gray hair slicked back into a painfully tight bun, squinted at Judith through the screen door when she knocked.

"You're wasting your time. I never buy anything from peddlers," she said stonily.

"I'm not selling anything," Judith said. "I'm Dr. Hildebrand and I've come to see Deek."

Mrs. Atwater's mouth opened and closed twice without making a sound. Then she called out "Deacon!" with a tremor of disbelief in her voice. "You have a visitor."

"Tell him to go away!" came a voice from overhead.

All right. He's in the attic, not the basement. I was still close.

"But it's a lady visitor, son."

"Then tell *her* to go away."

"Deek, it's Judith," she called.

He came tromping down the steep set of stairs so fast, she was afraid he'd fall and break his neck before she could convince him to do her bidding.

He skidded to a stop before her, but couldn't quite bring himself to meet her eyes.

"What are you doing here?" he asked.

"Deacon, have you forgotten all your home training?" his mother said reprovingly. "That's not how we treat guests. Ask the lady if she'd like a glass of lemonade."

"She doesn't want any," Deek said woodenly. "Lemons are highly acidic and can erode tooth enamel."

"Deacon!"

Judith saw a quick way to score with the kid, so she took it. "Actually, Deek's right. I don't want lemonade." His smile was pathetically grateful. "And I'm not really a guest, you see. I've come to ask Deek for help."

"Then you might do him the courtesy of using his given name," his mother muttered. "Why does everyone have to call him something that rhymes with 'squeak'?"

Because Deek the Geek is too good to pass up, Judith thought but couldn't say. Not if she wanted his help. "Is there someplace we can speak in private?"

His eyes widened, but he motioned for her to follow him up the stairs.

"Deacon, this is wrong. Ladies aren't supposed to push themselves forward like this," his mother scolded, her voice climbing in both pitch and decibels as Judith headed toward the foot of the stairs. "Ma'am, you are far too old to be calling on my son."

Judith stifled a growl under her breath. She did everything she could to mask her age, from dressing as if she were much younger, to spending more than she could afford on cosmetics. Hearing someone call her "ma'am" always ruined her whole day. But she couldn't afford a temper tantrum just now.

"Don't worry, Mrs. Atwater," Judith said as she climbed the stairs behind Deek. "My visit is purely professional."

"That only makes it worse," the old woman muttered.

Deek had commandeered a peaked attic space that ran the entire length of the house. A door at the far end probably hid his actual bedroom. The rest of the space was dedicated to Deek's interests. In addition to an astonishing assortment of electronics, Deek's room also housed an exhaustive collection of Star Wars action figures and an insect collection Judith took pains not to examine too closely. Posters of anime characters were pinned to the sloping ceiling, and comic books in carefully cataloged acid-free dust covers were neatly arranged in alphabetical order, cataloged by superhero.

"What do you need help with . . . Judith?" he added shyly. It was the first time he'd called her anything besides Dr. Hildebrand.

"I know you have amazing computer skills. Everyone says so."

He blushed to the roots of his hair.

"I understand you sometimes slip into places on the Web where you haven't been invited."

"I'm not a black hat."

"Oh, I never thought that. Not for a minute," she said quickly. "You're definitely a well-meaning hacker."

"Hacker is an ugly word," he said in a clipped tone. "We call ourselves 'white hats,' and while I may have made an unauthorized entry from time to time, I never do any damage."

His preciousness about his self-image was starting to wear on her nerves. "Look, I'm not here to insult you. I just want to know if you have the chops to do what I need."

"What's that?"

She walked over to him, invading his imaginary eighteen inches of personal space. He might not be aware of when he did it to others, but he certainly didn't like it when someone did it to him. He took a step back.

"I need someone who's smart enough and brave enough to hack into the local law enforcement and the hospital."

"That'd be illegal."

"So is what I'm investigating. There's been a terrible injustice and a cover-up here in this little town. Do you think it's right that a young girl died and no one has been made to answer for it?"

"Who died?" he asked, blood draining from his already pale complexion.

"Jessica Walker."

"That happened ages ago," he said. "I was like, nine or ten."

"But you remember it?"

He rolled his eyes. "I remember everything. I remember I had sausage and biscuits for breakfast the morning they pulled her car out of the lake. Mother had oatmeal."

Judith bit her lip to keep from saying something that would surely offend him. "Then you must remember what people said about her death at the time."

"It was just an accident."

Judith shook her head. "It was much more and you're going to help me prove it. If you're man enough." One of the comic books caught her eye. "No, make that *hero* enough. I need someone to dig out the truth and fight for justice."

"I don't fight. Mother doesn't approve of violence."

"It's just an expression, Deek. Help me uncover the truth. You can fight from behind your computer screen, can't you?"

His chest expanded, and he turned on the nearest laptop. "Who are you investigating?"

"Heroes always have secrets they need to keep," she said. "Can I count on you to keep this search just between us?"

"Of course, Judith. It'll be our little secret. Something only we two share."

"OK." That sounded pretty creepy, but she was out of options. She couldn't get past that Latina dispatcher to search the sheriff's records no matter how often she threatened to invoke the Freedom of Information Act. And she was certain she'd never be able to legally see any hospital records without a court order.

"This'll take a minute." Deek's fingers flew over the keyboard. He pounded. He plugged devices into the ports that sent blinking lights dancing across the ceiling while Judith paced behind him. In a remarkably short time, he announced, "We're in."

"The hospital or sheriff's office?"

"Both. Which one do you want first?"

Against her better judgment, she threw her arms around him and gave him a hug. He stiffened.

"Um. You're touching me."

She straightened and stepped back. "Sorry. It won't happen again."

"I can't blame you. I'd hug me, too. After all, I douse myself in antibacterial soap every day. I'm the only one clean enough to touch myself." He cast her a sideways glance. "But you're a close second. So now, what do you want me to search for?"

"Every reference to Jessica Walker, of course," she said. "And Michael Evans."

Chapter 24

I don't want to be a bridezilla, but I want even less to play Fay Wray to my mother's King Kong. If I don't watch it, she'll turn my wedding ceremony into a remake of the *Bride of Frankenstein.* Jake has always wanted to elope. I'm this close to climbing out the window with him.

— Lacy Evans, after the Battle of the Bridesmaids' Dresses

Heather was always a careful driver, two hands on the wheel and all that, but she was concerned enough about Lacy to pull her gaze from the tree-lined street long enough to cast a sideways glance at her friend. Lacy was drumming her fingers on her thighs, nervous energy pulsing from her.

"Are you sure you're up for this?" Heather asked.

"Yeah. After what Jake and I went through

last night, I can face anything," Lacy said. "Even Mom's plans for the wedding."

"It's your wedding, Lace. You don't have to cave on everything just because she's going through cancer treatments," Heather said. "In fact, it'd be better for her if you didn't. The best thing you can do for your mom is treat her like you always do. She needs to feel normal."

"But what if butting heads on every little thing is our normal?"

"Come on. Your relationship isn't that bad."

"Yes, it is. Don't get me wrong. We love each other to pieces, but Mom and I haven't agreed on anything but the color of the sky since I was ten," Lacy said. "And even that's open to argument."

"But this is your wedding, not hers."

"True, but you gotta understand what's driving her," Lacy said. "She comes from a really poor hill family. When she married my dad, it was at the courthouse before a justice of the peace. She never got to have any frippery or frufurrahs. She made up for some of that with Crystal's over-the-top wedding, but it looks like she's still got some unresolved nuptial notions she's dealing with now."

"Well, let her win a few then. Pick your

battles and get your way on the stuff that's really important to you," Heather said. "And speaking of battles, what did you and Jake decide to do about that job offer?"

"We decided not to decide until after the wedding. What with Mom's cancer treatments and Michael being home, well, every family get-together feels like we're coiled tight as a bag of Slinkys. So Jake and I agreed to table the question of where we'll be living after we get married," Lacy said. "For now, anyway."

"How did you come to that arrangement?"

"Jake showed up on my doorstep at dawn this morning." She sighed deeply. "Oh, Heather, he looked so miserable. I couldn't stay mad at him. I love him so much it makes my chest hurt."

"Could be an aneurysm," Heather said, straight-faced.

Lacy rolled her eyes. "Yeah. Like you don't have the same goofy feelings for my brother. I've got eyes. You two are crazy about each other, whether you're willing to admit it or not."

"We're not talking about me and Mike now."

"Maybe we should. It'd be easier."

"For you." Heather still wasn't sure how

to name the ache that started inside her whenever she thought about Michael. It wasn't painful. Not exactly. But it sure wasn't comfortable either. "You were so set on heading back East last night. What did Jake say to make you change your mind?"

"No mind changing went on. We just tabled the issue, OK? But if it comes right down to it and if I have to give up the Cambridge job, so be it. I can't give up Jake."

Heather wished Lacy wasn't the only one doing the giving, but it wasn't her call. She didn't want Lacy to have regrets about a road not traveled later on. Still, if her friend was satisfied, Heather would make approving noises. Besides, a selfish part of her didn't want Lacy leaving town either.

When they pulled into the Evanses' drive, Heather realized someone had beaten them there. A white van was parked in front of the garage. "The Bride Side" was stenciled along the passenger door in delicate filigree. Pale pink flowers and silver swirls flowed over the rear wheel wells. The other side of the van was splashed with "Teeter Guns & Ammo." Under the stark red and black lettering, it said, "When only a shotgun will do . . ." The Teeters had caused quite a stir when they first had their Jekyll and Hyde vehicle painted like that, but it couldn't be helped. Mitzi Teeter had explained to Heather that her husband had refused to let her invest in a new van for her bridal shop unless he could use it for his business, too.

"But the first time he leaves it dirty and I get gun oil on a dress, I'm going all graffiti monkey on his side of the van with glitter-in-a-can," Mitzi had said adamantly. "And then I'll hide his keys."

Laura, Jake's pretty dark-eyed sister, was helping Mitzi unload a hanging bar draped with dozens of zippered bags. They fit the bar onto a wheeled cart and pushed it through the Evanses' open front door.

"Guess I should have asked before, but what are we doing today? I thought your mom said we were making table favors," Heather said.

"That's part of the program. She has her heart set on making votive holders out of Mason jars, burlap, and lace."

"That sounds pretty." Heather flexed her not-so-handy fingers. "Did I mention I'm no good with a glue gun?"

Mitzi came back out of the house and wheeled in another rack of dresses. Lacy eyed them doubtfully.

"Don't worry. It'll take the whole morning for me to try on all those gowns," Lacy said with resignation. "We probably won't get to the crafty portion of our day until later this afternoon. Since you have the perfect excuse of needing to be at work by three, you'll miss out on wielding a glue gun. This morning it seems I'm picking out my dress."

"You haven't done that yet?" Heather couldn't have been more surprised. "Lacy! Your wedding is only a month away. I thought finding the right gown was job number one on every bride's to-do list."

"To be honest, I thought I had it covered. Ever since I was a little girl, I've wanted to wear Grandmother Evans's wedding gown. It's up in the attic in a cedar chest, perfectly preserved."

"What's it like?"

"It's a beautiful design — sort of old Hollywood. Sleek and elegant in ivory satin with lace overlay. The train goes for miles."

"Does it fit?"

"Like it was made for me," Lacy said as the two of them walked toward the front door. "But Mom is set on me having a new gown. She says wearing an old one will make it look like Dad and she are skimping on me, and she can't have that. I can wear Grandma's pearls as something borrowed, she says, but the dress of my dreams stays in the attic."

Heather was about to suggest that this was a battle Lacy might have wanted to fight, but if her friend was satisfied with peace at any price, she should be too. "Maybe Mitzi has something like it."

"And maybe I'll sprout wings."

"Don't do that. We'll never find a dress to fit you."

Lacy's mother met them at the door. "Oh, good! You're here."

Mrs. Evans had gone a little heavy on the foundation that morning, but Heather still detected faint dark smudges below her eyes. Chemo was hard on anyone's beauty routine.

"Isn't this lovely?" Shirley Evans said. "When Mitzi heard I was a little under the weather, she knew I wouldn't enjoy shopping as much as I usually do. So, bless her heart, she's brought her shop to us."

Only Shirley Evans would describe fighting cancer as being "a little under the weather." Heather admired her resilience.

The Evanses' little Yorkie came out from under a sofa to greet them with yips and yelps, as if to warn them that the house was being overrun with garment bags, and human attention must be directed at this sudden infestation immediately. Lacy stooped to pet him and then scooped him into her arms. He settled immediately, no longer caring that there was anything unusual going on.

"Is Dad home?" Lacy asked.

"No," Shirley said. "I convinced him that the estrogen level in this house would be too high for his comfort today, so he's gone up to the senior center to call out numbers for the bingo tournament."

"You don't think he'll want to see Lacy's dress?" Heather asked.

"No. Whatever we decide on will be fine with him. My George isn't much of a shopper." She tactfully refrained from mentioning that he'd be more interested in seeing the price tag than the dress itself. According to Lacy, spending money was the main reason for his shopping avoidance. Not that Mr. Evans was tight, of course. He liked to say he was thrifty. Heather bet he would've loved the idea of Lacy wearing his mother's gown.

"I take after Dad, so that makes two anti-shoppers in the family," Lacy said with a grin. "Whip me, beat me. Don't make me shop."

Heather knew Lacy wasn't allergic to spending money. She'd happily go "buying" any time, but Lacy considered "shopping" without a firm objective a waste of time. She especially hated trying on clothes, preferring to order things over the Internet and then sending them back if she didn't like them once they arrived.

Heather couldn't do that. Her height made trying things on absolutely essential, but that was fine with her because she really loved the hunt. Finding a new piece to add to her wardrobe was always a win. And if she could find it on sale, so much the better.

Shirley sighed. "Yes, I'm afraid the shopping gene skipped my younger daughter. But I think I've found a way to fix that." She crooked her finger, signaling for them to follow. "Come with me."

Heather and Lacy trailed Shirley into the family room, where Laura was already setting out a tray of cookies and Crystal was filling tall frosty glasses with sweet tea.

"Hey, Lacy," Laura said, coming to give her future sister-in-law a quick hug. "Aren't you excited about trying on all these dresses?"

"No, she's probably not," Crystal said. "Unless she's shopping for a design client, Lacy's as bad as Dad."

"Well, that doesn't matter because I've got the perfect solution to the problem,"

Lacy's mom said. She beamed at Heather, Crystal, and Laura. "The three of you wear about the same dress size as Lacy, so you're going to be her models today."

"But how will that work? Heath— I mean, some of us are so much taller than Lacy," Crystal said.

Fighting the urge to slump, Heather straightened her spine. Crystal might have been able to make her feel awkward when they were kids, but not anymore.

"Doesn't matter," Mitzi said, as she took one of the garment bags off a rack. "A difference in height may change the hemline and maybe where the waist falls, but Lacy can still get a good idea about whether or not she likes the dress by seeing it on any of you."

"There, it's all settled," Shirley said. "Lacy and I are going to sit here together like ladies of leisure, eating gingersnaps and sipping iced tea, while the three of you try on the dresses and model them for us. Then when Lacy has narrowed her choice to just a couple of gowns, she can try those few on to make her final decision."

"Mom, you're wonderful." Lacy's eyes welled with tears, and she threw her arms around her mother. "Just when I think I've got you figured out. Thanks so much for understanding. And for having ginger-snaps."

"I know my girls and I know they're your favorite, honey. Just like I knew you'd hate trying on so many dresses." Shirley hugged her back and patted Lacy's head when she gave a little sob. "Hush, darling. This is for your day. We can't have you stressing over it, can we?"

"No, I guess not." Lacy dabbed at her eyes and then smiled at her mother. "This is going to be a lot more fun than I expected."

Shirley Evans is smarter than the average mother.

She'd found a way to make Lacy feel beholden to her for coming up with this sweet compromise. If she'd asked Lacy to parade down the aisle in a barrel with suspenders just then, she'd have agreed in a heartbeat.

"OK, then. Quick like a bunny, girls." Shirley clapped her hands three times fast. "Grab a dress, head up to my room and put it on. Then one at a time, you can make a grand entrance down the long staircase so we can see how beautiful you look."

Heather followed Laura and Crystal up to Mrs. E's big bedroom. At least, it would have been big if she hadn't centered a king-sized four-poster along one wall and ringed the rest with chests of drawers and occasional tables of every stripe. On every horizontal surface there were collectible figurines or colorful glassware. The room wasn't cluttered up to hoarder levels, but it was close.

Mitzi joined them to help with zippers and buttons. She buzzed around each of them as needed, like a honeybee tending a patch of daisies. Other than Mitzi's soft chatter, the room felt too quiet as they disrobed and slipped into satin and taffeta.

"I enjoyed Riley's recital the other night," Heather said to break the ice. "Thanks for including me."

"Ha. You know where liars go, Heather." Crystal rolled her eyes. "Riley was a total disaster."

"I thought she was a delight."

"I see Michael has been coloring your perceptions of her," Crystal said with a sigh. "I wish she was more like Ethan. Riley's a catastrophe waiting to happen. That child will be the death of me. She's far too much like her uncle for comfort. Oh, sorry."

"For what?"

"Well, you two are a couple now, so . . ."

A couple of what, I'd like to know. "Mike doesn't need me to defend him if that's what you mean." *But it sounds like Riley does.*

"Anyway, I'd hoped dance lessons would teach her something about the value of working with a group," Crystal went on, "but as you saw, Riley dances to a different drummer."

"She's charming."

"She's a handful," Crystal said, still refusing to accept a compliment for her daughter.

Oh, I'm so seeing therapy in that kid's future.

"So since ballet didn't work, I'm trying to talk Noah into signing her up for tumbling," Crystal said as she eyed her reflection critically and adjusted her pillbox hat and veil. She looked like a Jackie O throwback from the '60s, but Heather didn't say anything. Lacy's tastes were quirky enough that the style might appeal to her. "Gymnastics is a team sport, but it allows for individual participation."

"That might work well for Riley," Heather agreed to be agreeable. "Just be sure the gym has plenty of spotters around the trampoline. The hospital has a new pediatrician who won't take on any patients whose parents allow them to have a backyard trampoline."

"Well, that's a little heavy-handed." Laura joined the conversation for the first time.

"Dr. Stratton doesn't think so." Even if it was, Heather doubted Beckett Stratton would care. Like many of the doctors she worked with, the new pediatrician was afflicted with a bit of a god complex. Still, Coldwater General was lucky to have attracted the young doctor. Lots of small towns had no pediatric specialist at all. "He's pretty adamant about a strict no-tramp policy."

"Why is that?" Laura asked.

"I'm guessing he lost a patient or two to trampoline accidents back in Arizona. That's where he came from."

Laura stood still while Mitzi hooked a long row of buttons down her spine. With a sweetheart neckline and a waist that dipped in a low V in front, the gown was a Victorian confection, a froth of lace and seed pearls. The skirt was so wide it required a hooped slip beneath it.

"Well, Mom doesn't have a trampoline, so I guess he'd take my Zoey on," Laura said. "We don't have a pediatrician here yet."

"You have a daughter?" Heather said in surprise. After going to college in California, Laura had moved back in with her mom a month ago. Everyone said it was a blessing for Mary Tyler to have someone else in the house since she'd lost her husband. But somehow the fact that Laura had brought her a grandchild, too, had escaped the Coldwater gossip grapevine.

Laura smiled shyly. "Zoey's only six months old. We don't get out much."

Heather noticed for the first time that Laura was wearing a gold band on her left hand. She'd been about five years behind Heather in school, so she figured Laura was only twenty-four or so. "Forgive me, I didn't know you were married. I was still thinking you're a Tyler."

"I still am. We got married in Vegas one weekend when Trent was on leave. After that, I was head down trying to finish up my degree, and then Zoey came along pretty quickly, and what with school and planning for a baby and everything, I never got around to filling out the forms for a legal name change." Laura studied the oak floor before her with absorption. "Not much point now, I guess. I'm . . . I'm a widow. My husband was killed in a training accident at Camp Pendleton the week after Zoey was born."

Heather gasped. "Oh, Laura, I had no idea."

"You really should, you know," Crystal said, reapplying a fresh coat of Maybelline and smacking her lips together. "Get your name changed, I mean. The last thing a child needs in a town as small as Coldwater Cove is to grow up with her mother's maiden name. People talk."

Heather shot a dagger glare at Crystal and then turned back to Laura. "I'm so sorry for your loss."

It was what people said when they didn't know what to say, but in this case Heather meant every word. She couldn't imagine a harder row to hoe than raising a child alone.

"Do you plan to stay in Coldwater Cove?" Crystal asked.

"I don't know. It's been a comfort to be with my mom. She's still sort of at loose ends without Dad, even though he's been gone for a while now. She knows what I'm going through. And she's great help with Zoey."

"Well, you really should finish your degree," Crystal said. "Bates will grant transfer credits if your coursework can be shown to be comparable to ours."

As dean of admissions of tiny Bates College, Crystal was always touting the school's credentials, which were impeccable. Of course, most of the degrees it offered were terribly impractical. Graduates were pretty much guaranteed *not* to find employment in their field of study. But in a world gone mad for math and science, it could be argued that there was a crying need for liberal arts.

Heather slipped into the gown Mitzi had laid out for her. With trails of chiffon and twinkling crystals, it seemed ethereal and airy enough to be worn by a woodland nymph. The asymmetrical cut bodice was lightly boned so that the off-the-shoulder straps could be purely decorative instead of functional. The hemline was pooled in a froth at her feet, and a train of about a foot and a half floated behind her.

"This would be far too long for Lacy."

"We can always take it up," Mitzi said.

"That's a pretty gown, Heather," Laura said. "Looks like something the elves would wear in Rivendell."

"In where?" Crystal asked.

"Rivendell. Don't you read Tolkien?" Heather said, enjoying exposing a gap in Crystal's knowledge.

"Tall, strong, fierce and wise, yet beautiful," Laura said admiringly. "Tolkien's elves were a magnificent race. You'd fit right in, Heather."

"No pointy ears," she said as she adjusted a circlet of silk flowers around her head and smiled at her reflection. She'd never thought of herself as beautiful, but in this dress, she almost was.

"Well, we'd better get downstairs. If we leave Lacy and Mom alone together too long, there will be blood — metaphorically speaking, of course," Crystal said before she minced down the stairs, her posture perfectly erect, her heels clicking on the hardwood.

Laura followed her in the full-skirted Victorian, and Heather brought up the rear in the gown that made her feel more feminine than ever before in her life. She thought about slipping into her sandals.

Nuts to that. Any elf princess worth her salt would go barefoot.

Silent as a cat, she padded after the other two down the long staircase.

Chapter 25

A tux makes you sort of invisible. Putting on a penguin suit makes you look just like the other penguins.

— Michael Evans, who would never be confused with a penguin

The front door to his parents' home was ajar, so Michael went on in. He'd intended to drop in on his mom for a few minutes to see how she was feeling that morning, but he almost drove on by when he saw the driveway was full of vehicles. Then he'd recognized Heather's car as one of them and couldn't pass up a chance to see her.

But he almost didn't recognize her coming down the staircase.

A goddess was descending, her bare toes peeping from beneath a frothy hemline. With her hair loose and framing her face, and in that dress that defied gravity by staying up with no visible means of support, she was so otherworldly gorgeous, he almost expected her to have wings.

There was no hint of "Stilts" in this lithe and lovely apparition. The sternly efficient Nurse Walker was gone. Instead, this Heather looked soft. Vulnerable. As if she might actually need someone like him.

Everything in him longed to shelter her. He wished he had the right to protect her from all harm.

Down, boy. She's just independent enough to bean you for even thinking that she might need your protection.

"Careful, Michael." She stopped on the bottom step, and put a couple of fingers under his chin. "Someone might mistake you for a codfish."

Heather gently lifted her fingers to make him close his mouth, which he hadn't realized was hanging open. She tried to hide her amusement and failed miserably.

"I can't help it, Heather. You're . . . you're . . ."

"I'd appreciate making you speechless if your stammering didn't sound so very surprised," she said.

"It's just that you look . . ."

Amazing. Beautiful. Michael wasn't one for words, but tons of superlatives scrolled through his mind just then. The only problem was he couldn't find one that began to be fine enough for her.

"I don't look a bit like me, do I?" she said with a conspiratorial grin.

"No, you look entirely like you. Only . . . more so." The fact that the dress she was wearing was a bridal gown suddenly hit him in the temple with the force of a wild pitch. "Why are you in a wedding dress?"

She rolled her eyes. "It's not a hint."

Part of him was disappointed. Last night, when he and Jake were talking and drinking, the Marine vet had confided how crazy he was about Lacy, and how it made him stupid sometimes. Michael recognized the same reaction in himself. He knew he was a smart guy — in some ways, at least — but every time he was around Heather, he felt like a dimwit. She made him both strong and weak, confused and surprisingly clear.

Was that love?

"This dress is for Lacy," she explained. "Crystal, Laura, and I are modeling for her. There are tons of styles for us to try on, but I have a feeling this is the one she'll pick."

"If she doesn't, she's nuts. But my sister won't begin to look as good in it as you do." He pulled her close and she came willingly. Their foreheads touched. Their breaths mingled, and before he knew it, he was kissing her right there at the base of the wooden staircase he used to slide down while riding on a cookie sheet.

Heather's mouth was a much better ride, and he wouldn't end up with splinters in his butt.

Then she worked her hands between them and pressed her palms against his chest. When he broke off their kiss, she grabbed his shoulders and turned him around.

"Now, out, Mister," she said. "There's nothing but chiffon and satin and silk around here this morning. It's no place for a guy."

"Hey! Maybe Lacy would like a man's opinion." The thought of seeing Heather in more silk and satin made his mouth go dry.

She shook her head. "If a woman wants a man to have an opinion about her wedding dress, she'll give it to him. Now, go. I'll tell your mom you dropped by."

"We're still on for tonight, right?" He'd been looking forward to exploring the corn maze with her. Among other things . . .

A cute little wrinkle formed between her brows. "Oh, shoot. I forgot. Jane asked me to switch schedules with her. I have to work till eleven tonight."

Mike wasn't ready to give up on seeing her. "Perfect. The maze should be almost empty by then. I'll come by your place around eleven fifteen."

"Make it eleven thirty. I'll need a shower."

The thought of Heather all soapy and wet was even better than wrapped in silk and lace.

"Heather," Lacy called from the family room. "What's the holdup?"

She stood on tiptoe and gave him a smack on the cheek. "Thanks for understanding. Gotta go."

Then she turned, lifted her hem, and trotted down the hall toward the back of the house. Her hair bounced back and forth as it had when she was "Stilts" loping down the court.

Michael released a long sigh.

He'd always watched her, always wondered about her, always been drawn to that long-legged girl. Even when he'd had to leave town and there seemed little hope he'd ever see her again, much less have a shot with her, he carried the memory of the girl he hoped she was inside him.

Now he knew her for real. She was even better than he'd let himself imagine.

And he knew, then and there, he was going to marry Heather Walker someday.

No matter what it took.

■ ■ ■ ■

The night was brisk, the stars shivering pinpricks in the dark sky. But Michael's hand was warm when it closed over hers. They walked hand in hand for the few blocks from her place down to the public park on the lakeshore.

"There are more people still going through the maze than I thought there'd be. I thought it shut down before this," Heather said. "Coldwater usually turns up its toes when the news comes on at ten."

A chorus of howls and shrieks came from inside the construction of hay and cornstalks. Someone set off a string of firecrackers about fifty yards from the entrance, and the Rotarians who were collecting the required canned goods left their post to chase after the punk with the fuse. As soon as the entrance was unguarded, a full dozen high school kids ran in to join the group already inside the maze, without dropping a donation into the bins.

Mike shook his head. "That's something I would've done. Stupid kids."

"Makes you feel a little old though, doesn't it?"

"Yeah, I guess. Or maybe just a little wiser.

If those fireworks had gone wrong, a spark could have sent up the whole maze. But when I was their age, I never thought about what might happen either."

More howling came from the maze, followed by squeals of laughter.

"Maybe we should just walk along the lakeshore," Heather suggested. He nodded and put an arm around her waist as they changed direction. It felt so good to be beside him.

Almost as if it's meant to be.

"This doesn't bother you?" he finally said as they neared the softly lapping water.

Heather didn't pretend to misunderstand him. They'd stopped only a few yards from where Jessica had driven her car into Lake Jewel. "It used to. At first, I couldn't bear to even look at the lake. But after a while . . . well, time passes, summer, winter, snow and rain. It's not like the grief is ever completely washed away, but the ache I used to feel when I'm around the lake has faded."

She sat on a rock outcropping and let her legs swing over the edge. There was still a good two-foot drop to the water below her feet.

"Now when I come down to the lake, I remember the good times when Jess and I would go swimming. Or when Dad would rent a pontoon for the day and we'd lie out in the sun and get brown as berries."

"I remember that."

"You do?"

"I always noticed you, Heather."

"When you weren't calling me Stilts."

"That was noticing you too, in a goofy kid sort of way."

"How'd that work out for you?"

"Not very well." He settled on the rock beside her. "But speaking of work, several members of my team from New York are thinking about making a permanent move here."

"Really?" Heather had seen some of Michael's developers in town, stopping in at the Green Apple and other businesses around the Square. The girl with spiky purple hair who was his personal assistant was especially hard to miss.

"Yeah. The design group has been working out at the Ouachita Inn for the past couple of weeks and some of them really like the area," Michael said.

"Well, I'll be."

"Mostly the ones who have kids. Once they get the feel of grass under their feet, it's hard to go back to concrete," Mike said. "But there are a few singles who said they'd like to give small-town life a try, too."

"That's surprising."

"A city can be exciting, but it can also be a challenge if you're looking to make some real connections. You can get lost in a crowd, and my people are saying they've never met so many friendly folks as they have here."

"Are you planning to move the whole company?"

He shook his head. "I've got some die-hard New Yorkers on the payroll who don't think there's any civilization to speak of between there and LA."

"They might be right."

"Here's to being a hairy barbarian!" Michael grinned and hoisted an imaginary mug. "Anyway, I can't afford to lose that talent pool, so we'll keep the office in New York. Besides, I like the buzz of the city, too, sometimes, so I'll divide my time. The Ouachita Inn will become our satellite campus. If it works for Google to have multiple locations, it'll work for MoreCommas."

"Does that mean you'll be here for good?"

"If you want me to be." His baritone rumbled over her, caressing her with its chocolaty smoothness as he put his arms around her. She went all gooey inside. "Heather, I need to tell you something important."

She looked up at him. The moonlight reflecting off the lake divided his handsome face into light and shadow. Bright and dark — that was Michael Evans to a T. But even the dark places in him called to her.

He's going to tell me he loves me.

Heather felt the unspoken words dancing in the air around them. She tipped her face up to him, inviting him to kiss her. She'd been daydreaming about kissing Michael during her whole shift at the hospital, sometimes having to give herself a little shake to focus back on the moment. She owed it to her patients to be fully engaged, but Mike kept invading her head and her heart. He made it awfully hard to concentrate when all the time she was longing for him to kiss her.

He didn't disappoint.

It was like their souls mingled in that kiss, all tangled up so that even once it ended, they each carried a bit of the other still inside them. The lump in her chest turned to aching sweetness as she looked up at him.

Michael might have a sketchy past, but he was good inside. She was sure of it. And even if he was a little bad, well, that sort of gave her license to be bad, too. No matter how naughty she was feeling, she could count on him to be naughtier. It was a weird twist on a safety net, but it worked for her.

Heather pulled his head down and kissed him. She wished it would go on forever.

I could invite him back to my place.

Maybe this time Lacy wouldn't interrupt with a wedding emergency. Maybe tonight would be about her and Michael. Maybe they'd finally know each other, deeply, truly.

And when morning's sun glinted off Lake Jewel, the world would be a different place, because she wouldn't be alone anymore. She'd wake with Michael beside her.

When their lips parted, he didn't pull away. Still close, his Adam's apple bobbed as he swallowed hard.

"I was there that night," he said softly.

"What night?" *Wait a minute. Where's that 'I love you' I was expecting?* "What are you talking about?"

"The night your sister died. I was there."

CHAPTER 26

LOST AND FOUND

Lost: Grandpappy Bugtussle's urn. Sort of looks like a old coffee can, 'cuz that's what it is. We done took him out to the corn maze for Halloween on account of how he used to love seeing the kids dressed up in bed sheets and raisin' holy heck. Reckon one of us, ain't sayin' who but we're thinkin' it was Aaron since he's still a mite puny after his bout with appendicitis, leastways, he musta set Grandpappy down on a hay bale somewheres. Anyhoo, we'd dearly like to have him back. Great-Grandmammy and Uncle Oliver's cans look mighty lonesome on the mantel without him. Call 555-0169 and ask for Junior. Reward offered for safe return: One of Darlene's blue ribbon-winnin' pumpkin pies.

— *The Coldwater Gazette* classifieds

The sweetness in Heather's chest melted away, and her heart began to race in a hitching rhythm. "What do you mean you were there that night?"

"Just what he says. He's coming clean about that much anyway, him being at the scene and all," came a voice from the shadows. "But anything else he has to say about your sister's unfortunate death will no doubt be a bunch of self-serving lies."

A woman in oversized spectacles and seriously high heels stepped from behind a nearby arbutus tree and marched toward them.

Heather scrambled to her feet, and Michael rose with her. This person had been spying on them. Her growing uneasiness over whatever Mike was trying to tell her was quickly swamped by this new violation.

"Who are you?" Heather demanded.

"Hey, I know you." Mike cocked his head at the newcomer. "You're Stiletto Girl."

If the woman had been gifted with super powers, her malevolent glare would have reduced Michael to a pile of smoldering ash. But since she couldn't immolate him with a look, she turned from him with a sniff. "That's Dr. Judith Hildebrand to you, and who I am is the investigative producer of a new reality show about the dirty little secrets of the rich and infamous." She arched a brow at Michael and then looked back at Heather. "I intend to see justice done for your sister, Jessica, by exposing the truth about her death."

The hitching jitters in Heather's chest settled into a heavy lump instead.

"Come on, Heather." Mike grasped her elbow and would have pulled her away, but her feet seemed rooted to the spot. "Let's get out of here."

"Wait!" Heather's nursing training kicked in. *Gather information. Assess. Then act.* "How do you know this person?"

"Stiletto Girl was part of a reality show I got roped into years ago when I first landed in New York," Michael said. "It was a stupid thing that didn't go anywhere. I never even heard that it aired."

"My name is Dr. Hildebrand, not Stiletto Girl. And for your information, the show did air, but the network didn't give us the right time slot so we didn't find our audience quickly enough," the woman said to Mike in clipped tones before directing her piercing gaze back to Heather. "That reality show is where I first encountered Michael Evans. And that's where I discovered he had a deep, dark secret he didn't want to come out. A secret *I* have now uncovered."

She reached into her jacket pocket and held out a thumb drive. “He was starting to tell you about the night your sister died. Listen to his excuses if you wish, but if you want to know the truth, watch this.”

Mike reached for it, but Hildebrand snatched it back. “It’s not for you. It’s for her. And in case you’re wondering, I’ve got plenty more where this one came from. Several are on their way to my producer friends, who will love the idea of tarring the newest dot-com golden boy with a scandal surrounding the death of poor Jessica Walker. There’s no stopping this story, so you might as well admit it, Evans. You were in the whole sordid mess up to your eyeballs.” Then Dr. Hildebrand smiled — a truly ghastly expression. “Of course, if you want to tell viewers your side, I’ll be happy to shoot a rebuttal interview to add to the package.”

Michael didn’t answer. He didn’t protest. He didn’t deny. He just took a step back. Heather didn’t move at all. It was as if she’d made the mistake of looking behind her to the past, and it had turned her into a pillar of salt.

“You’re probably beyond the statute of limitations for the infractions that occurred, so you likely aren’t looking at jail time,” Dr.

Hildebrand said to Mike with a curled-lip expression that screamed disappointment. "But just think about what this news will do to your IPO."

She held out the thumb drive to Heather again, stretching a little farther toward her. "Take it. If you care about your sister at all, it'll be hard watching, but you'll thank me in the end."

Somehow, Heather held out her palm, and Dr. Hildebrand dropped the thumb drive into it. Without another word, the woman Mike called "Stiletto Girl" turned and stomped off. The night went still as a frozen pond. Even the kids in the maze at the far end of the lakeshore had quieted down.

Then the stillness was interrupted by the sound of a stumble and fall in the dark, followed by a muttered curse.

"I can't frickin' believe it! I broke another heel! Is there nothing to walk on but rocks and dirt and cobblestone in this God-forsaken town?"

After that, Dr. Hildebrand disappeared into the night and silence descended again. Wind soughed through the treetops, sending the last of the fall leaves to the ground in a dusty flurry. Still, Heather couldn't bring herself to move, much less say anything. Her thoughts chased each other around as if they were kids in the maze.

"Well," Michael finally said. "I guess we'd better go watch whatever's on that thumb drive."

"No." Heather's fingers closed over the little device. Michael had already admitted he was there that night. All this time, he knew more about her sister's death than anyone, and he hadn't said a word. It was as deep a betrayal as she could imagine. Tears pressed against her eyes. "We aren't going anywhere together. I need to watch it alone."

Heather lengthened her stride as she hurried back to her apartment. Michael followed, keeping pace easily, but she ignored him. She took the iron steps that led up to her place two at a time.

"Heather, will you slow down and let me explain?" he said as he stomped up the metal stairs behind her, making the whole staircase ring.

"You had plenty of time to do that." She unlocked her door quickly, zipped inside, slammed it in his face, and flipped the deadbolt. Then, ignoring his loud knock, she pulled out her laptop and booted it. With trembling fingers, she plugged in the thumb drive, and a jerky video appeared on the screen.

The sun was shining as the camera panned the shore of Lake Jewel, pausing for a moment on the park gazebo and the rock outcropping Heather and Mike had recently been sitting on. Then the videographer did a slow three-sixty, sliding the lens past the big Victorian houses that ringed the park. Pointing heavenward, the Methodist church steeple rose above nearby rooftops. Dr. Hildebrand's cheap video equipment managed to pick up the carillon clanging out a fragment of a hymn. Finally, the hill leading up to the Town Square and Heather's place came into view. From that angle, her wrought-iron deck and staircase resembled the architecture in New Orleans's French Quarter.

"Coldwater Cove, a sleepy little town filled with pleasant-seeming people and charming homes. Looks peaceful enough, doesn't it? What evil could happen here?" came Dr. Hildebrand's ominous voice-over. "But don't let the picket fences and church bells fool you. All is not as it appears. An evil secret lurks beneath layers of Americana and apple-pie goodness."

Hildebrand's tone was so melodramatic, if she hadn't told Heather the video held the secret to Jessica's death, she would have pulled it out of her computer. Instead, when her sister's senior picture appeared on the screen, she was determined to watch the whole thing.

Dr. Hildebrand spent a couple of minutes summarizing Jessica's childhood and teen years. Heather recognized pictures that had appeared in the *Coldwater Gazette* and in their school yearbooks — winning a gymnastics competition here, singing in the all-state choir there.

As if a life can be reduced to a few sound bites.

Then the disembodied voice of Dr. Hildebrand read the article that had appeared in the paper after Jess's death.

Verbatim.

Hildebrand's bug-eyed face filled the screen, her expression taut with condescension.

"This so-called article is a sorry whitewash of the true story. Jessica Walker didn't inexplicably lose control of her vehicle. Nor was she alone in the car. My investigation starts where inept police work and lackadaisical reporting in the local paper end. After much digging, I discovered an eyewitness who was never interviewed at the time of the incident."

The woman's face faded and was replaced by an out-of-focus image of Mrs. Chisholm in her wheelchair. Heather recognized the lace doilies and fussy furniture surrounding her and knew the interview was being conducted in the old lady's parlor.

"No, the sheriff never sent a deputy around to ask me if I saw a thing," Mrs. Chisholm said. "Nobody from the paper came by either. And me with a big picture window looking out on the whole lake. Not a one of them thought to ask."

"Did you call in with information?"

"Heavens, no. Why should I get involved? I make it a policy to mind my own business. No loose lips in this house . . . but since you asked, here's what happened." The old woman leaned so far forward, it was a wonder she didn't topple out of her chair. "I remember it was a warm night, so my windows were open. I was already in bed, where all good Christians should be after midnight, don't you know? Honestly, can anything good ever happen in the wee hours of the morning? Why, I remember a time when —"

"Mrs. Chisholm," Dr. Hildebrand interrupted. "You were going to tell me about what you saw on the night Jessica Walker died."

"Oh, yes. Where was I? Ah! I heard a car race by — really roaring, you understand — speeding toward the park. They left the roads and tore up the grass. The next day there were marks all over in the sod where the tires —"

"Mrs. Chisholm, back to that night, please."

The old lady arched a wiry brow. Heather recognized it as the expression that asked *Who's telling this story, you or me?* but Mrs. Chisholm went on. She rarely had such an attentive audience and was intent on making the most of it.

"Anyway, then I heard screaming and sort of a crashing sound, but not like the car had hit anything solid. I guess that's because the water isn't solid, is it?"

"What did you see?" Dr. Hildebrand asked.

"Well, not much right then on account of my being still in bed," she said sourly, as if Dr. Hildebrand were a not-quite-bright child. "And it took me a few minutes to get up and into the wheelchair all by myself. That lazy niece of mine sleeps like the dead, so after the evening news she's no help at all. What with me taking her in and all you'd think she'd be more —"

"Mrs. Chisholm," Dr. Hildebrand interrupted in a weary tone, "if you could just stick to the events of that night. Please."

"Only since you said 'please.' You'd be surprised how many young folk forget the value of simple good manners." The old lady gave an injured sniff. "Anyway, by the time I wheeled myself into the parlor and looked out on the lake, the car had already sunk."

Heather bit her lip. Unshed tears made her vision waver, but she couldn't look away. "Was there someone in the water?"

Mrs. Chisholm nodded. "There was a full moon that night so I saw him clearly. Splashing and sputtering around and then kicking his heels into the air to dive back down. But then I heard sirens and figured someone must have dialed 911. The kid in the lake must have heard them, too, because the next time he came up, he slogged out of the water and ran off into the night just as the deputies arrived."

"Were you able to see his face?"

"No. My house is too far away for me to see that kind of detail, but I'm sure it was a boy. No girl in this town ever had a set of shoulders like that."

"Did the deputies try to apprehend him?" Hildebrand asked.

"No, but to be fair, they likely couldn't have caught him. He lit out like his feet were on fire. And besides, there was still a girl in the water to be rescued. Of course, by then, she was gone already, most like." Mrs. Chisholm tapped her chin thoughtfully. "I've often wondered if they'd have been able to get the Walker girl out quicker . . . well, the water in that lake is pretty cold, you know. It's high summer before anyone can bear to spend much time in it. But on TV they're always telling about how children who fall through ice are sometimes able to be revived long after they ought to have died. Anyway, I've wondered about Jessica Walker and if the lake water was cold enough to give her that sort of a chance. If they'd been able to get her out soon enough, of course." Mrs. Chisholm shook her head sadly.

"Coldwater Cove isn't much of a town," Dr. Hildebrand said. "I doubt you have a diving team standing by. And I suspect your local hospital doesn't have a trauma center capable of handling such a situation either."

"Probably not, but then we don't have this sort of thing happening every day of the week." Mrs. Chisholm blinked hard and tears trembled on her eyelashes. "It's so very sad when the young are taken suddenly and the old live on to die a little, day in and day out."

The scene with the old lady and her

wheelchair faded, and Dr. Hildebrand's face appeared on the screen in a close selfie angle that was not as flattering as the doctor seemed to believe.

"Yes, indeed. It's a very sad thing," she pontificated. "Especially if the young person was taken before her time and was somehow helped into that lake."

A quick shot of the sheriff's office flashed on the screen.

"Mrs. Chisholm's testimony that someone else was in the car with the young Jessica Walker sent this reporter searching for the identity of that unknown male."

A stack of official-looking documents appeared in place of the still of the sheriff's office, but the focus was too poor for Heather to read even the header on the first page. If Dr. Hildebrand really intended for a network to pick this story up, it would have to be reshot. Heather was no judge of such things, but even to her untrained eyes, the production value was terrible.

"According to police reports, which had inexplicably been sealed by court order, a knife not belonging to the victim was found in the girl's car. It was a pocketknife with an inscription that allowed the authorities to identify the owner."

Heather felt cold all over, as if she'd been

suddenly dunked in Lake Jewel herself.

"A check of hospital records revealed that the morning after the unfortunate drowning, the owner of the knife was treated for a slash across his ribs that required thirty-six stitches. The doctor notes that the injury was consistent with a cut from broken automobile glass."

Dr. Hildebrand's face filled the screen again. "This reporter believes that the injured male was in the Walker vehicle when it went into the water. He kicked out the passenger-side window and swam for safety, leaving Jessica Walker to drown. Then in an unimaginably callous act, he realized he'd lost his pocketknife and dived back down, hoping to retrieve the incriminating blade from the car. But before he could find it, the sheriff's deputies arrived and he ran away."

Another official-looking brown folder appeared on the screen, followed by another selfie of Dr. Hildebrand.

"No mechanical problem was ever discovered in the victim's vehicle. This fact was glossed over by public reports, but in the packet of documents this reporter has painstakingly assembled, it is obvious that the driver of the vehicle purposely chose to drive her car into the cold waters of Lake Jewel."

Another picture of Jess appeared, this one of her as a member of the homecoming court. Her smile was as sparkling as the little tiara on her head.

"Jessica Walker was an honor student. She was popular and pretty. She was fortunate enough to have been accepted at Brown University and would have started there in the fall. So why would someone with all that going for her drive her new automobile into the lake?"

A still shot of Coldwater General Hospital replaced Jess's picture.

"The results of Jessica Walker's autopsy were never made public. The coroner's findings were not even disclosed to the victim's family because — and I quote from official documents — 'the Walkers have suffered enough.' " Dr. Hildebrand appeared on the screen. She removed her glasses, making her eyes seem to shrink in size without the distorting lenses in front of them. "But the truth is, Jessica Walker wasn't the only one who died that night. She took her unborn child with her."

Jess was pregnant? Heather felt as if someone had punched her in the gut. On the other side of the door, Michael called her name and rapped loudly. She ignored him.

"No paternity was ever established for the fetus, but this reporter believes the father of the child is none other than the owner of the pocketknife, the man who bears a long scar as a memento of that night but has escaped any other repercussion."

The selfie angle tightened until just Dr. Hildebrand's very red mouth filled the screen.

"Until now," the lips said. Then the shot scrolled back and her entire face was visible.

"That man," Hildebrand paused for effect, "is Michael Evans. Not only was his name engraved on the knife at the scene, medical records reveal that he received stitches for a gash to the torso the morning after the incident. Yes, it was Michael Evans. You may know that name. He is the reclusive creator and CEO of the wildly successful dot-com known as MoreCommas. Here in his hometown of Coldwater Cove, he's better known as the town screwup."

Dr. Hildebrand began to natter on about how Michael's involvement in Jessica's death had escaped public scrutiny because of the influence brought to bear by his father, who was a well-respected attorney.

She ranted about lax oversight of law enforcement and lack of availability of emergency personnel, which added to the tragedy.

But Heather had stopped listening. She closed the laptop on Hildebrand in mid-sentence. She knew the visiting doctor had cut some legal corners digging up those official documents. If a case had been sealed by court order, how had she obtained it? At the hospital, Heather was prohibited from accessing a patient's records unless she could demonstrate a need for them, on pain of reprimand or possible termination. How had this out-of-town snoop managed to see not only Michael's medical records, but also a copy of Jessica's autopsy?

Heather shoved that issue aside. Could Hildebrand be right? Had Michael been in the car with Jess? He'd already admitted to being there that night, so it was possible. Add the damning evidence of his pocketknife left in the vehicle and the injury he'd suffered, and it seemed a certainty.

But surely he hadn't fathered Jessica's baby. Just thinking about it made Heather's chest constrict. No, if Jess had been pregnant, the father had to be Skyler Sweazy. He and Jess had been a couple since their sophomore year. After graduation, they were heading east to the land of the Ivy League together.

But now that Heather thought about it, her sister and Skyler had been having a running argument that last week or so. Jess would never tell her what it was about. She'd only say the problem would work itself out, one way or another. Had Jess been hooking up with Michael on the side? Was that why she and Skyler were on the outs?

She realized that Michael had stopped banging on her door. It was her temples pounding now. It hurt to think.

Her sister was dead. That much hadn't changed.

Michael had been with her when she died.

That changed everything.

Chapter 27

I love Heather Walker. She can have my body anytime she wants. I just didn't expect to give it to her in pieces.

— Michael Evans, before he does the only thing he can think of to try to make things right

"This is an extreme solution to your problem," Jadis said to Michael as he continued to stuff things into his duffel. "Most men would not consider it."

"You of all people should know I'm not most men. 'Extreme' is my default position."

Jadis was aware of Michael's whole story. Since he'd first met her in that tattoo parlor in New York, they'd formed a bond as strong as any brother and sister ever had. She knew everything about him and his past because she was the only one wise enough to help him sort things out. He often joked that if Jiminy Cricket and Yoda had a love child, it would be Jadis — only she was much better looking. But even she couldn't puzzle out a way for Michael to convince Heather to listen to his side of things since she seemed intent on pretending he didn't exist.

After being ambushed by Stiletto Girl down by the lake, Michael had waited outside Heather's door for a solid hour, but she'd never answered his knock. He'd tried calling her the next day. She refused to pick up.

He texted her. She blocked his number.

Even when he showed up at choir, she never glanced his way once. When they broke for cookies and coffee mid-rehearsal, he tried to approach her, but every time he joined the group she was chatting with, she found a reason to be someplace else.

It was like he'd hit the stealth button. He was the Invisible Man as far as Heather was concerned.

"If you've got another idea, I'm all ears," he said to his assistant. "I should have told her everything before Stiletto Girl got to her. It would have been bad, but not as bad as this."

"You did not wish to hurt her by dragging up the past. That is always commendable,"

Jadis said. "But now you are planning to hurt yourself. Do not make a rash decision."

"It's not rash. I've been considering this since I first heard about it. Why do you think I had myself tested last time I was in Tulsa?" Michael zipped his duffel closed. "Ever since I found out I was a match, I've been psyching myself up to do it anyway. This thing with Heather is just the tipping point."

"Have you considered that risking yourself in this way may adversely affect those who depend on you?" She meant his workers. Jadis had suffered through a lot of instability as a kid. MoreCommas had become her family. She was like a momma grizzly when it came to the company and its employees.

"MoreCommas will do fine without me for a while. Besides, if all goes well, I'll be back at work in a couple of weeks."

"If all goes well," Jadis repeated, crossing her thin arms over her chest. "What about your sister's wedding?"

"I'll be up to full speed by the time that rolls around. May have to take it a little easy at the bachelor party, but Jake's not the kind who wants a blowout in Vegas anyway."

"Naturally, I support your decisions." Jadis sighed as he hefted his bag onto his shoulder. "Am I at least permitted to worry about you?"

"You'd better." Michael snorted and gave her a half smile. "No one else will."

Heather usually enjoyed the drive out to the ranch where she grew up, but after all the fall color was gone, late autumn was not the prettiest of times in the Ozarks. In the dying twilight, it was like some old-timey cowboy photograph. The hills and hollows were awash in shades of sepia. The naked trees shivered in the wind, their bony fingers scratching a gray sky.

The bleak landscape suited her mood. Michael's betrayal had sucked all the color from her world.

He kept trying to talk to her, but she figured her heart was safer behind the stone wall she'd hastily erected. Whatever he had to say, however he might try to explain things away, it wouldn't change the facts.

He'd been there with Jess at the end, and he hadn't saved her. He'd run away when she needed him most. How could she have fallen for someone so spineless? Heather wished she could slap herself silly. For once, she was grateful for the "command performance" invitation to dine with her parents. Keeping their interfering suggestions at bay would distract her from her dark thoughts, if only for a little while.

She turned off the main road onto a long blacktop drive that led to the sprawling white McMansion. Her mom had been weaned on the old *Dallas* TV show and had remade her home into an Oklahoma version of Southfork. A flashy red Beemer was parked by the double front doors. Heather didn't recognize the car, but she recognized a potential fix-up when she saw one. Whoever belonged to that vehicle was the parentally approved suitor of the day.

Her mother had obviously been watching for her, because she met Heather at the door before she could turn the knob herself.

"Now, darling, before you get your back up, I know you think we meddle, but I promise you that is not what we're doing tonight. Skyler just happens to be in town on business and it would have been rude not to have him out to the ranch."

"Skyler again. I thought he'd gone back to Massachusetts," Heather said wearily. Even if Skyler had made her insides flutter in the least, which he didn't, it would be beyond weird to hook up with Jessica's old boyfriend. "What business does a Boston lawyer have in Coldwater Cove?"

"Well, to be honest" — her mother knotted her fingers before her — "your father hired him to handle a rather complicated merger with a fracking company in New York."

Heather knew better than that. There were no mergers as far as her dad was concerned. This was an acquisition, and the owners were evidently holding out. But she was sure that her dad would win in the end. He wouldn't be satisfied until the Walker name meant energy production in all fifty states.

"And I suppose there are no attorneys in Coldwater Cove who are up to the challenge?" she asked. The practice Mr. Evans had built and then sold to his partner when he retired was still a going concern and had offices on the Town Square. As long as Heather could remember, her family had used Evans and Farley for all their legal needs.

"Yes, but we've known Skyler for years. He's almost family. *Was* almost family," she amended. Her mother linked arms with her and started to draw her along the broad gallery that led to the great room in one of the big house's wings. "And besides, he's your friend."

"No, he was Jessica's friend." Heather stopped in her tracks, refusing to be dragged toward the room where the men were waiting. "She was the one you always hoped would marry into the Sweazy family and unite the two giant piles of money."

"What a thing to say!"

"Doesn't make it less true."

Her mother sputtered, but couldn't seem to form a coherent reply.

Heather certainly never meant to unload, but she'd reached a breaking point, and all her pent-up fears started spilling out of her. "Mom, you can't remake me in her image. I'm not Jess. I never will be."

Her mother blinked hard, as if Heather had slapped her. Then she found her voice. "Is that why you're upset? Darling, I'd never want you to be like Jess. You and Jessica may have been twins, but you've always been your own person. The two of you were different from the womb, and your father and I wouldn't have it any other way." Her mother reached up and cupped Heather's cheeks. "You are our precious daughter. You're strong and smart and beautiful and we love you so very much." Tears filled her mom's eyes, and Heather felt her own water in sympathy. No one ever wept alone in her presence. "If we meddle, it's only because you're all we have."

Grief had been a private thing in the Walker household. Even during those early days after Jessica's death, her parents had rivaled the British in the "stiff upper lip" department, each of them being strong for the other. Now her mother's voice broke. "We just want you to be happy, sweetheart."

Heather wished she could protest that she was happy, but that would be a lie. She was utterly miserable, sick over Michael, suddenly tired of her demanding job, and feeling so very alone. So she fell into her mother's arms, and they hugged each other, clinging tightly for the first time in ages.

"So you don't wish it had been me taken instead of Jess," she said softly.

"Never. Not even for a blink. We could never make that sort of choice." Her mom patted her back for a few more seconds. Then she straightened and put on a bright smile as she dabbed at her eyes with the hanky she pulled from her pocket. "Look at that. You've made me ruin my mascara. Why don't you head on down and join the men while I fix my face?"

"And my face doesn't need fixing?"

"Of course not. You're always so pretty. Some people get all red in the face when they cry, like I do, but you can be dropping buckets and still look like a supermodel."

Wow.

Heather had always figured her parents tried to order her life because they felt sorry for their tall, gawky daughter, that they didn't believe she could manage on her own. She never dreamed her mother thought of her as a supermodel.

Buoyed up by this revelation, Heather went willingly to the great room to join her father and Skyler. She even enjoyed the easy conversation over the dinner of Cornish hens, roasted potatoes, and asparagus with Dijon-lemon sauce. Alma, the Walkers' live-in cook and housekeeper of many years, had put the meal together, but since Alma was getting long in the tooth, Heather's mom always sent her on to her room to rest in the evenings. Between Heather and her mom, the meal was served. Heather would volunteer to clean up later.

"Now, then, daughter," her dad said as he laid aside his linen napkin, "while I help your mother with dessert, why don't you take Skyler out on the back patio and see if you can catch any falling stars? The Taurids meteor shower should crest tonight."

"Dad's an astronomy buff. Let's make his night by sighting a few," Heather told Skyler as she stood. When she and Jess were little, her father would sometimes wake them and carry them out to the dark deck in their jammies to view some celestial event. She treasured those memories of wonder and beauty. It was always a magical moment.

"Keep a good count," her father said. "I want to put it in the log."

"Oh, and slip on a jacket. There should be a couple hanging by the door," her mother said as she began clearing the table. "It's getting cold out there."

"I can see that resistance is futile," Skyler said with a grin as he followed Heather to bundle up and slip out back. He latched the door softly behind them.

The deck on the back of the ranch house was perched over a ravine, a dark chasm that wound past the home and into the hills. It was occasionally filled with runoff when there was a hard rain, but now each sage brush and blade of grass was edged with frost, glinting silver in the starlight. Her parents' home was perfectly situated for stargazing, far enough from civilization that there was no light pollution to mar the view. Since there was a new moon that night, the Milky Way spilled in a bright cloudy mass across the dark vault.

Skyler loosed a low whistle. "I'd forgotten how many stars there are out here. You can't see any but the brightest of them in Boston. The sky always seems bigger here, too." He walked to the edge of the deck and leaned on the railing. "So where are we supposed to look for these meteors?"

Heather joined him to overlook the ravine. "They can show up anywhere, but will most likely seem to come from the area around Taurus, the Bull."

"OK, I'll say it. Where's the beef?"

Heather chuckled and pointed upward. "Taurus is between Orion and the Seven Sisters, just there." She traced Orion's Belt with the tip of her finger before drawing an invisible circle on the sky around the tiny dipper-like collection of stars most people called the Pleiades. Her dad always said they were a group of sisters huddled together in the sky, hiding behind the bull for protection from the Hunter, Orion, so that's how Heather liked to think of them, too. "See that bright star."

Skyler squinted upward. "Mmm-hmm."

"That's Aldebaran. It's the tip of the bull's left horn. Notice how the stars form a V."

"Oh, yeah."

"That's the face of Taurus."

At that moment, a spark streaked across the sky, flaming to nothingness. Heather suddenly wished it was Michael beside her instead of Skyler. If there was magic in the night sky, it was Mike she wanted to share it with.

Half a dozen more meteorites slashed the

night. Skyler made appreciative noises.

Or maybe it's just the idea *of Michael I want.* Her chest constricted. He wasn't really the man she'd thought he was. At every turn, some new secret popped out, most of them surprisingly good, but this last one so heinous, it overshadowed the positive things and made them seem shallow and unimportant.

The sky went quiet for several minutes, the stars softly pulsing but no more dropping from the heavens. That was how meteor showers went — it was either feasting or fasting. Sort of like her relationship with Michael. It was either bountifully wonderful or soul-suckingly awful. And there was no warning either. It just tipped one way or the other.

"That was amazing," Skyler said softly, and reached for her hand.

Heather pulled away gently. "Look, I'm sorry about the way my folks have thrown us together. They mean well, but I don't want you to feel pressured to spend any time with me while you're here in town."

"What if I want to? I'd hate to miss a chance to be with a Walker girl. You remind me of Jess, you know."

Well, that couldn't be creepier or more untrue.

"Skyler, I . . ." She turned away from him. "I'm kind of off men for a while."

"Really?" His tone hardened. "I'd heard you were into Michael Evans."

"I was. I am." She met his gaze. "It's complicated."

"Yeah. It always is with Mike. Want to talk about it?"

She almost said no, but who besides Skyler would understand? He and Michael had been best friends back in the day. He'd loved Jessica. Besides, he deserved to know that Mike had been with her at the end.

So she told him about Dr. Hildebrand and most of the sordid details her investigation had turned up. Heather decided not to bring up the pregnancy. If Skyler wasn't the father, it would only make him despise her sister.

"So you see why I can't be with Michael, even if I want to more than" — *More than I want to keep breathing,* she stopped herself from adding. But she couldn't get past the truth. "He was there, Skyler. He watched her die."

"But you love him." It wasn't a question.

A tear slipped out and streaked her cheek. "God help me."

Skyler sighed deeply. "Listen. What I'm about to tell you cannot leave this deck. Can

I count on your discretion?"

She nodded.

"Michael didn't watch Jess die. He tried to get her out." Skyler leaned again on the split-rail fence that ringed the deck. Stars began falling overhead once more, but he only seemed able to stare at the ground that fell away sharply beneath their feet. "You don't have the whole story."

"How do you know?"

"Because Michael wasn't in the car with Jess that night." He drew a shaky breath. "That was me."

Chapter 28

Don't be afraid, sissy. If it's not dark, you can't see the stars.

— Jessica Walker, when her twin was too chicken to slip out of bed to stargaze without their dad

Heather put her hand over Skyler's where it gripped the rail. "Tell me."

"I'm a fool to do this, but Mike's my friend. I owe him. And I've hated myself over this for years." He sucked in a deep breath. "But I don't think I could bear it if you hate me too."

Heather was silent with foreboding at what he might say. She couldn't promise she wouldn't hate him.

"I remember you and Jess had been arguing about something that last week, but she never would tell me what it was about," she prompted.

Skyler nodded. "We couldn't agree on

how to handle a problem."

Suddenly, it seemed there'd been so many secrets that no one could ever get to the heart of what really happened. Heather decided to lay it all out. Nothing could hurt Jessica now. "That problem wouldn't have been that she was pregnant, would it?"

His gaze jerked to her sharply. "I didn't know you knew."

"I didn't. Not until a few days ago. I wish she'd confided in me."

"We'd agreed not to say anything to anyone. This was something that needed to be handled . . . judiciously," he said, choosing his words like a lawyer instead of the scared kid he'd probably been. "You have to understand, Heather. I was headed for Harvard that fall. She was off to Brown, but we'd be close enough to see each other on weekends. We were going places. We had a life, or at least a five-year plan. But she wouldn't agree to . . . to end the pregnancy."

Thank God. That squared with everything she thought she knew about her sister. Jessica wasn't the sort to make someone else pay for her actions.

"So I decided to end our relationship," Skyler said.

Heather's insides did a slow burn. "I do hate you a bit now."

"It's OK. I guess I deserve it. I hate me a little, too, but I had good intentions. I wanted to let her down easy. So I was going to take her for a drive so we could talk, but when I met up with her, she wanted to show me the car your folks had given her, so I let her drive." He pounded the rail with his fist. "I'd give anything if I'd been behind the wheel that night."

"I'd give anything if you'd been man enough to step up and take responsibility for the child you created."

"We were children ourselves, can't you see that?"

"You're still a child." A spoiled baby in a bespoke suit.

He shrugged. "I won't argue. First thing I learned in law school was how to pick my cases, and I wouldn't win that one," he said softly. "Anyway, I tried to explain to Jess that we couldn't have a baby then. How could we have a kid and a normal college experience at the same time? I mean, who brings a diaper bag to a kegger? Where do you go for spring break with a stroller in tow? A baby would ruin everything."

Skyler was worried about how being a father would mess up his frat life. Heather hated him more than a little at that moment, but she stayed silent so Skyler would keep talking.

"Anyway, Jess was getting more and more upset, and she wasn't watching the road like she should have been." The muscle in his cheek jerked. "When the car jumped the curb, I'll always believe she hit the accelerator by accident. It was a new car. She wasn't used to it yet. I think she was going for the brake."

Heather wanted to believe that, too. The idea that her sister might have intentionally driven her car into the lake made her feel ill. "And then what?"

"It all happened so fast. And at the same time, it seemed like slow motion. We whizzed by the gazebo and the car flew off the rock and hit the water, but we didn't sink immediately. I tried to get the door open, but it wouldn't budge. My window was halfway down and as the car settled, water started pouring in. I . . . I panicked."

"You said Michael was there."

"Yeah, he was waiting for me in the gazebo. We'd planned to meet up later and TP all the trees in the park. It was almost graduation, and we wanted to leave the town something to remember us by."

"Mission accomplished," Heather said under her breath. Jessica's death had been sudden and senseless, a life full of promise snipped off before it had really begun. No one in the county would ever forget it.

"Anyway, Michael was suddenly splashing into the lake after us, and he showed up by my side of the car. He grabbed me by the collar and pulled me out of the half-open window before I knew what was what. Guess I was pretty skinny back then."

"What about Jess?" Heather demanded with impatience.

He hung his head. "She wouldn't stop screaming. I tried to help her before Mike pulled me out. Honest, I did, but we couldn't get her seat belt unfastened. I swam to shore and dialed 911. By some miracle, my phone still worked. I yelled at Mike to tell him the emergency crew was on its way, but he wouldn't leave the car. He broke out the window and dived through it. I heard later that he cut himself up pretty bad on the jagged glass."

"Why didn't you help him?"

"What could I do?" Skyler gave an involuntary shudder. "The water was just so cold. It takes your breath away. If I'd gone back in, I don't think I'd have come out."

"So Michael was with her at the end, just like he said." *But he was trying to save her.* He'd done everything he could. He was a hero, and Heather had treated him like he'd done something wrong. It was suddenly hard to breathe. Her hand went involuntarily to her chest.

"Yeah, there was really only room for one of us anyway," Skyler said, totally oblivious to Heather's distress. She wasn't sure her knees would hold her up and leaned heavily on the rail. "And Michael had a pocketknife. He was sawing at the seat belt as the car kept sinking. Even after it was completely submerged, he went down again and again."

"And where were you during all this?" she said through clenched teeth.

Skyler wouldn't meet her gaze. "Well, I'd called 911 and Michael was there to tell them what happened. Once when he came up for air, he told me to get out of there. No need for both of us to take the blame, so I . . . I ran off." He glanced at her, and then an expression that looked like shame drew his features taut. His gaze darted away. That shame was the only thing that kept Heather from ripping off the top rail and whacking him over the head. "You've got to understand. There was nothing I could do to help Jess. It was better for Michael to get caught up in that mess by the cops. He could take the heat. He wasn't going anywhere anyway."

That mess. Jessica's death was just a bump

on the road for Skyler. She didn't think she'd ever hated anyone, ever been tempted to do someone violence so much in her entire life. Heather squeezed her eyes shut and prayed. For Skyler and for his continued ability to breathe. She wanted him to live a long time with his cowardice.

"Hey, it was kind of a repayment, if you think about it. Mike wouldn't have even graduated if it weren't for me," he said defensively. "I did all his English homework that last year. Did you know that?"

"Yeah, you're a real humanitarian."

"Well, just so you get it. We agreed between us that he'd take the blame if things came to light. Michael had nothing to lose and I did."

"What about my sister? She lost everything."

"It wasn't my fault. Nobody could have saved her. Even Michael couldn't. He told me later that he accidentally dropped the knife while he was trying to cut her free."

And that knife was how the sheriff's office had connected her sister's death to Michael. As Dr. Hildebrand had said, Mike's father must have used all his influence to keep him out of trouble, and if Mr. Evans had learned Jess was pregnant, he might have suspected Michael was responsible for that as well. It might explain why he'd sent Michael away.

"Mike should have told his side of the story at the time," Heather said. It seemed clear now that Jessica's death had been an accident. But if Skyler had come clean, he would have been the one who looked guilty. She supposed that sort of scandal had a way of following a guy if he was bucking for partner in a big-name law firm. Instead, it had opened up a bigger schism between Michael and his father than the ravine behind her parents' house.

"Mike swore he wouldn't tell. And when Mike swears to something, he sticks with it. Besides, like I said, I'm the one who had plenty to lose. Michael wasn't headed for college. He didn't have any expectations to live up to and he wouldn't have even made it through high school without me. I figured he owed me."

Heather was silent for a few moments. There was no fixing this. Nothing would bring her sister back. But her parents didn't need the pain of reliving it all again. If Dr. Hildebrand sold her story to some network, her version of Jessica's death would be plastered all over TV. At the very least, she'd post it on YouTube and hope it went viral.

"But I guess I owe Mike, too. That's why I told you all this, but please don't tell your parents," Skyler said. "I can't lose another client."

Heather arched a brow at him.

"OK, you may as well know the truth. I'm not a partner. I'm barely a junior associate, and if I don't make a little rain soon, my head's on the block. I need your dad and the deal he wants me to make for him. If I negotiate a sweet enough agreement, maybe I can persuade your father to move the Walker accounts to my firm. I've convinced the partners he's a whale and I'll be doing more work for his company in the future. So, please, Heather, not a word."

"I see. But it may not matter if I tell the folks the truth about Jess or not. They're going to hear a version of it anyway." She reminded him about the reality show producer and her plan to go public with an exposé about Michael and his supposed part in Jessica's death. This time she didn't leave out the part about Jessica's pregnancy coming to light. "Wouldn't it be better for the truth to come out now? All of it?"

"No," Skyler said. "It would be better if I put the fear of God into this Dr. Hildebrand with a cease-and-desist order. And if she goes ahead with her exposé, I'll sue her six ways from Sunday. She'll wish she never set foot in Coldwater Cove."

"You think that'll work?"

"Watch me," he said, his legal game face firmly in place. "Nothing scares the pants off the media quicker than the threat of litigation. With a cloud of legal trouble hanging over her head, nobody's going to touch this Dr. Hildebrand or her story. Besides, you said the way she gathered some of her information was questionable."

"More than questionable. Hacking into sealed court records and old hospital charts — that's got to be against the law."

"It is," Skyler said, getting more excited by the minute. "In fact, since Dr. Hildebrand intends to profit from her hacking, that raises the ante. It's no longer a misdemeanor. It's a felony. Argued before the right judge, she could get five years." Skyler caught up both of Heather's hands. "So, if I make this thing with Mike and the bad doctor go away, are we good? You won't mess up the deal I'm doing for your dad?"

"All right, I'll keep quiet on two conditions," Heather said. "You fix this thing with Dr. Hildebrand — and I mean squash it, quickly and quietly."

"Yes, yes, consider it done. What else?"

"You tell Mike's dad the whole truth."

"Heather, I can't."

"You can and you will." She checked her

watch. "Make whatever excuse you want to my folks and head back into town right now. You'd better text me from the Evanses' front door by nine or I'm marching back into that house and you'll be out of a 'whale' of a client before the night's over."

"I must say, I'm surprised that Skyler had to leave so suddenly," Heather's mom said as she put his piece of peach pie back into the refrigerator.

"Don't worry, Mom. You'll be seeing plenty of him in the future."

Her mother arched a brow at her. "Something I should know? Will you be seeing him again?"

"No, no, nothing like that." *Not if Skyler were the last skeevy lawyer on earth!* "I just mean he'll likely be working for Dad quite a bit down the road. Skyler seems to be under the impression that Walker Enterprises will be moving all its legal business to his firm."

Her mother shrugged. "Your father handles that sort of thing, but I doubt he'd ever leave Evans and Farley. He's only using Skyler for this deal because Farley advised going with an East Coast firm for the negotiations. Then when Skyler presents his deal, they'll help us decide if it's what we really want to do. Evans and Farley are our trustees. They know everything about our business. When the time comes and you inherit all this, you can count on them."

"Mom, please don't talk like that." Heather might not get along with her parents all the time, but the thought of not having them around to fuss with was far worse.

"Well, how about this, then? Your father and I have booked a Thanksgiving cruise out of Houston and we'd love to have you with us. Belize is lovely this time of year. We had our travel agent put a hold on adjoining suites just in case you can make it. Want to come?"

"I can't." But for the first time, she was tempted. The idea of running away for a while held real appeal. "Lacy's wedding is the day after Thanksgiving and I'm the maid of honor, remember?"

"Oh, that's right." Her mother sighed. "Maybe we can plan for something around Christmas, then. I love taking holiday cruises — no big meals to fix."

"As if Alma doesn't do all the fixing around the ranch."

"Oh, you know what I mean." Her mother waved away Heather's statement of the obvious. "It's just easier not to be home on holidays."

Oh! Heather mentally smacked her own forehead and wished for a metaphorical V8. She finally understood why her parents always made a point of putting as much distance between themselves and home as possible during times when everyone else was gathering their families close. Jessica's place at the table was too glaringly empty on those special days, the house too full of holidays past and celebrations future that would never be. Heather's parents weren't trying to get away from her.

They were running from that empty chair.

"Well, I'm sorry you can't join us for the Thanksgiving cruise," her mom said as she gave the quartz countertop a quick wipe down. "Especially since this year we really have something to be thankful for."

"Oh?"

"Cousin Mary Margaret posted the good news all over the Facebook. Don't you follow her?"

"I rarely have time to check it." Heather had tried several times, with no success, to get her mother not to call it 'the' Facebook.

"Bet you're not on the Twitter either."

Heather hid her smile and shook her head. "Don't keep me in suspense. What's up?"

"Your cousin Levi's been waiting at St. John's, hoping for a transplant for the past week. Word is he's getting a new liver first thing tomorrow morning."

"I can't believe they found a match." Heather was shocked to her toes. Levi's blood type was O negative, rare enough to make finding a compatible liver unlikely in the extreme. But then she remembered that the source of her family's joy was another's sorrow. "I wish we could thank the donor's family."

"That's easy enough. You know them well. It's the Evanses." Her mother was scraping and rinsing the plates while Heather loaded the dishwasher, but her mom's words made her straighten to her full height. "That's right. Your old classmate Michael has come forward to volunteer a partial liver donation. Didn't your friend Lacy tell you?"

"I doubt she knows." Lacy would have been all over this if she had.

"Well, I must say, the family was surprised by his generous offer. And I don't think he'd ever even met Levi before this." She dropped a pod of detergent into the dishwasher, closed the door, and started the cycle. "Michael Evans is certainly not the young hellion I took him for when you ran off with him the night of the reunion dance."

Heather hadn't run off with him. She'd just used his bad-boy reputation to punish her mother and father a little.

Now she wished she *had* run off with him and never looked back. Michael was everything she'd ever wanted, but she was as guilty as her mother of judging him based on his past. Everything she'd thought she knew about Mike was wrong.

"Mom, I gotta go." She gave her mother a quick hug. "Tell Dad good-night for me."

"Where are you off to in such an all-fired hurry?"

"St. John's. I need to tell Michael Evans something in person."

"Well, tell him thank-you for us, too. This family thinks the world and all of Levi."

"I'll tell him," she called over her shoulder as she sprinted down the gallery toward the front door. She suddenly had lots to say to Michael Evans.

She just hoped she'd get there in time to say it.

CHAPTER 29

A second chance ain't worth a tinker's damn if you don't do nothing different from the first time 'round. Oops! I mean, tinker's darn. Glenda don't like it when I cuss so I'm tryin' to quit it. That plus workin' steady, givin' up drinking, and minding my temper is a full-time job, but if the payoff is that I get my wife back, I'll make that trade all day.

— Lester

The road was a dark ribbon winding through the hills, illuminated only by Heather's headlights. She forced herself to flick her gaze from right to left from time to time so the repetitive white strips down the middle of the two-lane highway didn't lull her into a semi-hypnotic fog. Using the voice-recognition feature on her phone, she tried to call Glenda Scott as she drove through the night toward Tulsa.

When she finally hit a patch of road that had cell service, the connection was made. There was static for a second and then a clatter, as if the phone had been dropped. Then a man's sleepy voice said, "What d'you want?"

"Oh! I must have the wrong number." Heather was surprised not to hear her CNA's upbeat voice answering the phone. "Who is this?"

"Who you callin'?"

"Glenda Scott."

"She's asleep."

"No, I'm not."

The voice in the background sounded like Glenda. If that was so, the man who'd answered must be Glenda's formerly estranged husband, Lester.

Evidently not so estranged at the moment.

"Gimme that phone," came a muffled order.

There was another moment or two of shuffling and static before a voice came through loud and clear. "Glenda here."

"So is Lester, I gather," Heather said, a smile curving her lips. "Sounds like you aren't making him stay on the porch anymore."

If a blush could be heard, Heather was sure one would have blasted over the phone in the slice of silence that followed.

"No, he's made his way back into my house and my heart. Looks like we're doing like that old song says. You know the one" — her voice dropped to a whisper — "about love being sweeter the second time around."

"Only the second time? Come on. The night is young. You and Lester can do better than that."

"Heather!"

She decided to stop teasing her friend. "Look, I need a favor. I'm not going to make it in for my shift tomorrow, and I don't expect to have time to call administration. I need you to go into scheduling and mark me off as on vacation for the next week."

"You never take vacation."

"Well, I'm taking one now."

"You want me to go into the software and make it look like this week off has been planned for a while?" Glenda asked.

"Can you do that?"

"You'd be amazed at what my ten talented fingers can do." In the background, Heather thought she heard Lester say something that sounded like, "Got that right." Then there was a dull thud, like the sound of a pillow hitting someone's face. Glenda came back on the line. "What's up?"

“I’ll tell you when I get back to town.”

“Come on. You know all my secrets. Give,” Glenda wheedled. “It’s something to do with Michael Evans, isn’t it? You two getting together?”

Heather figured she was sending a blush of her own. “Not right away.” Not so long as Michael was a patient in a transplant ward. But soon. “Let’s just say I think I’m ready to learn about that second time around stuff, too.”

The preoperative literature warned that live donors should expect a certain amount of pain following surgery. As Michael clawed his way back to full consciousness, he decided the morphine drip was his new best friend.

He tapped the self-dispensing button with his thumb and a fresh burst of painkiller flooded his IV. The deep ache in his abdomen subsided a little. It still hurt like blue blazes, but the morphine made him not care.

So far, he hadn’t encountered any surprises with the procedure, but he hadn’t been warned to expect hallucinations in post-op. An angel who looked suspiciously like Heather glided into his small curtained bay. There was even a bit of a glow around her as she drew near him.

They really do give you good drugs around here.

"Hey you," the angel said softly, and ran her cool fingertips across his forehead.

She was real!

He wanted to say something, but his tongue was feeling two sizes too big for his mouth. Besides, he was all wrapped up in warm blankets and the pulsing afterglow of general anesthesia. He must have been moving his lips though because she put a finger to them.

"Hush. I really shouldn't be here. They only allow family in post-op, but I convinced the nurses I was your favorite cousin. If they think I'm tiring you, they'll send me away, so don't try to talk."

But he had to. It might be his only chance. "How's Levi?" he whispered.

"He's out of surgery and in the ICU. His doctor says the graft is doing well."

Michael closed his eyes. "Thank God."

"Amen." There were those cool fingertips again, this time sliding from his temple down his cheek. If only she'd keep touching him, he'd never ask God for another single thing. Not ever in his whole life.

"And thanks to you too, Michael."

His mouth twitched, and he forced his

eyes open. "Kinda had to do it. Only way I could get you to talk to me."

"A little extreme, don't you think?"

"That's what Jadis said." The morphine was dragging him under again. He'd just rest his eyes for a moment or two. "But if you forgive me," he mumbled, "it was worth it."

"I can't forgive you, Michael."

His eyes popped open again.

"Because there's nothing to forgive. Skyler told me the whole story. I know you did everything you could to try to save my sister." Tears trembled on her lower lashes. "And now you've saved my cousin."

"All in a day's work for a son of Krypton," he said with a chuckle, and then regretted it sorely. Laughter, even the soft kind, hurt like the dickens.

Heather rearranged the pillows under his head and shoulders and then pulled a chair close to his bedside. She sat and leaned forward, taking one of his hands. He gripped hers hard, as if she might get away.

"You do go at everything hammer and tongs, you know," she chided. "What am I going to do with you?"

Love me, he mouthed. Then he drew a deep breath and gave voice to the words. "Love me."

"I do," she said simply.

"Good. 'Cuz I've always loved you, Stilts." Pain notwithstanding, he figured he was the happiest guy in the hospital. Then he remembered how she hated that nickname.

But she was still grinning at him as if Stilts was the sweetest thing he could have called her. Then she leaned forward and kissed him softly. He wanted to rock her world, to take her and pull her into bed with him, but he couldn't seem to make his arms work. It was like trying to swim through Jell-O.

"I didn't mean for you to take the cousins thing literally," she said when she leaned back again. "That kiss wouldn't even shock Mrs. Chisholm."

"I can do better. Honest." The morphine was making him slur his words. "Give me a day or two and you won't think I kiss like a cousin."

"How about if I give you a week?"

"OK. That sounds . . . pretty . . . good." The morphine beckoned, and he felt himself slipping under, but he dragged himself back up. "You'll stay?"

"I'm not going anywhere."

This time when the morphine pulled him under, he let himself go. Heather would be there when he woke.

Then, maybe, if he was luckier than he

deserved, he'd convince her to be there when he woke every day for the rest of his life.

For the next week, Heather spent every waking moment with Michael in the hospital. She cheered him on when he took his first walk up and down the hall. She wheeled him into Levi's room so he could get to know the guy to whom he'd given a second chance at life.

On about Wednesday, Michael threatened mutiny unless his healthy hospital diet was supplemented with a little something from the grease and salt food groups. Heather decided to join the rebellion and sneak a hamburger and fries past the nurses' station. But when she arrived back at his room, she discovered his parents were there. She hung back, just outside the door, to give them a little privacy.

"You should have told us you were doing this," Mrs. Evans scolded. She was as fretful as a sparrow, shifting her weight from one foot to the other, but otherwise, in Heather's clinical opinion, she looked good for a cancer patient. Unless someone knew her, they'd never guess she was undergoing chemotherapy. Her makeup was flawless, and the short silver-haired wig framed her face perfectly. "Your father and I would have been here for the surgery if we'd known."

"I didn't want to worry you," Michael said, holding his mother's hand. "Besides, you've got your own treatments to deal with."

"I'd have rescheduled them, honey."

"I couldn't let you do that," Mike said. "I know you've been trying to stick to the regimen so you'll be done with your course of chemo before Lacy's wedding."

"And it costs her plenty not to put each round of treatment off," his dad said gruffly. Clearly, his wife's illness was wearing him down, maybe even more than it did her. "But if your mother couldn't have made the trip, I'd have been here, son."

Heather's brows shot up. *That's a shocker.*

"It wasn't necessary for you to be here," Mike said. "I wasn't in danger."

"That's not true. All surgery carries risk," his father said, his forehead wrinkled with concern.

They always say people look like their pets, but Mr. Evans looks more like a Shar-Pei than a Yorkie.

"Besides, son, I needed to see you anyway. Skyler Sweazy came to see me a few days ago and he told your mother and me an interesting tale. Seems I misjudged you.

And you let me misjudge you," Mr. Evans continued. "Why didn't you tell me the truth?"

"I never lied to you, Dad," Michael said.

"No, but you let me believe the worst of you. For years."

"Now, George, whose fault is that?" Mrs. Evans said, nudging her husband with her elbow.

"I couldn't tell you," Mike said, "because I promised I'd keep Skyler's secret. I may not have had much going for me back then, but you always told me that a man was nothing if he didn't keep his word."

" 'He sweareth to his own hurt, and changeth not,' " Mr. Evans quoted softly.

"Why, George! You know Psalm 15." Mrs. Evans beamed. "I'm proud of you, dear."

"And more than a little surprised, I'll warrant," Mr. Evans said.

According to Mike, his mom was the theologian of the family. She was all about grace, whereas his legal eagle father was, not surprisingly, all about the letter of the law.

As Heather watched from the corridor, his dad put a hand on Michael's shoulder. Mike covered it with his own. Heather sucked in a quick breath, trying to muffle her surprise. Mr. Evans and Mike were finally making peace with each other.

This means everything to him. Heather felt his joy as if it were her own.

"We've wasted too much time apart, Mike." Mr. Evans's voice broke as he continued, "I'm so sorry, son. Can you forgive me?"

"Nothing to forgive. You didn't have all the facts. Seems to me a wise man once said there can be no justice if some of the facts are missing."

Mr. Evans smiled. Clearly, he was the "wise man" his son was quoting.

"Well, I won't make the mistake of doubting you again," his dad said. "Even if the facts seem to line up against you in the future, I'll remember that character trumps what *seems* to be the truth every time."

Then there was lots of hugging all around and more than a few tears. Even though the bag with Mike's hamburger and fries was getting soggy with grease, Heather wouldn't have interrupted the Evans family just then for worlds.

Chapter 30

Holidays are stressful enough without chemo, a son donating part of his liver, and a wedding thrown into the mix. Guess this year, I should have just stuffed the turkey with Xanax.

— Shirley Evans, when George laced her morning coffee with Bailey's the day after Thanksgiving. Against all expectations, she didn't complain a bit.

After Michael was released from the hospital and back in Coldwater Cove, whenever Heather wasn't working at Coldwater General, she was with him. They had supper or breakfast together, depending on her shift schedule. Since he was still recuperating from surgery, they spent their time cuddled on the couch, talking and watching old movies at her apartment. At the ranch house the MoreCommas team was like a bustling hive, bursting with new ideas and energy. It was impossible for Michael to truly unwind there.

To Heather's surprise, there was no talk of the future. It was as if they were in a time bubble. She loved Michael. He loved her. He grew stronger each day, and every moment together was enough.

Heather hosted a bridal shower in the Methodist fellowship hall, where Mrs. Evans reigned amid her signature excessive decorations, but even so, Lacy enjoyed opening gifts and basked in the well-wishes of all her parents' friends. In place of a bachelorette party, Heather treated Lacy, Crystal, and Jake's sister, Laura, to a day spa in Broken Bow. For once, even Crystal the perfectionist had nothing to complain about.

As Mike predicted, Jake wanted a low-key bachelor party. It consisted of an evening of thick steaks and single malt whiskey, followed by bad karaoke and a poker game at Jake's place that lasted till the wee hours of the morning. Jake and his brothers cleaned Michael out of all his walking-around cash — which was more than most folks in Coldwater lived on for a month — but Mike didn't seem to mind.

"Better for me to lose it to them while I've still got it," he said. The threat of Dr.

Hildebrand's exposé made him push back his company's IPO. Heather had left a text for Skyler asking about his progress with the cease-and-desist order, but he would only reply that he was working on it and would get back to her as soon as he knew something.

But for now, she decided no news was good news. Besides, the wedding of the century loomed.

To make up for her unscheduled week of vacation, Heather volunteered to work a double shift on Thanksgiving Day. After all, her parents were out of the country, bobbing around on a cruise ship somewhere in the Gulf of Mexico. Even though Michael had assured her she'd be welcome at the Evanses' table, she thought the family deserved a quiet holiday by themselves. If there were no extra guests, maybe Mrs. Evans would even take it easy and order the precooked holiday spread from Piggly Wiggly.

She obviously didn't know Michael's mother very well.

According to Mike, his mom pulled out all the stops, and, refusing to allow anyone to bring anything to add to her menu, she served up the mother of all Thanksgiving feasts. The sideboard groaned under platters of white and dark meat, candied yams, homemade noodles, fluffy biscuits, a special family recipe for green beans flavored with bacon, several types of molded salad, and cranberry sauce that didn't bear the slightest indentation marks from a can. There were three kinds of pie for dessert — pumpkin, chocolate, and peach — and for good measure, Shirley Evans had made her prize-winning cherry cheesecake as well.

"There's so much left over," Michael had told Heather, "you're obligated to help eat some of it on Friday, so my folks' refrigerator won't burst." He patted his flat belly. "Not to mention my stomach."

In fact, all the Evans siblings were required to bring at least one guest. Shirley had made sure the entire wedding party got an invitation, calling it the "prerehearsal brunch."

"Lacy's worried that she won't fit into her wedding dress tomorrow," Mike said as they pulled up to his parents' house. He'd ditched his Harley and was driving a Lincoln he'd had delivered from a dealer in Dallas. The contrast between the elegant, understated coupe and the garish red sports car Skyler drove was striking. "My sister's vowing not to eat again until the reception."

"Well, that's not good. Sounds like she's getting bridal jitters," Heather said. "I'll see if I can talk her off the hunger-strike ledge."

"She's not the one I'm worried about," Michael said as he parked and came around the car to open the door for her. "Crystal and Noah got into a fight before we all sat down to dinner yesterday. It was pretty intense while we passed the stuffing, but I figured it would all work out by the time we were deep in our turkey comas."

"It didn't?"

"During the meal, Noah and Crystal kept up a running hissy fit under their breaths. Finally, he got up from the table before dessert. He left the house and didn't come back."

Heather had sensed tension between the couple at Riley's recital, but she didn't think it was so bad that Noah would ditch his family on a holiday.

"Come in, come in!" Mr. Evans met them at the door, shooing them through the opening quickly. "Mayhew had a squirrel get into his house the other day when he didn't latch his door tight. Darn thing made off with a piece of plastic fruit from the lazy Susan on his dining table."

"No kidding?" Mike said.

"Of course, you can't blame the squirrel since Mayhew puts out feed for the vermin." A small smile lifted the corners of Mr.

Evans's lips. "A man who feeds a squirrel deserves whatever's coming to him."

"How is your wife feeling?" Heather asked.

"Oh, she's in fine fettle," Mr. Evans said. "Took her last treatment on Monday, so she's stronger every day."

"She was determined to finish the course before the wedding. Good for her," Heather said. "Why don't I see if I can help Mrs. Evans in the kitchen?"

"What would help her most is if you'd call her Shirley," Mr. Evans said. "And I'm George. No more of this Mrs. and Mr. stuff."

"Thank you . . . George."

That feels good. Almost like family.

Shirley and Lacy were both in the kitchen, each intent on doing the most work, each trying to get all the leftovers from the refrigerator and into serving bowls before the other one could do it. As a result, they spent more time in each other's way than actually getting anything accomplished.

"I was thinking that the decorations at the church and the Opera House look a little sparse," Mrs. Evans was saying as she put out the molded salads on the island. She obviously intended to use the space as a buffet, but since she and Lacy had different ideas about where each dish should go, there was much arranging and rearranging going on. After greeting them both with a hug, Heather decided the wise course was to offer to fill water glasses and otherwise stay out of their way.

"We already talked about the decorations, Mom," Lacy said as she wrestled a big bowl of green beans from her mother's hands and put them in a pan to warm. "The florist will bring the fresh flowers tomorrow morning and it'll be fine."

"I'll admit those silk bows are pretty, but you're only putting a spray of blossoms on every other pew and a sparse spray at that."

"Less is more, Mom."

"Honey, that makes no sense. Less is not more. That's why they call it less. And you, my dear, deserve more." Mrs. Evans poured some heavy cream into a bowl and began whipping it into submission. "I've got two dozen silk arrangements, all in your pink, navy, and ivory, loaded up in the back of the van. If we put those silks above the bows on the pews that don't have fresh flowers, think how pretty they'd look in the pictures. It would certainly help fill in the space."

"Mom, sometimes you don't need to fill the space. You just need space." Lacy's mouth drew into a tight line, and her jaw seemed carved in granite.

Heather recognized that look. The decoration of the church and reception hall was a sore spot between Lacy and her mother that Heather thought had already been settled. Clearly, the mother of the bride wasn't of the same opinion and wanted to reopen negotiations on the day before the ceremony. The bride was reaching the breaking point.

Heather needed to change the subject stat, so she sniffed the air appreciatively. "Mmm, something smells wonderful."

"That's Mom's Day-After-Thanksgiving Turkey Potpie," Lacy said, tossing Heather a wink and a look of gratitude.

"Well, it's nothing fancy," Shirley said, with a smug grin that wasn't anywhere near as humble as her words. "It's just a little something I throw together to make Thanksgiving leftovers feel more like a real meal."

"Don't you believe a word she says," Lacy said, grabbing up the conversational ball and streaking for the hoop. "Mom's dish is nothing short of a culinary miracle. She takes leftover turkey and noodles, adds some peas and carrots and a puff pastry top and voilà! Heaven in a baking pan!"

Lacy might be laying it on a little thick, but it seemed to be working. Shirley showed no sign of returning to the Great Silk

Flower Debate. The last of the meal preparation went without incident, and soon the entire Evans clan, along with a good bit of the Tyler family, gathered to say grace. Then they filled their plates and divided into two groups roughly along gender lines. Heather; Jake's mother, Mary Tyler; Lacy and her mother and sister, Crystal, along with Crystal's children, settled around the dining table. The men and Laura, who was a devoted football fan, adjourned to the family room to eat while watching the game.

"Doesn't matter who's playing," Shirley said. "My George claims any game is a good game."

Heather dug into her meal. After the second bite of pie, she cocked her head at the serving on her plate. "What did you say is in this pie again?"

"My turkey potpie is a bit of a catchall, I'm afraid. Noodles, veggies and — oh, no!" The whites showed all the way around Shirley's eyes. "I forgot to put in the turkey."

"Well, that's unfortunate. Whoever heard of turkey potpie without any turkey? Even for a mostly family meal," Crystal said, thoughtlessly ignoring the distress on her mother's face.

Hard to call it a family meal when your husband is AWOL, danced on Heather's tongue, but she bit the words back. Not only were they unkind, they didn't need to be heard by Crystal's kids either.

Besides, Shirley needed her attention more than Crystal needed a rebuke. Lacy's mom was tearing up. Her sweet face crumpled.

"Oh, I'm such a dunderhead," Shirley said. "How could I forget the turkey?"

"You're just coming off chemo. You've got a daughter getting married tomorrow," Heather said. "There's a lot on your plate at the moment."

"Yeah, but none of it is turkey," Shirley's grandson Ethan looked up from his tablet long enough to say.

Like mother, like son.

"Come with me, young man, and we'll get you some," Heather told the little twit in clipped tones.

Both Ethan and Riley trailed her into the kitchen. She took the platters of turkey from the refrigerator and warmed them. Then she gave the children their choice of light or dark meat before offering the platters around to the football fans. The men and Laura were so wrapped up in what was happening on the gridiron, they hadn't even noticed the meat was missing from the main dish. But as long as Heather didn't block their view of the TV screen, they were grateful for a slice of turkey or two.

By the time Heather returned to the dining room to eat her meal, Shirley was all smiles. Lacy, however, looked like a storm cloud.

"What's up?" Heather whispered while Crystal and Shirley debated the comparative merits of Lenox and Wedgwood bone china.

"Mom wouldn't stop berating herself about the potpie, so I agreed to let her decorate the church and reception hall with those stupid silk flowers just to cheer her up. The tears turned off like a spigot," Lacy muttered. "If I didn't know better, I'd bet she forgot that turkey on purpose."

"Sounds like a sucker bet to me," Heather said. "No takers here."

CHAPTER 31

I don't get all the junk with the caterers and florists and colors and music when a wedding all boils down to one of the shortest sentences in the English language. I do. Why is there so much fuss over two little words?

— Michael Evans

The women, except for Laura, spent the afternoon at the church and Opera House, finalizing the decorations. In a groundbreaking compromise, they added only half of Shirley's beloved silk arrangements. Later that evening, the wedding rehearsal went off without a hitch, though there was a bit of confusion for the musicians. Lacy wanted the bridal party and the groom to process from the side entrances while the hand-bell choir played. Then once everyone was in place, the organ would take over. As a fluty rendition of Pachelbel's *Canon in D* began, the rear doors of the sanctuary would open, and Mr. Evans would escort his younger daughter down the aisle.

Heather arrived at the church the next morning an hour before the ceremony was set to begin. She peeked in the sanctuary, where the florist with real flowers was trying in vain to find a place to put her creations. Shirley had evidently returned after the rehearsal dinner and added a few more "pretties" — a huge silk arrangement on the altar, and ropes of artificial blooms strangling two candelabra on either side, along with the rest of the sprays on the pews.

"More is definitely . . . more," she muttered.

On her way to the Sunday school room on the second floor that had been set aside as the bridal dressing room, Heather ran into Michael on the stairs. He looked so handsome in his navy tux, she had to remind herself to breathe.

"Hey, gorgeous," he said as he drew her into his arms and bent to kiss her. "And before you ask, yes, the groom is here. Jake's getting into his dress blues."

"Good," Heather said. "And good thing it's not bad luck for the best man to see the maid of honor."

"Lacy and Jake don't need luck. They've

got each other."

"Yeah, if they can just get through the wedding," Heather said. "Did you see what your mother has done to the sanctuary? Or more importantly, has Lacy seen it?"

He lifted a quizzical brow at her, as if he didn't understand her concern.

Men.

"Yeah, she saw it. The family came through that way when we arrived."

"What did she say?"

"Nothing."

That was ominous. "Really?"

"Yeah, come to think of it, she'd been chattering like a squirrel up until then, but she didn't say a word after that. Not even when we parted company upstairs." When he kissed her forehead, she realized she'd been frowning. "Don't worry. It'll be OK."

"Michael, haven't you ever heard that calm comes before the storm?"

"It's just stuff, Heather, all the decorations and menus and junk. It's not important."

"It's important to your sister." *And to pretty much every woman on the planet.* "A woman wants her wedding to be an expression of who she is and what she wants for her future."

"When Lacy comes down that aisle, all

she'll see is Jake waiting for her at the end of it. Isn't that her future? Isn't that what matters?"

"I guess." Now if she could just convince the bride.

When she ducked into the changing room, Lacy, her mother, Crystal, and Laura were all there. With her mother's help, Lacy was stepping into her gown, but the bridesmaids were already in their dresses.

"They're pink!" Heather said. Not only were they pink, they were hurt-your-eyes pink. Lacy had wanted soft pink as an accent, a bare hint of color to balance the strong navy. Two heavy hues would look like the battle of the sexes on a color wheel.

"I know," Shirley said, beaming. "I was concerned there might be a mix-up, and sure enough, the company sent the dresses in navy to the Bride Side. And they came at the last minute, too, so there wouldn't have been time to return them. But while I was in Tulsa visiting Michael in the hospital, I dropped by a shop there and picked up the pink ones, just in case. Oh, I'm so glad I did. Aren't they just to die for?"

If you want to go out as a giant flamingo queen.

From across the room, Lacy looked at her wearily, as if to say, *Resistance is futile. Just put on the dress.*

Even though Heather was sick about having to wear a color that would be more at home on a Rio beach during Mardi Gras, she didn't want to cause any more problems, so she slipped into the eye-popping sheath.

At least Shirley hadn't thought to buy matching pumps.

Thank God for small mercies.

Shirley's attention was distracted by the fact that Crystal's eye makeup was smudged, so Heather took the opportunity to have a quiet word with Lacy as she helped her adjust her veil.

"You look beautiful. Are you OK?"

"I'll do," Lacy said grimly. "At the end of the day, I'll be married to Jake, and I'd walk through fire for that man, so Mom's gauntlet of shocking pink and death by silk roses won't stop me." The bride sighed. "But to tell the truth, I feel like this wedding already has two strikes against it."

Heather thought about trying Michael's argument that the details didn't matter, but she could see that to Lacy, they did. So she smoothed her friend's hair and made sure the beautiful bouquet of real blooms the florist had brought found its way into Lacy's shaky hands before Shirley could replace it with one made of her "forever flowers."

"Oh, for goodness' sake, look at the time!" Shirley said when Lacy's dad rapped on the door so he could escort his daughter down the stairs. She scurried away to be paraded to her seat in the front row, while Heather, Crystal, and Laura made their way to the left side entrance to the sanctuary.

Heather hoped George had some calming words for his daughter, because Lacy was barely holding it together.

The hand-bell choir began a piece that could charitably be described as a "joyful noise," and the bridal party coordinated their entrances. Each bridesmaid briefly met the corresponding groomsman at the front of the nave and then separated to either the bride's or groom's side. Riley went in before Heather, dropping clumps of rose petals on her way. Her basket was empty long before she met her brother Ethan, whose iPad had been pried from his hands and replaced with a pillow bearing the rings. When Heather and Michael met, her heart nearly banged its way out of her chest. He was so handsome. She felt sure the whole congregation could feel the attraction vibrating between them.

Before Heather turned and walked up a couple of steps leading to the raised area before the choir loft, she let herself wonder how it would feel to be meeting Michael at the altar, not as maid of honor and best man, but as bride and groom.

Would she care about the decorations and details or would she only see the man?

The point was moot. *He hasn't asked you, silly.*

As the hand bells were building to their clanging climax, Jake, flanked by Pastor Mark, joined them at the altar. Once the last chime died away, Heather turned to face the back of the church, where her friend in all her bridal glory would soon appear.

In the days that followed, several theories arose about what happened next. Some said Pastor Mark's head was down, scanning the order of service likely, and thus, he was distracted. Mrs. Chisholm, ever the ray of sunshine, opined that he must have had a ministroke and was unaware of his surroundings on that account. Some said it wasn't the pastor's fault at all because clearly the organist had fallen asleep, though how anyone could sleep through that bombastic hand-bell piece was a mystery as deep as the miracle at Cana.

At any rate, the organist didn't immediately launch into the music that signaled the bride's entrance. And in that slice of silence, Pastor Mark began the ceremony without her.

"Dearly Beloved . . ." he droned, his gaze still glued to the order of service.

This cannot be happening.

In the right transept, where the hand bells were set up, Mr. Mariano was practically jumping up and down. He waved his hands frantically, trying to catch the pastor's eye.

"The bride! You need the bride!" the director mouthed.

Pastor Mark continued his opening remarks undeterred.

Lacy must be beside herself. We're having her wedding without her.

"Pastor," Heather whispered.

He gave her a quick glare and went on with his timeworn opening. He barely paused for a breath when he asked if anyone had just cause for why the marriage should not take place.

How about there's no bride?

Finally, he wound down with "Who gives this woman to be married to this man?"

When there was no answer, the pastor looked up, blinked like a mole blinded by sunlight, and said, "Oh. I guess we need the bride."

As if that were her cue, the organist launched into a rousing rendition of *Here*

Comes the Bride, instead of the ethereal *Canon in D.* The doors at the back of the church swung open anyway.

But the only person standing there was Mr. Evans.

For a man who was missing a leg from the knee down, Jake could move surprisingly fast. Like the former all-state halfback he'd been, he bolted down the aisle toward his future father-in-law, with Michael on his heels. The gathered congregation released a collective gasp as Heather lifted her hem and followed suit.

She couldn't blame Lacy for being upset. What bride wants to be forgotten at her own wedding? But if her sudden disappearance was about more than that, well, the day had turned from gaff-riddled to disastrous.

As they neared the dressing room, her sobs could be heard through the shut door.

Jake put a hand to the doorknob, but stopped himself and knocked instead. "Lacy, honey, can I come in?"

The sobs only grew louder.

"She's being a drama queen just like when we were kids." Michael shouldered him out of the way. "Never ask a hysterical woman what she wants. Chances are she has no idea."

He pushed into the room with Heather and Jake close behind. To Heather's relief, Lacy ran across the room and threw herself into Jake's arms.

"I'm so sorry," she repeated, burying her face in the crook of his neck. "It's not you. It . . . it's just everything."

"Well, that doesn't sound good," Heather whispered as she took Michael's hand. He gave hers a squeeze.

"Let them hash it out," Mike whispered back.

"Don't you want to marry me?" Jake asked.

Lacy palmed his cheeks. "More than anything, but look at what happened. Everything's gone wrong. It's a sign."

"I don't believe that."

"But maybe it is. I mean, even if we get through this circus, what then?" Lacy pulled away from him. "We still haven't decided what we're doing after the honeymoon."

"You still want to take that contract job in Cambridge?"

Lacy nodded, her face a study in misery.

"Then, Cambridge, here we come."

"You mean it?" When he nodded, she was back in his arms faster than a rumor on the Methodist prayer chain.

"I've been saving this news for the honeymoon, but the truth is," Jake said, "I figure the Green Apple's gone about as far as it can go with a jarhead at the grill. So I've been looking into a cooking school in Boston."

"What about the Green Apple while you're gone?"

"My sister, Laura, can take over running it. She needs something to do and Ethel needs someone to bully besides Lester and me."

Lacy laughed and dried her eyes. Heather sighed in relief. Even though Lacy's wedding had a few speed bumps, her friend was going to get her happily ever after anyway.

"The school back East offers a two-year course, so I'll graduate by the time your contract's up," Jake explained.

"And then?"

"Who knows? We can decide what to do next when the time comes. Lacy, we can't map out our whole lives today. Things happen. Good things, bad things. Either way, we have to get through them." Jake took both her hands in his. "I just want to make sure we get through them together."

"Oh, Jake, I want that, too. Let's go get this wedding over with."

"No," he said. "I don't want our wedding to be something you just want to be over.

Like you said, it might be a sign. Your dad offered me a ladder to elope. Let's do it."

Lacy's face lit up like a thousand candles. "We're going on a cruise for our honeymoon. We can have the captain marry us once we're on board."

"You mean I'm paying for a wedding and nobody's getting married?" Mr. Evans was standing outside the open door.

"Hang on a minute, Dad. Maybe someone will." Michael turned to Heather and dropped to one knee.

She gasped, a hand to her heart.

"Heather, you know I love you. I've been trying to figure out how to ask you to marry me. You don't know how many times I've thought about trying to romance you, to whisk you off to Paris and propose on the bank of the Seine, but the truth is, where I ask you doesn't matter if I'm not the one you want. Can you ignore the details and just see the man?"

She was afraid her voice wouldn't work, but it did. "I can, if the man is you."

When he rose to his feet and kissed her deeply, the world seemed to slow and teeter just a bit on its axis. There was only Michael. Only her. And wherever they were, they were quite enough.

"Will you mind getting married in a borrowed ceremony?"

"I'm in favor of anything that gets me out of this flamingo suit."

Michael kissed her again, a toe-curling, knee-weakening kiss. "And just so you know, I'm taking you to Paris anyway."

Lacy clapped her hands loudly.

"All right, that's settled. Everybody with a Y chromosome, hit the road! Help me out of this gown, Heather. I always thought it suited you more than me anyway," Lacy said, taking charge as thoroughly as her mother would have. "I'll wear your flamingo suit."

"Oh, Lacy, I can't let you do that."

"Hey, you were willing to wear it for me," Lacy said. "Jake, get down to the sanctuary and let the guests know a wedding is still on before they start slipping away. On the double, mister."

He grinned and clapped Michael on the back. "Come on, bro. Let's go let everyone know there's been a change in the lineup."

In a few minutes, Heather and Lacy had exchanged dresses. Her friend hurried into the sanctuary to take her place as maid of honor, and to Heather's surprise, Mr. Evans was waiting by the open door.

"Welcome to the family, dear," he said, giving her a kiss on the cheek. "Since your parents aren't present, I thought I might walk you down the aisle."

"Oh, that would be lovely." She gave Michael's dad a hug. "And just so you know, the bride's family always pays for the wedding. My folks will reimburse you when they get back."

In the write-up for the *Coldwater Gazette,* Wanda Cruikshank reported that the bride's smile lit up the sanctuary, but the happiest man at the wedding — barring the groom, of course — was Mr. Evans.

Epilogue

Several weeks later, in the Coldwater Cove Courthouse . . .

"And in summary, Your Honor, we ask that you rule against Ms. Hildebrand and find her guilty of libel against Michael Evans," Skyler Sweazy said in his most lawyerly tone. "Not only were her accusations untrue, her intent was to maliciously harm him and his business interests."

Judge Barbara Mueller looked down from the bench at the defendant. "Do you have anything to add before I pronounce my verdict, Ms. Hildebrand?"

"It's Doctor."

"Excuse me?

"My name. It's *Dr.* Hildebrand," Judith said. "I earned it. I expect you to use it."

The judge removed her glasses and cleaned them slowly on the sleeve of her gown. "Very well, *Dr.* Hildebrand, do you have any further testimony to offer?"

"Only that a court like this one cannot possibly understand the complexities of the media," Judith said with a sniff. "I'm a journalist. The first amendment protects free speech, you know. Or perhaps you don't, Ms. Mueller."

"That's 'Judge.' "

"What?"

"*Judge* Mueller. I earned it. I expect you to use it."

Judith swallowed hard.

"There being no further testimony, I hereby pronounce you guilty of libel —"

"But —"

"Unless you wish me to hold you in contempt and reopen negotiations with the district attorney about charges involving how you came by the information you disseminated about Mr. Evans, I suggest you keep still," Judge Mueller said. "The maximum penalty is a thousand dollars or a year in jail."

"But I haven't got a thousand dollars," Judith protested.

"Then welcome to Coldwater Cove, Dr. Hildebrand." The judge banged her gavel. "You're going to be with us for a while."

Recipes from Coldwater Cove

HOMEMADE EGG NOODLES

When I first learned to cook, I was so frustrated by the good cooks in my family who didn't have exact measurements for their recipes. My mother-in-law always claimed she started at one end of the kitchen and kept going till she reached the other, dirtying every pot and pan in the place. My mother claims she adds ingredients "until it feels right."

Grrr! How could I ever fix anything with advice like that?

So let me apologize in advance if my noodle recipe seems a bit loosey-goosey. Mom was right. Sometimes, you do have to rely on feelings. And my M-I-L would be happy to know that making my noodles spreads flour in all directions, so my kitchen is far from spotless by the time I'm done. But my family loves them, so here's what I do:

Ingredients

Eggs, 2–4 (*depending on how many noodles you want*)
1/3 cup milk (*Add more if you want more noodles. Are you seeing a pattern here?*)
1/4 teaspoon cream of tartar
1/2 teaspoon salt
All-purpose flour, 2–4 cups (*again, depending on how many noodles you want*)
1/4 teaspoon baking powder
Broth — turkey, chicken or beef (*enough to fill a stock pot halfway*)

See. I warned you this was a slippery sort of recipe.

Directions

Start the night before you mean to serve the noodles! (*Very important! If the noodles don't dry before you cut them, you'll be in a world of hurt.*)

Whip the eggs and milk together in a large bowl.

Add the cream of tartar, baking powder, and salt, stirring vigorously. (*Get some kids or a highly motivated husband involved at this point!*)

Begin adding flour one cup at a time, and mix it thoroughly with the wet ingredients. Eventually, you'll need to use your hands to work the flour in. But don't knead it too much or the noodles will be tough.

Spread some of the leftover flour onto a pastry cloth, putting a pile of flour in the center.

Form your noodle dough into a ball and place on the center of your cloth, nestled in the flour pile. Pour the last of the flour on top and then roll out the dough to the desired thickness (*It depends on whether you want fat or thin noodles! Remember, they will rise a bit because of the baking powder.*) with a well-floured rolling pin.

Cover with a cloth and let dry overnight.

The next morning, cut the dough into noodles (*preferably while having occasional sips of coffee fixed for you by someone who appreciates all the work you're putting into the noodles!*).

Heat a stock pot of broth to a rolling boil. (*There are different schools of thought in my family about whether to use store-bought stock or to make your own or just use the drippings from the turkey you're probably roasting to go with the noodles. I'm a pragmatist. I use a little of all three!*)

Add noodles a handful at a time. Once they've boiled for 5 minutes under your watchful eye, and stirring spoon, turn the heat down until the noodles are barely bubbling. Set a timer and stir every 5 minutes so nothing sticks to the bottom of the pot.

Do not stir in a circle or you'll end up with the world's largest dumpling!

(*Yes, that is the voice of sad experience you hear!*)

After the noodles have cooked for an hour, serve to your grateful family. They'll love them! You can make the noodles well in advance and freeze them. Once cooked, they are great left over and can be worked into casseroles and soups.

Which brings us to our next recipe . . .

VEGAN TURKEY CASSEROLE

OK. In A Coldwater Warm Hearts Wedding, *Shirley Evans's casserole is only vegan because she forgot to add the turkey. But this is my mom's recipe and she contends that the main point of making a turkey casserole is using up your leftover turkey.*

So don't forget to add the turkey!

Filling

Leftover noodles with thickened broth (*If you used the noodle recipe on page 316, they'll be just right!*)
Peas
Diced carrots (*optional*)
Leftover turkey, cut into bite-sized pieces (*NOT optional!*)

Ingredients for a pie crust to fit a 9″ × 12″ baking pan

2 cups Crisco
Dash of salt

4 cups flour

16 tablespoons water (*To make it fit the larger pan, my mom just doubles her single pie crust recipe, which calls for 8 tablespoons of water. Just FYI: 16 tablespoons equals 1 cup.*)

Directions

Mix noodles, peas, carrots, and turkey (*especially the turkey. Do NOT forget the turkey!*) in a large bowl. Set aside.

In a mixing bowl, combine Crisco, salt, and a cup or so of flour. Gently mix. (*This means "by hand."*) Add some of the water and more flour (*by no means all!*), being careful not to overstir or beat. Go by feel until the dough is cohesive enough to pour out onto a floured board. Knead more flour into it.

(*I have been strongly cautioned NOT to work the dough too much. You want the ingredients blended but not flogged into toughness. Also, my mother confesses she doesn't mix all the flour the recipe calls for into the dough. Some of it is used to roll out the crusts.*)

Divide the dough into two balls, a larger one for the bottom of the 9″ × 13″ baking pan and a small one that will be the top crust. Roll to a one-eighth-inch thickness. (*Here's a tip from my mom: Once you have the dough rolled out, fold it over to lift it up and into the baking pan. Make sure there's enough to go up the sides and hang over the lip a bit.*)

Use a fork to poke holes in the bottom and sides of the crust.

Fill the bottom crust with the noodle, peas, carrots, and turkey mixture.

Cut two curved slits in the top crust before you cover the noodles, peas, carrots, and turkey. (*This is your last chance to make sure you didn't forget the turkey!*)

Flute the edges of the dough to join the top and bottom halves as if you were making a pie. (*Now that I think about it, I wonder why my family has always called this a turkey casserole when it's clearly a turkey potpie! Oh, well . . . whatever you call it, it'll still taste good.*)

Bake at 350 degrees for 50–55 minutes until golden brown.

If you're a little frustrated by these recipes, imagine how I felt back when I couldn't boil water. But through trial and error (many errors, as it turned out), I learned how to use them to make these family favorites.

What is life but a series of trials and errors? Don't we go "by feel" on most things? And fortunately, I have a forgiving family who's willing to help me get rid of most of my mistakes.

By eating them.

ACKNOWLEDGMENTS

No book comes to life as the result of one person's effort. *A Coldwater Warm Hearts Wedding* is no exception. There are tons of people I should thank, but these are the ones I can fit on this page:

Alicia Condon, my delightful editor, for believing in my stories and shepherding my books into the Kensington fold. Kudos to Kristine Noble, Tom Hallman, Paula Reedy, Brittany Dowdle, Carla Derr, Jane Nutter, Lauren Jernigan, Rebecca Raskin, and the rest of the Kensington gang who market, copyedit, and design my amazing covers. What a wonderful team!

Natasha Kern, my amazing agent, for believing in me! She's such a source of encouragement and guidance.

Ashlyn Chase, my long-suffering critique partner, for hours of "read alouds" and for her friendship.

Marcy Weinbeck, my beta reader and my friend. I rely on her exquisite taste and keen eye.

YOU, my dear reader. Yes, you, holding this book in your hands right now. Without you and your imagination added to my words, nothing happens.

And lastly, my Dear Husband. We've been together for forty years and he still knows how to show a girl a good time! He is, and always will be, the reason I write about love.

■ ■ ■ ■

A Reading Group Guide: A Coldwater Warm Hearts Wedding

LEXI EDDINGS

■ ■ ■ ■

About This Guide

The suggested questions are included to enhance your group's reading of this book.

DISCUSSION QUESTIONS

1. A hospital setting tends to put relationships into laser-like focus. Everything becomes both intensely significant and of no import at all. How are the members of the Evans family dealing with Shirley's cancer? With each other? What does Heather Walker see as her role in the situation?

2. Michael Evans has been wildly successful since he left Coldwater Cove in disgrace. He seems to want to keep his wealth and position a secret at first. Why do you think he came back on a Harley instead of in a limo?

3. Heather's relationship with her parents is fraught with unexpressed feelings. How does her twin's death continue to affect how they relate to each other?

4. Lester and Glenda Scott have been married a long time, but they haven't lived as husband and wife for over a decade. Do you think people can change enough for a second chance to work?

5. Heather's family is one of the wealthiest in the county. Why does she insist on making her own way in the world and not taking money from her parents? How do you think that makes her parents feel? Might they be unable to express their love in any other way and feel rejected when she won't accept their financial help?

6. Why do you think Michael called Heather "Stilts"? What makes middle school boys act weird around girls they like? Do they sometimes revert to type as men when they feel unworthy of the women in their lives?

7. Michael has been misjudged for most of his life — by his teachers, his family, and sometimes by Heather. He and his father were estranged for a decade. What do you think would have happened if he hadn't hidden the truth about the night Heather's sister died? Would he and Heather have gotten together sooner? Would he still have

volunteered to be a partial liver donor for her cousin?

8. Were you surprised when Michael realized that home might be the best medicine for his mother? And that him being there was an important part of her recuperation? What part does faith and the participation in church activities play in the story?

9. Why is Judith Hildebrand so intent on bringing Michael down? Does she bear any responsibility for the downward spiral in her life and career?

10. Weddings don't always turn out as planned. Were you surprised by what happened at Jake and Lacy's wedding? What lies ahead for them and for Michael and Heather? Where do you see them all in five years?

If you'd like to learn more about Coldwater Cove and the folks who live there, please visit: www.LexiEddings.com!

ABOUT THE AUTHOR

Lexi Eddings is the pen name of multi-published author Diana Groe, who has written for Kensington, Sourcebooks, and Entangled. A classically trained soprano, she calls her historical work a cross between Grand Opera and Gilbert and Sullivan. Her historical romances have received glowing reviews from *Booklist, Publishers Weekly,* and *RT Book Reviews.*

The employees of Thorndike Press hope you have enjoyed this Large Print book. All our Thorndike, Wheeler, and Kennebec Large Print titles are designed for easy reading, and all our books are made to last. Other Thorndike Press Large Print books are available at your library, through selected bookstores, or directly from us.

For information about titles, please call:
(800) 223-1244

or visit our website at:
gale.com/thorndike

To share your comments, please write:

Publisher
Thorndike Press
10 Water St., Suite 310
Waterville, ME 04901